Work of Art

JOHN BLACK

WWW.JOHNBLACKWRITER.COM

To my parents.

CONTENTS

We are born with a scream; we come into life with a scream, and maybe love is a mosquito net between the fear of living and the fear of death.
— Francis Bacon

Paint, not the thing, but the effect it produces.
— Stéphane Mallarmé

PROLOGUE

Think of the worst day of your life.

I know mine exactly – the thirtieth of November, nineteen ninety-nine. Ironically, it should have been one of the best.

But back to your day. Let me take a wild guess – somebody died, right?

I mean there are other personal disasters. You can lose your job – your life's vocation suddenly evaporating in front of you. You can come home to see that note telling you the love of your life has left you for another. However, by far the worst is when someone near and dear to you dies.

But perhaps you think you are too young to have experienced the loss of someone close? Maybe, but I bet it still cut you up when you put poor little Fluffy in an old shoe box and buried them at the bottom of the garden, right? Well, remember that and times it by about a thousand. Loss of a pet may be harsh, but the loss of person, a person close to you, is true trauma. Their death leaves a void that will never quite be filled because – and it will catch in your throat when you suddenly realise this – you can never see them, talk to them or touch them, ever again. All at once it spears you, crushes you and numbs you – like God has taken time out from his busy schedule just to personally piss all over your life.

Suicide is even worse – their life taken by their own hands. You will be asking yourself, over and over: *Why did they do it? Surely, I should have seen it coming? Surely, I could have done something about it?*

That was me.

The love of my life, my Catherine, the women who had just accepted my marriage proposal, had killed herself. And on the thirtieth of November nineteen ninety-nine, after being honoured with the Turner Prize for my art, I found the note. And it wasn't just the typical suicide note. It had an extra little kicker – it was also a 'Dear John'.

She had killed herself in a lovers' pact.

Leapt off a cliff, hand-in-hand, with the person she loved.

Not me, obviously.

From the highest turret of my life I found myself crashing down to the lowest dungeon.

So what did I do? Enjoy festering in my own misery for a time before eventually joining them? If only it had been that simple. No, I had to pick at it, worry and gnaw at it, take hold of a spade, prise up the stone flags covering that dungeon floor and start digging.

Because, cuckolded and bereaved – that was nothing.

It was going to get much worse than that.

1 NUDE FIGURE STUDY

Rain streamed down the window, smearing the view into an Impressionist landscape. However this was no traditional masterpiece – no pond choked with water lilies, no hot poppies or the spindly poplars of the French countryside. Under a dull grey sky, this was just a field in eastern Lincolnshire and not even the hard Dutch geometry, the Mondrian regularity, of the Fenlands. Nothing as exciting. But it was just the view I wanted – a field of deep brown earth covered with a haze of green from where the first spring crop of the millennium was just starting to show through, surrounded by a ragged over-cropped hedgerow studded with a few ivy-smothered oaks and ashes. The natural tones were only marred by two highlights of bright artificiality at the far end of the field. Two dabs of colour, one a fiery orange, the other an intense blue, trudged along the hedgerow. Without consciously thinking about it, I analysed the scene – memorising shape, tone and hue – for later reproduction.

A sudden brief squall caught the window, rattling the sash in its frame and splattering the raindrops hard against the glass like pellets from a shotgun.

I suddenly remembered where I was, and why I was there. And the urge to reproduce the view was gone.

Tomorrow. I thought. *I'll start painting tomorrow.*

The night before, as I slept on the bare floor, I had dreamed of her. Dreamed of her body, wave-battered and washed up on some deserted beach. Her clothes half dragged from her body. Her hair matted with fronds of rotting seaweed and encrusted with sand. Her lips rimmed with evaporated salt, brine pooled in her open mouth.

Gulls, screaming, flocked over her, taking turns to flutter down and peck at her dead white flesh; peck at her clouded eyes.

Then it was me lying there. Me, screaming with the gulls.

I woke, twisted up in my sweat-soaked sleeping bag.

A light in the darkness. The moon, high up in the corner of the bare window. Bright and just a shade off full – gibbous. I stared at it for a long time until sleep finally came again. Remembering. Remembering her in the moonlight.

I had been in the cottage for only a few days. And when I say 'cottage' don't imagine some twee, white-walled, oak-beamed, thatched-roof postcard image. This red-brick construction was as utilitarian as the food-factory fields that surrounded it. No longer needed after its land had been bought by a neighbouring farm, the property had been unloved and uninhabited for many years. The cottage's damp and pokey rooms, with a few abandoned battered pieces of furniture, rank carpets and damp-stained peeling wall-paper – with patterns that might just have been popular half a century ago – along with its remote location had ensured it had been on the market for some time.

However the place was perfect for my needs and, more importantly, exactly suited my mood.

I had done a deal and moved in with a sleeping bag, some basic survival equipment, a couple of pairs of camouflaged combat trousers, several plain olive T-shirts and sweatshirts, and as many brushes, paints, crayons, pencils, canvases, pads of card and paper and other art materials as I could stuff into a rucksack. I headed out by train and bus and foot, leaving my motorcycle and everything else behind.

The plan was to rent the place for a year and use it as a base for sketching and painting the local scenery. I wanted to show the changing countryside of the county of my birth, through spring, autumn and on into the cold of winter. And then to finally lock the door on the house turned gallery, with walls covered with my art, and to walk east to the coast.

And once I reached the unforgiving iron grey of the North Sea to just keep walking, to finally join my love.

Skegness, the town itself, had been too busy for me, even this early in the season. And the coast swarmed with flocks of twitchers – that peculiarly intense species of bird-watcher. An army of them, with binoculars slung round their necks and tripods and telescopes shouldered like pikes, scoured the landscape for the rarities that had been blown off course during the spring migration. So I had had to come inland a few miles. It may have been the county of my birth but I was a long way from home.

However Skegness was the perfect location – it was the place where I had been so close to death before.

It was a family trip out to the seaside. A day that I now only remember snatches of. I was supposedly too old – in my mid-teens – to still be able to enjoy that sort of thing. I should have been totally mired in teenage truculence but I was actually looking forward to it – a day's escape from the unexciting small market town that I lived in. A broad spread of our family-tree, three generations deep, had crammed into several cars. A convoy formed as we picked up more relatives from towns and villages on the way as we headed east.

At that time, in the early eighties, Skegness had not quite descended into total tackiness and there was still cheap fun to be had in shops that sold marvellous gaudy rubbish – from plastic space aliens to figurines of milkmaids, sticks of mint-flavoured hard rock with the red blur all the way through that was supposed to be the town's name, 'Kiss-Me-Quick – Squeeze-Me-Slow' hats and racks of rude postcards that I was now old enough to fully appreciate with a dark chuckle.

Naturally splitting into age-defined groups, I teamed up with two cousins I barely knew and we hit the arcades. Although carefully admonished to 'be sensible', once we were away from parental oversight we did nothing of the sort – racing down the prom, we hollered like Viking invaders. Coppers soon disappeared into the slot-racers and coin cascades and ten-pences were swallowed by the spinning wheels of the bandits and fed the beeping bright lights of the video games of *Phoenix* and *Star Wars*. We lunched on bags of chips washed down with blue pop. The last few chips were flung out onto the pavement to be immediately snatched up by screaming gulls. Then we moved on to the rides at the far end of the seafront, buying a long strip of pink two-for-a-ride tickets. Soon we swirled through the distorted pop that blared out on the waltzers and were jolted by sadistic collisions on the dodgems. A big wheel took us high above the smells of stale beer, sharp vomit and sweet sickly candy floss.

Then finally, as the weather started to dull, there was the solitary roller coaster. This was no modern, computer-designed, theme park attraction; this was a big rattling ride of the old school. Two bulbs were missing from the rows that spelt out *Xynacon* and the paint-work around the sign was sun-blistered and peeling at the edges.

The rest of the day might now be snapshot images, but that ride is always complete cinema as I can remember every moment.

I had never been happy about heights even before then and I was not exactly eager at first, expecting it to be something to be mostly endured rather than enjoyed. However, as we queued, watching the roller coaster's cars whip around, I found it all too easy to convince myself that the dragging, pulling feeling that ran from my throat down through to my guts, was a growing anticipation of thrill not fright. Plus there was no way I was going to stand at the bottom and watch my two cousins take the challenge on their own, waiting for the inevitable piss-taking that I would be on the receiving end of for the rest of the day.

All too soon we were at the head of the queue and we clambered into the small red four man ride-car. While my cousins had climbed in the front I had sat down on my own in the middle of the bench seat behind. It had been my choice – the view from the front seemed a scary step too far.

The ride attendant – some weather-beaten old man wearing a cheap baseball cap – took our tickets then slammed down safety bars across our laps. He gave the car a shove and it trundled along its rails around a corner to the start of the ride. There was a sharp *clack* as one of the hooks on the chain between the rails caught on the underneath of our car, followed by a drawn out *takka takka takka* as the chain pulled us up the long steep slope to the ride's summit.

The red vinyl fabric of my seat had split, been patched and then split again. It was uncomfortably warm and fleshy to the touch, having soaked up the long day's sun. In contrast my feet rested in a damp seat well that obviously never completely dried out each time it rained. In one corner there was a rust-edged hole that I could poke the toe of my trainer through. Although there was shiny metal grab-bar running along the top of the back of the seat in front of me, my hands gripped the safety bar on either side of my thighs. My cousins in the front shouted and pointed far out to sea at the few ships that were in view. I tried to look straight ahead.

As the car reached the top of the ride, dark clouds were starting to obscure the sun and a chill was descending that gave notice of approaching rain.

We crawled around the short bend that led to the first drop.

Then we plunged over.

And my safety bar popped out.

Physics had always been one of my favourite subjects at school so on one level I knew the logic of it all as it was happening to me. As the car dropped away down the slope my body's momentum meant it wanted to keep moving in the same direction as it had been, so relative to the car, I was thrown upwards. I have never been exactly slim but always more stocky than fat. The martial arts training I then did twice a week ensured I was fit and solid, the endless press-ups adding a muscular upper body to the hard thighs that I had gained from daily cycling to school. And muscle is much denser than fat.

All that weight was thrust up against the safety bar, via the tight grip of my hands and the impact of my thighs slamming into it – weight that became a force that acted against the mechanism that held the bar in place. I never know whether the bar had not been secured properly in the first place or if the locking device failed. Whatever, the effect was the same – I flew out of my seat.

As I pitched upwards I gripped the bar so hard my knuckles ached. Between my fingers and my toes, as they tried to dig through my trainers' soles into the car's floor, every muscle locked solid. My body was forced over into a bent-legged crouch, like some Soviet Olympic weightlifter straining for gold, as I struggled to stay in the car. My senses focused into a perfect sharp clarity as my bloodstream was flooded with adrenaline.

The one thing that I always found strange thinking back was that there was no fear at all. That had gone completely, to be replaced with a feeling of dull sickness, a cold realisation that I could be moments from my own death. My cousins, oblivious to my situation, screamed out in fun but I said almost nothing as time slowed down. A quiet, half-whispered, swearword was all that escaped my lips as I hung on.

And then after a few scant seconds, that could have been hours to me, we hit the bottom of the hill. I was pitched backwards into the seat and the bar slammed down again as we careered upwards. Then, as the car plunged down the following slope, out came the safely bar again. This time I was prepared as I sailed forward but it made the experience – again half-crouched forward with all muscles locked – no less sickening. Back up the next slope and I was back in my seat again. The ride nearly over, we swirled down from the top to the bottom in a tight spiral, the track forming a dark barrel, the centrifugal force keeping me in the car. One final small dip that barely took me out of the seat and it was all over.

The car trundled to a halt and my cousins leapt out, shouting and laughing. I staggered after on weak shaky legs.

All the reaction I got from the old man running the ride was a harsh whispered, *'You fucking idiot'* as I went past.

I said nothing, still stunned. Sometimes, thinking back, I wished I had shouted and screamed at him – that his shoddy ride had nearly killed me. But I had survived and at that age you think yourself immortal – a near brush with death can be casually cast aside as you move straight onto the next adventure.

The day was nearly over. Soon it was raining, a shower that turned into a thundering downpour. In a now deserted far corner of the fun fair we waited for our respective parents. Sheltering under a covered wooden veranda that looked out over a small artificial lake we captained a fleet of coin-operated radio-controlled model boats whilst the rainwater streamed off their decks. Probably like a million other children before us, we tried our best to ram and sink each other but it was to no avail.

Thud! Thud!

A loud pounding at the front door and by reflex I was there, was opening it, even as I was thinking – *But no one knows I'm here?*

'Bobolink?'

It was the two splodges, orange and blue, that I had last seen at the far end of the field. Up close they were revealed to be a pair of middle-aged bird-watchers in bright-coloured waterproof jackets. Water dripped off bulky black binocular cases slung round their necks, balanced by twin small rucksacks behind. They both stared owlishly back at me through rain-spattered glasses.

The man in blue was paused, fist raised, mid-thump.

'Bobolink?' He asked me again. The accent was thick, Germanic.

'Sorry?'

'Bobolink! Have you been seeing the bobolink?'

'Bobolink!' I exploded. *'Bobolink! What are the fuck are you fucking talking about? What...? How...? I don't...'*

I spluttered to a halt as I saw shock and fear in their faces.

'Ah, sorry to be disturbing you,' The man said, taking a step backwards and turning to go.

'No, I'm the one who's sorry.' I said, taking a deep breath and shaking my head. 'I'll start again. What do you want?'

'Bobo–'

I raised my hand to stop him.

'That part I've got ...let me guess. A bird?'

'Yes. Can you help us?' The woman in orange replied. 'My husband was looking for a bird. A bobolink. And now we're lost, I think.'

I paused for a second. Then I sighed, shrugged and tried to smile.

'You had better come in. I've got a map inside.'

As I led them into the back of the house towards the kitchen, apologising for the state the house was in, I was suddenly screaming in my head. *You idiot! You were supposed to spending a year on your own. In total isolation. To grieve. To mourn. To do penance. And how long did it last? Five Minutes. Is that how much she was worth to you? Five fucking minutes! You should be moping in your misery, not grinning like a loon at two German bird-watchers dripping water in your kitchen.*

The room, like the rest of the house, was not exactly overflowing with comforts. There was a disconnected electric cooker smeared with grease but all the cupboards had been ripped out, leaving patches in the paint-work where they had been mounted on the walls and scars in the plaster from their fittings.

The only furniture were two odd chairs and a Formica covered drop-leaf table shoved up against the wall under the window. On top was a cardboard box filled with supplies I had struggled to carry from the – not very – local shop plus some of the survival equipment I had brought with me from a camping shop back in London. I found a clean towel among the camping stove, plastic plates and other bits and pieces and offered it to them. They gratefully wiped their faces. I went into the largest room on the ground floor – a lounge-diner, empty of furniture, straight off the kitchen, where I had dumped all my art materials – to take down the Ordinance Survey map that was Blue-Taced to the wall.

For a long while I have been more than slightly obsessed with maps, always having one, usually several at different scales, covering wherever I happened to live at the time. Spend more than five minutes in a city and I'm buying an *A-Z*. Go on holiday and I'm straight down the *Tourist Information* for all the maps, plans and guides they have. I always wanted to know where I was, what was around me, how to get away and how to get back again.

I spread the map out on the kitchen table and showed the birdwatchers where the cottage was. They realised the hunt for their bird was now a forlorn quest; the rain would have driven it to cover. We quickly managed to work out between us where they had come from and the way back.

'Hang on.' I said, after returning briefly to the main room to fetch a sketchpad and pen. 'I'll draw you a route.'

'That is too good paper.' The women said, looking over my shoulder as I started quickly sketching in the details of the most direct route back to their car. 'You don't want to waste it with us.'

'No, it's alright,' I said. 'I've got plenty.'

While I explained the route to her husband, she moved to the doorway leading to the main room. I glanced up and saw she was looking at my sketches scattered across the floor – a few quick pencil drawings of the local area I had finished that morning before the rain drove me back inside.

'These are very good.' She said, picking one up. 'Are you a professional?'

'Kind of…' Finished, I handed my sketch-map to her husband then walked over to her. 'But this is something new.'

'With me it is mainly the birds.' Her husband said by way explanation from behind us. 'But with Clara it is the art.'

'I love these.' She put down the drawing she was holding and picked up an old sketchbook. 'Is anything for sale?'

'Er, no. It's just preliminary work for a project I'm about to start.'

A bolt of panic shot through me as I suddenly realised exactly which sketchbook she held. The panic flashed to anger and I made to snatch the book out of her hands.

'I'm sorry, but that's private!'

But she had already started flicking through the images I had made of my love. She stopped on one of the last I ever did, a simple rough pencil sketch, a nude figure study. She was sleeping when I could not, lying across our leather sofa, posed like a Pre-Raphaelite heroine, illuminated in soft sunlight coming from a side window, glowing radiant as an angel, as ethereal as the ghost she would soon become.

She would never pose for me and I had had to keep the pad hidden from her. My secret. A deadly secret.

But it was not so much the drawings that I did not want the woman to see, but what was on the last page – my love's contribution, her final message to me.

'Oh, I'm sorry.' She said softy, seeing my anguish but misinterpreting it. 'Your wife?'

I took the pad from her and slowly closed it.

'No, my girlfriend. Fiancée. She… She's dead.'

'I'm so sorry. Recently?'

My head slumped forward. The sketchbook slipped from my fingers to the floor. 'Yes.'

'Was she ill?'

'No, she… drowned.'

I stepped back from her, wiping my eyes with my hand.

'Oh, sorry. You do not need this.' She said.

I looked up to see them exchange a glance.

'Two years ago, our daughter was killed in a car accident,' the women continued. 'Death can come for no reason. You will never … but time, time can heal, as they say. Time is a great healer.'

'Thank you.' I said.

I looked up and out of the window. The view beyond had become much brighter, the grey sky laced with blue. I smiled. 'Look, it's stopped raining.'

'Ah, then we had better be going.' The man said.

I led them to the door then watched them walk away until they vanished behind the hedge at the end of lane. I breathed deep on the ozone-rich post-rain air.

Time is a great healer? I thought. *Bollocks will it be for me.*

I walked back into the main room of the cottage, to where my sleeping bag was rumpled up in one corner. Next to it was my old leather jacket

I reached down and picked it up then slowly slipped my arms into the sleeves. It had been my one constant over the years from right back when I first met Catherine.

Death can come for no reason.

Yes, but this had had a reason.

Why? Why did she do it? That bullshit she left on that video didn't count. That she did it for art. That she did it to protect me – from herself, from everything. That was no explanation.

Art is supposed to be all about seeing. Seeing the world not only as it is, but as it could or should be, reinterpreting it in your mind's eye, and then creating something new. It's supposed to be all about seeing, but I did not see… Not see that she belonged to another.

I drew you but did I ever see the real you?

Over the years — so many secrets. So much that she had kept from me.

I had been so blind. Right from the beginning, I had been so blind.

Protect me.

From herself?

From everything?

So there was more. More secrets.

I had to know, I realised. That I could not die… not now even think of dying, without knowing. Knowing the truth of it. The truth of all of it.

I zipped up the jacket and, only pausing to pick up the sketchbook, I walked out of the room and out of the house.

2 LIQUID SHOCK ABSORBER

'Snap!'

I looked up from staring down into my half-finished pint of bitter.

'Sor…?' I started, before my voice evaporated away.

She was beautiful.

Maybe not to everyone, maybe not classically attractive, but to me, to my eyes, she was perfect.

Like an antique bust carved by some old master, her strong features – her wide smiling mouth, sharp cheekbones and prominent nose – were all perfectly balanced. And her skin was as pale as marble. With slate-grey eyes and silver-blonde hair, the only colour to her face was a slash of thin red lips, the same scarlet colour as her fingernails.

'S… Sorry?' I tried again.

She leaned forward and a hint of perfume, something subtle and expensive, wafted towards me.

'Snap! We've both got the same jacket.' Her voice was light, the accent Home Counties. 'Well, almost.' She added, pointing to my leather biker's jacket lying on the bench-seat beside me.

Although the jacket she was wearing was cut with the same wide shoulders and was similarly studded, hers was a feminised designer version with thin supple unworn leather and the studs were small and silver. The studs in her ears were a close match but she wore no rings on her fingers, I noticed. The rest of her clothes were black and white and as stylish as her jacket and cut to accent her tall slim figure – a plain white cotton blouse, black jeans and shiny black ankle boots. Plus she carried a large black shoulder bag that was all buckles and straps. In sharp contrast to my deliberately dressed-down look of old combat trousers, baggy sweatshirt and worn trainers.

'And I think we are here for the same reason,' she continued. 'Do you mind if I join you?'

Instead of pulling out one of the empty chairs on the far side of the table she nodded down at my jacket.

'No, of course not.' I said, snatching up the jacket and laying it on down on the windowsill behind my bench seat. Dropping her bag to the floor, she sat down beside me. She moved with an easy grace, her slim leg finishing a bare inch from my thigh.

'Cat.' She twisted round offering me her hand; slim fingers and a cool narrow palm slid against my own hand.

She smiled at my frown. 'Cat, as in Catherine.'

'Ah, right. I'm Jason.' I reluctantly let her hand go and nodded towards the bar. 'Can I get you a drink?'

'Thank-you. I'll have half of whatever you're drinking.'

The bored looking young barman was sitting on a stool on the customers' side of the bar smoking while he read a copy of *The Mirror*. He stood as I approached.

It was the mid-afternoon low-point – the country's drinking habits, ingrained for seventy years, had yet to adjust to the recent novelty of all-day opening. The only other drinkers were two pensioners, a couple of tables away, who were watching the racing on a television mounted near the ceiling at the other end of the bar. The pub seemed to be a confirmed locals establishment – a tawdry oasis in a spruced-up student area; usually a type to be avoided with its chipped paint on the window frames matched by nicotine-stained wallpaper on the inside. But the name, *The Marquis of Granby*, and the fact it was a Free House had persuaded me to step inside. The fine selection of beer had further enticed me to stay for a least one, to kill some time.

'So you are here for the interviews, as well?' I asked Cat when I returned with her drink.

'Yeah.' She touched her glass to mine and then drank. 'Cheers. And good luck.'

I took a long swallow of bitter London beer.

'Nervous?' Cat said, with a raised eyebrow, before tipping back her own glass again.

'A bit… maybe. Well, I wasn't until I handed in my portfolio. That suddenly made it real. So I thought I had better get a pint or three of liquid shock absorber inside me.' I smiled then drained my glass.

Cat laughed. 'I know what you mean!'

I saw she had finished her own drink. A single long finger wiped the froth from the corners of her mouth – a delicate process I noticed, to ensure she did not smudge her lipstick.

'Another?' She asked.

'Please.' I replied.

I felt a pang of guilt as I found myself watching the play of her buttocks as she went over to the bar. I chided myself that I should be trying to psyche myself up for the imminent interrogation, not lusting after someone I'd only just met, someone who was well out of my league anyway. I thought of making my excuses and leaving but then Cat turned away from the bar with two full pints.

'London Pride, proper London beer.' She said placing one of the pints down in front of me while sipping the head off her own. 'Hope you don't mind me drinking a pint.'

'Oh, Christ no!'

'Thank goodness. I hate those 'women-should-not-drink-pints' wankers. And yeah, I certainly didn't want to hang around in the canteen back there drinking tea.'

'Sure, but I better slow down a bit. I don't want to get too pissed.'

'Oh, I don't know. Cannot do you much harm, I reckon – relaxant and all that.' She grinned. Then, casually, she reached down behind the seat and lifted up my jacket. 'So you have a motorbike then, to go with this? Or is it just for the image – like mine.' She let go of my jacket and pointed back to her own.

'No, I've got a bike. But it's nothing flash… you?'

'I've got a car, Daddy bought it for me. A brand-new Renault Clio.'

'Ahhh… Papa! Nicole!'

She raised one corner of her mouth into a half-smile.

'I know. Bit of an embarrassment when you are supposed to be a starving student. Have you come far?'

'Birmingham.'

'That's not a Birmingham accent though, is it?'

'No, I'm originally from the East Midlands, Lincolnshire. Not far from this bloke's place actually.' I waved my hand around to indicate the pub.

'Sorry? What bloke?' She frowned.

'Oh, I mean the pub name, *The Marquis of Granby*. The village of Granby's not far from where I grew up, just over the county border in Nottinghamshire, in the Vale of Belvoir. The Duke of Rutland – who owns Belvoir Castle and the surrounding estate – well his eldest son inherits the title The Marquis of Granby. Way back in the seventeen hundreds, the then Marquis was Commander in Chief of the Army. He was known for his bravery, always used to lead his troops into battle – which was exceptional for the time. In one battle he was that keen to get stuck-in he charged so fast his wig flew off! The often use that image for the pub sign, like here.'

Cat grinned. 'Yes, the sign outside, I wondered about that!'

'He loved his men,' I continued. 'And, also very unusually for the time, gave them a pension out of his own pocket when they retired. Many started pubs with the money and by way of thanks, named them after him.'

I sighed and slowly shook my head.

'What's the matter?' Cat asked.

'I've just realised all that must make me sound a right sad git.'

'No, but you do sound like you know a lot about pubs!' Cat smiled. 'That's not a bad thing, no?'

'I suppose so. But if I ever see a *Marquis of Granby* I like to have a drink. Raise a glass to the old Marquis.' I did just that. 'The Marquis!'

'And all his pubs!' Cat joined in, chinking her glass against my own. She shifted slightly and her leg touched mine. But then she moved again and the brief contact was gone.

I saw her drink was nearly finished already.

'You can certainly pack it way!'

'You calling me an alcoholic?' She gave me a raised eyebrow again. 'Don't worry I'll slow down. If you can't take the pace.'

I laughed.

'I can take a hint,' I said, standing to swallow what remained of my drink and gather up the empty glasses. Then she glanced at my jacket.

'Ah, but if you have to ride…?'

'Oh no.' I said, interrupting her as I turned for the bar. 'I'm stopping the night at a hotel, already ditched the bike there.'

I dropped the glasses off at the bar and while the barmen refilled them I walked into the pub's back-room looking for the toilet.

When I came out of the toilet she was gone. Sudden emotion surged up through me – shock, quickly followed by disappointment then the first sputterings of anger.

'Over here!'

I spun round.

Jacket-less, Cat was standing behind the pool table in the back-room next to the jukebox.

'Thought I'd run out on you?'

I smiled. 'Yeah, did it show?'

'Just a little.'

She finished her selection and picked up a cue.

This is Radio Freedom! Announced the start of a KLF track I recognised. Cat smacked the lone white ball to rocket off three cushions before sinking into a pocket.

'Not bad.' I applauded her. 'And good choice of music.'

Cat nodded over at the jukebox. 'Judging from what's on there they must get some students in here. Anyway, want a game?'

'Sure.'

I saw that Cat had already brought over both our jackets and piled them on top of each other on a stool next to a side table, her bag by them on the floor. I fetched our drinks over to the table while she racked up the balls.

Cat lost the toss and I broke, fluking a yellow.

'So what brings you to applying for the MA at Goldsmiths.' She said, as I lined up my next shot. 'You doing art at Birmingham University?'

'Oh, no… I'm pretty much unqualified as far as art goes. I'm trying to get in on the 'unqualified amateur with talent' thing.'

Cat laughed. I sunk an easy plant and moved on to the next shot.

'I was actually working in computing, a programer.'

'Impressive.' She said with raised eyebrows.

'You think so? No, not really… just something I stumbled into. I was always good at sciences at school, did engineering at university. I liked computers – well found them easy to work with. So for lack of anything else to do I found myself walking into a job with them.'

I managed a risky long shot but left myself with nothing obvious.

'Computers are cool.' Cat said, as I pondered my next shot. 'Daddy's got one for his business. One of those new personal computer clones. But you said, 'was'.'

I tried to play safe but botched the snooker.

'Oh yeah, 'was'.' I said.

Cat leaned over the table to cue up her shot. For the first time I noticed a thin white line of a scar that ran from the back of left hand up her forearm. She saw me looking.

'Oh, that's just where I fell off a horse once.'

'Sorry, I didn't–'

'Don't worry about it.' She said, sinking a double.

'Anyway computers are cool to play around with, or play games on, or whatever.' I said as I re-chalked my cue, watching Cat start clearing up the table. 'But sitting there all day, debugging stock control systems, with the same desk, the same four walls, the same faces staring back at you every time you look up. Hell on Earth. Every day I had to walk down this long corridor to my office… One day I just could not get to the end of it. I don't know if it was a panic attack or something but I just could not breathe… each step was like a noose being pulled tighter. I went back outside for some air and just kept walking, well virtually running, back to the car park, to my bike. I rode back to my flat and wrote out a resignation letter as soon as I stepped through the door. My friends, my parents, all thought I was mad but it was like someone had been smothering me all the time I was there, it was just so good to be able to breathe at last. Anyway, while I was wondering what to do next, I read about this course in the paper and thought 'why the hell not?' I always loved art, from way back, wandering round galleries between lectures at college, watching art docs on the telly, doing a bit of drawing and painting in my spare time. Whenever anyone I worked with was going – 'Modern art, it's all bullshit!' I was going – 'No, you are just so wrong!' I did do art at school – never took it past O Level – but I've been thinking perhaps I should have. Just found maths and the sciences easy, that's all. Art's always been hard work for me, but much more satisfying in the end.'

While I had been talking Cat had potted all her reds. I paused as she lined up a long black to a bottom corner pocket. She just missed, the ball rattling in the pocket's jaws.

'Well, that's me. How about you, what brings you here?' I asked her.

'Me? Too dim for anything else besides art, despite my public school education.'

'Don't do yourself down. It's obvious you are not stupid.'

Cat was standing close to me as I looked over the table, working-out an order to clear up the remaining yellows while avoiding the pocket she had now covered. I cued-up and sank the first one.

'Well okay, perhaps you could just say I'm not academic.' Cat said. 'Art was the only thing I've ever had any talent for, apart from horse-riding, but I wasn't ever going to be good enough to be a pro there. So off I went to the Slade to do Fine Art. I was actually engaged for a while. That was before I realised he was a fucking horrible gormless wanker. By that time, I'd started to enjoy my art. I mean really enjoy it, pushing myself into new areas, wanting to do something radical, stopping up all night sketching, then painting all the next day or out with my camera. My fiancé wasn't very happy about that, wanted me to settle down, be the little doting wifey while he was busy being 'something in the City'. Well fuck that. I ditched him… And my parents were very unhappy about that, let me tell you. But it was time to move on. See if I can make it as a proper artist. If all else fails I'll get an assistant job in a gallery, wait for my trust fund to come through and carry on doing my art in my spare time. I'm not going to stop now.'

I had cleared up all my yellows and I was now on the black. It still hung over the bottom pocket from Cat's last attempt to pot it and I easily knocked it in.

'Well done.' Cat said.

'Thanks. Another?'

'Yeah,' Cat smiled, and then winked. 'Now I'm used to this cue, I'll cream you'

'You can try. I won't be so easy on you this time.' I grinned as I crouched down at the side of the table to feed in some change. 'It's a different world to me – trust fund, public school, horse riding. Not like the council estate I grew up on.'

'Oh, you'd soon tire of it, I assure you.' She racked the balls again. 'The best artists on my course were the ones who had to struggle up.'

'Well…'

Cat sighed and dropped her head forward, turning slightly to give me a sideways look round the edge of hair.

'Oh God, I must sound so patronising. I grew up in such a fucking bubble. Wasn't until The Slade that I actually started to meet some real people.'

'Well, I wouldn't tire of the money. And it has to be more interesting than my home-town.'

'Granby, was it?' She said as she bent down to break.

'No, Grantham. The 'most boring town in Britain'. Official.'

'Really?' The split was less open than the last game. I tried and failed to find an easy pot.

'Yeah, there's been a national vote and everything, was in several of the tabloids. The local paper was trying to drum up support that it's not, of course. Fat chance, it's like *Twin Peaks* without the excitement.'

I cut one red into a side pocket but fluffed my position. I played safe on the next shot.

'So who do you reckon killed Laura Palmer, then?' Cat asked as she assessed the table. She took on a long shot.

'God knows, my money's on the Log Lady… or Hannibal Lecter'

'*Ugh!*' She pulled a face, as she missed the shot. '*Silence of the Lambs*… didn't like that all.'

Cat finished her beer as I returned to the table.

'Another?' She asked, waving her empty glass at me.

I paused, but then convinced myself one more pint would not make much difference. I was now in a drinking mood, in the groove where booze was loosening me up nicely without any great detrimental effects as yet. And I was enjoying the company.

'Yeah, go on.' I said.

Whilst Cat was at the bar I managed to pot another couple of balls before I missed a tight cut, playing it too soft.

'I knew Grantham was important for something.' Cat said smiling as she came back with two more pints. 'Just remembered it's the divine Margaret's home town.' She added with a sarcastic edge to her voice. She placed down the drinks on the side table then spun out a halo above her head with one long finger.

'I take it you're not a fan then.' I said.

'Ah no, a bit too middle class for me.' She curled up her lip in a fake sneer then laughed. 'Grocer's daughter, marrying money. Fancy that running the country.'

'God, I drank so much the day she was booted out.'

'Oh, yes. I remember her crying. I was too, with laughter.'

She aimed up a long shot and this time she was spot on.

'I would've have thought you were a Tory.'

'Perhaps, I am... bah, probably too posh for that. Most of the family tends to beyond politics. Traditional cross-benchers.' She efficiently moved around the table quickly sinking two more difficult pots.

I gave her a sideways look.

'Cross-benchers. House of Lords. You're titled then?'

She stopped playing and turned to face me, walking around to my side of the table.

'Well... yes, but only minor.'

'Ah, only 'minor' nobility... just a small castle then?'

'No, not quite, but we do have a family place out in Kent.'

'A stately home? How many servants?'

'Stop it!' She gave me a mock punch on the arm then shook her head. 'This is all so embarrassing. I try not to tell people straight away. I don't want people getting the wrong idea.'

'Come the revolution, I'll try to see to it that you're spared.'

'Thanks,' she said. 'Yeah, here's to Prime Minster Kinnock.'

We raised our glasses.

'So, anyway, you're the art expert.' I said to Cat as she returned to the game.

'Not quite.' She put me into a difficult snooker. It was the beginning of a safety battle – neither of us having easy pots on our last few balls –- and we started exchanging snooker after snooker, nipping pots were we could.

'Yeah, but more than me. You any idea what sort of questions they will be asking?'

'Well, *Freeze* is bound to come up. This guy called Damien Hirst organised it, he's their rising star.'

'Oh yeah, that show the students put on themselves after graduating? I've read about it. It got a fair bit of press interest.'

'Apart from that,' Cat continued. 'Just be enthusiastic about what you want to do. Like you have been with me. Don't blather on about theory. Craig-Martin's on the panel, he hates that and he will be able to spot any bullshit a mile off.'

'Right,' I lifted up my near empty pint. 'He's the 'Oak Tree' guy.'

'Yeah, glass of water on a high shelf – Is it an oak tree?'

'I just laughed when I first heard it. But then after a while I thought it was brilliant… You can't reach up to touch it, so how do you know it's not an oak tree that *just happens* to look like a glass of water? You can't prove it isn't. It's like one of those Zen things… what's the sound of one hand clapping, or if a tree – an oak tree in fact – falls in a forest and no one's there, does it make a sound? A total mind-fuck. Well, I think that's what it means.'

'I don't think it has any final meaning,' Cat said. 'Like the best art. It's supposed to question what sculpture actually is… What makes it different to just any old object. But only mention it in passing, if at all. Don't stress on it.' She potted her last yellow. 'What's in your portfolio? That's what is important.'

'Ah, that's my weak spot. Some sketches and drawings, ideas for the future. There is also this.' I picked up my leather jacket and fished out a sheet of rolled up graph paper from the inside pocket. I had started filling in every second tiny square with blue Biro, to create the start of an intricate chequer board pattern. 'I'm starting to think it's just a mad idea. 'An Infinite Capacity for Cruelty' I've called it. Still working on it. I'm aiming to do one for every school day of the year. It was a punishment at my old school. One sick fucker in the sixth form came up with it, a nice variation on lines. You fill in every odd square with a pen. It takes absolutely fucking forever. And if you weren't neat enough – you tried to be too quick and missed squares or went over the lines too often – you had to do it again. I had an idea it would make a good metaphor for how cruel man is and also how pointless and cruel a lot of our so-called education system is.' My enthusiasm petered out and I sighed. 'Terrible, isn't it?'

'No, that's a great idea! Sell it to them just like you did with me.' She smiled. 'They'll love it.'

'I hope so.' I smiled back. 'Also got some sketches for something I'm planning of doing about the built verses natural environment, bring my engineering into it.'

'Yeah, play on that... it's your unique selling point – your non-arty background. It's a lot more than I have, anyway. Just some self-portraits and vague plans about themes of identity.' Cat said as she leaned over the table. She cued up on the black and nodded at a side pocket.

'Tricky.' I said.

She just changed her angle and suddenly I saw it was an easy double. The black rolled into the pocket.

'Not that tricky then, well played.' I said.

'Thanks,' She said as came round to my side of the table again to join me and picked up her drink. 'Best of three?'

I glanced down at my watch.

'Fuck, no! I'm due on in ten minutes!' I shoved the sheet of graph paper back into my jacket pocket and knocked back the rest of my pint. I threw on my jacket, swaying from the effects of drinking so much in so short a time.

'Wait a second!' Catherine crouched down next to her bag. She pulled out a notepad and pen and scribbled something down. Standing, she ripped out the page and leaning in close to me to push it into one of my jacket pockets.

'My phone number. Let me know how you get on.' A quick kiss, her lips hot against mine, her hands at my waist. 'Good luck.'

I stared at her open-mouthed as she stepped back and flicked her head towards the door.

'Go on, be off with you!'

I sailed into that interview three sheets to the wind.

But I stormed it.

3 BIN BAGS

I stared up at our studio. Stared up at the window that had illuminated Catherine the last time I had drawn her. To anyone else it would be nothing special – just one window on the top floor of a turn-of-the-century warehouse in a small square of other similar buildings in the middle of London. One building like a thousand others spread out across the capital.

But this was Hoxton. And a stones-throw from Hoxton Square itself – the ground-zero of the strange other-world that was the British art business in the closing years of the twentieth century. Studios, galleries and other miscellaneous viewing spaces – from one-room ex-shop-fronts to huge warehouses – plus the offices of dealers, framers, specialist PR companies and a dozen other associated hangers-on had spread out through the borough like a rapidly-mutating fungus, corrupting the original intent of the buildings with this new post-modern industry, encrusting the drab Victoriana, the post-war building boom, Sixties Brutalism with a gaudy new intent.

In the square where I was standing, the old workshops on the other three sides had had funky designed, garishly coloured and deliberately intriguing logos added next to their entrances – with names like 'Kaos Kreation', 'Dollars and Sense', 'The Wire Office' and 'Twenty Three' in the currently most fashionable typefaces.

Ours just had 'Five Feathers Studio' engraved into a brass plaque with the conservative seriffed letters you might see outside any solicitors or doctors' surgery. Above was a discreet version of our official logo – five differently styled feathers.

It was so quiet that morning that I found it hard to recreate in my mind the times when the square had been flooded with noise, crammed to overflowing during the after-show parties. And although the early sun warmed my back I could not help feeling chilled as different memories came flooding back.

Memories of the bad times.

And the worst time of all.

The key ring was in my hand. My hand stretched out to the lock but then it slowed. Stopped, wavering. The sun glinted off the edge of the key pointing towards the lock as it swayed in front of me; the bright light lasered into my eye. I squinted and turned my head from it, blinking away the after image.

Not now.

Not yet.

Our studio on the fourth floor I could face, but not the stairs. And especially not the third floor.

Not when the memory of climbing that staircase one chill night was suddenly so close to me. Something I thought I had buried but was now so raw and so vivid, skittering and scratching on the edge of my consciousness like a rat trapped in the wall space of an abandoned building.

A faint sweet smell of decay drifted in from the alley behind me, a familiar Sunday-morning smell. A dark bouquet from the detritus of the previous night – from the pools of vomit and the discarded half-filled glasses left on pub window ledges, but most of all from the piles of black bin bags thrown onto the street outside the local restaurants and takeaways. Some of which had split so that their contents spilled out into the street, leaving them looking like the carcasses of dead aliens after an unsuccessful invasion, their bright multi-textured, multicoloured innards cast out onto the pavement.

I put the key ring with its Five Feathers logo fob back in my pocket, turned and walked away down the alley.

The studio had seemed the obvious place to start. The only place to start, really. Since the night I had found Catherine's suicide note I had not been back to the place – living in hotels while I sorted the funeral arrangements and bought my potential final gallery.

I had left the farmhouse the previous day, leaving everything bar the clothes I was wearing and the sketchbook filled with my drawings of Catherine. I had dropped the latter off at my solicitors when I had picked up the keys to studios – the temptation to lose myself constantly flicking through it was just too strong.

The local mini-store was the same as ever, even down to its smell, a faint soapy-lemony fragrance of floor cleaner that no-one else ever seemed to use.

'Are you all right?'

I looked up.

'I said, are you all right?' It was Mr Singh from behind the counter. It was the first time I could remember ever seeing him not smiling.

'Oh yes, sorry…' I said as I walked up to the counter. 'It's just…'

'I understand.' He looked over to the rack of newspapers. 'I read about it of course. We are very sorry for your loss. I wondered if I would see you again.'

All I could do was mumble a thank-you back at him.

A dark arm, wreathed with jangling bangles, pulled aside the plastic strips of the curtain that separated the stock room from the rest of the shop and his wife stepped forward to stand beside him. She handed him a mug of some hot drink then looked straight at me, her large eyes filled with sympathy.

'It must be terrible for you.'

I was suddenly embarrassed by their concern. I found myself moving away from the counter, down the narrow aisle crammed full with produce to the fridges at the back grabbing cartons of orange juice and milk. As I returned to Mr Singh I forced a smile on my face.

'I will be here for a bit, I think. While I… while I sort of put my affairs in order. After that I don't really know.'

I placed the cartons on the counter. Mr Singh produced a carrier bag.

'I understand. I will miss you if you do go. And Miss Catherine of course. I will always miss her. It is sad. She seemed so happy.'

I pulled a sliced loaf off a shelf.

'Yes.' His wife said. 'I think it will be for the best if you think of her when she was happy'

'I'll try to.' I said as I went back to the fridges for ham and cheese.

'I did not know you were artists until I read it in the newspapers.' Mr Singh said when I returned. He started putting my goods into a bag after his wife had rang up the prices on the till. 'Most of it is not to my taste… animals cut in half and the rest. But I suppose I should have guessed. That you were artists. Living round here. And the other thing.'

'We didn't like to shout about it.' I said. 'People can get some funny ideas.'

'I can see why.' He said. 'It is not often I have a naked woman walk into my shop.'

Mr Singh now smiled at me. Grinned in fact. As did his wife.

I stared back at him open-mouthed.

'What? Sorry?'

'A naked woman. Especially one *that* naked.'

And then I remembered.

I remembered waking one Sunday, horrifically hung-over to see Catherine standing over me naked, a career bag dangling from one hand. Naked and bald. Shaved bald everywhere.

'Just been to the shop,' she said. 'You looked like you needed a lie-in for once.'

I groaned. Then suddenly my eyes were wide open.

'Oh, dear God. Don't tell me you went there and back stark-bollock naked!'

Catherine raised an eyebrow – her eyebrows and eyelashes being her only concession to total depilation. 'Of course. It's what we agreed last night.'

'Yes, but I thought you would be spending the whole day in doors.' I half sat up, propping myself up on one elbow. 'I didn't think you would be waltzing down to the shop like Lady Godiva sans horse! Wait a minute... did anyone see you?'

'Of course people saw me! I got quite a few wolf whistles, I'm proud to say.'

'But anything could have... '

'Well, it didn't.' She pouted her lips. 'And I don't know why you are being such a prude. It's not like half the world won't be seeing me like this in my photographs tonight. Well, slightly more hirsute. But they will see me in all my glory at the viewing.'

'Look, I still really don't think that is a good idea. Especially now that you have… I think…'

She dropped down to her knees, straddling me. The carrier bag fell to one side, the contents spewing out over the floor.

'My mind's made up.' She said. 'I won't be changing it'

Catherine leaned in close, smiled a tight feral smile and kissed me quick on the lips. She jerked her head away before I could kiss her back. Placing her hands on my shoulder, Catherine cocked her head to one side then frowned.

'Now, you want me to make you some breakfast or…' She slowly looked down her own naked body, then stared straight into my own eyes. 'Perhaps you want to eat something else.'

'Breakfast.' I grinned backed at her. 'First.'

'Oh god, I'm sorry.' I said.

The apology was automatic but I had started smiling myself.

'It was part of an art project.' I continued. 'The being bald and naked thing. But I didn't realise she was going to go out like that! You never mentioned it… I mean I avoided coming back here for weeks. And when I did, you never mentioned it at all. I finally thought she must have just been joking with me.'

'I thought you might have been avoiding me because of that.' Mr Singh laughed. 'I thought if I brought it up you might desert me forever.'

I paid Mr Singh and he handed me the bag full of groceries.

'I told him,' His wife said, laughing too. "Every customer is still a customer… Even naked ones!"

As I walked out the shop I realised I had started laughing with them; laughing for the first time that I could remember.

But the laughter soon died away and as I walked away from the shop back towards the studio.

I stopped.

Dropped the bag of shopping down beside me.

Looked again.

Looked again up the street ahead of me because just for a second I thought I had seen her. I thought I had seen Catherine, running ahead of me and ducking down a side street, long coat and long hair streaming out being her. The way she would sometimes teased me, playing tag, tapping me on the shoulder then skipping out in front me, turning back and waving at me — 'first one back to the studio makes breakfast!' — and running off.

I rubbed my eyes like some silent movie actor.

No. No way. Must have imagined it.

I crouched down and gathered up my spilled shopping.

This is such bullshit! Pull yourself together. She would not thank you for it. Grieving like some weakling until you crack up.

I stood up.

And all at once it came to me.

The way forward was to do what she would have done. Stuck? Blocked? Then just put on a new mask. Take on a new identity and work forward.

If I was going to get to the bottom of what happened — to investigate it, to find out why she did it — I was going to have to become an investigator myself. A Private Investigator. A

PI. A hard-bitten cynical world-weary PI who gets the job done, even if he doesn't get the dame in the final reel. Like in one of those old movies me and Catherine used to watch together… a Philip Marlowe or especially a Sam Spade. After all, although *Casablanca* was our favourite film, *The Maltese Falcon* was not far behind.

I squared up my imaginary fedora and with renewed purpose walked down those – well if not exactly mean, then familiar streets – back to our studio.

After the sun-drenched yard the stairway was cool and clammy and I almost shivered as I started climbing the stairs. But Sam Spade would not have shivered so I ignored it and pushed on.

Taking the steps two at a time, I found I was past the third floor before I had even begun thinking about it.

Remember that classic episode of *Steptoe and Son*, the one where they split the house in two? That was what me and Catherine did to our studio space. During the conversion we had taken out all the dividing walls, stripping the whole place back to brick and bare boards. The top floor of the warehouse was now one long open space that we had divided into two, working exclusively in our own halves.

When we had first moved into the studio together, the chaos that had ensued, with each other's materials and equipment becoming intermingled and lost, almost bumping into each other all the time as we stepped around each other's work and having to negotiate space for larger projects had been a nightmare. I had suggested converting the space into two separate studios, or even one of us moving out, but

Catherine had come up with the current plan and it had worked well ever since.

For most of the day, Walkmen on, we had been locked into our own creative worlds. But not completely isolated from each other; we often discussed ideas together at meal times and on into the evenings.

There were no physical barriers but there were very much a psychological ones. Naturally with my map obsession I had planned all this out on paper, then carefully measured and divided the bare wooden floor up with silver gaffer tape.

Most people thought we were crazy when they heard about our arrangement but it worked for us, enabling the two of us to work productively together in the same room but on different projects at the same time.

And we did share the rest of the space. At the far wall we had boxed-off a small bathroom – that had ended up so stuffed with house plants it was like bathing in the fern house at Kew. In a larger room alongside we plumbed in a couple more sinks to create a darkroom for Catherine. At the other end was an open-plan kitchen area with stark designer units and, in contrast, a large old oak dining table with several odd chairs that we had picked up at flea-markets and second-hand shops. There was another smaller neutral no man's land in the middle – with our futon and leather sofa, television, video recorder, PlayStation and sound system. On the wall behind, facing the row of windows, was a large metal framed photograph of the moon.

So although we worked physically apart in the shared space we always came back together in our shared areas. Plus no matter how separate we tried to be there was always a little of each of us in the other's half – a borrowed pen, a sketch of an idea that had come in the middle of the night that might help the other's current project, the discarded remains of a snack one had made for the other. Some *ying* in the others *yang*.

But as a rule we never physically ventured into each other's work space.

There was a strong sweet smell when I opened the door to the studio; a pungent variation on the odour from the bin bags earlier. I immediately spotted what was the cause of it. In the middle of the dining table was a bowl of fruit, that had now decayed down to a mush of semi-liquefied brown-tinged apples and white mould encrusted oranges. The artist in me was thinking it would make a good subject for a memento mori for my beloved, that I should be finding a camera to record it. However my more practical side had me already in action, dumping the lot, bowl and all, into a black bin liner I had ripped from a roll I found under the sink. I delved further among the bottles of bleach, surface cleaner and washing-up liquid, cans of spray polish, boxes of soap powder and other cleaning products and found a can of air freshener. I sprayed the pine scent all around the inside of the studio to cover the cloying smell. I finished in the middle of the floor next to the sofa.

I paused and took my time looking over the whole room.

There was something about the room that was not right, but it was something that I could not quite place. Something small but significant.

I walked over to my half of the studio.

Two drawing boards were set up to catch the light from the window, a high stool behind them. A row of filing cabinets and a couple of desks were shoved up against the far wall, a PC and Mac on one. A row of plastic fishing-tackle boxes on the floor were overflowing with art supplies. On the floor and plastered over every available surface were sketches and photos that I had set up for a television interview for the Turner Prize. Plus there was research material on tombs, crematoria, abandoned graveyards and related statuary – angels and the like, and in contrast computer printouts of simple geometric forms. There were several piles of books I had been using for reference: mathematical text books, histories of science, second-hand pulp horror novels from the Seventies, a stack of *New Scientist*. Other scattered detritus included test tubes of soil samples, several small strips of polished wood, a light bulb painted white, two videos of the film *Scanners*, a copy of Paul Strand's 'Blind Woman' torn from a textbook on the history of photography and a photocopy of Dürer's 'Melencolia I'.

At one time this stuff had meant everything to me – the base materials for what I had thought at the time was my life's greatest work. Now, after what had happened, it was all nothing to me. Just a pile of rubbish.

But what was it? What was wrong with the room?

Had something changed here?

I looked over it all again.

No.

I turned towards Catherine's side.

The dark eye of a video camera perched on top of a tripod stared right back at me.

Video had been the new thing for her. She had been moving towards it stepping away from her photography, as I had been moving away from maps and towards something else entirely.

I briefly flashed back to watching the grainy footage of the video found at the site of her suicide that had been recorded bare minutes before she had jumped. Their last will and testament and their supposed explanation for the act.

There must have been a reason.

A real reason, not the nonsensical stuff on the tape. There had to be.

Her side was a lot barer than mine.

A hell of lot.

I realised then that she must have planned that her work was coming to an end and had tidied everything neatly away. There was a washing basket full of carefully folded backdrops and a clothes rail of bagged costumes. On a table there were her cameras – both film and video – packed away in their cases and bags plus boxed up lenses, filters and other photographic equipment all in neat perfectly spaced rows. A collection of dismantled lighting rigs and folded reflectors lay on the floor. Against the far wall was a small fridge that she kept her film in. Next to the fridge, beneath the light-bulb surrounded mirror – that always looked like it belonged in a theatrical dressing room – was a table covered with the lipsticks, blushers and mascaras again all arranged in neat lines.

I must have spent hours looking over at her half of the room, watching her work, mostly when she had not been aware that I was doing it.

And now there was… something?

Something about it was not quite right, I was certain now. Something had changed but I could not see what it was.

Then I remembered the Room World project.

When I was a kid, like a lot of boys at the time, I went through a phase of making model aeroplanes. A whole squadron of them had hung from my bedroom ceiling on the end of cotton threads and I had imagined dogfights between them as they circled the lampshade. Plus I had fought many pretend skirmishes across the carpet with platoons of plastic soldiers; staged armoured assaults around the bed with Airfix tanks.

A few weeks before Catherine's suicide, while thinking back to those times, I had come up with the idea for the 'Room World'. A way to refer back to my older work but also to springboard off into something new, side-stepping trying to build on what had won me the Turner prize – which I knew, once I completed it, despite the plaudits, was a creative dead-end.

The idea was to look at the room I lived and worked in at a new scale. Room World – to make the room a world. To blow up the scale from my wargaming days, but instead of the floor being limited to battlefield, to think of it as a whole world. To think of it as the physical, three-dimensional map of the surface of some surreal planet. The floor became a flat bare desert. The furniture became mountain ranges with strange sheer cliff edges. Then I thought further and saw the place flooded with an imaginary ocean. Then the tops of the tables and other furniture became island counties. In my mind, our two different work areas became the basis for two civilisations. My side were militaristic map-making explorers, who mined the scrap at the bottom of their oceans to create fleets of iron battleships. Catherine's were harsh portrait-painting obsessives who worshipped the sun-nova gods that were her camera flashes and built squadrons of glass aeroplanes. The kitchen area remained an unexplored place filled with weird crashed alien spacecraft. The bathroom an equally mysterious swamp-like jungle.

When I told Catherine about it she had added the idea of 'Fuck Island'. Our futon become a place where two star-crossed lovers – one fleeing from each of the civilisations – could meet and fall in love.

Initially seeing a series of paintings I thought it could be taken beyond into other media. Perhaps even a children's illustrated story-book.

Probably change the name of 'Fuck Island' in the latter case, though.

I had not got very far with the project before Catherine's death had changed everything; only producing just a few scribbled notes.

Except for one other thing.

In a fit of enthusiasm I had borrowed a Polaroid camera from Catherine and spent an afternoon firing off shot after shot, to create an accurate record of the studio at one moment in time. The next step would have been to use them to create some maps and plans. That had never happened but I knew I still had the Polaroids.

Quickly, I pulled open the draws of the filing cabinet until I found the photographs – several thick elastic-banded bundles of them.

I snapped off the bands and started flicking through them. Holding each one up, I compared what I had photographed to how things were now.

Nothing was exactly the same of course – the half-drunk blue and white stripped mug of coffee next to my drawing board in one Polaroid had long been washed up and re-used many times and was currently sitting on the draining board next to the sink – but I was sure what I was looking for, what was nagging at me, was something that was beyond the superficial. On the other hand it also had to be something subtle, something un-obvious, that I could not see straight away.

Moving around the room from each exact spot that I taken a photo from to the next, I compared before and after, recreating my movements I had taken around the room those long weeks ago.

Then I saw it.

From where I was standing by the windows I looked over Catherine's side of the room to the rear wall.

The fridge had been moved.

The small refrigerator near her dressing table that Catherine kept her film in was in a different position to what it had been.

I crouched slightly, took one step to the side to line up the photo exactly, holding it at the end of my outstretched arm swinging it in and out of my field of view to double check.

It was so obvious now... the relative position of the fridge to Catherine's make-up table was totally different. Only a couple of inches, but the fridge had definitely been moved.

'Yes.' I hissed under my breath, dropping the photographs to the floor.

I hesitated to step over into her half of the room.

But only for a second, there were no third floor horrors to go past this time.

I walked straight over to the fridge. Closer, I saw a couple of new brighter scratches in the wooden floorboards in front of the fridge, where it had obviously been pulled out then shoved back in a slightly different position. I leaned forward. Something had been crammed in behind. I grabbed both sides of the fridge and dragged it away from the wall, spinning it around to one side.

A large padded envelope has been shoved down the back behind the black metal cooling coils. I pulled it out. The envelope was addressed to Catherine via some PO box.

It had already been opened. I reached in and pulled out the contents – a letter, an A4 card folder and two loose Yale keys.

The card folder contained a set of pen and ink drawings, plus some photocopies of the originals. The drawings were clearly in Catherine's hand. I could clearly recognise her style, even though these were a pastiche of Victorian illustration.

The first had a young woman smartly dressed with a silk top-hat, riding a horse. Then what was obviously the same woman, but this time she was wearing a parlour maid's uniform, standing head-bowed in front of a stern-looking moustached older gentleman. The next showed the maid pouring water from a jug down the naked back of another woman in a bath. I was shocked to see the following drawing had the maid bent over a chair crying, dress pulled up to show her bloomers while the gentlemen from before was standing over her, looking on lasciviously, bending a cane bent in his outstretched hands. After that the last few drawings became positively pornographic.

When the hell did she do these?

I turned to the letter and quickly scanned through it. From some publishing company called 'Oyster Press' it thanked Catherine for her illustrations for their forth-coming novel, *Maid to Measure*.

One particular phrase toward the end caught my eye.

'We have no problems with you using the pseudonym 'Fanny Dore'.'

Fanny Dore?

Fanny Dore. Phantom Door. The Ghost Door! At that party in the second term!

When… When I. No, when we…

4 CROP CIRCLE

'Oh god, no, it was awful,' Mark said. He drew deep on his cigarette until the tip glowed brightly, then blew out a long dragon-like stream of smoke over our heads. 'Like walking into a room full of naked jockeys or something.'

I had just come downstairs back to the entrance hall where Mark was standing near the front door, talking to two clowns. I was about to start a second circuit of the party, to see if I had missed Cat the first time around. This particular large shared student house in New Cross was unfamiliar to me, and I was wondering if I might have a skipped a room on the first circuit. However this sounded like it could be a conversation worth stopping and listening to, at least for a short while.

'No, it wasn't like you would think at all.' Mark continued, with a shake of his head.

As usual he was looking more like a mechanic than an artist, with greasy-looking jeans and a baggy dark wool jumper. He had obviously not bothered to shave for a couple of days but his shaggy hair was looking shorter than the last time I had seen him. However, judging by the way it jutted out in clumps, he had hacked it back himself.

As he waved away the remaining smoke in front of him with the back of his hand ash fell from the end of his half-smoked cigarette and scattered down the front of his grubby jumper.

'Shit.' He tried to brush away the ash, only making it worse – rubbing it into the wool, leaving a long pale streak behind.

I noticed a new plaster on one finger that was already smeared grey with dirt. His hands – thin and delicate as a pianist's – were spattered with a collection of scabbed minor cuts and healing burn-marks. His bitten-down nails and the cuticles of his fingers always seemed to be stained with thin dark streaks of grime so that his finger nails ended up looking like a beach after a tanker disaster, with new streaks of oil-stained sand left behind by each retreating tide.

'*Oooo!* I don't know! Sounds a bit of all-right to me, dear.' Fred, the taller, fatter of the two clowns said, sounding camper than a *Carry On* film.

His head was shaved bald and smothered with thick white make-up, except for a large black splat on the top of his crown that looked like a enormous dead spider had been squashed flat there. A red heart surrounded one eye and the lips were out-lined in purple. He wore an old dress with a large bright yellow flower pattern on it that looked like it came from a charity shop.

Ginger, the smaller, shorter clown, was done up like Chaplain in baggy black suit and a bowler hat – too large, and pulled down so the brim was just above the eyes. The eyes were crossed with lines of make-up and the outfit was completed with the traditional red nose.

The front door opened with a blast of cold air as more people streamed in, obviously Goldsmiths' students but no-one I recognised.

Mark reached down to pick up an unlabelled plastic bottle filled with some dark fluid from the floor.

'Let's get in here and out of these people's way.' Mark said around the cigarette now clamped between his lips, pointing with his bottle at the doorway to the front room.

There was music blaring out in the back of the house somewhere – 'Jump Around' blended into 'Ebeneezer Goode' as we moved out of the corridor – but inside the room it was relatively quiet, and almost unoccupied.

All the large high-ceilinged downstairs rooms had been emptied of furniture for the party and this one had been half-heartedly tarted-up. The walls were hung with large old bed sheets that had been covered with derivative Pollock-like paint dribbles and splashes.

The door had been pushed back as far against the wall inside the room as it would go. Mark leaned back against it and took a swig from his bottle.

I had a couple of cans of Stella in my jacket pocket, having dumped the rest of the six-pack I had brought with me in the kitchen on my first tour of the party. I fished a can out and pulled back the ring-pull.

'You see,' Mark said. 'I thought it was going to be the experience of a life-time but it was suddenly like being in an audition for the Diddy Men or something. Which puts you off your stride somewhat.'

'Is there some explanation to all this or is it just some surreal fantasy of yours?' I asked him.

Mark turned to me with a half-grin.

'Last summer I ended up hanging around with a load of gay porn stars. Got invited to an orgy. But the thing is they are all short-arses. Not one above five-foot six. Because when they are on screen it makes their dicks look bigger. In reality, like, most blokes' cocks are roughly the same size. So a smaller man's dick looks bigger in proportion, especially on screen. Like how they use small dinner plates in adverts.'

'Well, speak for yourself. Mine is fucking massive!' Ginger suddenly piped up with a high-pitched squeak.

'Mine too, dear!' Fred said.

'I think this is all coming under way too much information.' I added, mainly to myself, thinking maybe this was not a conversation I really wanted to be part of after all.

'But I tell you what it really made me think of,' Mark continued. 'That film… the one based on the kid's book. The one in the psychedelic sweet factory. It was like seeing a room full of those dwarves in it. Umpa Lumpas? All shagging each other. God, what's it called?'

'Charlie and the Chocolate Factory.' Fred said.

'That's the name of the book,' I found myself saying. 'The film's actually called *Willy Wonka and the Chocolate Factory.'*

When I saw the look of disdain Fred gave me I instantly regretted my pedantry. I looked down and sipped on my Stella.

'Whatever,' Fred said, turning back to Mark. 'But a room full of porn stars…? My willy would have been totally wonkared, I can tell you!'

I nearly choked on my lager, as I laughed with everyone else.

'So, Mark,' Fred continued, pointing at me. 'Is this a new member of your fan club? You've not told us about him have you, you naughty boy?'

'Nah,' Mark said. 'Jason's just on my course.'

'Not that we ever see much of what art Mark actually does.' I said.

Mark shrugged. 'I keep telling you, I'm being deliberately secretive. Most of the stuff I make is just too big to drag into college that's all.'

'But if these two are your fan club,' I said nodding at Fred and Ginger, 'then perhaps they can tell me?'

'Oh no, dear.' Fred said. 'He keeps it all a big secret from us too. And I would have thought that all us gay artists should stick together.'

'Ah, well, I'm not... gay, that is. But... erm–' I tried to stutter an answer.

'Only teasing,' Fred cut in. 'Though I'm surprised he hasn't turned you yet!' He held up a hand to me before I could say anything to that. 'No! No! We are off. There are others who will better appreciate our devotion. Mark is obviously so butch now he's forgotten he's gay.'

'Yes.' Ginger added. 'He might make us straight!'

With perfect timing they both turned on their heels and paraded out of the room.

Mark slowly shook his head. 'Those two are so over the top even I find it trying some times. God knows what you think.'

'Well, err...' I said slowly, not knowing quite what to say. 'Was that when you were in the States? That, err, party?'

'Yeah, last summer,' Mark said. 'Pity, I can't afford to go back any time soon. I was hoping to nip over to Yugoslavia this Easter. Beautiful country. But no chance of that now.'

'Real shame. Never been myself but I heard it was always a good place for a cheap holiday. Poor sods.'

I was interrupted as more people I vaguely recognised from college streamed into the room. No one I was particularly friends with but we exchanged nods as Mark and I stepped back out of the way to let them past.

'They should have taken this door off.' Mark said, pointing with his bottle to where the door met the frame. 'Make things a lot easier. See, you can take it right off its hinges. You don't even need a screwdriver. It's a lift-off hinge.'

I looked closer and saw the door was a cheap lightweight replacement to whatever had been there originally. The hinges were not the normal type – with flanges attached to both door and frame with a separate pin going through the middle of them – the door-frame halves of the hinges here were just fixed pins that each door-hinge, consisting of a single half flange, slotted down on to.

'Look,' Mark said. Holding his cigarette between his lips and resting his bottle of drink on the floor, he took hold of the door. He lifted the door until the door-hinges were almost off the pins.

'Easy.' He added as he lowered the door back again.

'Don't give people ideas.' I said. 'Someone will walk off with it for an 'art project' or something.'

'What, like Trish?' He laughed.

'Who did you think? Her 'magpie' thing or whatever it was.' I took another swig of my larger. 'I tell you one thing. I did not really think it would be like this. I mean I had a pretty active social life as a student first time around but this is…' I waved my can around the room at where the people who had just come in were talking and drinking. 'I could be out every night if I wanted to, to things like this. Plus all the free viewing at galleries, with wine of course.'

'Yeah, the Christmas party season just seems to be going on forever.'

'Only a few weeks and it will be Easter.'

'Never mind the course,' Mark said. 'I cannot believe how fast last year seemed to go. First year of the decade over and we are into the next one already. Be the end of the decade – the end of the bloody century – before you know it.'

'Jesus, that's a depressing idea. You're getting old before your time.'

'Maybe, but the end of year show will be on us before you know it. Definitely have to start thinking about what to do for that soon.'

'That's when it really starts, I suppose.' I said. 'When you get to find out if you have the talent to make it as a real artist. A professional. See if real people want to pay real money for your stuff.'

'Now you're depressing me.'

'Sorry.' I finished off the can of larger I was drinking. There was a small pile of empties in the corner of the room and I went over and added my can to them.

'Want a swig of this?' Mark said when I returned. He offered me the bottle he had been drinking from.

'What is it?'

'Cocktail. My own concoction. Vodka and coke mainly. Plus a few extras.'

'Nah, you all right, thanks. I'll stick with my Stella.' I pulled out the other can from my jacket and pulled back the ring-pull.

'So where's your girlfriend then?'

'Who?'

'Cat.'

I shook my head. 'She's not my girlfriend.'

'Could have fooled me, the amount of time you spend together.'

'Yeah, well… we are just friends, that's all. I think she's seeing someone else anyway.'

'Who?'

'No one we know, I think. No one on the course anyway.'

'But… she's not exactly said anything has she?'

'No. But she's sort of hinted.'

'You've not asked her? And not tried it on with her either, I take it?'

'No. To be honest I don't want to ruin the relationship… the friendship, we have. We've sort of discussed collaborating on something. Don't want ruin the chance of that. I'm not her sort, anyway.'

'What is her sort? I doubt she'll want to go out with another Hooray Henry like she was engaged to any time soon.'

'You know about that?'

'Hey, you're not the only one she talks to, you know. Anyway, you get the chance… don't forget, Titanic her and she'll love you forever.'

'What?'

Mark tutted like it was oh-so-obvious.

'Titanic her. You know… the Titanic.' I must have still looked clueless. He sighed, then continued in a sing-song voice. 'With women, always go down on the first voyage, and they'll love you forever.'

'Oh great… I'm getting sex advice from a gay man.'

'The best kind, sister!'

Mark looked over towards the doorway.

'Hello Hiawatha, like the new look.'

I turned around to see Trisha standing behind me.

'What you two talking about?' She asked, in her usual airy tones.

'Sex. Same as usual.' Mark said.

Trisha had feathers in hair – woven into her long light auburn hair that had been plaited to fall over one shoulder and down her front. They appeared to be lack crow and grey pigeon feathers, plus a long peacock feather hanging from the end of the plait. And not just in her hair – there were more feathers, small colourful fluffy ones, pinned to the front of her dress like a row of medal ribbons. The dress itself was obviously hand-made, patched together from bright patches of remnant cloth. She wore white tennis shoes over which she had drawn intricate leaf-like patterns with a red Biro.

'Bird-Girl dressing like a bird now.' I said.

'Yes!' Her bright green eyes flashed and she fluttered her fingers over her hair and down to the end of the plait. She held the end of the plait between her fingertips and flicked the peacock feather across the end of my nose.

I had thought the word 'bird' the first time I had seen her, with her small frame, bright eyes and sharp nose and chin – even before I knew her self-appointed nick-name. A fluttering mad bird, with her exaggerated hand-gestures and broken speech patterns and sing-song voice – I never could work out whether it was all an act, a pose, or if she was genuinely like that.

'And screw you, Oil-Boy.' She smiled at Mark.

'So I take it you are not planning to make a crop circle now?' I asked her.

She cocked her head to one side.

'Crop circle is now a no no. Those two old codgers ruined it. Them with their plank of wood and bit of old rope. Now yesterday's news. Mystery gone. Spoilt.'

'It's ridiculous.' I said. 'The tabloids make out they did them all. Like they would know all the maths – the trig and geometry – for even the most basic multi-circle patterns, never mind the full-on fractals stuff like a Mandelbrot set. It's a real pity though, I was getting keen on writing a computer program to sort out all those patterns for you'

'Well, now, think of some other thing.' She said. 'For the end of year.'

'What about that stolen art idea…? It had legs I thought.'

'Yeah, maybe? Could be?'

She stepped close to me and looped an arm around mine. She pointed with her free hand through the doorway to the stairs beyond.

'Anyway, Computer-Man. Bird-Girl wants to show you something. Something interesting. Something amazing.'

She started to steer me out of the room.

'Don't forget… Titanic her!' Mark called out from behind us as we left.

'Fuck off!' I shouted back.

Trisha led me upstairs to one of the bedrooms. Dimly lit inside, the air was fugged thick with smoke – from dope, judging by the smell. Except for a television in one corner this room was as devoid of furniture as those downstairs. Trisha closed the door behind me. While my eyes adjusted to the gloom I looked over at the television's flickering screen. Half a dozen people were sitting on the floor in front of it. Reflected onto their slack faces a blue hedgehog was chasing golden rings. While I stared the game controller was passed in one direction and a joint passed in the other.

'This way, Computer Man.'

Trisha was waving me over to a large pale marble fireplace. Highly carved, it stood out incongruously in the otherwise plain room. Perched on top was a glowing blue lava lamp. As I approached I saw the white marble of the fireplace was Dalmatian-spotted with dark U-shaped splotches.

'Amazing, isn't it?' With a big theatrical gesture, she curved her arm up and around and then spiralled a finger down onto one of the shapes illuminated by the pool of blue light cast by the lamp. 'This?'

'It's a fossil!' I said, tapping the shape she was pointing at. 'They all are. Did you know?'

'Thought it might be. Thought you would recognise it. You the geologist.'

'Well, I'm no expert. Just did it at A-level.'

'What is it? Trilobite? Ammonite? Dinosaur?'

I looked closer and drew a finger along the saw-toothed edged twin-lobes of the fossil.

'Nah, no dinosaur. But still interesting. Graptolites. Ancient sea creatures that lived on coral reefs. Filter feeders, they looked like plants but were actually animals. Millions of years ago they would have lived. Millions of years. The reef is buried and over the years slowly turns to limestone then some time later it's crushed and baked into marble. All those millions of years in the ground then dug up and carved into this fireplace by some long forgotten craftsman. Then… Well, then I suppose, a hundred or so years sitting here in this room.'

'Until us, right now, looking at it. Amazing!'

'Amazing, it is.' I agreed, still staring down at the fossil. I could see it, the graptolite, swaying in the hot primordial ocean. An ammonite floated past. Then a swift long-necked Nessy-like plesiosaur swooped down to snatch the ammonite in its spine-toothed mouth. Then–

'Wonder if Bird-Girl could work it for year-end show?'

'Wha?'

I looked up at Trisha. I rubbed at my face to counteract the effects the room's thick air was having on me.

'I tell you not? Other idea. May be? Standing stones. Stone circles. Paganism. Magic and all that stuff. Another trick or treat. Another fool-them-all. Create a false standing stone circle or something.' Trisha fingered the end of her plait then swept the long peacock feather along the edge of the fireplace. 'Ditch that idea for found art. Move away from jokes. Stolen art. Magpie-ing. Love fossils. Use them. Or create new fossils somehow. Us, our waste stuff. Fossils of us, in furniture of the far future. Alien furniture…' She looked back towards me. 'You understand even half of that…? I don't know, Computer Man? Fossil. Feather.

Something. Nearly there. So close...' She reached into the air in front of her, stretching fingers out towards something she could only see. 'Just can't grasp it. And it seemed so obvious at four this morning.'

'It always does.'

Trish looked right at me.

'You think I'm mad don't you?'

'I think you might just be the sanest person at this party, Trisha.'

She held up a finger and wagged it at me.

'Don't call me that. Call me Bird-Girl.'

'But that always sounds so silly.'

'But it's what I am. Like Computer-Man, like what you are. Like Horse-Girl. Hello.'

'What?'

'You not saying hello, then?' A voice from behind me. A very familiar voice.

Cat?

I span around.

No, not Cat.

Someone I had never seen before. A stranger. A woman with black spiky hair, short on top but longer at the back, almost a mullet. Lots of dark make-up around the eyes. She wore a long male army coat that reached down nearly to her feet, gaping open to show a black T-shirt. It was ripped at the front to show some pale skin above the belly and a hint of rib. Short dark skirt. Bare legs. Doctor Martin boots. Tough-looking, slightly androgynous, but feminine and sexy – all at the same time. She held a pint glass that was filled with some sort of frothy lager.

But Cat's voice?

No, it was her!

Suddenly, I could see. She was so changed but her figure, the shape of her face, the cheek-bones, the eyes, her smile –

grinning at me as I grinned back at her — all the same, as beautiful as ever.

'You recognise me then?'

'I do now.'

She flipped up one arm up and thrust out her hip into a model's pose.

'As you can see I've had a bit of change.' She said. 'Get to know me long enough and you'll see this is a regular thing. You like it?'

'It'll take a bit of getting used to.'

'I'm sure you'll manage,' She said. 'I've been keeping an eye on you since you came in, you know?'

'I'm sure you have. Very amusing. This one of Trish's tricks?'

'No, it's all my own work I'm proud to say. I was seeing how long it would take you recognise me.'

'Well it would have taken some time. If at all. I've probably already looked past you a couple of times.'

'You have. It was very funny.'

'So why did you break your cover?'

'Oh, Simon wants a word.'

'What about?'

'Some big idea he's got.'

'Well, we had better not keep him waiting then.'

Simon took us all into the yard at the back of the house.

He gathered us together at the wall at the far end, by the bins and a motor scooter covered in plastic sheeting, as far away from the light of the kitchen window as he could. The concrete flags were greasy underfoot with a coming frost; the air so cold now you could see your breath. The booze I had drunk went someway to keeping me warm but I still zipped up my jacket.

Cat was standing beside me, her coat open but her arms crossed. On the other side of her, Trisha rocked from one foot to the other. She had put on a short jacket – as patchwork as her dress – but she still seemed to be shivering slightly. Next to her was Mark, a padded coat over his jumper. Simon completed the circle.

'So what's the big secret?' Mark said to him. 'Let's get this over with so we can get back inside.'

Simon ran his hand through his black hair, smoothing it back into the usual Bryl-Creamed parting after it had collapsed onto his forehead as he had bustled us out of the house. He pulled his white scarf tighter and tucked it down the front of what appeared to be a new donkey jacket he had bought since the last time I had seen him. He looked at us all with his intense dark eyes then clapped his hands together.

'Right, I've had an idea about the end of the year show,' Simon said. 'My idea is not to go.'

'What?' Mark said.

'We do it ourselves.'

'I don't understand.' Cat said.

'We do our own separate exhibition.'

'But what's the point of that?' I asked.

'Yeah, all the collectors… the gallery owners, everyone, goes to the end of year show.' Mark added. 'Let's–'

'No,' Simon interrupted, turning to him. 'I've thought about this a lot. We do it right – we'll get a ton of publicity and stand out from the crowd. It will catapult all our careers up over everyone else.'

'Or we get no publicity and are humiliated.' Mark said, shaking his head.

'Might work,' Trisha said, not looking at us but looking down at the ground as she traced a circle with the toe of one of her self-illustrated tennis shoes. 'Might just work. Call it art strike.' She looked up at us and smiled. 'A strike against the cowardice of art.'

'I don't know,' I said 'It's all a bit punk rock. A bit Situationist.'

"Situationist!' Oooh, spot the art scholar.' Mark laughed.

'So, I've been doing some reading up on art history.' I said, bristling slightly. 'What's wrong with that?'

'Nothing.' Mark said. 'Except no one gives a fuck about art history now. But you would not–'

'Don't pick on–' Cat started to say.

Trish ignored us, cutting in. 'A union. A collective.'

'What?' Mark said.

'A collective.'

'That's it!' Cat said. 'We could form a collective.'

Mark looked over at Simon. 'But why us? Surely there are other people on the course who would be much more suited to your scheme though? More flamboyant that us lot. More craving of your 'publicity'.'

'No.' Simon said. 'Well, we do need that, and I think we do actually have it, but showmanship will only get you so far. I've been watching the others on the course carefully and we are the only ones with real ideas. And I think we can work well together. We're already friends and our art styles complement each other as well.'

'Maybe,' I said, then smiled. 'Except we don't know what Mark's style actually is.'

'Simon does.' Mark said, looking down, his voice low.

'What?'

'Yeah,' Mark continued, raising his head. 'He came out to the workshop I rent the other day. Had a good nosy about.'

'And it's bloody good what you are doing.' Simon said, pointing at Mark then sweeping his hand around the rest of us in the circle. 'All of you! Real fucking art for god's sake!

Not like those wankers and leeches, and yes, those fucking cowards in there.'

'But what if nobody comes?' Mark insisted.

'Oh, they will come all right. If we start causing enough fuss right now we can build up a real momentum.'

'I've got a couple of contacts in the media. Old school friends, friends of the family and the like,' Cat said. 'I can start something straight away on that score.'

'We can have a massive party for the opening.' Simon said. 'Invite absolutely everyone to it. It will be like *Freeze* only ten times bigger.'

'So this collective?' Mark said. 'If we do it, what are we going to call it?'

'What about ... if we are against 'the cowardice of art' we show that they are the cowards?' I said thinking aloud. 'A white flag, not for our surrender but theirs... and the opposite of the black flag of the anarchists–'

'White feathers.'

We all turned to look at Trisha.

'White feathers. Women gave them to men that did not fight.'

'Yes!' Said Cat. 'Like in that film.'

'What film?' Mark asked her.

'*The Five Feathers.*' Cat replied. 'I watched it the other afternoon. 'About the First World War. They gave white feathers to those that did not want to fight.'

'No.' I said. 'It was some colonial conflict. Africa or something. And I'm sure it's *Four Feathers*, not *Five*. It's based on a classic novel.'

Cat turned and smiled at me. 'That doesn't matter now ... there's five of us so 'Five Feathers' is the best name. Five white feathers. We can send then out with our press pack.'

'No,' I said. 'Just send the feathers first. Nothing else. Anonymous. Everyone will start talking about it then.'

'We could send out hundreds of feathers.' Simon said. 'Start a phenomena. We need to get working. Sort the feathers. From a farm or something. Or who makes pillows? But we need to keep it secret.'

'We could all have our own feather.' Cat said. 'A different bird. Or something.'

'Own design of feather.' Trisha said. 'For each of us. Design ourselves. Our own art style. Our own art.'

'Great idea!' Simon said. 'That's exactly what we will do. Right, so it's decided then.'

Simon looked at each of us and we nodded in turn.

'Course I've no clue what I'll do for the actual show.'

We all laughed at that.

'Right,' Simon continued. 'That's enough for tonight. Let's meet up tomorrow afternoon at college and we can get some more plans worked out.'

'Yeah, it's bloody freezing.' Mark said.

Cat turned to me. 'Come on. Let's get a drink.'

Cat led me into the large kitchen. Three or four students were clustered around the cooker making toast. Off to one side a table was covered in drinks – bottles, wine boxes and cans. In the middle of the room two more students were building a tower from empty beer cans. It was already three-quarters of the way to the ceiling. I passed one of them my last empty as I made my way to the table.

'Thanks,' he said to me, then turned to the other tower's constructor. 'Look, we can't glue them together.'

'But it's not stable enough.' His friend said, crouched down carefully nudging some cans at the base of the tower.

'We would never get it out of the door. Just accept it's going to be temporary. It's not the bloody 'Kiss' for Christ's sake!'

'That's besides the point. I think–'

'But–'

'No–'

I left them to their argument. Cat had lifted up a carrier bag from under the table. She pulled out a large bottle of Diamond White cider and a can of Special Brew. While I watched she part-filled a pint glass with the cider, popped the can of Special and poured in the contents, then topped up the pint with the cider again to make herself a thick-headed snakebite.

'That's a bit hardcore.' I said as she took a large sip. 'Snakebite with ordinary cider and lager is bad enough never mind that evil concoction.'

'This is only my third.' She licked away the froth moustache. 'Want me to pour you one?'

'Think I'll stick with my Stella, thanks.' I said, finding the last on my Stella on the table.

'So you think it's a good idea?' I said once I had opened a can. 'Doing our own show?'

'It will get us out of the crowd, he's right about that. Unless you are totally brilliant, your work can end up getting lost in all those end of year shows. So we don't actually lose that much if it doesn't work. And I actually think it will, as long as we get the main people to it.' She took another long drink then looked right at me. 'Look, I have been thinking … of getting my own space when the course finishes, after the show. A studio. I was wondering if you might want to share? I think we can work well together.'

'Yeah?' I said. 'But I would have thought you would want to move in with this boyfriend of yours you keep hinting at?'

She looked away from me, looked at the tower of cans. One of the students was now sitting on the other's shoulders. He reached up and placed a can on the top of the tower, close to the ceiling. He scolded the one below him to stand up straight and stop wobbling.

'Maybe there is no boyfriend.' Cat said taking another drink. 'Or maybe it doesn't matter. Or maybe I would not want to move in with them even if they do exist.'

'Right...'

'Sorry, but I have to have some secrets.' She then looked back at me and grinned, grabbing my arm, her face suddenly animated with excitement. 'But I will tell you one thing – a secret – I'm thinking of changing my name! For the art at least.'

'Oh yeah? What to?'

'Wendy Plinge!'

'What!'

'Well, it should be Walter Plinge but I wanted something vaguely feminine.'

'You are going to have to explain that.'

'I found it looking though an old book on identity while I was looking for inspiration for my self-portraits. It's to show I'm a different artist. A new artist whose name does not matter, only the work. Walter Plinge – it's a non-de-plume actors use. It's for when an actor has to play two different roles in a play and they don't want it to be obvious. In the program they say the second part is being played by 'Walter Plinge'. In America they use George Spelvin. So you could have Georgina Spelvin. But I don't like Georgina. Or Spelvin. There's also Jane Doe.'

'Well, that name I do know.'

'Yeah, too obvious. So Wendy Plinge.'

'But, Plinge.' I shook my head then grinned at her. 'It just sounds daft. Too close to 'minge'. It's like calling yourself Miss Fanny or something. Alright for a joke, but not for something serious.'

'You think so?'

'I know so.'

Cat took another long swallow of snakebite. 'There's also Lauren Ibsen. That's another one I've thought of'

'That's much better. Rings a bell, though. Another stage name?'

'No, it's from Lorem Ipsom. That standard block of random text they use for print design mock-ups. Looks a bit like Latin. I thought it was a good idea for something to reflect anonymity.'

'It is good, in fact—'

Cat suddenly pointed back over my shoulder.

'We've got a ghost!'

I turned to look where she was indicated. Oblivious to the others in the room a door was floating past behind the beer can tower. The door, I realised, that Mark had been leaning against earlier with its lift-off hinges.

'A ghost door, that's a new one.' Cat said.

Then, as the door came closer I could see that was not floating after all. Trisha was carrying it, carefully manoeuvring it out of the kitchen. I laughed then rushed over to her.

'Had the idea to magpie anyway.' She said when she saw me. 'Even if do not do the stolen art thing, I'm sure it will come in useful.'

'Bloody hell! You sure? What, just take the door? Whose house is this anyway?'

'Heh, joking.' She laughed. 'No. Not take it home. Leave it in back garden or something. A surprise for them. Use the idea. The idea for something.'

'For a minute, we thought we had a ghost. 'A ghost door', Cat said.'

'Yes. Ghost door. Like that. Maybe use if for the name of a painting. Or sculpture. A haunted door.' Trisha smiled. 'A phantom door!'

'Phantom Door! Fanny Dore that's it!' Cat had walked over to stand besides us. 'That's the pseudonym I need! Nothing funny about that!'

'No, not at all.' I said, laughing.

'Welcome to it, Horse-Girl' Trisha said, laughing as well.

'Yeah, well, maybe not.' Cat said as Trisha hefted the door up to carry it out of the kitchen.

I saw Cat eyes narrow.

'Actually, I think I've just been far too serious about all this.' She turned to me with a raised eyebrow. 'Fuck it. Fancy a dance?'

'What?'

'You know. Dance me, romance me, prance me?'

'You want?'

'You heard.'

She turned and walked out of the room. There was nothing I could do but follow her.

Just before I left the kitchen I heard a can clatter to the floor.

I looked back from the threshold of the room.

'Oh, fuck.'

The students, still on each other's shoulders slowly backed away from their construction.

There was one long pause as everyone in the room stared at the tower in silence.

And then in one metallic rush of noise, it collapsed, with cans flooding out to all corners of the room.

'I told you to glue it!'

No one was dancing in the room where Cat led me. There was no music – the last CD or tape had reached its end and no one had bothered to change it. There was a cheap midi-unit on the floor in one corner with speakers on chairs placed as far away from the main unit as their cables would allow. There were a stack of CDs on top of the midi unit and an open attaché-case style cassette box half-filled with tapes on the floor next to it. I picked up the CDs and started looking through them while Cat crouched down by the tape. I soon came to Nigel Kennedy's *Four Seasons*. Someone had written 'TWAT!' on the cover in thick black pen. I held it up to Cat.

'I don't think so.' She said. 'But it's good to see that insightful criticism isn't dead. Here, try this.'

She handed me a cassette with 'Party Mix #3' hand-written on the label. I put the tape on, turned the volume up. Soon the introductory chords of what I immediately recognised as Vic Reeves and the Wonder Stuff's 'Dizzy' blasted out.

'Good choice!' Cat shouted as she stood up, tearing off her coat and flinging it to the floor. 'Come on!'

She grabbed one of my hands in both of hers then pulled me into the centre of the room and spun me round. Even with confidence fuelled by booze I felt self-conscious as she started dancing around me, flinging her hands about her head and shouting 'Dizzy!' in time with the singer. Especially as everyone else in the room just seemed to be watching us. But I joined in with Cat as best I could. Then when 'Smells Like Teen Spirit' came on after, several people joined us to dance and I felt much better. I let myself go, throwing myself into the music.

When Right Said Fred followed the Nirvana track Cat pulled me over to one side of the room.

'I'm too sexy for this party!' She said, loud over the music. 'You know... I don't live far from here...'

She looked straight at me. I suddenly realised how close she was.

'Want walking home, then?' I asked her, trying to sound casual despite my raised voice.

'That's what I was thinking.'

The streets were quiet. The only disturbance was Cat softly singing 'Dizzy' as she strolled along beside me, leading me from New Cross towards Camberwell. In the pools of light cast by the street-lamps the pavement was starting to sparkle. The booze had been acting like a second coat against the cold but the chill air was now starting to seep through to my skin. I rubbed my hands together.

'Is it far?' I said to Cat.

'No, not far.'

'Giddy up then Horse-Girl! I'm frozen!' I said, making to stride ahead.

'Oh, don't say that. I don't like it.' She looked away from me.

'Sorry. Will 'Kitty Cat' do instead then?'

'Yeah, that will do.' She looked down and smiled to herself.

The top button on her coat was already undone and as we walked she unfastened the next one down.

'You're not cold?' I asked her.

'Nah. I'm a country girl. I'm used to it.'

'Well, I'm not exactly a townie myself you know.'

'Townie! Not heard that for a while.' She moved closer to me, walking in step. 'Here, I'll keep you warm.'

She slipped her arm around my waist and rested her head against my shoulder.

We walked along in silence for a while, her leaning against me.

Cat stopped at the next corner. She checked each road, slowly turning to look down each of the choices of direction.

'Sorry,' she said. 'Went a different way to the party from the pub.'

I reached inside my jacket.

'No, it's all right.' She said, when she saw me pull out my *A-Z*. 'I'm not lost. It's just these streets get a bit samey, especially at night.'

'Nah, this is for me,' I said, flicking open the map book to the page I had dog-eared earlier. The page where I had marked the location of the party with a cross.

I quickly worked out what streets we had just walked down, then turned to index at the back. Pulling a pen out from the spiral binding, I ticked off the streets' names, writing the date next to each of them. I tutted to myself as I realised it was now past midnight and changed the dates.

'This is a bit of a project.' I continued. 'I make a note the first time I walk done any particular street in London. I'm thinking of trying to do as many as possible.'

'Sounds cool. This way anyway.' Cat led me across the road when I had finished.

'Actually. There's an interesting story behind the *A-Z*.'

I turned to her and she smiled back at me.

'Oh, yeah?'

'I'm doing it again, aren't I? Going all nerd on you.'

She grasped my hand in hers and swung it in time to our footsteps.

'No, go on. I was just as nerdy earlier with the new name thing. Your turn now. I wanna hear it.'

'Well a woman had the idea for it. The *A-Z*.'

'I didn't know that.'

'Yeah, Phyllis Pearsall her name is. Funnily enough it started with a party as well. The maps back then were so bad she got lost trying to find the street a particular party was on. So she decided we needed a more useful map. Nobody else was interested so she ended up mapping the whole city herself and started her own publishing company to print it. Spent eighteen-hour days walking down all the streets... all bloody twenty odd thousand of them. She persuaded *WH Smiths* to buy two hundred and fifty copies and delivered them herself in a wheelbarrow. Never looked back, still runs the company.'

'That sounds like some woman.'

'Oh, yes. Not sure how I can get an art work out of it though. Can't just have an old *A-Z* with few street names ticked off and dates written against it like a fucking train spotter!'

Cat laughed.

'Perhaps you can create another record? Something more visual? Draw on the maps? Take photos or something?'

I took a deep breath and blew it out in a long sigh that left a white cloud of mist behind.

'I don't know.' I said shaking my head. 'To be honest, I just don't know what fuck I'm doing.'

'Hey,' Cat said, jerking on my arm. She stopped and I came to halt next to her, turning back to her. 'Don't give me that!' She said, frowning. 'You think I do? You think anyone else does? We're all just groping in the dark.'

'I don't know... Some are so confident about what they do. Simon. Mark.'

'Don't you worry. They are the ones that are most worried. Be sure of that.' She started walking again. 'Come on. Nearly there.'

We walked on together in silence for a while then a few minutes later Cat suddenly announced, 'You think I'm a nice girl?'

'Where's that come from? Of course I do.'

'Or a nasty girl?'

'What? You're not nasty!'

'Oh, ignore me, it's nothing. We are here now.'

Cat led me into the porch of the large Victorian town house we were just passing.

Inside the porch, just in front of the door she turned back to me. Shadow from the porch's eve fell over one side of her face – the rest brightly lit by the yellow glow of the street lamp directly outside the house. She swayed backwards and forwards. The shadow chased across her face. Her eyes turned from dark fathomless pits to bright and glinting.

'Thanks for that,' she said. 'Walking me home, that is.'

She leaned forward again and kissed me, soft and quick our lips hardly touching.

'Oh, and there's nobody else,' she whispered. 'Only you.'

I leaned forward to kiss her back, slipping my hands around her over the course fabric of the army coat.

'Let's go inside, Kitty-Cat,' I whispered.

She slid her hands up between us and placed them flat on my chest. She pressed against me, pushing me away from her.

'No, sorry'

I went to step back.

'Ah, okay. No, I'm sorry. I got the wrong idea... I'll be...'

'No, it's not that. I share with a nurse and she's on early shift. I can't ask you in.' She reached up and touched my cheek. 'Your face... so anyway you'll have to take me round the back'

'Wah?'

Cat grinned.

'Don't get any ideas. I mean the back garden. Come on.'

She led me from the porch into the dark passageway dividing her building from the next one. She unlatched the gate at the end and, taking my hand, led me into the garden into the inky darkness beyond.

No street lamps reached back here and there were no lit windows in view; the only light came from the thin crescent moon.

Cat sensed my hesitation and turned to me – her face a pale blur floating in the dark.

'What, don't you want to?'

'No, it's not that. It's pitch-black. I don't want to break my neck!'

'Ah, don't be a wimp!'

'Woman, I'll show you what a wimp I am!'

I strode forward and immediately tripped over.

'You okay?' Cat asked when she had stopped giggling and I had clambered to my feet.

'Yeah, I think so. Only dignity damaged.'

My eyes were now growing used to the darkness but I still stepped forward more casualty. Surrounded by looming silhouettes of large bushes and trees, I could now make out a lawn so overgrown that it resembled an unmown hay meadow.

'Blimey Cat, it's like a jungle.'

'Don't worry. Give me a hand.'

She stepped onto the lawn and started to walk around in a small circle, tramping the grass down. I joined her.

And then I started to laugh.

'What?' She asked. 'What is it?'

'It's a crop circle! We've made a crop circle. Got to make one after all. Trish will be jealous.'

Cat looked down at our handiwork.

'Hmmm, maybe…'

She slipped her coat off and spread it on the ground.

'Sure you are not cold?' I asked.

'I told you, I'm a country girl. This won't be the first bit of alfresco sex I've had on a winter's night you know.'

She me pulled me close to her and then down.

We sat down together on the coat and kissed – for a long time, this time.

She suddenly moved closer towards me, arms around me. I slid a hand through the rip in her T-shirt. My fingers groped upward. She was not wearing a bra and I cupped her breast, palm against the nipple, hand twisting. The T-shirt ripped further.

'Jesus, sorry.'

'Hey, you're eager. I like it. Come on.'

She leaned back and pulled up her skirt. Pale thighs flashed in the moonlight. She yanked down her knickers then reached over to shove them into my jacket pocket.

'Trophy for you.' She whispered.

I spread her legs open and knelt between them. I slowly ran the fingertips of one hand up her thigh towards the dark shadows of her crotch. I dipped down and started kissing along the path my hand had taken.

'What are you doing?'

'Well, I–'

'Oh, God.' She sighed. 'You've not been listening to Mark have you?'

Her hands were on my shoulders pushing me back.

'But–' I started.

'We can't be here all night.' She said. 'I'm not totally immune to the cold. Just hurry up and fuck me.'

She scrabbled up the edge of the coat and dug underneath it. She fished into one of the pockets and pulled out a condom packet.

Her grinning teeth gleamed bright as she held up the silver foil packet in front of my eyes like a magician un-vanishing a coin.

'And put this on. I don't want fertilising.'

After a while she rolled us over and crouched above me.

'You don't mind do you?' She breathed. 'I'll come quicker like this.'

'God, no.'

She guided me back into her, hot as a furnace against the chill of the night. My hands slid under her T-shirt and up the twin ladders of her ribs until my thumbs found her nipples.

Her thighs gripped me hard as she ground against me.

Her harsh breathing soon became gasps then moans as we worked hard against each other. Like an engine. Like a machine.

The fog of our joined breath, moonlit silver, became a halo above her head

Cat yowled like her namesake when she came.

5 SERPENTINE CABLING

I looked out of the same studio window that yesterday I had stared up at from the yard below. I sipped from a mug of strong black coffee as I looked over the other buildings in the square, the squabbling pigeons on the roofs and through the gaps in the buildings to the rest of London beyond.

Looking out, drinking coffee while I collected my thoughts had become an ingrained habit before starting the day's work. Technically I had already started earlier, but I needed another caffeine kick to keep me going after a sleepless night. And after pouring boiled water onto two spoons of Gold Blend I had found myself automatically wandering over to the window.

Movement below caught my eye and I looked down.

Two people, young and dressed on the smart side of trendy had just appeared at the entrance to the yard. The woman was carrying a large art portfolio under her arm. The man slung a laptop bag off his shoulder to unlock the door into one of the buildings opposite the studio. They chatted and laughed together. I remembered them as the young couple who a few months ago had arranged to rent some space to open a print design shop. They must have moved in while I had been away.

I should go down and say hello… but then what?

I had not seen them since Catherine had died so all that would have to be resurrected. The conversation would be very polite with platitudes offered and thanks given, all very English, but just excruciatingly embarrassing on all sides. And the temptation would be to slip back into mourning, back into the pit of grief I was starting to climb out of.

I went back over to the kitchen area of the studio. I had placed the phone onto the table. Next to it was a notepad, a pen and a pile of loose papers – Catherine's drawings and the letter from Oyster Press I had discovered yesterday. I had already put the keys I had found with them onto my key ring. I picked up her drawings and, moving the empty fruit bowl to one side, placed them out in front of me across the table in a neat row.

I sat down and read the letter and gazed over the drawings again, for what seemed about the hundredth time.

Why?

I drained the rest of the coffee in one swallow.

Why? Well, now was the time to find out.

I picked up the phone and dialled.

I had spent the previous night away from our studio. After discovering the drawings I had started to feel overwhelmed, both from what I had just discovered and being alone in the place I had shared with Catherine for so long. Plus the adrenaline rush that came from my determination to get to the bottom of everything – becoming the Private Investigator, the PI – was starting to peter out. I had to get away, if only for a short while.

For the rest of the day I had travelled around London on near empty tube trains, getting on and off at random. I ate bars of Fruit and Nut and drank tins of Coke bought from vending machines and kiosks, scanned through newspapers abandoned on the carriage floors without really reading them.

As I stared out of the tube carriage window, through my reflection, at the tunnel walls and the dark serpentine cabling streaming past I thought over the implications of the drawings and the other things I had found. Why had she done them? What locks were the keys for? Catherine had always said she would keep a secret or two from me – would never tell me everything – and I had grown to live with that. But I had never thought she could be doing anything like this behind my back. Pornography. For the first time since leaving the cottage I had doubts.

What else had she kept from me? Did I really want to know?

But of course I did. I had started on a journey that I knew I could not turn back from. I had to find the real Catherine, not the person she had presented to me. The first step was to find out everything I could about the drawings and I had planned out how.

I travelled out on the overland section of the District line as the sun set and darkness crept over me and fatigue seeped through me. Finally leaving the Underground I walked around Turnham Green until I came to a small dingy hotel down a side street. I spent most of the night staring at the ceiling but I eventually fell asleep, only to wake sweating from an unremembered nightmare a few hours later. Dawn was filtering through the room's thin curtains, filling the room with a watery light. Lurching out of bed, I pulled on some clothes then staggered along the hotel's barely lit corridors to the shared bathroom for a shower, feeling queasy and strung out.

A full English breakfast in the nearest café, with multiple cups of tea, made me feel at least an approximation of alive and my determination and resolve built back up to what it had been. I headed over to Oxford Street, looking for the first business suit I had bought in years. Walking into the nearest department store I came to out of the Tube Station, I pulled a dark grey single-breasted off the rack along with a couple of white shirts, a plain blue tie and the black leather shoes to go with it, plus a few changes of socks and underwear. I had the shop assistant cut off the price tags from the suit and unwrap one of the shirts. Getting changed before I left the store, I left my old clothes behind me in the fitting room, taking the first step in my plan to become fully my new persona.

From there I headed straight back to the studio. I had a lot less hesitation in coming through the door this time, but I still ran quickly past the third floor.

Brrr-Brrr. Brrr-Brrr. Dial tone filled the dead space of waiting.

'Hello, Oyster Press.' A woman's voice, confident and well spoken.

'Ah, yes. I wonder if you could help me?'

'Yes?'

'I'm working for a firm of solicitors… helping with the estate of Catherine Shorley.'

'I'm sorry?'

'I believe she did some work for you.'

'Let me look at my files.'

I heard a *clunk* as the phone was put down. I waited impatiently – straining to listen to any background noise, any clue. I thought I could hear filing cabinet draws being rolled open then slammed shut.

'Ah, yes. I remember now.' The woman said a few moments later, when she returned to the phone. 'I had been wondering why she had not got back to me… Excuse me, but you say 'estate'? Do you mean she's died?'

'Yes, unfortunately she has.'

'Oh, I'm very sorry to hear that. How–?'

'Did you know she was an artist?' I said, interrupting, anxious to get on with things.

'Well of course, she was doing some illustrations for us… For one of our books.'

'Yes, but the stuff she did for you was totally different to what she normally did. She was actually better known as a modern artist. Photography mainly. She's had several major exhibitions.'

'Oh, I never realised.' The woman said, 'She certainly never mentioned it herself. To be honest I don't take much of an interest in that sort of thing.'

'Yes, well, I'm just sorting out some of the more peripheral details of the estate. Tying up loose ends and the like. Did you have a contract with her? Can you tell–?'

'Who did you say you were?' She interrupted. 'It's just in this business I…'

'Sorry, thought I mentioned it. I represent the solicitors dealing with the estate. I need to get back all the work you may have of hers that is not covered by contract… plus sort out any contracts you do have. To be honest this is a bit of a tricky situation… we had no idea she might have been involved in something like this. I'm hoping to make the arrangements as simple and smooth as possible. For both parties. This sort of thing can end up being very expensive and time consuming. Solicitor's letters going backwards and forwards and the like. Plus I had hoped to keep the relatives out of it… given the nature of the drawings I've seen.'

There was a pause.

'Well, I will have to ring you back.' She was suddenly much more formal, almost clipped in her speech.

'I'm actually in town today.' I said, leaning forward, trying to put some urgency into my words, rushing them out before she could put the phone down on me. 'Just for today, unfortunately. I really need to sort this out as soon as possible. I hoped I could visit you, just to get things started. I won't take up much of your time, I promise. Just a few minutes.'

She sighed.

'Well okay, if you promise not to take too long. I'm very busy myself. Give me your name so I can tell reception to look out for you.'

My name? What was my name. Jesus, who am I now? The one thing I'd not thought about. Think! A detective. Sam Spade?

'Yes, my name is Sam...' *What? Spade, no! Fork? Garden?* 'Sam Garden... er... Samuel Gardener. Sorry just got distracted there.'

'Company?'

'Samuel Gardener Investigations.'

'Do you have an address?'

'No, I'm... recently started. Have a contract with the family solicitors. I've just took it over. The man who used to do it retired. I used to work for him in fact. But I started my own company... well, it's all for complicated tax reasons. And this has fallen into my lap before I can sort anything out – no time to sort out premises for my own offices. I'm currently based at Ms Shorely's old studio but–'

'Okay, okay. I will be able to give you some time this afternoon. Just bring something I can show to my solicitors. A letter.'

'Thank you... give me your address and I'll be there straight after lunch.'

After we had said our goodbyes I sat back, took a deep breath and smiled.

It would be the easiest thing in the world to print up some name-cards and some official looking letters to flesh out my identity. I had had enough experience dealing with solicitors to knock out something that looked right.

Especially as I knew exactly where to find two young print designers to help me.

Oyster Press were located in an anonymous five-story office block out west just beyond Ruislip. A number of small businesses shared the building. In the entranceway was a plaque with names and logos arranged by floor and it seemed Oyster Press shared its floor with several other concerns.

The security guard behind the desk in the foyer had my name down on his roster. I scribbled my new signature next to it – I had practised it a few times whilst I had been waiting for the paperwork to be printed.

Once in the lift I shivered from the over-chilled, air-conditioned air as I ascended. The top half of the rear wall was one large mirror. I stared at my pale reflection – eyes blood-shot, shadowed underneath from lack of sleep. I looked hard into my own eyes.

The PI.

Remember you are the Private Investigator now.

I smiled a tight smile to myself then looked away.

A print-out of Oyster Press's logo was framed on the wall alongside their door. The two words of the company's name were drawn-out in a hand-written flowing font, whose embellishments swirled round the letters like seaweed flowing with the tide. Between the two words was a drawing of an oyster, gaping open slightly, with just the hint of a pearl inside.

The door was ajar.

'Come straight in.' A disembodied voice came from the room, the same woman's voice that had answered the phone.

I slowly opened the door and entered.

Half the floor space in the small room beyond was taken up with a number of large cardboard boxes. Most had been opened, and were surrounded by small stacks of books along with shredded paper, sheets of bubble-wrap and other packing materials, pages of computer printout and other receipts. Book titles I could see included *Oyster Collection No. 16, The Memoirs of Lucy Draws* and *Nuns and Nurses.*

The left-hand wall of the room was taken up with floor to ceiling shelves crammed full with books. Many were multiple numbers of the same title, such as *Thrashington Manor, The Ins and Outs of a Swiss Finishing School* and *An English Vampyress On Lesbos.* The opposite wall was lined with grey filing cabinets.

The woman was on the far side of the room, her back to me, leaning over a desk that was smothered with papers.

'Come in, come in,' she said. 'Don't stand on ceremony.'

The room was hot, the air stuffy, with a faint newsprint tang from all the freshly printed books.

The woman turned to me.

She was startlingly beautiful.

Tall, with an hour-glass figure that her tailored business suit flattered.

She looked at me over black rimmed glasses perched on the end of her nose. Her thin lips were lipsticked bright scarlet, her cheeks flushed pink – I assumed from all the recent exertion of opening and emptying all the boxes. Her dark hair was pulled back in a tight bun-like chignon. A few hairs had come loose from the arrangement and hung down over her face.

She was still young – in her late twenties, I guessed – but she had the manner, the bearing, of someone much older.

Her beauty came from something unconventional. I could not quite place it, but somewhere in all her obvious femininity there was a touch of masculine which only seemed to emphasise the rest of her womanliness.

'Close the door, please'

I reached back and pushed the door shut.

'Mr Gardener, I take it?'

I slowly made my way across the room being very careful to avoid knocking over any of the stacks of books.

'What? Oh, yes. Thank you for seeing me.'

I flipped open my folder and fished out one of the business cards. I held it out to her.

She reached to take it from me. After quickly glancing at it she threw it down on top of the papers scattered across her desk. Then she reached out again to shake my hand.

'Stephanie Smith.' Grasping my hand firmly then letting go first.

She leant over and took a couple more books off the chair in front of the desk and put them on the floor. She nodded down at the chair.

As I sat she perched on the edge of the desk and took off her glasses, placing them down behind her. She leaned back and crossed one leg over the other twisting around so she was side on to me. Her skirt rode up her legs exposing seeming acres of thigh. From my position I thought I could see just the dark edge of stocking tops.

It was so hot in the room. Airless. Suddenly my new shirt collar seemed far too tight. I looked away over the piles of books and paper.

'Sorry, it is so chaotic.' She said. 'I've just had a load of stuff come in from the printers.'

I looked back, looked up at her.

'So, it's just the one sort of books do you publish, err, Miss, Mrs Smith?'

'It's Ms, but can call me Stephanie. Coffee? I've just made some?'

'Please… Stephanie. Black, no sugar.'

Stephanie slid off the desk and went over to the filter coffee maker that was perched on top of the nearest filing cabinet next to a tray of cups.

'So… the kind of fiction you publish…?' I asked again as she poured.

'Yes, it's erotica, or pornography depending on your point of view. I'm certainly not ashamed of it. Many titles, some contemporary but mainly Victoriana. A lot of reprints in fine bindings for the collectors' market. Some new stuff. But mainly new versions of old out-of-copyright books… very popular with a certain class of gentlemen and lady.'

'Do you run the business on your own?' I asked her as she came back to me with the coffee.

Stephanie smiled at that. She sat back onto the desk and sipped her coffee, looking down at me over the edge of her cup.

'Oh, I think you will find I am more than capable.' She purred at me.

'Ah, right.'

I gulped a mouthful of the coffee, wincing at the heat. It had an odd spicy aftertaste to it, some blend I had never tasted before.

'Well,' I said. 'I found these whilst I was creating an inventory at my client's daughter's studio.'

With my spare hand I flipped open the file again. I pulled out the drawings and handed them over to Stephanie.

She pushed some papers aside to expose a small area of bare desk and put down her coffee then looked over the drawings.

'Yes, this is for a book I was planning to publish soon. She did a good job. I was about to write back to her to see if she wanted to do any more.'

'That's what's confusing me. I mean there is nothing like this in her other work. She had done some nude work, but nothing like this. I just wanted to check it really was the same woman to be honest.'

Stephanie laughed.

'Oh, Mr Gardner! In this business... well, you see all sorts – writing and illustrating. And more women than men. You get one or two of the most outrageous flamboyant types of course. But I've had the most prim and proper people walking in here – really spinsterish librarian types. You would not believe what goes on in their heads.'

'So you meet all your writers and illustrators?'

'Usually, though most of the business is done by post or over the phone. I only met Catherine the once but she seemed very nice. And you say she died? That's terribly sad.'

'Yes, it's a tragedy.'

'So young. May I ask how she died?'

'It was suicide. She... she threw herself off a cliff.'

'Did she say why? Did she leave a note?'

'Yes, but it was very brief. She also left a video ... she had set up a video to record the event itself and had recorded an explanation to why she was doing it before. But it was very incoherent...' I cleared my throat. 'Or so I've been told. I've not seen it myself,' I tried to lie.

'You said she was a photographer?'

'Yes. Self-portraits, mainly'

'That makes sense. I had wondered why she insisted on arranging her own photographs.'

'What photographs?'

'For the inside of the dust jacket. As the illustrator.'

I frowned and pulled out the letter from the folder. 'I thought she wanted to be anonymous? 'Fanny Dore' it says here.'

'Yes, well… like many of our writers and artists. But she got around that. Let me show you. Here, I've got a copy. I pulled out her file before you came.'

She picked up a box file off the desk, opened it and pulled out a large glossy photograph. She held it up to me. The photograph showed the naked back of a woman. The picture cut off just where her hips started to flare out She had long blonde, almost white, hair that looked like a wig. Her hand was raised with a pencil poised. The edge of an easel and a canvas could just be seen over her shoulder. There were the first few pencil marks of a drawing.

It was Catherine.

There were hints of a Victorian bedroom with plush cascades of draperies. Catherine was drawing a naked woman who lay in on a bed in the background, only her bare legs in the shot. Catherine again, I realised. She had combined two photographs of herself. Her drawing a woman asleep, like I had often drawn her. Drawing herself, another self-portrait.

Then I saw it. At the edge of her hair at the top of her raised arm, near her shoulder. A mark. I looked closer. There was a black vertical line, with two other shorter diagonal lines on the left hand side that ran down to join the main line at an acute angle

'What's this? Oh her shoulder?'

Stephanie looked at where I was pointing.

'Oh, it's a tattoo isn't it?'

For a second I could not say anything.

A tattoo! She'd had a tattoo!

'Oh, I didn't know she had this.' I said, doing my best trying to appear natural and calm. 'I've not seen it in any other photos. It looks like a diagram of the flight end of an arrow... half of one, anyway.'

'Really? I assumed it was a stylised 'F'. F for Fanny Dore? That she must have flipped the negative over when she processed it. Liked her pose better that way or something. But forgot the tattoo would be reversed.'

'When did she send you this?'

She flicked through the file.

'This was one of the last things she sent me.'

We had not seen each other much in the final days. So busy. But how could...?

Then I remembered the bandage on her arm. She said she had hurt herself, caught her arm on some scaffolding during a photo shoot.

I stared down at the tattoo. I could see it looked raw around the edges, the flesh reddened and raised. Freshly done.

The room was so hot. I felt like I was sinking. Drowning. I breathed deep.

Pornography. Now this.

'F for Fanny' was an obvious interpretation but, even flipped the symbol would not look much like a F...

What the hell did it mean?

At least the next step was easy.

I was certain there could be only one place she could have had that tattoo done.

6 SPELEOLOGY

'I'm thinking of getting a tattoo,' Cat said.

'What?'

We were waiting at a red light somewhere in centre of Croydon – I was not sure exactly where and that was beginning to irritate me.

I had not needed to navigate, Cat – driving her red Renault Clio – knew exactly where we going. However, it was the first time that I had taken this particular journey, so I had been tracking the route in my *A-Z*. Later, once we were in the countryside, I was planning to switch to the newly bought *AA Road Atlas* lying in the seat well beneath my outstretched legs.

Unfortunately I had been increasing distracted, partly by our recent conversations but mainly in just watching Cat drive. There was something in the interplay between woman and machine – the way her hands lightly danced around then firmly gripped the steering wheel, the way her arm flexed when she changed gear, the interplay of the muscles in her legs as worked the pedals – that was just undeniably sexy.

So, annoyingly, I had lost track of the last few streets we had just driven down and I was staring down at the *A-Z* spread open on my lap, trying to work out exactly where we were when Cat had spoken.

'I said, I'm thinking of getting a tattoo.' She repeated.

'I heard you the first time—'

Then I spotted it. My finger stabbed down at the point on the map where the arrangement of printed roads exactly matched the configuration of the junction we were now stopped at. Satisfied, I looked back at Cat.

'Sorry, I did hear you. My 'what?' was more an exclamation than an enquiry. Anyway, tattoo? Where has this suddenly come from?'

'I've had it at the back of my mind for ages,' Cat said. 'But that place made me think of it again just now.'

She flicked her head to the right.

As I leaned forward and around her to look, the lights changed and Cat sharply accelerated away. I had to twist around in my seat to look back behind her – through the rear side window, then the rear window itself – to see where she had nodded towards. Just before it was obscured by the traffic following us, I saw a shop-front with twin long sinuous dragons emblazoned around the edges of the window, flying round the words 'Tattoo You' written in faux oriental writing. Bright sunlight glinted off the window and I could see nothing beyond as our car sped away.

I looked back at Cat. She glanced at me and smiled.

'Why?' She said with a raised eyebrow. 'Don't you think it's a good idea?'

'No,' I said emphatically. 'I don't.'

Cat had arrived at my place early that morning and we had breakfasted together sitting on my battered old sofa in my pokey flat.

The day had started bright and fine and the forecast was good for the whole of the forthcoming Easter weekend.

So we both wore shorts. Mine where self-mutilated – an old pair of dark green combat trousers that I had hacked off just above the knee, level with the bottoms of the deep side pockets.

Cat's were some navy-coloured tailored variety – designer, expensive, and a lot shorter than my pair. She wore an equally stylish plain lemon yellow halter-top. Plus, I could not help noticing, she was wearing a bra for the first time since I had met her.

In contrast, I had just pulled on one of my many plain black T-shirts and I felt a right scruff next to her. But she said I was fine; had insisted, in fact, that I dressed down, joked that she would have left me standing at the curb if I had gone posh like I had hinted I would.

Cat had been growing her hair out since she had last cropped it short. It now reached down to the nape of her neck and I was having to get used to the new colour – a dark mousey blonde. I should have expected it really. She had told me the previous evening that she could not come round as she would be busy doing her hair.

'So, how do you like the new look?' She eventually asked as she bit into a slice of buttered toast.

'I like it. Though it's a bit straight isn't it? I hardly recognised you this morning. I wasn't expecting 'Miss Conventional'. Not given how you've dressed before. Your other looks.'

'Well, I don't want to shock my parents too much.' She brought a hand up to flick her fringe to one side. 'That's why this colour. It's just about my natural shade.'

'Yeah, I thought so.' I reached out with one leg and ran my foot down the side of calf. 'At least collar and cuffs should match now.'

Cat sighed and rolled her eyes. 'Well, you won't be able to check for a while. There will be no nookie at my parent's house, I'm afraid. It will be separate bedrooms and everything.'

'What!'

The car slowed as we approached another set of red lights. I put the spread open *A-Z* down on top of the *Road Atlas* beneath my legs and turned to Cat.

'No. No tattoos,' I said, dabbing a finger at the top of her bare arm.

I tapped with my fingertip on the faint blemish where she had had her tuberculosis jab then ran my finger down to her forearm and along to the back of her hand tracing along the more obvious scar.

'Don't want to mark this anymore.'

'Ah,' she said. 'But perhaps I could get you to design the tattoo for me? One of your maps? Be a walking canvas of it. Be the ultimate collaboration.'

'Jesus, Cat, that's far too much responsibility. To come up with something so permanent?' I shook my head. 'Anyway, tattoos are not fashionable now.'

'Fashion!' She scoffed. 'That should be something we make, not follow.'

'I could... draw. Draw on you.' I mused, almost to myself, my finger tracing out absent-minded abstract swirls over her skin. 'A tattoo that isn't a tattoo. Temporary. Body art. Something non-permanent but seeming permanent.'

I moved my hand away to allow her to chang gear but I continued to stare down at her arm. The pale skin. The faint tracery of blue veins underneath. I followed one down towards her wrist.

I thought of the flesh beneath. Musty memories of boring science lessons came back to me. I remembered diagrams in old biology textbooks.

'I could draw out your veins, arteries. Make a map of it. The blue veins becoming rivers, the arteries roads. Arterial routes out of the cities… where? The organs… The heart? Heart of the city…?'

My ideas petered out and I paused. The car was crawling now as we reached the end of a queue of stationary vehicles.

'Well, I could paint it all on your body.' I said, as the car came to a halt.

'Then I could photograph it! Photograph myself!' Catherine exclaimed, obviously excited by the idea. 'That will be a fantastic collaboration. Yeah, that would be real cool. Nude, of course. But not too revealing. Close-ups. Make it abstract. Yes, that'll work. That will work fine.'

She leaned over and pecked me on the cheek.

'Great idea.' She said.

'Pleasure.'

I placed my hand near the top of her bare thigh, gave the inside a slight squeeze.

'There's also that deep dark damp cave system at the top of this long long valley. The one with the thicket of bush above the entrance. I think it might need mapping in some detail. Maybe even a field trip, some speleology. I've heard rumours that there's this short stubby stalactite hidden above the entrance somewhere that's so geologically sensitive it can trigger earthquakes if dis—*owww!*'

Cat had play-punched me on the leg.

'Enough of that!' She mock-scolded me. 'Keep such pornographic geography to yourself. I've told you, there will be no sex at my parents' house. We won't even be sleeping together.'

'It's early, we could stop on the way,' I said. 'Find some woods or an overgrown field or something?'

'No sex outdoors, either. We're not savages.'

'What about the first time? I don't remember any qualms from you then. I distinctly remember you taking the lead, practically dragging me into your back garden.'

'I was desperate then. Anyway, have patience. It's only for a couple of nights. You are the first boyfriend I've taken home to meet me parents for some time. I want them to have a good impression of you and me.'

'Yeah, well, okay. Let's just make sure we make it a fast journey home, all right? *Owwwww!*'

'Not far, now,' Cat said.

We were just heading back out into the countryside on the other side of Tonbridge Wells.

'Oh, yes.' I said.

On the open *Road Atlas* I checked the distance from the edge of the town to the cross I had drawn in pencil at the point where Cat had told me her parents lived.

'It's very nice of your family to have us all over,' I continued. 'To let us have the meeting there.'

'Well, we normally have a family get-together at Easter anyway. Have a bit of a party. Invite some friends over. I just thought it would be convenient for us all to meet up at the same time, sort out all the details for the exhibition.'

'Too right. I got a phone call from Trisha last night, by the way. She should be arriving early after all. Soon after lunch, in fact. Sounded like she has been worrying herself to death about the exhibition though.'

'Oh dear. Last time I was speaking to her she was getting all stressed about it. I told her not to worry, that what she was planning to do was fine.'

'She's not the only one who's worried. It's not long now and still so much to do. I've hardly started on my own artwork for it, never mind all the organising.'

'I keep telling you – and her – It'll all be fine. I'm hoping that getting out of the city for once will give us all a fresh prospective. Anyway, it's good she is arriving early. It means you won't be alone this afternoon.'

'Hey, I told you not to worry about that.'

Cat smiled and patted my leg.

'I know, but I didn't really want to leave you behind with a bunch of strangers while I go off riding on my own. It would have been totally selfish.'

'Well, now you can enjoy having a good gallop with a clear conscience.' I said. 'So I call you Catherine, right? In front of your parents, I mean.'

'Yeah, using Catherine will show you are serious about me. My name in the family, or Cathy. Oh and you might hear Kate, but I don't really like that myself.'

'I don't suppose 'Kitty Cat' either then, then?'

'No, not really.'

'Or 'Hot Pussy'?'

'Definitely not! And I've told you!' She raised her arm up. fist clenched and held it poised, threateningly, over my leg.

'Sorry.' I laughed and she withdrew her hand. 'I think I prefer Catherine anyway. Have you settled on a name? For the art I mean?'

'*Hmm.* Well, I'm thinking of sticking with Jane Doe. Yeah, it'll probably be that. Parents might be a bit a little annoyed by it. I can see it now – 'Are you ashamed of the family name? Once a Shorley, always a Shorley.' All that. But want to get away from the family name, really.'

'What? Because you are an aristo? What is it again? Countess Shorley? Princess Shorley?'

'Don't start.' Catherine said. 'Anyway the name's famous in other circles as well. The family business. Architecture. Well a tradition, a hobby, more that a business. Really. There always seems to be someone in each generation who wants to keep on with it.'

'Just tell them you want to move away from all that. That you want the work to stand alone, to be all you own effort. To prove that is has real value and not just, buying your way to success.'

'Oh yeah, I'm not that worried, they should be fine about it eventually. I hope so, anyway. Oh, and I should warn you that some of people who will be there this afternoon can be a bit... well, eccentric.'

'Don't worry about it.' I reached out and took her hand, squeezed it for a second. 'I'm sure they're all be fine.'

'And there's one another thing.' Catherine frowned. 'Things got a bit tense between myself and my parents when I ditched the fiancé, but I've got you to show off to them.'

'Yeah? I am honoured, but I just wish you'd let me put some posh clothes on. I feel a right oik next to you.'

'I've told you. It's 'working class credibility'. I want to show you're not a posh brainless idiot like the last one.'

'I certainly don't think they will be making that mistake – well the posh part at least.'

'Here we are.' Catherine said.

We were driving down a narrow hedge-lined country road. Well out in the countryside proper, we had not seen any buildings since the last village, a few miles back. Coming up on my side of the road there appeared to be the beginnings of a wood – mature oaks and ashes that were just coming into leaf towered up from behind a long brick wall.

Catherine slowed. There was a gateway, with open iron gates, that she steered the Renault into. Beyond was a long winding tree-lined driveway.

'There it is, the family homestead, Shorley Manor.' Catherine said as she brought the car to a halt at the last bend of the driveway.

Out across a wide expanse of lawn framed by the twin verticals of the final pair of trees, I saw, for the first time, Catherine's home.

'Bloody hell!' I exclaimed.

'That's the usual reaction.'

The complex edifice in front of me seemed to be divided three main sections, each of which had its own distinct architectural style.

The left side was three stories high and built from dark red brick. The few windows were narrow and tall, some extending up over several stories, and arched at the top. The slate roof was steeply pitched. At the far corner a tower extended a further two stories higher than the main building and topped with a steep conical roof – reminiscent of the Kentish oast houses we had seen on our journey here.

The central section was slightly higher and done in a more classical style – with a flatter roof and faced in pale stone. The windows were square and regularly placed across this section's frontage. In front of the main door there was a row of columns that gave the appearance of the entrance to a Greek temple.

The right side was also brick built but used lighter, more yellowish bricks – from the parts I could see that were not smothered in ivy. This was the lowest section, being only two stories high but more sprawling in appearance than the left, with small higgledy-piggledy windows and a pan-tiled roof. At the far end a white-painted orangery extended away out from the main building.

Looking over the whole building again I saw that there had obviously been a number of alterations added to the three main sections since they had been built. Some windows were bricked up while several more had been added. What looked like a new room was poking up out of a section of roof. Plus there were a number of small extensions – one even with a thatched roof.

'Wow,' I said. 'It looks like it's been built by a load of different people who just completely ignored what everybody else had done.'

'Well spotted,' Catherine said. 'That's just about what happened.' She started up the car again and drove straight up to the building, to where a number of cars were already parked up around the gravel oval in front of the main entrance. 'Our family has been interested in building and architecture for several generations. And just about each one decided to add something to the house.'

'Where's your contribution?' I asked jokingly.

'It's not been built yet.' Catherine replied in all seriousness as she got out of the car. 'I've been talking with my brother about adding something sculptural around the back.'

Catherine had parked up next to a Bentley and I noticed there was nothing cheap about the other cars either – at least two Mercedes and a Porsche as well as several Range Rovers.

Catherine came around to my side of the car whilst I got out. She pointed up towards the top of the tower.

'Up there's my old bedroom'

'So you were a princess, then? A princess in her tower?' I slipped my hand around her waist and pulled her close to me.

'Oh, stop–' Then she smiled and kissed me on the cheek. 'No, actually you're right!'

She took my hand and led me up to the main double doors of the entrance.

The doors were unlocked and we went through into the large open hall beyond. A wide stairway, guarded by two suits of armour, curved up and around the white painted walls. Proceeding up the wall alongside the stairs was a series of photographs and paintings – generations of Catherine's family heading back into the past. I walked over towards them. The nearest was a row of four separate family portraits, all done by the same artist. Catherine's mother and father plus her older twin brother and sister, by the descriptions she had given me, were all portrayed sitting on the same coach in the same room. Catherine's portrait was different, with herself on a horse, a small grey. And obviously a self-portrait, I recognised her style from the few early examples of her work that she had allowed me to see.

'Oh, that's horrible.' Catherine said, from behind me. 'One of my early daubs.'

I pointed to the four paintings of her family. 'Missed out on this then?'

'Yeah, well he painted me as well... but I never liked it, and my parents hung my painting up as a compromise and...'

Her voice died away as she saw that I was already looking up past her self-portrait, following the line of paintings and photographs around up the stairs. Some were formally posed family groups with self-satisfied looking Englishmen standing next to their seated subdued wives with smug children or dogs at their feet. But there were also hunting scenes with red-jacketed huntsman on horseback alongside packs of hounds charging across the countryside. Plus there were photographs – in black and white and sepia – showing great white hunters dressed in shorts and sola topis. One was standing proud next to the hummock of a dead elephant with a long-barrelled rifle in hand. Another was crouching down next to a dead tiger, the head of which was held up by a smiling native bearer by the flesh of its cheeks for the better display of the fangs.

Then, once the paintings had finished, lining the balconies of the upper stories, and coming down the walls to either side of us I stared at the actual physical trophies of all the family's hunting. A cascade of fox and stag heads, plus other beasts from all ends of the empire – decapitated lions and tigers, long-horned antelope, a number of bears including one polar, rhino and elephant tusks and the outstretched striped and spotted skins of leopard, jaguar and zebra.

I turned back to Catherine. She was looking right at me. At my expression.

'Yes, right. Bugger.' She finally said, then sighed. 'The one thing I forgot to tell you. I really should have mentioned it. The other family tradition. Hunting.'

'Well…' I said. 'A country land-owning family. I suppose I should expect it. It's just… such a display.'

'We don't do it anymore.' Catherine quickly said. 'Well, fox-hunting we do, but not things like that anyway.' She pointed toward the nearest tiger skin. 'In fact we support the World Wildlife Fund. And– Oh shit, listen to me. It must just look horrible… all this dead stuff!'

I walked back to her.

'It's all right. I was just surprised by it, that's all. But you don't have to defend what your family does. What they did in the past. Christ, whatever they do. What I'm trying to say is you can't judge by the past.'

'Yeah, but we still do it… I've been fox-hunting myself. Not for a while, but–'

'I'm not going to condemn you for it.'

'Thanks.' She said with a small tight smile.

I looked back at the display.

'But Trisha's not going to like it, is she?'

'She knows already. I did think to tell her.'

I slipped my hand around her waist again and hugged her.

'Come on, introduce me to your family.'

'Yes, probably out the back.' She said as she started to lead me through to the rear of the building. 'Already started on lunch.'

We walked through a spacious sitting room, with the sort of large expensive furniture that I had only ever seen on the television before, and then through the French doors at the far end. Beyond were flowerbeds surrounded by low clipped hedges. A number of trees were dotted across the expanse of grass behind – in ones and twos and then further out more gathered into small copses until in the distance they merged into a small wood proper. There were the same oaks and ashes from the front of the house but I also saw a couple of large horse chestnuts, a number of cherry trees, a solitary elm, several types of conifer plus more unusual species that I did not recognise.

Between the flowerbeds and the first trees on the lawn a square had been divided off where two young couples in shorts and shirtsleeves played croquet.

'I suppose I should have expected it.' I said, pausing to watch. 'The sport of the aristocracy.'

'Hey, it's a great game. The tactics of chess, the skill of snooker and the viciousness of boxing. I do sometimes think us poshos keep it to ourselves because it's so good. I'll have to teach you.'

'As good as pool?'

'Better. And that's our arboretum.' Catherine said, pointing past the croquet square to the trees. 'It was planted by a cousin who was not interested in architecture, more into landscape design.' She pulled a mock frown then winked at me. 'We don't like to talk about it.'

'Sort of the green sheep of the family, then?'

'Yeah, that's right.'

She took my hand again and led me left along the back of the building. We went through a break in a taller hedge. Beyond, a stone-flagged patio ran from the rear of the house up to the edge of a large rectangular swimming pool. At the far end of the pool, where some kids were splashing in the water, was a modernist looking pool house – all curves of white painted concrete and wide sheets of glass.

Closer to us several people were sitting around the patio on wrought iron garden furniture or lying back on wooden sun-loungers. Off to one side, a barbecue had been set up and lit.

A woman smartly dressed in a light sundress and with a sweep of brunette hair brushed back over one shoulder stood up on seeing us. It was Catherine's mother, I recognised her from the picture I had just seen in the hall. She took off her large gold-rimmed sunglasses and smiled as Catherine ran over to her. They embraced and kissed.

The man behind the barbecue waved and walked over to me. Tall and beefy and not really showing his age bar a few wrinkles around his eyes and a dusting of grey in his blonde hair, it was Catherine's father. He was dressed in old jeans and an open necked hunter-checked shirt but had added the stylish point of a red paisley cravat.

He reached out his hand and we shook.

'Ah, the famous Jason,' he said. 'I'm Catherine's father. We have heard so much about you from her.'

'All good I hope.'

'Oh yes, good! Very good!' He smiled. 'And this exhibition thing sounds splendid.'

'Yes. I'm sure it will be.' I smiled back. 'I hope so, anyway.'

'Well, I want you to tell me all about it later. Here's the twins. I had better get back to my barbecue!'

As he returned Catherine led over the final two from the paintings, her elder brother and sister. They were tall and well built, taking after their father in stature but they had both inherited the dark hair of their mother. Hers was a cut into a designer bob, whilst his was long and pulled back into a pony tail. Like the rest of the family they were dressed informally but with an easy casual elegance.

'So these are the twins. Clarke and Polly.'

'And this is the man who likes maps, that our Cathy has developed such an interest in.' Clarke said to me.

'I'm afraid so.' I said as we shook hands.

Clarke turned towards Catherine.

'I've worked up the plans for the sculpture, sis. I think it will fit in well with the rest of the old pile.' He said, pointing up at the back of the building.

'Yeah, but I think they'll be maybe a couple of changes.

'There's no rush.' Clarke said. 'We can always do a redesign if you want. So you taking this art thing seriously then? I suppose we still can't persuade you to join in the family business.'

'Oh god, no fear.' Catherine said. 'You know I'm too thick for that. All the sums involved.'

Clarke looked over at me

'She do that 'I'm too dim!' act with you too?' He asked.

'Oh yes,' I replied. 'I don't believe her either.'

'I think it's just her way of avoiding work.'

'Hey, you two!' Catherine exclaimed. 'I am here!'

'Yes, don't pick on her' Polly said. 'We can't all be architects.'

'Not, in the business then?' I asked her.

'Oh no, I don't work at all. I married as soon as I could.' She waved over at the man I assumed was her husband who was relaxing in a recliner by the pool, a glass in hand. He waved back her. 'I'm afraid I'm one of the idle rich.'

'You know I'm only kidding, sis.' Clarke said. 'Besides this sculpture will be good. It's keeping the family tradition, but just that bit different.'

'Like papa's.'

'Exactly.'

Catherine saw my confused frown. 'My father designed and built the pool and pool house.'

'Oh yes, it's very nice. Beautiful, practical—'

'What a fine filly you have grown into, Kate!' A voice interrupted us. 'Lovely rump!'

'Oww!' Cat cried out.

I turned to see her rubbing her bottom. A tall, auburn-haired middle-aged man was shuffling around from behind Catherine to join us. His face was flushed and his blue eyes were tinged red. His hair, including his trimmed moustache, had the even flat hue of an obvious dye-job. He was bending over slightly, as he walked with the aid of cane. I looked down and saw he had a plaster-cast pot on one foot.

'What happened to you?' Polly asked him.

'Took a tumble off the old nag. Bloody nuisance! But I'll soon be fully fit and able,' he said. 'And it gets a lot of sympathy from the fairer sex, I must say. Even some from the memsahib! I might take this up permanently.' He added, waving the cane.

'Hello, Uncle Rupert.' Catherine said with a sigh. 'See you haven't changed.'

'You certainly have, my dear. Flowered into a very beautiful bloom I must say. You'll make a lovely wife for some lucky man one of these days.' He pointed his stick up at me. 'Like this one. I presume'

'We're certainly not ready for that yet!' Catherine exclaimed.

He ignored her and shuffled over to me. 'Yes, you are very lucky man.'

Now he was closer I could not help noticing that his flies were undone. He looked down to where I was staring.

'Oh sorry!' He said as he zipped back up. 'But you know. Always ready for action!'

He laughed loud and slapped me on the back.

'You are incorrigible, Rupe!' Catherine said. 'If Pa hears you talking like that he'll horse-whip you!'

'We'll just have to make sure he doesn't.' He smiled at Catherine. 'Now let me find the bloody booze. Can't have lunch without a couple of decent G and Ts inside me.'

'Randy old sod!' I tutted when he was gone. 'He one of those 'eccentrics' you were warning me about?'

'I'm afraid so... But you'll get used to him. No doubt you'll meet his new wife later. She's calmed him down a lot.'

'You mean he was worse!'

Catherine just smiled and took my hand. 'Come on, a drink sounds like a good idea, actually.'

I reached the top of the tower out of breath from running. On the door in front of me was a porcelain plaque with 'Catherine's Room' written below a cartoon image of a lucky horseshoe. I took hold of the doorknob but paused whilst I let my breathing return to normal, listening to Catherine moving about in the room beyond.

I let go of the doorknob and knocked.

'Who is it?' Catherine called out.

'Er, me. Jason.'

'Don't be silly! Come on in. You didn't have to knock!'

I opened the door and entered the room. Catherine was standing, her back to me, reaching inside her wardrobe. She was wearing a white blouse with a long tail that just about covered her bottom. Below, her legs were clad only in pale tights.

The wardrobe was small, painted white with gold highlights, like all the rest of the furniture – just the sort of delicate dolls-housey stuff that a girl would choose. The rest of the room was equally juvenile, with posters of horses on the walls and a dressing table that was strewn with bright, cheap-looking make-up and jewellery. The narrow single bed had a pink duvet cover with a repeated pattern of white hearts scattered across it.

The one adult exception to all this was the half-drunk glass of wine sitting on edge of the dressing table.

Catherine pulled out a pair of cream trousers on a hanger from the wardrobe and turned to me.

'Yeah, I know.' She said with a half smile. 'It's all a bit girlish isn't it? Spending all my time away at school and college, I've not had chance to change it much since my teens.'

'Actually,' I said. 'I think it's kinda sweet.'

She reached down to pat the end of the bed.

'And of course, another reason for not sharing my room is there just isn't the space.'

'I'm sure I'll survive. My room's great. I feel like a lord. Which I suppose isn't that far from the truth.'

She reached over and picked up the wineglass. She took a slow sip, looking at me from over the rim of the glass.

'It's still only my second, you know.' Catherine said as she put the glass down.

'Did I say it wasn't?'

'I never drink and drive. Don't drink and ride, either.'

She started pulling on her trousers – jodhpurs, I suddenly realised. I wandered over to the window and looked down at the pool at the rear of the house, then over at the arboretum and then past it to the fields and orchards and hills of the Weald beyond.

'You get a fantastic view from up here.' I said.

'Oh yes, very inspirational when I was growing up.' Catherine said from behind me. 'I've got some sketches of it somewhere. But you know, seeing it again I was thinking it's funny how your ideas change. I grew up in the countryside and yet my art has nothing to do with it now.'

I turned back to her to look at her.

'I know what you mean,' I said. 'Mine too, in a way. Certainly more urban-influenced than my upbringing.'

'And Trish, she grew up in the city but everything she does now is sort of to do with the countryside. But the others… well, I suppose they mostly keep to their backgrounds. My theory sort of breaks down there.'

Catherine stood and pulled up the jodhpurs, tucking in her blouse before fastening them. She smoothed the material down over her legs and backside.

'So, I still can't persuade you to come, then?' She asked me.

'God, no fear. I've already tried it once – Pony-trekking when I was on family holiday. Never again.'

'You're not frightened of horses are you?' Catherine said with raised eyebrows.

'Oh, no. It's just… the next day it felt like someone had taken a baseball bat to my bollocks.'

Catherine laughed.

'Oh, you just have to learn to do a proper rising trot.' She said. 'It's easy, I can show you.'

'Nah, you don't want me holding you up, trying to teach me. Not when you've not been for ages. And besides I've got boxers on. I think you are supposed to wear something… tighter. They don't call them jockey shorts for nothing.'

Catherine laughed again then sat back on the bed.

'Okay, okay.' She held up a hand in surrender.

She reached out for her wine again and finished the glass in one swallow. 'But I still feel guilty about leaving you on your own. I can wait until Trish gets here, you know? Or go tomorrow.'

'Don't be ridiculous.' I said, shaking my head. 'Anyway we can spend tomorrow together.'

'Yes, I can teach you how to play croquet.'

'Turn me into a proper toff, you mean!'

'I told you, it's not–'

'I know, I know.' I said, interrupting, holding my hands up in mock surrender.

Catherine started putting on a pair of trainers.

'What about those?' I asked, nodding at the pair of tall riding boots that were standing at the end of her bed.

'Oh, I can't drive wearing them. I always put my boots on when I get there.'

'Go on, show me now. I'd like to see what you look like with them on. And all the rest of your gear.'

She paused for a second, as if thinking it over. She pursed her lips.

'It'll make you feel less guilty.' I said.

Catherine grinned.

'Oh, all right.' She said.

She quickly took off the trainers and then stood and stepped into her boots. She took a dark riding jacket of the hanger on the back of the door, slipped it on and buttoned it up. Finally, she grabbed her riding hat from the top of the wardrobe and pulled it on a jaunty angle.

'So, what do you think?' She asked me, grinning. She brought her hands up in front of her holding pretend reins, bending her knees. 'Giddy up!' She added, slapping her thigh, bouncing as if riding.

'Giddy up, indeed.' I said. 'Two looks in one day. I'm honoured. And why is it that women in jodhpurs are so sexy?'

Catherine straightened up and then slowly walked towards me.

'You think everything I wear is sexy.' Catherine said, her voice low. 'You are as bad as old uncle Rupert…'

'Oh, yeah?'

'He's not my real uncle you know… just been a friend of the family for years. I sometimes wonder why my father puts up with him and all his 'toodle pip' nonsense.'

'He's got one thing right, you are a fine filly.' I said.

Catherine stepped right up to me until we were almost touching. She put one hand on my shoulder and looked into my eyes. Her expression was serious, unreadable. Then she reached around with one leg and slowly rubbed the side of her boot against my bare calf. She leaned in close and whispered.

'You know… I suppose, we could… If we're quick.'

'I thought you said no sex in your parents' house?'

'Hmmm, maybe I was a bit hasty in deciding that.'

I kissed her, quick at first then long and slow. Her boot moved higher as her hands grabbed my shoulders tightly. Hooking her leg around the back of my thighs, she held me hard against her.

While we kissed her hands drooped down to my waist, and her raised foot slid back to the floor. She took a step towards the bed. I got the hint and we shuffled over. I lowered her down with our mouths locked together, tongues still entwined, one hand at her back, the other sliding down to her crotch. She squirmed and suddenly crossed her legs, trapping my palm against the heat of her. Her fingers were at my shorts, hastily unbuttoning my fly.

'Cathy dear!' A voice called up from below us, Catherine's mother. 'Your friend's here!'

We suddenly parted, then both of us laughed.

'Oh, great timing.' I said.

'Ah, well.' Catherine said. 'You had better go and say hello.'

'Yes, I suppose I'd better.'

I moved to the door.

'Jason,' Catherine called to me as I was leaving the room.

I turned back to her. Her eyes met mine as she started pulling off her boots. 'Come to me,' she said. 'Come to me, tonight.'

Trisha and I walked across the lawn, past the last of the small groups of trees, towards the arboretum proper. Ahead of us there was an obvious path of stone flags that led into the larger plantation and we followed it.

Trisha walked with her head down.

'Look,' I said pointing, as a bird fluttered into the sky at our approach.

'Ahh,' Trisha said, glancing up. 'Only a magpie. Magpie is common. But still pretty. But one for sorrow.'

We had just waved Catherine off from the front of the house. Then I had asked Trisha if she had wanted something to eat. But she had told me that Bird-Girl was not hungry. That she just wanted to walk the grounds.

She was wearing a short version of her usual patchwork skirt with a pair of long odd socks – one black, one pink – and a pair of canvas sandals with long rope-like laces that criss-crossed up her legs to her knees. The baggy navy-coloured T-shirt she was wearing looked home-made with a semi-abstract design screen-printed on it – black curly 'W's on splashes of pale blue that formed flocks of child-drawn bird shapes. She had pinned some old broach high on her chest, which with the large cracked amber-coloured stone at its centre, added a sun to her sky.

Her hair, golden red in the real sunlight, had been plated into two braids that ran down her back.

'One for sorrow?' I said. 'Oh yes, how's that rhyme go? One for sorrow, two for joy, three for a girl, four for a boy... er...'

'Five for silver, six for gold, seven for secret never to be told.' Trisha finished for me, her head down again.

'That's it.' I said.

'Magpie likes the bright and shiny. Like me.'

'You not planning any more tricks today are you! Not planning to steal something from here?'

She still did not look up.

'No, no tricks. Not today.' She said. 'Today we be serious, Bird-Girl thinks.'

'Not too serious, I hope.'

We walked along the path in silence for a while as it wound around the trees of the arboretum. The plantation was well-managed and felt more like a park than a wood, with clipped lawn still extending between the artfully spaced trees with small wooden signs near the bases of their trunks giving their names in both English and Latin.

'So Horse Girl, horse riding.' Trisha said. 'That's good. She like that, I think.'

'Yeah,' I said. 'In a way. She was glad you've arrived. She was worried to be leaving me with strangers. Felt guilty about it.'

'Really? Not guilty for leaving you with Bird-Girl?'

'Of course not!' I said. 'Jesus, Trish are you okay? I thought you wanted to see the countryside. But you have hardly looked up once.'

'I suppose,' She said, her head still down. 'But Bird-Girl disappointed. This is not the real countryside.'

'Yes, it is a bit over-managed. Let's go that way.' I said, pointing at the beginning of a tramped down dirt-trail that went off through a cluster of conifer trees to one side. I could see a thicker copse of deciduous trees behind the evergreens. 'It looks a bit wilder over there.'

'Also, Bird-Girl worried.' Trish said as we started following the new path. 'No ideas. Nothing for the show.'

'Don't say that! Catherine was telling me about the cover design you are doing for the catalogue. It sounded great. A feather for each of us. In our own art style.'

'Not that. My own. My own stuff.'

'But that fossils from the future thing. They will work.'

'Maybe. But left it too late. I think.'

'Oh, everyone thinks they have left it too late!' I said. 'Anyway Simon will bully us all into getting our stuff finished I'm sure of it.'

She smiled then. 'I suppose so.'

We walked past the conifers. Trisha's head lifted at last and she smiled. She stopped and I came to a halt beside her. Ahead of us was more natural woodland with thick undergrowth under the closely growing trees. A slight breeze blew at our faces, stirring the branches above us, chasing dappled shadows across our feet.

'This better.' Trisha said. 'Bird-Girl like this much better.' She turned to me. 'So Computer Guy and Horse Girl? Getting on well together?'

'Oh, yes,' I said, as we started walking again. 'We were just talking earlier about collaborating on something for the exhibition.'

'Collaborating. Oh yes, indeed.' She said. 'Collaborating on something else. Bird-Girl thinks so.'

I smiled. 'Is it that obvious?'

'Very obvious.'

'Yeah, I'm very lucky,' I said.

'Perfect couple.'

'Think so? I worry though… that it's all too intense, that's it's all going too fast. That we will burn out and it won't last past college. We have planned to get somewhere together after the course. But I don't know… I've thought of trying to put the brakes on, but I'm frightened that will kill it stone dead.'

'Hah, keep it going. Make it more intense! Ride the storm.'

'Yeah?'

'Yes. Bird-Girl see true love in Horse-Girl's eyes.'

'You think so?'

'Think so? I know so. Bird-Girl saw that once. Bird-Girl thinks she will never see it again.'

I looked over at her but she was looking away from me.

'Oh, don't say that,' I said. 'I'm sure the right man is just around the corner for you. The man of your dreams.' I abstractedly waved ahead of us. 'He's out there. Somewhere.'

'A man, for me? No.'

She stopped and grabbed my hand, pulled me around to face her. She looked up at me.

'I don't dream about men.' She raised her eyebrows. 'At all.'

'Ah.' I said, finally understanding. 'I must be so stupid. I never get things like that.'

'Like men though. Just not like that.'

She led me on, still holding my hand, swinging my arm in time to her steps.

'Went to private school. All girl.' Her voice was now pitched lower I noticed, all the usual Bird-Girl inflections and cadences gone. 'A lot of girlie love. Not everyone. But a lot. Most stopped when they left. But some carried on after. Like me. And my love. Together. But then last summer my parents found out, found us together. Threw me out of the nest. Then she goes off with a man. Says she's going to get married. That she's always had a boyfriend. That I was just some sort of 'experiment'. World went dull back then. Dull for Bird-Girl.'

'Trish, I never realised. I'm so sorry—'

'Don't be. Forget it.' She pointed down at her clothes. 'Now Bird-Girl uses colour to keep away the dull.'

The path ran up a shallow slope ahead of us. Trisha let go of my hand and ran out up to the top of the incline. She turned back to me and waved me towards her.

'Come on!'

I jogged up to her.

'Bird-Girl happy now. Really.' She said, her normal sing-song voice returning. 'Bird-Girl be all right.'

'Yeah.' I said. 'And the exhibition. Just throw something together. Don't even think about it. That's what me and Catherine are going to do.'

We started walking again down the other slope that I could now see led up to the edge of the wood.

'White doves on snow.' Trisha suddenly said as

'Sorry?'

'You know… like polar bears in an Arctic storm?'

'What?' I said. 'I don't understand.'

'Barn owls flying in front of bed sheets hanging from a washing line…?' She said to me as if was oh so obvious. 'Bird-Girl paint a load of canvases white. Just give them clever titles.'

I slapped my forehead.

'Genius!'

The path turned to run alongside an old wooden fence that cut across in front of us. The fence-posts were green with lichen and moss, all but smothered by thick bushes and brambles that had grown up around them. There was cornfield beyond.

Trisha stopped and we looked out over at the hills of the Weald that rose up behind the field.

'Maybe I'm just not cut out to be an artist.' Trisha said, her voice serious again.

'What? You can't say that… you have lots of good ideas.'

'But I don't follow them through. Reach the depth that others do.' She reached out with both hands, arms outstretched, at the countryside in front of us. 'You know, all that is so beautiful. I grew up in the city. Never seeing any of this. All this beauty and we have such a short time to appreciate it.' He hands fell to her sides. She kicked out at one of the more decayed posts. 'All is gone. Eventually. Everything, gone. All gone to rot and dust.'

'Trisha…?' I said, reaching out to her.

'Oh dear.' She said. 'You must think I'm totally crazy.'

'No–'

'Well, perhaps I am mad.' She looked at me. I had never seen her look so serious. 'But I've tried being sane. Normal. I didn't like it for long. Didn't like it one bit.' She looked up back over the field. 'But I'm not mad like poor Vincent. You seen his last painting?'

'Van Gogh? Yes, I have.'

'Sometimes I wish I had that passion, even if it did mean madness. True madness before he shot himself. In those stabbing brush marks; the cornfield, the crows. You can see all his passion and pain made solid in that thick paint – I cried the first time I stood in front of it. No, I'm not mad like that… eccentric-mad not mad-mad. A Dali instead of a Van Gogh.' She turned to me with a huge grin on her face. 'Yes, Bird-Girl will be Da-*liiiiiii!*' She drew out the last syllable in her high bird-song voice. She posed, looking up to the sky, flicking her fingers up on both side of her face.

'I don't think the moustache will suit you.' I said.

She laughed, grabbed my hand and turned me around. 'Come on, the others might be here by now.'

'Anyway,' I said, as we started walking again. 'I've heard the only difference between madness and eccentricity is how expensive a doctor you can afford.'

'Oh, yeah.' Trisha said. 'You know. One day, you will marry the Horse Girl. You be rich.' She pointed around us with one long sweeping gesture that ended pointing back towards the house. 'All this be yours.'

'Oh god, I can't even begin to think about that. I'm just a poor working class lad at heart.'

'Bird-Girl thinks you would suffer it. For Horse Girl's sake.'

'Look, I think we should call it a day for now.' Mark said. He reached forward to stub out his cigarette in the ornate cut-glass ashtray on the table in front of him.

I glanced down at my watch – surprised to see it was already past nine.

We were all sat around one end of a long table that could have easily have seated twenty. The dining room was in a part of the house some distance from the main locus of the party. However, during our discussions, we had occasionally been reminded of it by the sounds of distant merriment floating through to us from an open window.

'Yes,' said Trisha. 'Done lots.'

'Okay,' Simon said. He was at the head of the table – head down at moment, his hair fallen over his face – scanning through the notes spread out in front of him. 'I think we have just about covered everything anyway. Let me just check.'

'Plus, I think your missus might be getting worried about you.' Mark said. He reached up under his jumper to scratch at his chest, then stretched his arms out above his head and yawned. 'Don't you need to get back to her? *Siii-mon?*' Mark pulled out the last word into the long whine in a fair impression of what we had all come to recognise as the voice of Simon's girlfriend, Julie. Catherine, right next to me, nudged me in the ribs. I tried very hard not to laugh, not daring to look at her.

After coming back from riding Catherine had changed into clothes very similar to what she had been wearing earlier, except now the halter-top was bright green and the shorts showed even more leg. I was still in the same shorts and T-shirt I had arrived in. Throughout the meeting Catherine had been distracting me by pressing her bare thigh up against mine.

'Yeah, maybe.' Simon said, his head still down scribbling something at the bottom of one his pages.

He was wearing a powder blue shirt, the collar undone. A black pinstriped suit jacket had been slung onto the back of his chair. Over the last few weeks I had noticed he was starting to look more the businessman than an artist. He had actually worn a tie when he had arrived but had eventually taken if off after some gentle teasing from Mark.

'I think we have made some real progress tonight, anyway.' Catherine said. She sipped from a large tumbler of whisky sour.

'Well, I definitely feel happier.' I said, then drained my own glass of wine. I reached out to check the bottle in front of me, holding it up to the light and shaking it. Empty.

'Yeah, but Bird-Girl still worried.' Trisha said. 'A bit. What if no one comes?'

'Build it and they will come!' I said in a mock-ominous voice.

There was some laughter and a groan from Mark as it was a repeat of a joke I had made earlier.

'Come on, Simon.' Catherine urged. 'I want to make a start at working the crowd here tonight before they all get too pissed.' She reached under the table to squeeze my leg. 'And have some fun.'

'Well.' Simon said looking up at last. He put his pen down and ran one hand back through his hair. 'There's just a couple more things we do need to sort out.'

'Yeah, but not right now, I bet. Not this minute.' Mark said, shaking out another cigarette from his packet. 'I think we have been going around in circles for a while now anyway.'

'Okay,' Simon said. 'But I just want to double-check what we will all be doing between now and the next meeting, then we'll call it a night.' He turned to Catherine. 'As you've just said, start to press those contacts. See if there is any feedback from what we've done already. Try and see how far the rumours about the feathers have gone. In fact we can all do that – plus start some more gossip about it, if you can. 'You heard about these feathers? Know what they mean?' Things like that.'

'Hopefully we've not sent one to anyone who's violently allergic to them.' Mark said with raised eyebrows.

'At least it will be a reaction.' I laughed.

'You okay to be in charge of the money, Jason?' Simon asked me.

'I suppose so,' I said. 'But why do I feel I have been suckered into it?'

Catherine patted my arm.

'Because you will be best at it.'

'Don't forget to check out the grant situation.' Simon said. 'Also don't forget to liaise with Catherine. See if she can gets some corporate sponsors interested. '

'No problems there, Bird-Girl thinks.' Trisha smiled. 'Liaising.'

'Try and get as much sponsorship as you can.' Simon said, ignoring her. 'Actually at this stage that is more important that the buzz from the feathers.'

'But we can still do it without?' I said. 'If we can't get enough sponsors, I mean. Scrape together enough money from credit cards, loans or whatever?'

'That's your job now.' Simon said. 'But I think so.'

'Right, I'll find some accountants next week and get the business set up, all of us joint shareholders. Get the books started, sort out some petty cash and all that.'

'And you worry that you won't be able to do the job.' Catherine smiled. 'You sound pretty confident about it to me.'

'Yeah?' I said. 'Just remember to get receipts for everything you buy, that much I do know.'

Simon turned to Mark. 'You fine with what you are doing?'

'Oh, yeah.' He said, tapping on the table with the end of his unlit cigarette. 'I'll go back to the sites I told you about. Narrow it down to the best few so we can all go and see and decide on one. As I said I think I can do a deal with some builders I know. Clear up the site, make it secure and all the rest. I'll get an estimate once we've picked a place.'

'Great.' Finally, Simon turned to Trisha. 'That just leaves you with the catalogue.'

'Bird-Girl get design finished. Soon. Very soon.'

'Need to sort out the descriptions of the work you are going to submit.' Simon said, looking back to all of us. 'Even if you've not completed them all. Plus get some photographs of the ones you have finished.'

'I can help with that,' Catherine said.

'That's all then?' I asked.

'It will do for now,' Simon said. 'Right, next meeting same time… well a different place, obviously, I'll phone you all to sort out a location. Any questions?'

We all shook our heads.

'Good. Oh, and remember any problems between now and the next time we get together don't hesitate in coming straight back to me.'

'You know, I actually think we might really do this.' Mark said, pushing back his chair as he stood.

'I've never doubted it.' Simon said, gathering up his papers. 'Never.'

I slumped deeper into the designer couch. It was a huge tan marsh-mellow, one of three in a spacious, softly lit and minimally decorated lounge area. There were half a dozen people quietly chatting on the other sofas or on the floor in the front of them, or in one case slumped against the wall near the door asleep.

Catherine had temporarily deserted me and gone off to talk to the last person on her list. I had cried off going along with her, saying I was too tired to meet any more new people. She had promised me she would be giving me her full attention when she had finished – her very full attention, she had added with a wink.

As midnight had approached I had slowed down my drinking, switching from wine to spirits, gin and tonics with lots of tonic and lots of ice. Not something I would normally drink but it seemed appropriate somehow given the location, the people and the atmosphere. Light jazz was playing in the background and I mellowed out to it.

The sofa shifted, breaking my trance. Catherine's father sat down beside me, a large tumbler of whisky in his hand.

'You look bored.'

'Oh no, just relaxing.' I said. 'Catherine's gone off to give the hard-sell to someone.'

'Well, if you want me to introduce you to some people?'

'Ah, Catherine's already done that.' I pulled myself more upright, turning to him. 'Too many, I think. I'm sure I can't remember what even half of them look like now, never mind what their names are.'

'I can imagine.' He laughed. 'So this meeting of yours went all right? Everything sorted?'

'God no, there's still a ton of stuff to do. We were mainly sorting out areas of responsibilities. But I think we'll start making some real progress now.'

'Oh yes, Cathy told me. I heard you got saddled with the treasurer role.'

'Unfortunately. It's because I'm the only one who's had a proper job before. Well some of them have had temp jobs, but I'm the only one with real work experience. Like that makes me an expert on starting up a business! And just because I've programed financial software doesn't mean I know all the necessary tax rules back to front. I sort of kidded I didn't want to do it because it sounded boring but really it's because I'm frightened I'll just completely cock it up.'

'Don't worry about it. I can give you some help. Introduce you to the accountancy firm we use for a start. They'll sort out most of it for you anyway. And I think we'll – the architecture business, I mean – be able to sponsor you as well. Give you some cash to get you going, certainly.'

'That sounds fantastic,' I said. 'I didn't want to ask but... Thanks anyway.'

He paused, looking away from me for a few seconds. He swallowed a mouthful of whiskey.

'So how you getting on with Catherine then?' He asked.

'Great.' I said.

'I'm sure. It's just, well…' He spoke slowly as if reaching for the words. 'I, well we, her mother – well, everyone really, we… we worry about her. The twins settled down so quickly. And Catherine… Well, we just worry about her. It's just it didn't end too well with Julian.'

'Julian?'

'Her fiancé.'

'Ah yes, she has mentioned it.'

'I can see straight away that it's different with you. I'm sure she will be fine… It's just, she can be a funny girl, at times.' He laughed to himself. 'Dearie me, when she was a kid… for almost a year she said she was a princess. Because she lived up in the tower. Would only answer to 'Princess Catherine'.' He looked at down at the whisky in his glass as if seeing it for the first time. 'Yes, she can be a funny girl.'

He laughed again then pushed himself up off the sofa to stand over me. 'Ah, well. I had better go and find my wife, I suppose.' He continued. 'It's just… a father worries. You know?'

'Yes, of course.'

'Right.' He turned from me and made his way out of the room.

I finished my drink thinking over what he had said, then hauled myself out of the sofa.

I bumped into Simon in the corridor outside.

'Have you seen Catherine?' I asked him.

'No, not for a while. I was looking for you, actually. Can I have quick word?' Simon asked. 'I just wanted to check you're really all right with the financial stuff?'

'Oh, course I am. I might gripe and moan, but to be honest, now I've had time to get used to the idea, I think it might be interesting.' I smiled. 'Plus I've just had a word with Catherine's dad. He's gonna help me out.'

'Good,' Simon said. He swigged from a bottle of Pills. 'Good. And you on track to get your stuff finished for the exhibition? You'll have enough?'

'Think so. I've just about finished the map stuff I've been working on.'

'Good.' He smiled. 'So, I guess you and Catherine will be working closely together in the future. Very close.'

'And I thought we being so discreet. Turns out everyone knows.' I shook my head then leaned back against the door frame. 'And I suppose you are already finished, Mr Organised.'

'Well, yes. Of course I am!'

We both laughed.

'Mark's still got a way to go but I think he's back on plan.' Simon added. 'He's told me he's putting in some long hours so I think he'll get it all done.'

'It will be interesting to see what he's working on, finally.' I said. 'I was talking to Trisha earlier. She was worried about not having anything, that she has no new decent ideas… but I told her the ideas she's already got are good enough. And she's come up with something new today. Still, she might need some extra encouragement.'

'I'll have a word with her.'

'Yeah, we should just keep egging her along.' I said. 'I had…'

Simon ignored me. He stepped out into the middle of the corridor. He spread both hands wide in a theatrical gesture.

'This place. Amazing isn't it?'

'Oh yes, it was nice of Catherine's parents to have us for the weekend.' I said. 'Actually I was–'

'It's real eye-opener.' Simon interrupted me. 'I wouldn't mind having a bit of this in the future.' He leaned in close, swaying, breathing beer fumes into my face. 'That's what being an artist is all about, really. Manipulation. Imposing your vision on reality. Melding it to your means. Making your personal philosophy into life. If you want to be rich – just, be rich.'

'Maybe, I suppose.'

'Oh, yes.' He said, pointing the bottle at my chest. 'I think we are lot alike, you and me. Two poor lads on the up. We'll have to work at being rich and successful, but that only makes it all the better when we get it. And makes us work all the harder to get there. Just like Maggie said. I tell you, growing up no-one I knew – my family, no-one at school – would ever had guessed I would end up in this sort of company, in this sort of place. And this will just be the start. And with Major back in there won't be Labour putting on the breaks. I bet this lot were happy about that.'

'I think they all vote Liberal actually. Kind of a traditional thing.' I said. 'I don't know… sometimes, I don't think I even deserve to be here, on the course, never mind partying in a place like this.'

'I don't want to hear that. You deserve it. We all do.'

'Simon!' A voice called out from along the corridor. We both turned to see Simon's girlfriend, Julie, running up to us. Slim with long dark hair pulled back, her make-up was garish and unsubtle, the same as her clothes.

'I've been looking all over for you.' She said to Simon, throwing her arms around him.

'I know pet, but I had work to do.'

'Come and talk to me, for a bit. It's only knobs here who take the piss out me. Even your boring art bollocks is better than that.' Julie laid her head against his chest. *'Pleeeeease.'* She added with a pleading whine.

He sighed.

'That 'boring art bollocks' will make you rich one day,' he said, patting her head.

'Maybe.' I added.

'Be sure of it.' He said.

His eyes met mine over her shoulder.

'Well,' I said. 'I'll leave you to it.'

I turned away from both of them.

At the end of the corridor was a room dominated by a large circular table, the top of which was a sea of glass — multiple bottles of wine, beer, spirits and mixers plus clusters of glasses in all sizes. I saw Mark standing on the far side making himself some sort of cocktail.

'Seen Catherine?' I asked as I approached him.

'Last time I saw her she was outside.'

Now I was closer I saw how bloodshot his eyes were, and thought back to what Simon had said.

'You're working too hard.'

'Tell me about it.' He said. 'But I'm nearly back on schedule. Then I'll take it easy. Well, easier.'

'Hello, gentlemen.' The tall man with the plaster-cast on his foot who I had met earlier lurched into the room. Uncle Rupert, I remembered. 'Choices, choices. Eh?' He said, looking over the table. He turned to Mark. 'What's that you're making?'

'Cocktail. My own recipe.'

'Oh really? Well make us one too, my lad. Always willing to try something new.'

'Oh no! On no, you don't!'

I turned towards the shrill voice. It came from a short slender oriental woman of indeterminate age who now standing behind us. She was wearing a Chinese-style mini-dress made from some bright turquoise spangly material with orange embroidery, her black hair was long except where it framed her face with a sharp fringe. She would have been almost perfect in her beauty if not for a slight squint plus her face was currently screwed up in anger.

'You drink too much!' She pulled at Rupert's arm.

'Bloody hell, woman – I've barely had a drop.'

'No, you come away.' She yanked at his arm again. 'Now! Or no rumpo!'

'Oh, all right, dear.' He said, a note of resignation in his voice as he turned away from the table. 'Anything for a quiet life.'

Some of the anger left the woman's face. She put her arm around his waist, let him lean against her as she helped him hobble out of the room.

He looked back to us as he reached the doorway. 'Sometimes, I'm sure they sent me the wrong one.'

She tutted. 'Always with 'they sent the wrong one!''

'Oh, come on dear, you know I'm joking. And that I love you.' He put his hand around her shoulders. 'Can't I just have one more drink?'

At first she shook her head but then she smiled.

'No, but maybe one later.' She started to lead him out of the room. 'Just one.'

They shuffled away down the corridor.

'Jesus, I hope you and Catherine don't end up like that.' Mark said when they were gone.

'I'll make sure we don't. Better go find her, anyway.'

I rediscovered the room from where Catherine had led me out of the back of the house when we had arrived. Although the party was now starting to wind down this seemed to be the epicentre of what remained and was still filled with people.

Suddenly a hand was on my arm. Catherine's sister, Polly.

'Jason, I need to have a word.'

I waved out towards the garden with my free hand, making to go past her. 'I just going to catch up with Catherine.'

She looked right at me.

'This is about Catherine. And you really need to hear it. Now.'

I let myself be led to some spare straight-backed chairs tucked away in the corner of the room. We sat and Polly turned to me.

'My father's spoken to you, hasn't he?' She said in a low voice.

'Yes.' I replied. 'Sort of, I'm not too sure what he was getting at.'

She sighed. 'He means well. But sometimes... He just does more harm than good. How much has he told you? He mention Princess Peculiar?'

'Yes. Well no, he said something about Princess Catherine, I think.'

'So he didn't mention the bullying I take it?'

'No, what bullying?'

'Some kids at her school found out about it – the Princess thing. I mean it had all happened years ago by then but she was still bullied over it – calling her Princess Peculiar. Girls can be just as vicious as boys with that sort of thing. More so sometimes – jealously, who's in the in-crowd, who's teacher's pet, all that nonsense. She was also going through a growth spurt at the time – looking real gawky, which didn't help her self-confidence at all.'

'She's never mentioned any of this to me.'

'She wouldn't. She moved schools eventually – but she was bad for a while, even after that. I mean properly depressed. Lost weight, a lot – borderline anorexia, actually. Once she came home covered in bruises. We thought it was the bullying again but it turned out she was doing it to herself. Self-harm, they called it. Then sometimes she would smash things up, temper tantrums.'

'I've not seen anything like that in her.' I said. 'And it was a while ago, I take it. She must be over it by now?'

'We all thought so.' Polly said. 'Until she split up with her fiancé. Then it all started again.'

'She told me she threw herself into her art. Might have been a bit manic for while, but surely not that bad?'

'She tried to kill herself.'

'What!'

'Swallowed handfuls of pills. It wasn't the first time either... but that time was very close. Too close. Real touch and go.'

'Oh, god.'

'She had to go away for a while. Hospital. But the art helped her – seemed to pull her out, kept her on the level. One of the reasons that father gives her so much support in it.'

'I can't believe this,' I said, 'It's just... I've never seen it in her. I've never seen her depressed. Not at all.'

'I thought I had better warn you. That if you see her getting depressed again, let me know. Maybe, I'm being over-sensitive but she's my little sister. She's so talented, so beautiful. But she's so fragile as well.'

I went outside to find Catherine. She had not gone far. She and her friends had moved on to the pool area.

As I had walked from the garden towards the pool, two of them ran back past me, holding hands, shouting. I turned to watch them charge through the garden then run off out over the lawn towards the arboretum.

It looked like a sudden storm had blown across the patio and the pool – sun-loungers, chairs and tables had been haphazardly rearranged; a single croquet mallet had been cast aside; a sun-lounger floated in the pool itself. All around and over the scattered lawn furniture were strewn glasses, bottles and plates. To one side, on a table shoved up against the wall a midi-stereo had been set up, speakers out on chairs, an extension power cable extending back into the house through an open door – Shakespears Sister played.

Some of Catherine's friends were clustered around a table over by the house. Others had changed into swimming costumes and lounged, semi-submerged, in the pool. One, burly and hairy-chested, was eating a bap – filled with bacon by the smell. He backed away swearing from a busty woman in a red bikini who was trying to splash him.

Catherine laughed at them both. She was perched on the edge of the pool, bare feet dangling in the water.

Most of the house lights were now off but the pool was lit from below by blue lights embedded beneath the surface of the water. Ripples of light chased across Catherine's face so that she appeared to be sitting underwater herself, like a mermaid on a reef.

'Ah, Jason lover.' She said, turning as I walked up to her. She looked at me, head on one side, with sleepy eyes and a lop-sided smile. 'There you are. I was just about to come and find you.'

'Catherine, I could do with having a word. In private.'

'"Private', right.' She winked at her friends and received a few catcalls in return. 'That's a good idea.'

She giggled to herself then pulled her feet out of the pool and stood up. Stepping into her shoes she reached down to pick up a bottle of Brut from the poolside.

'Come, walk with me, then.'

She looped her arm around mine then led me alongside the pool away from the house. Her footsteps were deliberately placed as she leaned against me. We were twined by our spectral reflections in the glass frontage of the pool house. She led me on behind it.

The plain rear wall of the building blocked what little light that still came from the house, creating a long deep shadow that stretched out across the lawn towards the distant trees.

Cat slipped her arm from me and leaned back against the wall then lowered herself to sit down on the lawn.

She took a long swig of the Brut then held the bottle up to me with one outstretched arm. I took it from her hand, sitting down besides her. I sipped from the bottle. It was nearly empty, and what Champagne was left was tepid and flat.

'I used to sleep out here sometimes.' Catherine said, her voice light and dreamy. 'In the summer. When it was too hot.' She reached up over her head and slapped her hand against the wall of the pool house. 'Or in there when I was too pissed to climb all those stairs.'

'Look, Catherine. I–'

She reached across me for the bottle of Brut.

'Give us the champers. If you're not drinking it, I'll finish it off.'

As she stretched she unbalanced and slumped against me.

'Oh, sorry.' She slurred, her mouth close to my ear. 'You know, we could do it now. It's a bit naughty, but–'

'Cat–'

Loosely draping her arms around me, she planted wet kisses down the side of my face.

'No. Look–' I said.

'We can slip away to the arboretum. We–'

She suddenly unbalanced completely. Sliding down off me she collapsed down into a heap, her head in my lap.

'Whoops,' she giggled, as she pulled herself upright, finally grabbing the bottle of Champagne.

'Jesus, Cat! Don't you think you have had enough?'

'Oh, don't be such a fuddy-duddy. You're as bad as Su Lynn.'

'Who?'

'Uncle Rupert's wife.'

'Oh, her. Hardly.' I said. 'Look, Catherine… It may not be the best time. But… I don't think it can wait. I need to ask you about something.'

Catherine ignored me. She braced herself against the wall with one hand to get to her knees, then to stand. She turned from me and swigged back the rest of the Champagne. Then she flung the empty bottle out across the lawn.

'That's where I'm going to build my statue!' She pointed out to where I could just see the bottle now rested. 'It's going to magnificent! Three giant-sized chess pieces.'

She turned and then threw herself down on top of me. I managed to catch her in my arms.

'Big and handsome like you.' She gave me another sloppy kiss, right on the lips this time.

Her hands were trying to pull my T-shirt up. I took hold of them.

'Look, Catherine I have to ask you something…'

'What?' She whined. 'Make it quick. I want sexing.'

'It's about your past. When you were at school… but also after you split up with Julian.'

She jerked back from me.

'I'm not going to talk about any of that.' He voice was cold.

She pulled herself off me and quickly stood again.

'Catherine, I think–' I said, as I clambered to my own feet.

'No!'

She turned and stepped from me, striding back towards the pool.

'Cat, I'm sorry. But–'

I reached for her arm but she snatched it away.

'No, just fuck off!'

She broke into a run. I sprinted after her and caught up with her at the front of the pool house. Grabbing both her shoulders I spun her around to face me.

'Catherine! Please!'

'I told you!' She cried. 'I told you there were things I would never talk about! I told you that!'

'But, I never thought it was something like this. Your sister, your father told me. I mean suicide...'

She said nothing then. Just stared at me, eyes wide, mouth tightly closed. I was shocked. I had never seen such anger, such venom, in her.

'They never should have told you.' Her was voice low and cold again, her words slow and deliberate. 'It all came out in my last relationship. It did not help. At all. It made it worse. It turned him against me.'

'But I would never do that; Catherine. You know I wouldn't. I'm only trying to help you. I–'

'Leave me alone!' I could see there were tears in her eyes. 'You don't own me!'

She squirmed out of my grasp. Turned and started to run again.

I tried to grab her.

'Fuck off!' She screamed. *Fuck off!*'

Spinning around, arms stretched out, fingers splayed, she tried to push me away from herself. But, lighter and already unbalanced, she only pushed herself back and made herself even more unstable. She stumbled backwards, trying to recover. She stepped onto a discarded bottle and lost her balance completely as it rolled out from under her foot.

She fell, fully outstretched, into the pool.

She hit the water with a splash that turned the heads of all those near the pool that had not already been staring at our argument. Others had started to come out of the house.

I ran to the edge of the water. Catherine was twisting round under the surface of the water so that she faced the bottom of the pool. I watched her kick against the poolside and swim two powerful strokes away from me. Surfacing, she swam the rest of the pool's length. Then, not looking back, she started to climb out at the other end.

'*Catherine!*' I cried, running along the side of the pool towards her.

She said nothing, ignored me, and the concern of her friends and others now around her. Sodden clothes hung plastered against her skin. Her fingers pulled her wet hair away from her face. I heard a single sob, then she sprinted back towards the house, water streaming down off her clothes to splatter a dark trail across the flags of the patio.

Catherine's sister stopped me following her into house.

'Leave her,' she said. 'For now.'

I hesitated, then turned away from the house. I grabbed the first bottle that came to hand and strode away towards the arboretum.

I collapsed down against the trunk of a large oak and swigged from the bottle – gin, tasting vile without a mixer. Disgusted, I cast the bottle aside. Liquid sloshed out onto the grass.

Then I just stayed sitting there for a while, alone, my head in my hands.

Suddenly I jerked awake, shivering slightly. Head swimming, my mouth felt like it was lined with old carpet. Cursing to myself I stood and made my way out of the trees.

A risen full moon had turned the lawn to a lake of silver. The house itself was quiet and the only signs of life were a few lit windows on the upper floors.

I found the French doors closed but not locked and I slipped inside as stealthy as a burglar. Among all the discarded bottles and glasses, I spotted the familiar curves of a full bottle of Perrier. I seized it like a drowning man grabbing a life jacket and eagerly swallowed down the fizzy water.

The bottle empty, I left it behind as I crept through the house to the bottom of the stairs that led up to Catherine's room. Slowly ascending, I planned my apologies.

But her room was deserted.

I had no idea where else to look.

Eventually I found the bedroom I had been assigned. However when I opened the door I saw somebody was already sprawled on the bed. Or rather two somebodies – Uncle Rupert was lying on his back, lightly snoring, with Su Lynn half on top of him, naked, her small breasts flattened against his chest.

'Wha–?' Rupert mumbled, as they both woke. His wife shushed and soothed him, a hand to his face.

I carefully shut the door on the both of them.

Thinking of nothing better I made my way back outside again. I found that the door to the pool house was unlocked and I dragged one of the sun-loungers inside.

A ghost came to me.

A pale blur of a white lady, that became Catherine, as my eyes focused. She was standing over me, illuminated by the moonlight shining through the glass wall of the pool house, hair swept back, face free of make-up, a long cream-coloured dressing gown loosely draped around her.

Her cool hand on my face had woken me.

'Oh god, Catherine. I'm so sorry. I looked for you. Your room, then my room...' My voice petered out.

She just smiled down at me.

'Move over.'

I shifted onto my side and she lay down beside me. She smelled fresh and clean, a faint hint of wild flowers in her hair.

'I was in the bath,' she said. 'For a long time. Fell asleep. Then I came looking for you. But Uncle Rupert had crashed out in your room. I saw you weren't in my bedroom and then I thought of here. Thought of what I told you about sleeping out here...' She sighed then continued. 'God, I never should have told you about that. It was here. Right here.'

'What was here?'

'Where I tried to kill myself.'

Silent tears glittered on her face. I put my arms around her, held her to me.

'Oh, I'm—'

But she angrily brought a hand up between us. She wiped at her face then pushed a single upright finger hard against my lips to quieten me.

'No!' She urged. 'Let's say nothing more now.'

She stood again and quickly pulled off the dressing gown and threw it to the floor. She was naked underneath – monochrome in the moonlight, all silver and shade. I gazed up at her breasts, at the inky points of her nipples, then down the shadowed hollow under her ribs to her navel, to the dark fur beneath.

Then her hands were reaching down to me.

I helped her to pull off my T-shirt. She kissed me then pushed me back down.

She turned her back to me and then swung her leg across my body so that she straddled me. She unfastened and pulled down my shorts and boxers. I reached for her hips.

Then she did say one word. Sighed it out into the night as she pushed her groin to my mouth, as she bent forward to envelop me with her own. 'Speleology.'

After our bodies had cooled, our combined sweat evaporated, she spread the dressing gown across the both of us.

'So, I suppose, technically, that wasn't in your parent's house.' I said.

'Yup, and technically it wasn't sex either.'

We both laughed. I reached for her, and she turned to me, lying on her side. I stroked from her shoulder past her breast, swooping down into the valley of her waist then up again to finally rest my hand on the flare of her hip.

'Our first argument then.' I said.

'Yes, I think it was. Stupid. I should be happy you worry over me. But... all those things are in the past now. Please don't... let's just agree not to talk of them again.'

'Okay.'

'And there's one more thing.' She said. 'We get along real well together and we're friends and the sex is fantastic and we've survived a big argument and everything and well... I know it's stupid... but I just don't want to ever spoil it. Because every time I've – or they've – said it in the past... Well, that's been the beginning of the end.'

'Right you've lost me now. What are you talking about? Said what?'

'The l-word. The falling in... the l-word.'

'*Ahhh...*' I said, understanding. I pulled her closer and lightly kissed the tip of her nose. 'All right, I'll never say it. Never, ever.'

'I'm serious now. Feel it. Show it. But don't say it. Ever. Promise.'

'Promise.'

'Good.' Then she lay head on my shoulder and hugged me tight before murmuring something more.

'Say it again?' I whispered. Then I moved my head, pressing my ear close to her mouth.

'Hold me.' She breathed the words. 'Hold me, I'm yours now.'

7 HEARTS AND DAGGERS

Designs swirled in front of my eyes.

I flicked through the pages of tattoo-pattern samples in the lever-arch files spread open on the counter-top in front of me -- from the traditional macho hearts and daggers, skulls and anchors to the modern feminine dolphins and unicorns. Mickey Mouse shared a page with Yosemite Sam, Winnie-the-Pooh with Hello Kitty. Familiar film stars were displayed next to portraits of anonymous loved ones – their original photograph alongside to show off the skill of the reproduction. Pages of rock-band logos vied with trade-marked symbols of multi-million dollar corporations. Celtic crosses and knot-work were displayed alongside Maori inspired abstract swirls.

From every tattoo parlour I had ever seen depicted on screen, I had been expecting the walls of the reception area to be plastered with sample designs. Instead, to my surprise they were bare with only a few framed professionally shot photographs of attractive, alternative-looking, models with interesting artwork inked on their skins. The minimalist design continued with the room's furnishings with only a couple of plain sofas and a glass-topped island counter towards the rear of the room

However I soon discovered that the island counter was where sample tattoos could be looked over in three thick lever-arch folders.

After a few minutes my studies had been briefly interrupted when the tattooist himself suddenly leaned out over the saloon-style doors that separated off the back room of the parlour to tell me he would be free in a few minutes. Then he had just as quickly disappeared and the metallic buzz of the tattoo ink gun – that had been the constant and annoying background noise from the moment I walked in the place – started up again.

The place had been harder to find that I had expected. Once I arrived in Croydon I began to realise just how much time had gone by since me and Catherine had first drove past the tattoo parlour, and I struggled to find it again.

As I wandered the streets, breathing in car fumes, my lack of sleep from the previous nights made it like wading through water. I cursed the fact that I had come straight from the publishers and not gone back to the studio to dig out the maps where I had recorded the old journey. However, just at the point I was about to admit defeat, and go back for the map, I found it.

I saw the search had been made doubly difficult by the fact that the place had obviously changed hands, or had been given a major make-over at least. It had been transformed from the traditional tattoo parlour that I rememberd into a sleek new studio. The garish dragons of my memory had been replaced with a solid field of cerulean covering the bottom half of the window, out of which a new name had been cut out, the clear glass letters spelling out – *Black and Blue.*

After quickly flicking past oriental ideograms and Arabic writing samples, I slowed as I reached pages filled with examples of the English alphabet, plus numerals and punctuation marks all, in different fonts.

I had placed my own folder down on the glass countertop and now I opened it and pulled out the sketch I had made of Catherine's tattoo from the publisher's photograph – the half arrow flight or the stylised reversed 'F' as I now thought of it. I spent several minutes studying all the lettering samples carefully but there was none that even remotely resembled the tattoo.

The letters suddenly seemed to swirl around in front of me like a swarm of angry bees. I looked away, rubbing at my tired itchy eyes.

'See anything you like?'

I looked back to see the tattooist was now standing behind the counter.

He was tall and rangy with short spiky hair shaved down to bare skin at the sides of his head. There were multiple hoops in both of his ears and two through one side of his nose. A baggy sleeveless red singlet with a 'Chicago Bulls' logo hung off his bony shoulders.

The whole of his right arm, from the shoulder down to the back of his hand was one long intricate kaleidoscope of tattoos. In stark contrast his left arm was completely unadorned, bare and pale. His hands rested on the counter. On the top finger joints of his right hand thick inked letters spelled out 'S-C-A-B'. His left hand, like the arm was bare.

'You're left-handed, I take it.' I said.

He smirked.

'Well spotted,' Scab ran his left hand along down his right arm. 'You would not believe how many offers I've had to ink the bits I can't reach but I want to keep it all my own work.'

He nodded down at the design folders.

'So, see anything you like?' He asked. 'If it's simple I can probably fit you in when I'm finished in the back – say in half an hour? Otherwise, I'll book you in for an appointment.'

'I'm just interested in this.' I said.

I slid over the drawing of Catherine's tattoo. Scab looked down at the design for what seemed a long time then slowly picked it up. He blinked twice then looked at me again.

'That's easy enough. Exactly like that? All black? Certainly do that for you today.'

He placed the drawing back onto the counter.

'I don't want the tattoo.' I said. 'I just wondered if you know anything about it, what it might mean, or the person who may have had that done. I think someone may have had it done here.'

'Sorry, I don't discuss other clients.'

'Look, I–'

'Are you the filth?'

'No, but–'

'Then piss off.'

He turned his back to me and went straight into the back room before I could say anything else.

I walked away from the saloon with the late afternoon sun at my back, staring down at the pavement at my shadow stretching away from me.

Was that it? The end of the line.

I stopped.

No. Not the end.

There was something else back there. I was sure of it.

Something in the way Scab had reacted when he saw the tattoo. Something in his eyes.

Recognition.

He had seen it before, I suddenly realised. I was sure of it.

Sudden cold anger seethed in me.

He was not going to keep it from me. No fucking way.

I chided myself on being such a poor detective. I should have badgered him, not accepted the brush off.

Questioned him properly.

Pressed him.

I turned around and rushed back to *Black and Blue,* breaking into a run as I went through the door. I threw my folder back down onto the counter as I dashed past it and crashed through the saloon doors.

The small back room was dominated by a black leather reclining seat set almost fully back. Lying face down on top was a rather plump woman. She had a white blouse on but nothing else. Scab, perched on the edge of a stool, was leaning over her, white-gloved like a surgeon. He was adding colour into the black outline of a large butterfly that had already been inked onto one of her bare buttocks.

The woman lifted her head up to stare back at me as I stormed into room. She yelped. She tried to cover her backside with her hands.

Scab jerked around towards me.

'What the fuck!'

I barrelled into him, slamming the heel of my hand up under his ribs, lifting him back and off the stool.

'I want some answers, Scab!'

My full weight plus weeks of bottled up grief, anger and frustration were behind the blow. A martial arts move I had half-remembered from my teens proved to be rusty, the angle off, some of the power dissipated back up my arm, hurting my wrist in the process. But I barely noticed and the blow was still enough to make Scab gasp for breath as he staggered back a few steps.

The woman tried to get up, one hand still trying to cover her bottom, fingers splayed. I pushed her back down with my hand between her shoulder blades.

'Stay there.'

She wailed into the leather of the bench.

I quickly spun back to Scab, shoved him in the chest before he had a chance to fully recover. He was taller than me but I had an obvious weight advantage. Plus, judging by his ashen face and his wide eyes, nervously glancing from my hands to my own eyes then back down again, he wasn't going to put up much of an argument anyway.

My hand went to his neck, pushing up under his jaw. Forcing his head back, I backed him up to the wall. The tattoo gun hung loosely in his surgical-gloved hand and I snatched it from his limp fingers. The gun was nearly at the end of its flex but I was still able to bring it up to Scab's face, millimetres from his cheek. I pulled the trigger a couple of times, that irritating buzz suddenly loud between us.

'You want to see some impromptu art work?' I spat the words into his face. 'Add a little something to that precious bare skin of yours?'

'Oh god, no! Please!' He gasped.

'Then fucking tell me all about that tattoo I showed you. You've seen it before haven't you?'

'It was just some woman!'

I brought the tattoo gun down and pressed it hard against the top of his bare left arm.

'What woman? When? Tell me all about her. Everything!'

'Alright, alright!' Scab pleaded. 'Just put it down. Please!'

I pulled the gun back from his arm, and letting go of his throat, I moved back a step, breathing hard.

Now the adrenaline surge had dissipated, I felt sickened by my previous aggression.

'Just tell me.' I said, my voice flat.

'She just came into the shop one day, had the design on a piece of paper just like you did.'

'When was this?'

'Last year, around autumn I think.' He spoke rapidly. 'Later October, early November, sometime like that. She was attractive. Smart, like a businesswoman. But that's not unusual, we get all sorts here. She did seem a bit strange though... Almost sad that she was getting the tattoo.'

'And you still did it?' I said, scathingly.

Scab looked down, rubbing his throat.

'I've seen people like that before. They're getting a tattoo to commemorate a loved one who's just died or something. A portrait or their name or just an initial. They can be bit upset about it. I assumed that's what it was.' Then he suddenly looked up at me, meeting my eyes.

'What gives, man?' He continued. 'Is that it? Did she loose someone? If she did, I'm sorry!'

'It's none of your fucking business.' I snapped. 'Now is there anything else?'

'No... well, apart from the art stuff.'

'What art stuff?'

'While I was inking her we got talking about art. She told me she was a part-time illustrator. Talked to her about it... and about her maybe doing some designs for tattoos in the future. She left a business card so I could get in touch if anyone wanted something similar to what she was working on. She was supposed to be sending me some samples but she never did.'

'Have you still got it? The business card.'

'Maybe. It will be in there if I have.' He nodded over at a desk in one corner of the room.

'Get it,' I said, reaching out to turn him towards the desk with my free hand. Scab stepped over and started rooting though one draw filled with various papers.

I looked back to the woman. She was still lying on the couch but reached out with one arm to the chair where her jeans and knickers were neatly folded. She could not quite reach – her hand clawing at the air tantilisingly close, only inches away - because she was still trying to cover her bare backside with her other hand, fingers splayed.

I shook my head.

Scab pulled out a business card and held it up to me.

'That's it. Lexington. That was her.'

I took it from him.

Lexington? Another name? Another identity?

Scab continued. 'She said she had run out of her illustrator business cards so she gave me that.'

I glanced at the card, turning away from him.

Nichola Lexington – Discreet Private Massage and Executive Escort Service.'

Beneath were printed two phone numbers, one a mobile, and an address for a flat in Camden.

A sinking feeling settled back over me – the same airless disorientation I had felt when I had seen Catherine's tattooed skin in the photograph.

'Jesus Christ.' I said softly to myself.

'Yeah, it surprised me too.' Scab said from behind me. 'She didn't look the sort to be a part-time whore.'

My shoulders stiffened and I spun round, a sharp stab of emotion cutting through me.

Scab quailed away, hands raised.

'Sorry! I didn't mean to–'

I made a step towards him then stopped.

I let the tattoo gun fall clattering to the floor, then turned to the door and left.

I went straight to nearest phone box and punched in the first number on the card.

I listened to an answerphone message – just a bland request to leave some contact details. The voice was more clipped, more precise and professional that I had been used to – and the pitch was lower than the normal – but it was unmistakably Catherine. And the lower pitch I had heard before. She often employed it during our love-play, to add an extra edge of seduction to her words.

Now just a ghost on the line.

Almost uncontrollable emotion swelled up inside of me, but there were no more tears. They seemed all burned out of me.

The phone box seemed to spin and I slumped against the side of it, suddenly nauseous from the rising tide of emotion combined with my deep fatigue. I crashed the phone down on Catherine's words and pressed my forehead against the cool glass until the chill of the glass seeping through my brow into my skull provided a temporary respite to my bone-tiredness and the sick feeling ebbed away.

Then I remembered back to that other time; that other phone box call.

Cold sweat on my back.

My hand was at the door.

No. I had to see it through.

I redialled the number. Second time around Catherine's voice already had a less drastic effect and I was able to listen to the actual words. The message itself was spare – boringly so, with just a request to leave a name and number.

I dialled the other number on the card but, as expected, the message was near identical.

153

I put the receiver down again, picked up my folder, and scooped up the loose change I had piled on the phone for the call. As I slipped the coins back in my pocket my fingers ran along the jagged edges of my keys. I pulled out my key ring. Holding it by the Five Feather's fob I stared at its two recent additions. The ones that I had added the day before. The keys that I had found with Catherine's drawings. I looked back at the business card. At the address. A flat.

Two keys. One key for the main building? The other for the flat itself?

The key fit.

Well one did at least, into the lock of the building's main outer door. The address on the card had led me to a recently built large block of apartments in Camden, obviously expensive and anonymous – the entrance had been discreetly designed, hidden away round the back along with the off-road parking.

The concierge hardly looked up from reading his library book as I walked across the foyer towards the stairs. The number of the flat suggested it was on the second floor. I trudged along the hallways alone until I found it. The only other indications of humanity in the place were muffled music or the occasional low mumble of televisions showing the early evening news leaking through the walls of some of the other flats.

The second key unlocked the apartment itself but the door jammed as I opened it. I shoved hard and gained another couple of inches. I could just squeeze around the door's edge. Looking down I saw a pile of envelopes and flyers and free newspapers crushed up behind the bottom of the door. I crouched down and sifted through it, yanking out the ones wedged under the door itself. It was all junk, nothing personal. I stood and closed the door behind me.

The place had a slight stuffy musty smell of long abandonment but nothing like as ripe as the studio had been.

In the main room, against unadorned white-painted walls and a pale sandy-coloured carpet, there were just a few pieces of furniture – two beige sofas and a low table – that could have been bought from any upmarket interior design specialist. In fact the room could have graced the 'Living' section of any Sunday newspaper supplement, but even they would have added some personal touches to add some sort of story to the photograph. There were no personal nick-nacks on display, no ornaments, nothing. And no signs of entertainment – no television, no music system, no books.

The kitchen was just as spartan, with only a kettle out on the worktop. The small cooker looked completely unused but there was an open packet of Ariel on top of the washing machine. There was some cutlery in a draw, a couple of mugs and plates in the cupboard below, but no saucepans or other cooking equipment. The food cupboards were all empty as well – except in one there was a half-full jar of Nescafé, a near empty box of Tesco teabags, and two unopened packets of Digestives – but that was all. The fridge was empty except for milk – two well out-of-date plastic bottles that bulged with what must be nearly yoghurt. I shut the door on them.

My tiredness was now near overwhelming. Putting my folder down on one of the work surfaces, I took the opportunity to make myself a strong black coffee. I sipped it while I explored the rest of the apartment.

The bathroom looked like it saw more use than the kitchen. There were a whole array of soaps and bottles of shampoo lined up around the edge of the bath. Three expensive looking thick white fluffy towels were neatly folded over the heated towel-rail. There was toothpaste and a single toothbrush in a glass on the shelf above the sink along with a pink-handled razor. Next to them was a large bottle of Listerine. The bathroom cabinet had a mirrored door. The only mirror I had seen in the whole apartment. Inside, on the top shelf were a packet of Superdrug aspirin, some Rennies and a packet of Tampax. Below were a few cosmetics – bright scarlet lipstick, blue eye shadow, black eyeliner.

Then finally the bedroom. This room had been decorated and furnished in a complete contrast to the other rooms' bland styling, with a thick wine carpet and dark-stained furniture. Around the black-painted walls were hung silver-framed black and white photographs of naked women. The shots were cropped tight and unusually framed – perhaps to preserve the subjects' anonymity or make them look more artistic that the usual pin-up: a close-up of a breast with one nipple just at the far edge of the frame; a shot of the abdomen, from navel down to the edge of pubic hair; one isolated thigh; the lower part of the back merging into the top half of the buttocks.

But not women. All one woman, I realised. Catherine, all of them, I was sure.

The only bedding on the double bed were two white pillows and a matching fitted sheet. On the other side of the bed was a set of draws. On the top, clustered together, were three stubby silver candlestick holders with half-melted red candles stuck in the top of them.

Facing the bed, against the far wall, was a large television on top of a cabinet. Next to the television was a wardrobe. I opened it. Inside hung a row of costumes – a nurse's outfit, a French maid, a female police officer, a St Trinian's style school uniform, a nun's habit. Plus there were more generic outfits that could be easily fitted into other obvious roles – the business suit of the secretary or teacher, the skimpy slutty clothes of the easily available tart. Hats, bags and belts and other matching accessories were stuffed onto shelves. There was a pile of shoes at the bottom – all high-heels.

They were all in Catherine's size.

I closed the wardrobe and went around to the other side of the bed. I put the coffee mug down on top of the set of draws and opened each one in turn. The bottom one was filled with underwear – bra and knickers sets, garter belts and basques in gaudy cheap-looking black, white and red – that looked like they came straight from Ann Summers. Off to one side were rolled-up stockings, most of them fishnet.

I opened the top draw and glimpsed jars of massage oils, tubes of lubrication gel, boxes of condoms, the bright pink and white torpedoes of sex toys.

I slammed the draw shut. Picking my coffee up I left the room, pausing only to check the cabinet below the television. There was a video player on a shelf, and, as I now expected to see, a row of porn tapes below.

I went back to the kitchen, closed the door on the rest of the flat and finished my coffee.

Catherine, a prostitute?

I just could not believe it.

It had to be something... something else. *Something different.*

An art work?

A new art work!

That's what it was, I realised. Just another new look. But going further this time, not only dressing as them, but providing a space for them to exist in. A living space with all the props needed for them to appear true. Taking her art to the next level.

She would have been planning to photograph herself in the role later or film it. Maybe – once she had fully developed her idea – include me in on it; to collaborate with her, help her photograph or film it, like she had done in the past.

Now I thought about it I realised all the stuff in bedroom, the costumes, the porn and the rest of it seemed much too obvious, like the idea of what the bedroom of a prostitute should be – a hyper-reality, a parody on what the reality would actually be. A criticism on it, on the men that used such a service, on the society that allowed it, that needed it. It would have made a great piece.

And not only 'Nichola Lexington – Discreet Private Massage and Executive Escort Service' there was also 'Fanny Dore – erotic illustrator', as well. Another identity. Another art piece?

Was this it? The 'everything' she had referred to in the video? Why she had done it?

Fanny Dore and Nichola Lexington? Just a bit of pornography and play acting? Killed herself over that?

No, there had to be something else.

Another project? Something I might have missed, back at the studio?

I cursed myself for not looking further than I had done, at jumping on the first clue I had come across.

I rubbed at my gritty eyes, stifling a yawn. The coffee had not had much of an effect. I decided to call it day, start again at the studio in the morning.

I turned to leave the kitchen and saw something I had not seen the first time I had been in the room. Behind the door, next to a telephone fixed onto the wall, was a calendar.

Last year's, it was open on November. I took it down off the wall and flicked through the months each accompanied by a Picasso painting, the artist's more obvious works depicted – 'Guernica', 'Les Demoiselles d'Avignon', 'Three Musicians', some Blue Period still-life.

November itself was blank, as was the first half of the year. However in the weeks from late summer and on into autumn, initials and times, in Catherine's handwriting, had been added to a number of dates. At first only occasionally, once a week or so, then increasing in frequency to one every couple of days. Imaginary customers, I presumed – a nice touch. Then in October the word 'SPA' joined them, again with increasing frequency.

I hung the calendar back up and turned to the telephone. It had a built-in answerphone and I found playback. I listened to the message I had heard back in the phone box followed by a number of frustrated or angry sounding male voices, wondering where she was, why had she missed her appointments, what had happened to her. They were all time-stamped after the day Catherine had died.

I suddenly felt numb. This seemed too real, too prosaic to fit in with the fantasy art scenario I had just devised.

Why would men be calling with messages like this...? Had she actually set up appointments?

No, it had to be part of the artwork, somehow. She would have paid actors—

The string of male voices were suddenly interrupted by a female one. She was much more sympathetic in tone, filled with concern at not hearing from 'Nicks' recently, asking her to ring the 'spa' whenever she wanted, if she wanted to come back. She left a number.

I stopped the playback. Grabbing a pen from my folder, I replayed the woman's message and scribbled down the phone number onto the back of the Nicola Lexington business card.

I dialled the number immediately, if only to try and fend off the growing realisations in my mind.

'Carlton Health Spa, can I have your membership number please?' The voice was female, but it wasn't the same as the one on the message I had just heard.

'Oh, err, I'm not a member.' I stumbled at first, then improvised, 'someone said I should ring this number.'

'And their name is?'

'Nicola Lexington.'

'Just a second.' I heard a keyboard clattering in the background. 'Yes, she's one of our consultants. Well, was — we've not heard from her for some time.'

'Yes, it would have been a while back.'

'That's okay. We can sort your membership out when you visit in person and book any treatments you may want. Let me take your name now and I'll book you as a preliminary member.'

'Sam Gardener. What about tonight?'

'That's no problem. We don't close until ten, but there's no entry after eight.'

'Oh, I'll be there before then.' I paused, then added. 'What was the address again?'

She told me some street and number in Chelsea and I copied it down on the back of the business card below the number. We exchanged final goodbyes and I put the phone down.

I realised I had been staring at the calendar throughout the conversation. Certain days in November had been marked after all. Printed on the calendar, as well as notable dates — All Saints' Day, Armistice Day, Thanksgiving, St Andrew's Day, spaced out through the month were the phases of the moon: Last Quarter, Waning Crescent, New, Waxing Crescent, First Quarter, Waxing Gibbous, Full, Waning Gibbous…

I had not noticed it at first but now I looked I saw each 'Gibbous' had been carefully underlined.

They were the only marks on the calendar for that month. I checked back. Throughout the autumn, at least one 'Gibbous' per month had a line drawn under in. Plus there were initials added under each occurrence.

Fuck me under a gibbous moon.

It was all true. She had been a whore.

I remembered back to one mild late autumn day, towards the end of our first year together. Another trip over to her parents and an evening spent alone together in a pub in a nearby village. After closing Catherine had taken my arm as we walked across the car park. Her hand had clasped around mine and she steered me away from her car.

'I don't want to go straight back. Let's go for a little walk.' She grinned up at me, her face pixie-like and mischievous.

She had led me in a slow tour around the village. As the few other drinkers disappeared into their own houses or drove away into the night, we were soon alone together in the dark. After spending the whole evening talking we were now happily quiet in each other's company. Catherine pushed up close against me as we walked. She wore jeans, one of my old shirts, a long mac over shoulders, her hair was near shoulder-length, dyed back to her natural colour again.

Patchy cloud scudded across the sky, mostly obscuring the stars, but a hint of moon sometimes appeared above the roofs. There was little other light except the occasional lit window in the houses we passed – the streetlights were sparsely placed with large inky pools of blackness between them.

We approached the village church from the rear, its dark stone tower looming over us above the wall separating the path from the churchyard. Catherine led me around to the other side, to the litchgate huddled beneath tall ancient yews. She pulled me inside.

Now shrouded from all direct light, under the roof of the lichgate, Catherine was almost invisible. Just faint glints off the edge of her hair and eyes showed where she was. A row of thick vertical lines, opposite the entrance, black against the grey of the church, became a gate as my eyes grew accustomed to the increased darkness. Behind Catherine pale rectangles floated in the gloom, the printed-up minutes of the parish council pinned to a notice-board. Beneath there was a bench seat that ran from the front to the back of the gateway. Catherine shrugged off her coat and laid it down on top. She took my hand again and led me over to sit down beside her, on top of her coat. She turned to me. I could feel her breath on the side of my face.

'Most of my relatives are buried here. My parents were married in the church. Brother, sister, too. They expected me to but, well...' I saw her teeth flash briefly in the darkness as she smiled. 'Maybe, they still do. But no chance of that.'

Catherine let go of my hand and stood, turning. She sat back down on my lap, side on, grabbing both of my shoulders. I put my hands around her waist and she leaned forward to kiss me quickly on the lips.

'I'd take you into the churchyard but they lock the gate at night.' She said. 'And climbing over the wall seems a bit undignified.'

I dipped my head forward and down looking out of the gateway's entrance across the village green. The odd house still had a light on but there were no other signs of life.

'Don't worry, it's all quiet.' Catherine whispered, draping her arms around my neck. 'Why did you think I'd brought you here? The rule.'

I had to laugh at that, a quiet chuckle.

'Christ, Cat. We bloody live together now. Your parents know that. And they've not made any fuss about us sharing a room this weekend.'

'Yeah, but a rule is a rule. Plus, it's fun.'

My head flicked towards the church on the other side of the gate. 'Isn't it a bit sacrilegious?'

'Don't be silly. You're not afraid of a few ghosts are you?'

'No, but… No, I suppose not.'

'And it's a full moon again.' She said. 'Just like the first time at my parents.'

I turned, bending forward to see where she pointed. The cloud had thinned. The moon was now clear. It hung low in the sky, just above the roofs of the houses on the other side of the green.

'Fuck me. Fuck me under a full moon.'

'But it's not a full moon.' I said. 'Not yet… a couple of days to go. It's still gibbous.'

'All right, know-it-all.' Her pale toothy smile, floated in the darkness in front me. 'Fuck me under a gibbous moon, then.'

And it became one of those in-jokes that couples have, one of our euphemisms for wanting to have sex – 'Is it a gibbous moon?' So her underlining of the work 'gibbous' in this context could only mean one thing – she had been prostitute.

Dark clouds fluttered at the edge of my vision as that hot wind blew back through me.

I lurched from the kitchen and into the lounge. Slumped down on one of the sofas. Closed my eyes.

She had kept so much hidden from me.

A whole secret life. Secret lives, plural, actually.

To the outside, as a couple, we always seemed so happy and so perfect, so bright and shiny. Just like the collective as a whole. However all dazzle and glare was just like the bright accretion cloud that forms around a black hole, as matter spirals down to oblivion.

If I was going to get to the bottom of it all – why she had killed herself – I was going to have to face up to that fact. Accept it. All of it. No longer push it to the back of my mind like I had done. I had to acknowledge the dark pit, the black hole, at the core of the collective.

Astronomers can only hope to detect a black hole by the effect it has on its surroundings, the massive gravitational effect it has on nearby objects. They can only see the bright accretion cloud that forms around it as matter spirals down to oblivion —not the singularity itself.

We, the collective, were the same. Outsiders could only see our accretion cloud, the dazzle, the glare. But at our core was a darkness, that could not be seen, not even by ourselves at first. But, like a black hole grows as more mass falls into it, over time it had slowly expanded. To the outside world we had seemed so strong and resolute, even during the worst of the bad times, the horror of the third floor and the rest. But unaddressed, the darkness grew, until like a black hole it had pulled everything else into it.

And I knew exactly were that inner darkness had started.

When the good began to go so very bad.

The Five Feathers Exhibition.

8 PRICE TO PAY

'Jesus, Cat! I've missed you!'

I rushed down the marquee towards her, as quickly as I could without spilling the tray of teas I was carrying. She was crouched down, placing a large aluminium framed photograph against the bottom of a display board. In the background a techno track started with – *Let me hear you say 'Yeah!'*

'What?' Catherine turned towards me. 'It's only been a couple of days?'

She stood and I briefly kissed her on the lips. She took a styrofoam cup of tea off the tray and pealed back the lid.

She was casually dressed in jeans and an old grey sweatshirt of mine that I had seen her in before, but the cherry-red pair of Doctor Martins were new to me, as was the clashing shade of her bright scarlet-dyed hair.

'Only a couple of days!' I said with mock outrage. 'It seemed like a life-time to me.'

Catherine sipped from her tea, barely suppressing a grin.

'Yeah, well, I missed you too,' she said. 'But it's a small price to pay in order to get all these looking right. Now, I'm just sorting out the best order to display them.'

Catherine stepped out into the middle of the marquee then turned back to inspect her work. She slowly scanned along the row of display boards that ran down one full side of the marquee, each with a framed photograph resting against it. Behind her was a similar row of boards but the photographs to be displayed on these were still waiting to be arranged, stacked against one board in the far corner. It was hard to make out the full detail of the dark sepia-stained photographs in the dim light. The only illumination came from the square of pale daylight at the marquee's entrance plus what weak sunlight filtered through the fabric walls.

At the far end of the marquee two riggers from a display lighting company were bent over, busily connecting up cables. The radio playing the techno track was theirs. I left Catherine as she went back to her photographs and swooped two around. The riggers gratefully accepted the teas I offered.

'Want to give it a go now, Terry?' The older one said after taking a mouthful of tea.

The marquee was suddenly flooded with light. From a gantry above our heads it illuminated a spot on the display boards where each photograph would be mounted, whilst a warm glow was cast up the fabric walls of the marquee by lamps hidden behind the boards.

'That looks great!' Catherine shouted over to us.

As the younger lighting technician started to gather together spare lengths of cable his older supervisor turned to me.

'I'll check they've done the red-head's all right.' He said, then paused and gave a half-smile. 'The other red head, I mean. But that should have been straightforward. It's the big tent that's going to be the trouble. But we will get it done on time. Tell the other guy that.'

'Oh, don't worry. I will.'

I watched them leave, drinking my tea. Catherine stepped back to study her new arrangement. Without turning she reached out an arm to beckon me towards her.

Returning to her I slipped my hand around her waist then slid it down over her hip to her bottom, giving it a gentle pat. I rested it there as she leaned against me.

'Looks good.' I said.

'Yeah, I was worried I was going to have to arrange them all in the dark.' She turned to me and sighed. 'Jesus Jace, do you think it'll be all finished in time?'

'I don't see why not. They're a little bit behind time, but they seem to know what they are doing'

'No, I don't mean the lighting. I mean us… the whole thing, really.'

'We got the rest of today to get all the big stuff done. Then most of tomorrow to get it all tidied up before the grand opening. Don't you worry, we'll get it done.'

'I'm just sorry I couldn't make it last night,' she said. 'Bloody lab cocking things up! Stress I don't need.'

'You had to sort it out and to be honest you didn't miss much – just a quick chat to sort out a few of the final things. I just thought we could have had a few hours off together by ourselves before the final mayhem, that's all.'

Catherine smiled.

'When this is all over we'll have plenty of time together. Get away for a bit of a holiday.'

'I don't know, Catherine. My contribution to the finances has just about busted me.'

'It need not cost much. Some friends of my parents have a villa near Lake Como. It's going spare for a week. Anyway, call it a working holiday. A chance to top up the batteries and think about what to do next.'

I smiled then.

'Oh, I think I know that already.' I said. 'Came to me last night.'

'Really, what?'

'Too early to really say – just half an idea at the moment. A direction to go in. I need to think about it for a bit more – try a few things out to see if it's viable. But I think it could lead to something interesting.' I shrugged. 'Be a bit ironic if I had my best idea too late.'

'Oh, there will always be other shows.'

'Yeah, but only if this one works. If I sell some pieces. That's what I worry about.'

'You'll do all right.' She bit her bottom lip and a worried frown creased her brow as she contemplated her work again. 'It's my stuff that's rubbish.'

'No, it's really good!' I waved out at the display. 'They are even more impressive in this size. And seeing them as a whole… they really work.'

I stepped away from Catherine, bending down to look at the photographs closer.

Previously, she had only shown me a couple of contact prints in black and white. Now each of the photographs was sepia stained, the shade subtlety changing from one picture to the next – it was obtaining that precise gradual graduation in tone that had so troubled the lab. Their size and upright orientation were more suited for portraiture but at first glance they seemed landscapes, alternating between cityscape and countryside. In fact Catherine had initially called the piece as a whole, 'Town and Country'. It was only when you carefully studying them that you realised they were actually portraits. In each of the country ones there was a figure, obscured either by distance or part hidden behind a tree or the edge of a farm outbuilding or crouched down in the shadows of a hedgerow. In the city photographs the same figure could be seen sitting alone at the back of a café, face turned away from the camera or spotted walking away among the crowds of a busy shopping street. The figure was dressed in what would seem the opposite clothes for each location – a business suit in 'country', Wellingtons and waxed jacket for 'city'.

The figure was Catherine, of course.

'I like the way you're a part of the landscape.' I said, still staring. 'In both locations.'

'That's the idea.' Catherine said from behind me.

'So you finally settled on a name then?' I turned back to her.

She had started arranging the photographs on the other side of the marquee – picking them up in turn to rest them down against each board. She glanced back over her shoulder.

'Jane Doe. I suppose it had to be. Once it was in the catalogue.'

'And you've not named them?'

'No, only numbered. To extend the anonymity theme.'

'Makes sense.'

I went over to start helping her but we were interrupted by another workman walking into the tent. He was carrying a workbox, a long-barrelled powered screwdriver in the other hand. Catherine smiled, obviously recognising him.

'This is Bill I was telling you about.' Catherine continued when she saw my puzzled frown. 'You know, from the gallery I worked at last summer? He's doing us a big favour.'

'Of course.' I turned to him. 'I remember. Thanks for your help.'

He shrugged it off.

'So you ready to put these up, then?' He asked Catherine, pointing with his screwdriver at the row of already arranged photos.

'Yes,' she said. 'Middle of each board. I'll just finish off sorting these.'

'Fine.' He turned to me. 'And there's a delivery just arrived that needs signing for. Some catalogues I think.'

'Right, the book. I better take care of that.' I said, going back to the rear of the marquee to pick up the tray and gather together the empty cups before moving towards the exit.

I paused just before I left, turning back to blow Catherine a kiss but she was already turned away from me, absorbed in her work.

Someone had filled a shiny new dustbin outside the marquee with a dozen umbrellas. Simon had mentioned the idea at a meeting, but I had completely forgotten about it until now.

We had found a location for the exhibition close to the south bank of the Thames, not far from Greenwich. Much of the clearing of the site had gone on without me as I sorted the final financial work. When I finally saw the place – a partially demolished factory, the dead building given one last gasp of life – I had been surprised just how well it worked for our purpose. Even the garish hazard tape, and the warning signs and lights, erected to keep people away from the potentially unsafe areas, added to the effect. In fact, I suspected a lot more had been added than was strictly necessary, to keep in with the anarchic, rough-and-ready, do-it-yourself atmosphere of our whole venture.

The partition walls, along with most of the upper floor and roof of the factory had been removed in the earlier phases of the demolition, leaving the site open to the skies – hence the need for the umbrellas. Duck boarding – that would soon lit with strings of fairy-lights – ran over the old cracked and stained concrete floor, leading from one marquee to the other. The old entrance to the site had been widened so taxis and the cars we had hired could easily drop people off at the reception marquee, towards which I was now heading. A row of Tardis-like Portaloos seemed to have materialised next to it since the last time I had been past.

The other marquees were arranged in a rough horseshoe around the reception tent. Even under the overcast sky the white-tented structures stood out in high contrast to the dark walls of the factory. Mark's was by far the largest. Nearly three stories in height and oval-shaped in plan, it looked more like a 'Big Top' circus tent than our wedding-reception-style rectangular marquees the rest of were using for our displays.

Mark had insisted on erecting it first and had then immediately disappeared into it, remaining hidden from us ever since. He had only emerged for trips in a rented lorry back to his studio, returning each time with a large number of crates of various sizes and several spools of wire.

The reception tent was filled with activity. Catering staff in matching blue polo shirts where bringing in supplies and unpacking glasses and plates, placing them out on a long cloth-covered table. On the other side was a smaller table with two large urns set up to keep the whole site supplied with tea and coffee. I tipped the empty cups into a plastic dustbin besides it and left the tray on top of the pile at the end of the table.

By the far entrance I spotted a uniformed deliveryman holding a clipboard. I signed and immediately opened one of the four boxes he had been standing next to.

As expected it was filled with catalogues for the show – our book. It was the first time I had seen a copy. Across the centre of a flat grey cover was a row of five different representations of feathers: a sepia-stained photograph of a blackbird's wing-feather lying on bare earth, a section of graph paper with the semi-abstract outline of a feather shape picked out with filled-in squares, a painted feather executed with a minimum of strokes in the palest shade of grey on white, the outline of a feather stamped out of a sheet of copper, resting on an old workbench, the word 'feather' hand-written in blue Biro on lined paper.

Above them all was written – *FIVE FEATHERS*. Below, 'Against The Cowardice Of Art.'

'Finally arrived. Good. Good.'

I turned around to see Trisha.

She was wearing a set of baggy overalls, stitched together diamond patches of contrasting cloth, mainly red and white, had the effect of a jester's motley. On one foot was a new white tennis shoe, the other a battered old red trainer. Her hair was loose, flowing down back over her shoulders. She was drinking from a large-size cup of coffee, looking even bigger in her small hands. Her face, half-hidden behind the cup, was pale.

'You all right, Trish?'

She gave me a quick smile.

'Bird-Girl not feeling well. But Bird-Girl will survive. Lots to do. But worried though. Worried about lights. Will you have a look? Look at Bird-Girl's work?'

'Of course I will,' I said.

But as we walked out of the reception tent, heading towards her marquee, Simon intercepted us.

'Ah, Jason, I've been looking for you. I need to talk. Urgently.'

'Right, but–' I looked towards Trisha

'It's okay. Bird-Girl can wait.'

Simon led to me to his marquee. His part of the exhibition had been completed some time ago and the space was quiet and deserted. His work was housed in a series of Victorian wood and brass glass-topped display cases salvaged from a museum during a refit to modernise its display galleries.

The only light came from small strip bulbs inside each case. Standing close, the light shining up from below threw strange shadows over our faces.

Simon had been conducting a series of postal exchanges – initiated by placing small ads in publications like *Loot* and *Private Eye*, asking for worthless objects from people's pasts that they no longer wanted. The results were displayed under the glass. I noticed a badge from some stately home visited on a school trip, a pen used for O-levels, a bruised cricket ball, a star cut out of silver foil and mounted on a straw among others. Alongside were the stories of each object, printed or written out longhand.

'The lighting people have finished Catherine's display.' I said. 'Trisha's as well – I was just going to have a look at it. Said they'll soon be finished with Mark's as well – despite the difficulties.'

'That's fine,' said Simon. 'You're doing a great job, Jason. All the books up to date I take it? We are covered, as planned?'

'Oh, yes. Almost all of the promised sponsorship has come in so that will match the expenses. Of course if we want to make an actual profit on the venture we will need to sell something.'

Simon looked back to the entrance of the marquee.

'That's what I wanted to talk to you about. In private, so we don't worry the others while they get finished. We need to be out banging the drum more. I want to get off-site and back to college. Do a final bit of fly-postering, ring up some of the most important people, confirm they are coming… or try and persuade them otherwise if not.' He turned towards me. 'Think you can handle stuff back here without me? It's mainly just checking everything's being done, hurrying people up if they are falling behind the schedule. I'll give you a check-list.'

'No problem. I do feel a bit of spare-wheel at the moment, to be honest.'

'I just don't want things to run behind while I make sure of the visitors. We need to get the right people here. The real buyers. The gallery people and the collectors – though I've heard some good noises in that direction. Catherine has done well there. The journalists – and not just the arts magazines, but the nationals if we can. But I need to follow it up.'

'You're still thinking big, then?' I smiled. 'It's certainly not the end of year show I was expecting when I started the course. I thought I'd be sharing a room with a load of other students; not having our own exhibition – having a whole tent to myself. I still worry we've tried to be too much too quickly.'

'But that's the way we had to do it, Jason.' Simon swept his arm around his own marquee. 'Don't just think big. Think bigger. Bigger than anyone else. The ones back at college – the ones following the rules – they'll be the ones left behind.' He looked back over towards the entrance to the marquee. 'I tell you something, there's a change in the air. I can feel it. The nineties are really starting now. We are finally leaving the eighties behind and starting a new decade with new art... and new politics. The Tories aren't going to stay in forever. That's obvious. Not with Labour finally getting their act together. So a change in the old order. We can take advantage of that. Labour have always traditionally put money in the arts.'

'I thought you supported the Tories?'

He turned back to me.

'Major isn't no Thatcher, that's for sure. The revolution's grinding to a halt. Cabinet full of dead wood and cronies.'

A silhouette appeared at the entrance to the marquee.

'So, this is where you have got to.' It was Julie, Simon's girlfriend. She walked into the marquee to join us. 'I thought you were finished with this one.'

'We are,' Simon said. 'Just having a chat – a bit of business I needed to sort out. But we're finished now. I'm off back to college. You want to help me with some leaflets, pet?'

'I can't. I was just looking for you to say I'm off as well – to go shopping. I need a frock for tomorrow. What with all your posh friends coming, I don't want to look like a total scruff. Embarrass myself.'

'I think you'll be fine whatever you wear. But if you think so. Sorry, I can't come with you.' Simon replied. He turned to me. 'I'll leave the checklist in the reception tent, then Jason. If you're fine to be in charge?'

'Of course,' I said. 'But I'd better go and see Trisha first.'

Trisha was on her own in the corner of her marquee. She was sitting on the floor with her knees pulled up under her chin. She looked very small compared to her artwork. Five huge slabs of white canvas, reaching from the floor to the roof of the marquee and covering the whole width of the sides and rear, towered over her like icebergs.

Seeing me enter she slowly pulled herself to her feet then walked to the centre of the marquee to meet me.

'It's too bright.' She said.

The paintings were directly illuminated from the sides by lamps fastened to spindly metal columns.

'No, it's just right,' I said. 'Perfect. You don't want to make it too obvious. Let the viewer discover the true meaning in their own time.'

I walked slowly around her, looking at each painting in turn.

At first, in the strong light, the paintings appeared to be just flat colour fields. However, after closer inspection, you noticed a few abstract marks of the very palest of off-white grey. Then, as you moved past them, and noticed the changing play of light over their surface, their true nature was revealed. Created in the brush strokes of the paint, in the delicate shadows formed from the faint ridges and furrows, aided by the grey hints – suddenly no longer abstractions, but added depth and shadow – were birds in flight. They were different on each canvas – white doves, Arctic owls, swans, herons and cranes. Flying across frozen lakes, or forests of frost-shrouded trees, or fields smothered in snow. All traced out in minimal flowing lines.

'It's magic.' I said, finally standing beside Trisha. 'Just what you wanted.'

She frowned.

'Not too un-obvious? Too subtle? Too hard to figure out?

'No, it's just right'

'But it reproduces so hard. So difficult to see in the book. The catalogue.'

'But that's what makes it the most magical. That you can only get the full effect in real life. By standing in front of them.'

'The literal titles too much a joke? 'White Doves on Snow' and all that.'

'No, they are perfect.' I turned to her and put my hand on her shoulder. 'Stop worrying about it.'

'Bird-Girl does worry.' She looked down. 'Bird-Girl has to worry. Bird-Girl flying now. But when Bird-Girl lands, worry what comes next. Nothing. Nothing there. No more magic. The fires of creation burnt out for Bird-Girl.'

I shook my head.

'But we all feel like that.' I said. 'What with the big rush for the show and everything. When it's all over the ideas will flood back. They came in the past, they will come again in the future. Just don't worry about it, Trisha.'

She looked directly at me then raised a finger and pointed at herself.

'Not Trisha, you know that. Bird-Girl.'

I smiled.

'Sorry. Bird-Girl.'

I saw her beginning to smile back at me, but then her face fell again. A single tear ran down the side of her cheek.

'Oh god, I'm so worried. About the show.' She rubbed at her eye. 'I feel terrible. I've been up for days. So tired.'

I put my arms around her and hugged her to me. Her head nestled against my shoulder.

'It will all be okay. You just need some sleep. We all do.'

I could feel her start shivering in my arms.

'Tomorrow is the most important day of my life.' She whispered. 'It just all needs to go perfectly. I need to–'

I lifted her head up and looked into her eyes, now shining wet with tears.

'Trish, go home and sleep now. You've done everything that you need to. Go home, sleep, and you'll feel a million times better tomorrow.'

'Yes,' Trisha said, I saw her smile again – fully this time – before she brought her hand up to her mouth and performed a spectacular mock-yawn. 'Yes, Bird-Girl thinks you are right.'

As I made my way back to the reception marquee I saw Mark standing outside his tent, smoking. I detoured over to him.

'Finished?' I asked.

He took a last drag on the cigarette and stubbed it out in an old tobacco tin that he slipped back into his pocket.

'Not quite, just taking a fag break. Still a lot to do. But I'm getting there.'

'No chance of a quick preview then?'

'I told you. Only on the day. And no trying to sneak in round the back like Simon.'

'The catalogue's arrived. I could just look in there.'

He laughed. 'Be my guest. You'll see nothing but a few abstract close-ups photos of shining metal surfaces and some cryptic hints in the write-up as to what they may mean. Trust me, you'll appreciate the surprise.'

'Are you going to walk me through it then?'

It was my tutor, Call-Me-Grant, looking as ever the old hippy, with his denims and ponytail and beard. I had not spotted him hidden in the cluster of people who had entered my marquee a few minutes before. The show was starting to fill up and twenty to thirty people slowly circulating my marquee, examining my work. It was an odd feeling to watch them; to see them look at work that had, up until a few hours ago been private to myself and my friends.

'I was just going to look for Catherine...' I started, but my tutor ignored me, walking over to my first piece.

I had not seen her since earlier when she had disappeared to change, hinting that she would be wearing something 'rather splendid'. I still wore the usual uniform of combats, boots and sweatshirt that I had had on all day.

I followed Grant and tried to excuse myself.

'Sorry, but–'

'Surely she can wait for five minutes?' Grant said, turning back to me. 'I know you've done all this dropping-out thing.'

'We've not dropped out. Technically.'

'Yes I'm sure the powers that be are still pondering your end of year exhibitions that consist of advertisements for the student's own separate show. But anyway, I'm sure even an anarchist like yourself wouldn't mind a few comments? Yes? You've done some interesting things here.' He turned back to my artwork. 'This I remember from your interview. You finished it I see. It looks good.'

In front of him was the now completed 'An Infinite Capacity For Cruelty' – over two hundred sheets of graph paper, each one cheaply protected by a clip frame and the whole array mounted on a single sheet of white MDF that ran one full length of the marquee. The first few sheets had had every odd square filled-in by a cheap blue Biro pen, forming a chequer board pattern. From a distance they were a soft blur but closer the pattern seemed to crawl and swarm in front of your eyes like electric blue static. As the array progressed, gradually less and less of the sheet's squares were filled in, creating holes in the chequer board, clouds in the blue. The holes grew slowly larger – joining with each other – until the filled squares became a random lacework that shrunk away, unravelling, until blank space dominated, creating islands of ink that themselves shrunk smaller and smaller until they finally vanished. The final sheets were just bare graph paper.

'Yes.' I said. 'I like the way it turned out, but it's not what I planned. It was just taking too long to fill in all the squares on every sheet.'

'To be honest, I thought at the time you were being too ambitious.' Grant slowly walked down the side of the marquee. 'But I'm sure you could have got some people to help if you had asked.'

'Oh, Catherine offered, for a start. But it's the artist's hand thing. I wanted to do them all on my own. And anyway, if I got others involved, I'd just be spreading the punishment.'

'I see,' Grant said, stepping back a few paces to take in the whole of the piece. 'But I like the way you got the pattern out of it. You can move on from that – do more patterns. If you wanted to.'

'Well, I suppose this is a development from it.' I said turning around.

On the other side of the marquee were framed prints of asymmetric roundels and targets. They were divided into random segments by converging lines of varying thickness, some of the segments subdivided by various patterns and stripes and grids. They had initially been hand-drawn with an old steel pen that had given an alternately scratchy or blotchy quality to the line, adding some organic randomness to the hard mathematical geometries.

'Yes, I like how you have done some prints.' Grant said, following me. 'Any particular reason to not just leave them as paintings?'

I produced a sheepish smile.

'Well, nothing artistic. I just thought that I could do a load of cheap stuff that more people would be able to buy.'

'Ah, the dread hand of commerce. You trying for some sort of optical-art effect though? With these and the previous work?'

'Not really. If anything, I was starting to move away from it – something easier on the eyes. I've got really interested in developing this mapping thing.'

The final part of my display that we moved towards was the framed pages from my *A-Z* and *Road Atlas*. The work charted my various travels across London and beyond with a pen line drawn along the printed streets and roads, with the odd cryptic symbol added alongside. Some of the symbols were explained – for example, the cafés were I had stopped to eat, or the points I had descended down into the Tube. Others, especially those that indicated the places I had had sex with Catherine, were left very much unexplained. Alongside were notes of the time and date of the journeys and observations like weather conditions plus quick sketches of things seen – a post-box, some weeds sprouting out of a patch of rough ground, a man walking his dog across a park – to create the impression of the notes of an explorer as they surveyed a new land. Via these reports of my explorations of the commonplace, I was trying to raise the ordinary to the extraordinary, to hopefully entice people to look again at their familiar surroundings as something new.

The only significant journey not recorded was the first to Catherine's parents' place out in the country. She had suggested it would not be a good idea to include any of our homes on the maps and I agreed, happy to not have to be reminded of the time and place of our sole major argument.

'Yes,' Grant said. 'I think it could be an interesting direction.'

'I'm thinking of tying them together somehow.' I said. 'The maps and the geometric stuff. The next step.'

'That might work. Though you don't just have to do one thing of course.'

'Well, that's the direction I'm thinking off. Exploring the place where art and science meet… there's more but it's complicated.' I said with a shrug.

'No, go on.' Grant urged.

'Okay.' I continued. 'On one level a map is just a tool, but it can also be an aesthetic image in its own right. But sometimes it can go even beyond that… into, well, philosophy I suppose. Take the London Tube map. It's an abstraction of the actual rail network that exists. That was Harry Beck's, the bloke that designed it, genius. He created a schematic diagram, shifting the lines around, changing the distances between stations so they looked more even, making it easy to navigate the system – moving from the real to the abstract. And its simplicity creates an image that has real beauty. But here's the really interesting thing, the philosophy of it. It's gone on to be more than just a map, but a symbol for the Tube, and also an iconic symbol of London itself. I mean, you see it on postcards! The distance between the representational and the abstract closes in our minds so that we forget, for instance, that two stations that look distant on the map are practically next door to each other, that it would in fact be easier to walk between them. That's what I want to try to explore, those contradictions… but… but…' I shook my head as my voice trailed off. 'I don't know, it's hard to explain how I'm going to do it – to visualise it – but I think I can see what I want to do. The images I want to create.'

'Then just do it.' Grant said. 'Just start doing it and see where it leads you.'

'Good god, more rubbish!' A voice behind us cut through the background murmur of the crowd. 'Doodles and scribble on a ripped-up map. What…? Don't shush me woman! Oh, it's you… Jason isn't it?'

I turned around to see, as expected when I had first heard his voice, Uncle Rupert, his face flushed. He was wearing a black-tie dress-suit. His wife Su Lynn was at his side, in a pale green silk dress with a repeated bamboo pattern in a darker shade. She nodded towards her husband then gave me a slow shake of her head.

'Yes, yes. Ahem, err.' Uncle Rupert continued. He took a swig from the champagne flute he held tightly with fingers grasped around the stem. 'But I have to say you have done quite a job here! You, Catherine and the others. Must have taken some organising.' He moved closer to me and put his arm around my shoulders, turned me away from the others and leaned in to continue in a harsh whisper. 'Of course I think it's all a load of balderdash. But that's just me. What do I know? Just give me a Constable any time or a Stubbs. Great horse man, Stubbs. Catherine used to do some lovely horse paintings before she got interested in all this nonsense. I mean, they actually pay people to teach you this!'

'Yes,' I heard Grant say behind me. He cleared his throat then continued. 'I had better take a look at what the others have done.'

I turned back to him, pulling myself away from Rupert's grasp.

'Yes, err…' I started, wondering how to even begin explaining Rupert to Grant.

'It's all right.' Grant said, already stepping back from us. 'I've kept you occupied long enough.'

He turned and walked rapidly towards the marquee's exit before I could say any more.

'Who was that?' Rupert asked when he was gone

'Only my course tutor.'

Su Lynn tutted. 'I told you. Embarrassment! Drink too much!'

'Right, yes, foot in mouth time. Oh dear. But never mind.' Rupert said. 'I mean he actually teaches you? What? 'This is how to do some scribbles?''

I had to smile. 'They don't tend to be that explicit. It's more about enabling you to develop your ideas than giving specific directions.'

'Ah, right.' Rupert said. 'Though, to be honest, I can't even began to understand it. A hopeless heathen. But I must say you've got a good turnout. I just saw old Squibby! Says he's going to be buying something, the mad fool. Have you sold anything yet?'

I automatically scanned around the room, even though I knew there were no orange 'sold' stickers next to any of my work.

'No, not yet.'

He leaned in close with the loud whisper again. 'The memsahib's interested in your target things. Might have to put my hand in my pocket to keep her happy. But I don't want to think I'm patronising you. I'm sure Catherine's parents think the same or they would be buying loads of her stuff, and yours. Your family here?'

'Been and gone.'

'Hello, Uncle Rupert, you hassling my fellah when I need him.' It was Catherine. And she did indeed look splendid.

She was wearing a dress that was the exact shade of red as her newly dyed hair, now swept up and back and crowned with a ruby studded tiara. The jewels of the latter were matched by similar in a pair of pendent earrings. Her lip-stick and nail varnish were the exact same colour, as was the small bag hanging off one shoulder. The outfit was finished with shiny patent leather high heels of the same colour again.

The dress itself was a simple and elegant sheath of silk; its smoothness was only interrupted by the twin points of her nipples. A slit up the side showed a dangerously long hint of thigh as she walked. Like Rupert, she too held a glass of champagne, but delicately poised in her fingers.

'I thought I'd be Miss Scarlet tonight.' Catherine. said to me with a raised eyebrow as I took in her outfit.

'You are that, my dear.' Rupert said.

Catherine accepted a kiss off him then turned back to me and smiled. 'When you didn't turn up I thought I had better go looking for you.'

'Sorry, my tutor collared me, and then, well you can see, and–'

'We need to see the rest.' Su Lynn said, interrupting me. She turned to her husband. 'And these two want to be alone I think.'

'Yes,' Rupert said. He swigged back the last of his champagne. 'And I need another drink.'

Su Lynn looked instantly cross.

'No more drink!'

'But darling,' he started as they left the marquee. 'I've only had a couple!'

'Couple of bottles!'

As they continued to bicker, Catherine took my hand and, turned to me.

'So you don't mind me being the scarlet woman?'

'Of course not, though I think it's more of a ruby red.'

'And you don't think the tiara is too much?'

'No, it's makes you into a proper princess.'

She smiled.

'I used to wear it sometimes when I was a kid. Dressing up. Pretending. It's a family heirloom. For special occasions – I've always wanted the opportunity to wear it properly. The dress cost me a small fortune but you can't just wear jewellery like this with a party frock.'

'So it's not to match with Trisha then? The hair? Actually what's she wearing tonight? I've not seen her yet.'

'You've not heard then?'

'Heard what?'

'She's not here. Not coming. She's come down with some bug, taken to her bed.'

'Oh, that's a real shame. To miss her moment of glory with the rest of us.'

'Yeah, she rang up just as I arrived. She was in tears, poor thing.'

'She did look a bit poorly the last time I saw her. I sent her home. She's been working night and day – must have trashed her immune system. We'll have to do something special for her when we've finished. Make up for it.'

'Definitely.'

Catherine took a sip of champagne then suddenly grinned. 'Oh, I've not told you yet! I've sold some stuff!'

'Congratulations!'

'I couldn't believe it, when I saw!' She continued wide eyed. 'How about you?'

I shrugged. 'Nothing yet.'

She became serious.

'Ah, sorry. I should not be so jovial.'

'Don't' worry. It's early days.' I said. 'I think I'll sell some prints for sure. There's been quite a bit of interest in them.'

'That's good, so you been around the rest of the exhibition yet?'

'This afternoon.'

'But you won't have seen Mark's though?'

'You've been in? What's he done?'

'Sorry, can't say.' She shook her head.

'Oh, come on!'

'No, it's part of the piece! It's better if you don't know. But you have to see it.'

'Give us a hint.'

'No. No, hints. You really have to see the thing in its entirety. Without prior expectations.'

'But...?' I gestured with my champagne glass around the marquee.'Potential buyers. I've got to...'

'Being away for five minutes won't hurt. I can hold the fort.' She put her hand on my back and gave me a gentle nudge towards the marquee's entrance.

'Oh, all right.' I said, letting Catherine escort me.

Outside the coming dusk was transforming the exhibition – the factory walls falling away into the gloom as the lights strung between the tents above the walkways became more prominent.

'It's beautiful,' Catherine said. 'Like a fairy grotto.'

'Yes,' I agreed, pausing at the entrance arm in arm. I turned to Catherine and our lips briefly touched.

'Now go!'

A loose cluster of people waited in line at Mark's tent, standing between crash barriers strung with lights. Near the front, a sign stated that no more than ten people at a time would be admitted along with a warning to epilepsy sufferers of strobe lighting effects. Below the red numbers of an electronic clock counted down the last couple of minutes to the next viewing.

At the head of the line Mark was standing with a security guard by a flap in the side of the tent.

'Hey, Jason!' Mark saw me and waved, then turned to talk to a cluster of middle-aged women in front of him. 'Jason, here is another artist at the show, ladies.' He pointed back towards where my marquee was. 'Don't forget to go see his work when you have seen mine.' He waved me forward. 'Come to the front!'

The other people in line moved to one side, giving me room to pass, offering me smiles and nods as I made my way to the front, completely embarrassed by all this sudden public attention.

'And now he's finally got around to doing me the honour of seeing my own work.' Mark said, making a big fuss out of checking the clock as it counted down the last few seconds to zero. 'Just in time!'

The security guard held open the flap of the tent. A group of people came from the darkness beyond, blinking in the light cast from the nearby lamps. Mark accepted their congratulations and handshakes.

'Remember,' he said to them. 'Don't tell anyone anything about it. Let them see it for themselves.' He turned to me. 'Push through the drapes. Walk to the centre. Then just wait. And don't go outside the lines.' It was obviously a well-practised spiel.

Mark pointed to the flap in the tent still held open by the security guard. 'Go on then.'

I stepped forward then paused to look back at the people behind me. Mark had his hand held up to stop the others. 'I don't think they'll mind waiting for you to see it on your own.' He said, 'I think you deserve a solo show.'

'It had better be worth it.' I said with a smile and shake of head before turning stepping through the flap.

Ahead of me I could just make out another inner layer of dark cloth hanging down. I pushed against the heavy felt-like material and almost immediately found a gap between two overlapping sections. There was another layer close behind it. I pushed against them both and stepped through into the darkness beyond.

As my eyes adjusted to the lack of illumination I saw there were tiny red spots of light on the ground – lights inset into some form of walkway. Two parallel rows led up to the outline of a square in the centre of the space. Large arrows, outlined by more red dots, flickered on between the lines pointing to the middle of the square.

I walked slowly forward.

There was no sound. The background chatter of the exhibition and the low murmur of London beyond were deadened by the layers of cloth.

As I stepped over them I noticed the arrows disappearing as the lights winked out.

On either side of me I could just make out – perhaps sense more than I could see – large shapes out in the darkness.

As I reached the centre of the square I realised it was not completely silent. Something very quiet but definitely there. As I strained to listen it gradually increased in volume. A ticking clock. Low and solid like from an old long case – its *tick-tocks* widely spaced apart. It slowly grew louder still, and faster, shifting up in pitch. It merged into a another more rapid, lighter clock sound, then changed up again into something like a overwound alarm clock – its *tic-tic-tic-tic-tic-tic* annoyingly rapid.

And then suddenly, after a heart-beat pause of complete silence, a deafening crash followed by a montage of explosions. At the same time light blazed down from above me. Bright light that seared into my eyes from all around, scattered off a million sharp reflections on all sides.

Then, just as sudden, complete dark and silence again.

The snap of illumination had been so quick I had had not chance to fathom what I had seen.

As I blinked away the dull red after-images from my eyes, noise rose again, a low rumble of indistinct sounds. And then above it I heard a voice. A muffled crackling voice – 'Mary had a little lamb'.

More voices followed, starting with radio broadcasts from the beginning of the century. They were overlapped by newsreel and then the sound of television news broadcasts. As more voices came in others dropped out. News of the First World War. The Wall Street crash. The rise of Hitler and Stalin. Second World War. Cold War. Communism's collapse. Intersected with the news were snatches of music from movie soundtracks – I recognised *The King and I, Hello Dolly, Star Wars* and *Chariots Of Fire* among many others. Underneath all this was a bass rumble of machinery, cars and aircraft.

And with the sound came a lightshow, erupting with strobe-light flickers sparking around me. Longer and longer bursts of light followed that flowed and flickered around me like fire. I turned to follow them as they illuminated all that was around me.

Ahead a steam train seemed to bear down on me, on rails ten foot in the air. Behind me an aircraft – a Spitfire – dived at me. To one side, a car – an old Jaguar. Opposite that, a Cortina. Other, smaller vehicles between – motorbikes, a motorboat, a scooter. And in-between them, a multitude of missiles, rockets, torpedoes, bombs, bullets. All of them were suspended on invisible wires. Some real – salvaged scrap, some obviously fabricated mock-ups. All painted dark bronze. All pointed right down at me. The last hundred years surrounded me, hammered down on me from all sides.

Finally the sound died away into a crackle of static that then faded to nothingness. A diffuse warm orange glow of light that shone over the whole piece slowly shifted into a dull red that dimmed away to darkness.

Arrows appeared in the floor pointing back to where I can come in.

I walked out blinking into the light.

Mark looked at me expectantly. 'What do you think, then?'

'It's a bit phallic.'

He smiled. 'I never noticed that.'

'Sure you didn't. What have you called it?'

"Twentieth Century Fucks."

As I walked back to my own marquee along the duck-walk I saw two figures approaching me, half-familiar in the semi-darkness. Closer, under the fairy-lights, they resolved into the two clowns, Fred and Ginger. Fred was wearing a baggy white dress covered in large black polka dots. The dots continued randomly over the rest of him – down spotted tights to spotted shoes and, in thick black-on-white make-up, up over his face to the top of his shaved head. The other shorter and slimmer clown Ginger wore their usual Charlie Chaplin along with the crossed-eyes and red clown nose.

'We were just about to leave so we were glad we caught you.' Fred said to his partner.

'Oh, yes.' Ginger replied.

'We heard you work together now. With Catherine. Closely together. Very closely.' Fred continued with a very theatrical wink to me.

'Closer than us, even.' Ginger countered.

'I think we will have wedding bells soon.'

'Ding, dong!'

'I think you'll be waiting a long time before you see us in a church together!' I said shaking my head, but smiling.

'I was just telling Ginger,' Fred said, pointing around the marquee. 'How impressive this all is. Putting out your own show. But it was naughty of you to keep it a secret.'

'We could have helped.' Ginger added.

'Yes,' Fred said. 'Still at least we saw the invitations you left at your course-work exhibition. Allow us to keep our reputations – that we attend all the best parties. They will be talking about this for some time, won't they dear?'

'Oh, yes.' said Ginger.

'And it will put you right out in front of the rest of your class – in getting attention from buyers, galleries and the rest of it.'

'That's not–' I started.

'Oh, I'm certain you've got lots of artistic reasons for doing this.' Fred interrupted, leaning forward. 'But I'm also certain there will be a lot of jealousy. But don't worry about them. Just keep being fabulous.'

'Well, I– It's been nice talking but I've got to get back–' I indicated towards my marquee.

'Yes, we'll leave you to it,' Fred said. He took Ginger's arm. 'Come dear, let's take our magnificence elsewhere. Fred and Ginger are now leaving.'

He steered his partner away from me and with an airy wave from Fred they started skipping down the duck-walk away from me.

I turned back towards my own marquee.

At first I thought the reception tent was empty. Then I heard a voice off to one side.

'Wanna drink?'

It was Julie. She had pulled up a chair next to the long drinks' table. She held up a glass.

'I suppose so. Now the show's over.'

She lifted a champagne bottle from the table.

'I'm afraid there's only some champagne left and a bit of orange juice.'

'Bucks fizz it is then.'

I took the bottle from her. The rest of the table's surface was covered with a flood of dirty glasses, empty bottles and wine-boxes, the cloth beneath stained. I managed to find a glass that appeared to be clean and nearly filled it with champagne – sloshing it into the glass to try and give it some fizz once I realised it was nearly flat. Then I added the dregs of some juice from a cartoon. I sipped my cocktail. It was warm but drinkable.

'Where are the others?' Julie asked.

'I was wondering that myself. I thought the plan was to meet-up here after we had closed the show and sort out stripping it down.'

'I thought you were doing that tomorrow.'

'Most of it, yeah. Though I think Simon is planning to work through the night.'

'Yeah. I think he mentioned something about that.'

I found another chair at the end of the table, brought it back and sat down. I looked over at Julie. She had slipped the heel out of one of her gold high-heels and bounced it with her toes. I had not seen her wearing shoes like that before – the same with the gold cocktail dress. She had always seemed more a jeans, trainers and top type of girl. She had had her hair cut recently into a shorter, more angular style.

She looked up at me. 'Can I ask you something?'

'Sure, what?'

'You think Simon's gone off me?'

'What, no.' I said. 'At least I don't think so.'

'It's just well. It's not the same. I know I've changed. He's giving me a lot more confidence than I used to have. I know I'm a lot less clingy. Less whiney. Grown up a lot in the last few months, but I thought he liked that, that he wanted it. I mean it's him that introduced me to all this, to another life. Shown me things I could never imagine. Changed me. But I just don't know now, I think he preferred me as a I was.'

'Well, I…'

She glanced down at her watch then stood up and picked up a coat from the back of her chair.

'Anyway, I've got a taxi booked. If he's off doing art stuff elsewhere I'll go home on my own. He knows where I'll be.'

'Sold it!' I turned to the shout.

Mark had strode into the marquee, both arms raised to punch the air. He quickly walked over towards me and slapped me on the shoulder.

'Sold the bloody thing!' He laughed.

'Well done!' I said.

He reached into a pocket and pulled out a crumpled packet of cigarettes. As he lit one I glanced back to Julie but she had already gone.

'Yep, to Saatchi.' Mark said. I turned back to him. 'It was touch and go for a while but he took it in the end.'

'I was worried you had put all your eggs into one basket.'

I drained my drink and went back over to the table to make another one.

'Yeah, I know.' Mark said behind me. 'But it paid off in the end. And you've done alright haven't you?'

'Eventually.'

'And Catherine's sold out.' Mark continued. 'Trisha has sold most of hers too. It's a just pity Simon's not done so well though.'

'I saw that. But its equal shares – I think we'll all make a tidy sum overall.'

'We've done so fucking well!' Catherine was striding into the marquee, Simon close behind her. She raced over towards me and leapt up at me. I just managed to catch her, one hand on her backside, the other on her back to support her as she straddled me, the dress riding up. She kissed me on the cheek.

'You've sold so many!' She gasped in breathless excitement. Up close I could see her face was flushed. 'I could not believe how many stickers you had when I popped in towards the end!' She then seemed to notice the others, put her hand to my mine on her bottom. 'Let me down,' she giggled.

I let he go and she slipped off me. I went to kiss her again, but she was turning away from me, towards the table.

'Orange juice? I'm so thirsty.' She grabbed the drink I had just made.

'Buck's fizz.'

'Even better.'

She drained the glass in one long swallow.

'Lovely, I needed that.' Then she gasped. 'Oh sorry, was that yours? I'll make another. For us both.'

'Thanks.'

She kissed me then, the taste of oranges on her lips. Then she turned away from me, putting her bag down on the table and started to pour two drinks. I went over to Simon.

'Sorry you didn't do so well.' I said.

'Oh, I sold some, more than I expected really.' He said. 'And I was planning to move on from that stuff anyway.'

'You'll probably sell all the rest soon anyway. Once the publicity from tonight kicks in. And it's equals shares anyway.'

'Oh, yes.'

He stepped forward towards the table where Mark was now pouring himself a drink. I followed him back and Catherine handed me a glass of bucks fizz.

'Look,' Simon said to us all. 'It's been a long crazy day. I think it's better if we get some rest tonight. And then make an early start to clear the site tomorrow. We can have a bit of a celebration after.'

'Yeah, that's a good idea.' Mark said, yawning. 'I'm knackered. I wasn't looking forward to another all-nighter'

'Not, a celebration now? Damn!' Catherine pretended to sulk with a pouting bottom lip.

'I'm afraid so.' I said.

'Also,' Simon said. 'I've been thinking we can move on from this. As a group. Together.'

'Another exhibition?' Mark asked.

'Not straight away. But soon, maybe. We don't want to let the publicity die down completely. But I was thinking of something else – making the collective permanent. I thought we could get some premises together. Need to talk to Trisha of course, but I'm sure she'll be fine with it. Could use the profit from today to put down a deposit. If you all agree.'

'You sure that's a good idea?' Catherine said. 'Us all on top of each other.'

'I think it's great,' said Mark. 'Be a lot cheaper for us all to share. Especially if we have living as well as work space.'

'It'll have to be pretty big. We'll need space for four studios.' Catherine said, still sounding sceptical.

'Four? There's five of us?' I said.

'Sorry,' She turned to me a half smile. 'I assumed that you would be wanting to share with me.'

'Oh.' I smiled back and took her hand. 'Of course.'

'I think I know a couple of industrial places we can convert.' Mark said.

'But not right away.' Catherine said. 'Me and Jason are going to have a holiday at least.'

'I think we could all do with a bit of a holiday.' Simon said. 'Or at least a rest for a month or so. Then start looking for somewhere. Anyway let's call it a night. Get back here as early as you can tomorrow. We can share a ride.'

Catherine finished her drink, put down her glass and picked up her bag. She took my arm.

'We'll get another cab. I fancy a bit of a walk. One last look around here before it all goes.' She turned to me. 'If that's all right.'

'Sure.'

Outside it was raining. Catherine grabbed one of the umbrellas from the bin outside. She put the umbrella up, holding it over our heads as she strode down the duck-walk. The fairy lights above us were reflected in the puddles across the old factory floor – the sparse pools breaking up the strings of lights into Morse-like dots and dashes.

Catherine sung quietly to herself. It seemed nonsense at first – 'No! No! No, No No! No!' However when she finished with, 'There's no limit!' I recognised it as the chorus of track that had been playing on the radio when I had first entered her marquee earlier in the day.

We passed a security guard going in the other direction and exchanged nods.

As soon as the guard was behind us Catherine pulled me to one side, leading me off the walkway. I gave her questioning look but she just smiled back at me before we disappeared into the shadows between the two marquees. At the far end, close to one of the walls of the factory, she brought us to a halt.

'This'll do. I don't think anyone's going to come down here. Take this.' She handed me the umbrella. Then, dimly lit by an orange safety light off the in distance, she opened open her bag and pulled out a disposable lighter.

'What? You don't smoke?'

She ignored me and fished again in the bag producing a pre-rolled joint.

'Ah,' I said

'It's a special occasion.' She said to me.

She lit the joint and took a deep drag, holding it in for several long seconds. She finally let it out then took another drag before passing the roll-up to me. I dragged some of the hot air into my lungs, stifling a cough.

'You know I think this is the best day of my life.' Catherine said, swaying in front of me. 'I've dreamed so long for it. Hoped for it. And it's gone so well.'

'Yes, it's been much more of a success than I had ever imagined. Or dare imagined.' I admitted, passing her back the roll-up. 'Actual proper buyers turning up and putting their hands in their pockets for our stuff. And we might even be in the papers.'

'Yes, we're certainly not in Kansas anymore.'

'Sorry?'

Catherine nodded down at her red boots. She stood on her toes and clicked the heels together.

'Oh, I see.'

She took my hand and led me over to the wall. She leaned back against it and I did the same. We passed the joint between us, smoking. The glowing tip of the joint illuminated our faces in turn as we listened to the rain spattering on the umbrella. I could see the tower of Canary

Wharf, though a gap in the wall on the other side of the exhibition, out across the river.

'I don't want you to feel you've been railroaded.' Catherine broke the silence. 'About us working together, living together.'

'Oh no, I was going to ask you, actually. Eventually.'

'It's just I worry.'

'What?'

'That I'm too much… too much a thoroughbred for you.'

I laughed. 'Oh, and I suppose I'm just some sort of working-class carthorse, am I?'

'No, I don't mean that!' She threw down the joint and stubbed it out, grinding it under her boot heel. She turned to me. 'Not the class thing. It's… I know I've got problems. I'm too skittish, too temperamental.'

'We've been over that. I'm not going to pressure you.'

'I know, I know.' She sighed. 'It's just I worry. I worry that I'm too much for you. I'm just so stupid and weak sometimes. Acting on impulse and not thinking. And I'm frightened that it's just too good between us, that it'll all collapse. That it will all turn to ashes. Like it has in the past.'

'Don't be daft. Anyway it's only moving in together. We practically do that now. It's not like we are going to change much.'

'I know.' She looked deep into my eyes. 'I know I'm just being stupid. I suppose I'm just nervous about my life changing. Our lives. With the art taking off. Not being in Kansas.'

'Yeah, I'm a bit worried about that myself,' I smiled. 'Hey, that's something we can be frightened about!'

She laughed.

'Oh, just kiss me.'

And I did. I pushed her back, against the wall, stroking against her lean flesh through the thin fabric of her dress.

The umbrella slipped from the fingers of my other hand and fell to one side. I felt cool rain on the back of my neck.

Gasping, Catherine gently pushed me away from her.

'Let's go.' She said. 'I'm getting wet.'

'What? Oh, sorry.' I said, reaching for the umbrella.

She laughed then. Dark and deep.

'No, not from the rain.'

'Wake up!'

Catherine was leaning over me, shaking me. I was in bed, her bed. Bright light. Morning.

'Oh Jesus, Jason, please wake up! She's dead!'

Her face was close to mine. Flushed. Eyes pink. Tears ran down her cheeks.

I took her hands and sat upright.

'What the fuck? Who?'

'It's Trisha, Bird-Girl!'

I gathered her in my arms as her breath broke into sobs.

'She's dead. She's killed herself.'

9 BODY WASHES

There was a light in the alley, up ahead. Several lights, I saw as I approached. A blue cluster of illuminated letters picked out the name 'Carlton Health Spar' and 'Entrance' over the door. Next to them a shaded lamp, aimed down to cast a cone of white light over the entrance. Clear panels in the upper half of the door glowed with more light from inside.

I peered in. There was the edge of some sort of desk. Behind, a wall of blonde wood panelling and shelves lined with rows of stumpy glass and monochrome plastic bottles and the sort of small shiny logo-printed boxes you see behind perfume counters.

By the door was a console with a keypad and card-swipe slot. I reached out for the buzzer.

I had woken with a start. Wondering where the hell I was I pulled myself upright, rubbing the side of my face where it had been squashed up against the sofa's arm. Then it hit me – the flat of Nichola Lexington, Catherine's alter ego, masseuse and escort.

I staggered into the bathroom, flicking on lights. I swilled some water around the inside of my mouth then splashed some on my face, feeling more exhausted than before I fell asleep.

Then I remembered the earlier telephone conversation and automatically checked my watch. Nearly seven thirty. I could still just make it. I snatched up my folder and dashed from the apartment.

Grabbing a taxi I headed over to Chelsea. The address proved to be on a street leading off the King's Road. I had the taxi drop me off at the end and I walked past the frontages of brightly-lit restaurants looking for the place. I nearly missed it – the front window glass was frosted and dark, unlit behind. No sign of an entrance but I spotted a small sign pointed towards the alley at the side of the building, warning that the establishment was members-only. The lights drew me on.

My finger paused over the buzzer.

Yet another step. Did I want to take it? Did I really want to know more?

Then I noticed the camera. Mounted above the door, hidden in the shadows next to the light. Looking down at me standing there like a statue with my hand reaching out.

I pressed the buzzer. Almost immediately a disembodied voice hissed something unintelligible in reply. I leaned down towards the speaker next to the buzzer but before I could say anything I the door lock clicked and there was another tone from the buzzer. I pulled the door open.

The room beyond was warm, with the faint humidity of a swimming baths foyer, and a similar bleachy chlorine bass note in the air, but with a musky perfume on top. On the desk was a computer keyboard and monitor, a credit card reader to one side. Near the wall was a cluster of plants in colourfully painted pots. A variegated ivy spilled across the desk and trailed down towards where there were more pots of larger plants on the floor. On the rear wall, I could now see, were shelves of grooming products – soaps, shampoos, conditioners, body washes. All expensive brands I had never heard of.

A woman suddenly appeared though a doorway. She gave me a quick tight smile as she moved over to the desk. A curvy figure was half-hidden by a baggy olive green cardigan. Below were faded jeans and dark blue mules. Curls of chestnut coloured hair spilled onto her shoulders.

She sat down behind the computer. Her hand flicked the mouse.

'Can I help you?' A northern accent. She looked up at me with a tilt to her head. She wore little, if any, make-up. A professional smile with a few lines crinkled up around her eyes. I had first taken her for late twenties but now I thought early forties.

'I rang about joining.'

She moved the mouse, glancing at the monitor. She clicked on something.

'Oh yes. We were expecting you earlier.' She stood up and moved back to the room's entrance. 'Follow me.'

She led me down a narrow corridor where the blonde wood theme continued, quickly opening doors and flicking on lights to show me the rooms beyond.

'Solarium. Sauna. Treatment room. Changing room and storage lockers. We're mixed – it's all repeated upstairs – but kept separate. You can join now, but I'm afraid it's too late for any treatments.' She led me back to the first room again with its desk and computer. 'I sent the girls home. I thought you were not going to show and we had no other bookings.'

'Yes, sorry about that, something unexpected came up.'

She sat back behind the desk, hand to the mouse again.

'I'll just take some details.' She looked back at me. 'Who was it that told you about us?'

'Nichola Lexington.'

She flicked through screens on the computer, opening up a database.

'Ah yes, Nicks.' She said. 'Not heard from her in a while. What's she up too now?'

'Well, I–'

She turned in the seat and looked right at me with her large brown eyes. 'She didn't recommend you at all did she? Look, what is this?'

I opened my folder and produced a 'Samuel Gardener, PI' card.

'I'm working for her family. I'm just trying to find out more about her. Lexington wasn't her real name for a start. And I've been surprised by what she's been up to – massage and escorting and, well, prostitution.'

Sudden anger flashed across the woman's face. 'You think this is some sort of knocking shop! We're a legitimate establishment!' She leapt up, stepping towards me with a finger jabbing at my face. 'We don't do 'extras' or anything like that, none of my girls! I'm very careful about that. I don't know what Nicks has been doing when she's not been here or what she said to you–'

'*She's not said anything!*' I shouted back at her.

She stared back at me, her face hard, eyes unblinking.

I took a deep breath. 'She's dead.'

She glanced down, then held up my 'Samuel Gardener' card. Her face softened.

'That's a load of old crap, isn't it?' She dropped the card on desk. 'You're no investigator, you're her boyfriend aren't you?'

'What? How do you know?'

'You're a terrible liar for a start. And she mentioned you a lot. It wasn't hard to guess. Jason, isn't it?'

'Yes.'

'I'm Louise.' She gave me a quick smile. 'Let's go upstairs. It's more comfortable. Then we can start again.'

She led me out of the room again, turning lights off behind her. I followed her to the end of the corridor that ran through the building, then up two flights of stairs. At the top she unlocked a door and led me through into what was obviously the hallway of a flat, pale green walls and thick carpet. On one side I can see through half-open doors a kitchen and a bathroom. She pushed open the single door opposite.

'Make yourself at home. I'll get you a drink. You look like you need it. Gin and tonic all right?'

'Yes,' I said, walking into the lounge whilst she disappeared into the kitchen.

There was a dull-red square-edged sofa against the wall opposite the door, and I gratefully slumped down onto it, dropping my folder next to me. All my anguish from earlier in the day just seemed to have been replaced with a numbing dull weariness.

The room was small, obviously set in the roof space, with the upper half of the walls slopping in towards the low ceiling, giving it a cave-like appearance, making it seem smaller that what it actually was. Several small Persian-style rugs, patterned in red, orange, brown and ochre, were scattered across the floor. Some soap-opera burbled away quietly on the television in one corner near the window.

The wall facing where I was sitting was lined with bookshelves, half-filled with a number of fantasy novels, some modern romances and a sprinkling of the classics, plus a wide selection that had obviously come from the 'Mind, Body and Spirit' section of the bookshop – books on horoscopes, dreams, ghosts and yoga. Among the plants and art-deco style statues that filled the rest of the shelves I noticed two packs of tarot cards.

There was another closed door, next to the sofa, opposite to where I had come in.

Louise returned. She moved around the room turning on small lamps then turned off the main lights. As she passed she picked up the remote off the top of the television and turned it off as well. She handed me a drink, then, lifting up my folder and placing it on the floor, she sat down beside me. Slipping her feet out of her mules and turning to me, she tucked one leg up under the other. She pushed the sleeves up on her cardigan, showing bare brown arms beneath. She sipped on her drink. Ice clicked in her glass.

I nodded over at the cards on the shelf.

'No crystal ball then?'

She shook her head but smiled.

'You may mock. But I do all the girls who work here. And I'm usually right. It's my Romany heritage. Got the gift of sight.'

'I'll take your word for it.' I said, still sounding sceptical.

'Saw right through you, didn't I?' She sipped her drink.

'I'll give you that.' I nodded.

'It's harder with women. And especially with your girlfriend. She was always a hard one to read.'

I nodded. 'She was always good at disguising herself. Hiding things from others.'

'Nicks seemed happy enough on the outside but... you know, I'm sure there was something else.'

'Yeah, you're right there. Though it wasn't Nichola. Not to me. Her real name was Catherine. Nichola was this false identity she had. Another was Fanny Dore.'

Louise laughed. Then she saw me looking at her. 'Sorry.'

'No, it's all right. It was just some silly pen-name she used for some illustration work for this publisher, Oyster Press. Porn – well erotica. I found the illustrations after she'd died. She was an artist but I never realised she did anything like that.' I took a large swallow of my drink and looked back at Louise. 'And then I found out she was also a masseuse, an escort and prostitute as well, then when I found I she was working here–'

'So you thought she would be doing sex stuff here too.' Louise nodded. 'You wouldn't be the first jealous boyfriend I've had storming in here.'

'No, it's not that.'

I took another sip of my drink. I sighed and looked down. I felt Louise move closer.

'She did cheat on me.' I continued. 'Not just with the massage or escorting. Before that. For a long time before that, I think. I don't know… I've just been trying to find out more about her. Perhaps it's just selfishness. Pride. Wanting to know all her secrets, all she kept from me. I just don't know. I suppose I keep thinking I'm going to find the one answer to it all. But all I find is more questions.'

'You're not selfish.' Louise said. 'I can see that. You want me to get the cards? Do a reading? It can help, you know. Even if you don't believe, it can help to get your thoughts in order.'

'No, I'm really not into that sort of thing.' I smiled, turning to her. 'Though you are easy to talk to.'

'That's part of my job. Most of it, probably. The number of clients that use us as a confessional, once they get to know you. The girls too, over a coffee and that. But Nic– sorry, Catherine… she would never really open up to me. There was something dark in her. Something stopping it.'

'There was something dark alright. I tried to avoid confronting it. Thought it helped her. Not cause a fuss and all that. But the troubles buried in her past never really left her.'

'Troubles?'

'Anorexia, self-harm, suicide attempts. Depression. I don't think I ever saw the real her. Even at her most raw and naked. Maybe she didn't know either... She kept changing her image, taking on new identities. I thought it was part of her art, but it was all covering up.'

'Art? She never mentioned anything like that.'

'Yeah, modern art. Photography mainly. Though she moved onto video later. She got a bit of name for herself. In the papers and all that.'

'I wouldn't know, not my sort of thing.'

'She was always the artist no matter what... to the end. Until she died.'

'I had wondered what had happened to her. Suddenly leaving. Not answering her phone.' Louise put her hand on my shoulder.

'She killed herself. Fucking videoed it.' I sighed. 'Set up a camera and left it running... Made it into a bloody art work.'

'Look, if you don't want to talk–'

'No, I do. I really do.' I took a deep ragged breath. 'She threw herself off a cliff. Washed out to sea, lost forever.' I turned back to Louise. I took her hand and held it tight. 'And this is the worst thing. She threw herself off with her lover. A suicide pact. Not only did she keep that affair from me. Not only was she planning her own death, she planning to share it with him. That she felt so much more of him than me. That's the ultimate betrayal.' I shook my head. 'I am bloody jealous of him, aren't I? Jesus.'

'Did she not say anything? Anything at all? Before?'

'No. I've tortured myself over and over that she might have left some hints, but there was nothing. We were apart at lot towards the end – but nobody else thought anything like that might be coming… not her family, no one. We've had some bad times, but everything seemed to be going well.'

'So you've no idea—'

'Oh, she did leave a note. And a message, on the video recording, at the beginning. To me, personally. That she was taking herself away from me. That it would help me. Help my art. Protect me from her. That she was dragging me down. That she didn't know who she was any more… It was all pretty incoherent. I don't know.'

I let go of Louise's hand, finished my drink and put the glass on the floor. I relaxed back on the sofa. Louise joined me and leaned against me.

'How did you find out she was working here?' She asked.

'A phone message at the flat she was using as an escort; the address of which I found from the tattooists.' I tipped my head over towards Louise. 'I knew she had adopted other identities. Well, sort of – I always thought it was just play-acting, part of the art… something to be easily changed for the next one. But what really shocked me was the tattoo, such a permanent change.'

'Tattoo?'

'Saw it in a publicity photo at the publishers – I'd been led there by some illustrations of hers I found. It was like an 'F' but reversed.'

'Her lover?'

'No, doesn't match any of his names. I think it refers to one of her other identities. Though it was so stylised it could be anything.'

Louise patted my thigh. 'She never mentioned him, to me, by the way. Her lover. Talked about you a lot, though. If that helps.'

'Really?'

'Oh yes. I think she was expecting you to propose marriage soon. I thought that might have been why she disappeared. Starting a new life.' She twisted around on the sofa to face me. 'Actually, I've just thought. I've still got some stuff of hers. In her locker. Always thought she might be back to collect it… but you'd better have it. I'll have to dig out the spare key. Will tomorrow do for you?'

'Yeah, it's getting late. I had better be off.' I sat up. 'I'll get a taxi or… no, I'll find a hotel nearby.'

'Don't be daft. You look like you're at the end of your tether. Sleep on the couch. That way I can sort the stuff out and give it to you first thing before we open.' She sat up beside me. 'And, after what you have just told me… I don't think either of us wants to alone.'

'Ah, no, but…'

She smiled at my reaction. She put her hand on my arm.

'You know I didn't mean that. Now, do you want a bath? Make you feel a lot better.'

I stepped back into the lounge with a large white towel wrapped around myself. The door on the far side was half open and blue light spilled across the carpet. Tarot cards were spread out in some cross-like arrangement on top of a dark cloth spread out on the floor in front of the sofa. Depicted on the centre card was a cartoonish cupid floating over a cluster of medieval figures, bow and arrow poised – 'The Lovers'.

A shadow moved through the light. I turned to see Louise standing naked in the doorway. She stepped towards me.

'You can't mourn her forever.'

Afterwards we lay on her bed, entwined together under her duvet in the blue light.

The bedroom was plain, only a Persian rug on the floor and another hanging on the wall. A blue cloth had been draped over the small lamp by the bed, which was either a narrow double or a wide single.

'Was that for real?' I asked.

'What?'

'The cards. 'The Lovers'. Like James Bond?'

'Sorry?'

'In that Roger Moore voodoo one. Where he palms 'The Lovers' to get Jane Seymour into bed with him.'

She laughed quietly. 'Oh, no. That's the way the cards came out. I'd never cheat.'

'You know I hit someone earlier today.'

'Very James Bond.'

It was my turn to laugh.

'I can't remember having a proper fight like that since I left school. It was ridiculous.'

'Yeah, I think you're more a lover than a fighter.' Louise said softly.

'No, actually, there was one other time… But no, I'm not the tough guy. The private eye. Not really. You saw through that.' I sighed. 'I think this is the end.'

'What?' She murmured.

'The end of my journey. I'll never get to know the real Catherine, I realise that now. I just have to give up on it. Start a new life. What do you think?'

But Louise was asleep.

Low golden afternoon sun filtered through the branches as I walked though the wood, glinting off clouds of midges. The ground under my feet was spongy with moss. A clean earthy smell filled the air. I heard birdsong and a slight rustling from a breeze blowing through the leaves.

Then a shadow passed over me.

A creaking sound behind.

I stopped.

The sound repeated, then again and again, as the shade passed back and forth in front of me.

The wind rose, cool against my back.

Another cloud of midges. No, not midges – flies.

I turned.

She was hanging from one long limb of a horse-chestnut tree. In a short crimson dress with white stockings and red shoes. Swaying back and forth from the leftover momentum of that final dance, from those frantically kicking legs – now forever still. The noose, tied from bright blue plastic cording, creaked like old ship rope.

There was the acrid smell of urine. Urine that had stained one stocking, and still dripped from the toe of one down-pointed red shoe.

Her face was twisted and swollen and flushed dark. The neck above the rope raw, from where she had clawed and scratched at it in dying desperation and regret.

The wind rose again – a bitter chill that flowed over and through me.

Her face twitched once and her eyes snapped open – deep pools of blood red.

She moaned, low at first then rising into a groan, a cry, a scream—

Louise held me, her hand on my face.

'A bad dream. Just a bad dream. Shush now.'

She soon slipped back into sleep again. But I stayed awake, staring at the ceiling. Cold, I pulled up the duvet back over both of us.

A bad dream all right. All a bad dream. Since Catherine died.

211

But long before that. Since Trisha… since Bird-Girl died. The nineties – one long bad dream. When the spring of our careers slowly turned to winter.

10 SNOW

Hidden in cold dark cloud, a single water droplet condensed onto a speck of dust, then froze. Rising on the air, as more ice formed around it, it grew into a crystal.

'Ever get the feeling you're not wanted?'

The speaker was a big bald man in a dark suit. I first assumed he was one of the relatives, but then he nodded over at the group of family members on the other side of the room – so that made him one of us, an artist. The dark suit was not typical, but this was a not a typical gathering – we were all wearing dark suits.

There had been little effort by the two sides to integrate. The family had not been very welcoming – a quick 'thank-you' greeting and a 'help yourself to something to eat and drink' once we had arrived at the house, but that was it.

In the dining room a large table had been moved to one side and covered with a white cloth. There were plates of sandwiches and cakes – both with the neatness and uniformity that made me think of a catering company. Plus tea and whiskey.

Some people had already moved out through the patio doors to the modest garden. But even out there, though less obviously divided, it still appeared that neither side were talking to each other.

And then I suddenly recognised him, the speaker. From the voice, plus the short-haired tom-boyish woman who suddenly appeared at his side, tea cup and saucer in hand. They were the two clowns, Fred and Ginger. And Ginger, it now turned out, was a woman.

'Didn't recognise us out of character then?' She gave me a small smile, her voice low. 'But I've been thinking that maybe Trisha would not have approved. Would have preferred us to dressed up more jolly. But we felt the family wouldn't have appreciated it.'

'You got an invitation?' I asked. 'I got the feeling we were only asked reluctantly.'

'We don't need an invitation, my dear.' Fred said with a grin. 'You should know that by now.'

'We go everywhere, no matter how sad.' Ginger added, sipping her tea.

A voice rose suddenly on the other side of the room, the punch line to some joke. A burst of laughter followed.

Fred sighed.

'No wonder she wanted to get out of here. So provincial. I bet she was glad to leave.' He dropped his voice, leaning forward towards the both of us. 'Even though I heard they chased her out. Couldn't stand having a dyke in the family. I bet they're regretting that now. But, too late for that.'

'Too late for us all.' Ginger added. 'Too late to make a difference anyway.'

'Yes,' I said, covering an uncomfortable pause in the conversation. 'Well, I think Catherine's outside.' I continued, taking a step towards the room's patio doors. 'I was going to take her a drink.'

They both nodded.

'And I think we shall depart.' Fred said. 'Hope to see you at something more cheerful next time.'

'Yes,' Ginger said. 'Much more cheerful.'

I nodded my farewell and made my way out to the garden, stopping off at the table to half-fill two tumblers with whisky and water.

Outside a gentle breeze countered against the warmth of the sun. Catherine was standing on the lawn with her back to the house. I passed her the drink. She smiled and mouthed 'thank you', then taking my arm she slowly led me away from the house.

The garden was neat to the point of obsession. The lawn, with its rotary washing line folded in the middle, was cropped and striped like a bowling green. Either side were ruler-straight rows of bedding plants in front of creosoted fences. At the far end was a vegetable garden next to a shed. The rows of cloches and pea-cane triangles were just as ordered as the flowerbeds.

The only exception to all this regimentation was a bird table at the front of the narrow gap between the shed and the fence. Hexagonal shaped with a small peaked roof, it was leaning at a pronounced angle, its green paint sun-blistered and chipped, exposing dark blue underneath. A few strands of cobweb extended from the roof down to the dusty surface of the main platform, fluttering in the breeze.

I glanced back and confirmed you would just be able to see it from the house.

Catherine took a final bite out of her sandwich. She quickly ripped up the crusts and scattered them over the surface of the bird table.

'Yes, I think that's what she would have wanted.' I said.

Catherine turned back to me. For the first time today I thought I could see a tear at the edge of her eye.

'Maybe.' She said. 'But I don't see many birds around, do you?'

Earlier that day we had travelled up together in Catherine's car. She had another new look – a plain dark suit with her hair pulled back and pinned up. She wore very little make-up.

I wore a newly-bought black suit, with a pale blue shirt and navy tie and a pair of decent black shoes. I had had to extend my credit to afford it but plenty of money would be coming to us all soon.

We barely spoke during the journey. Just a short discussion about where we were heading, Liverpool. Well the Wirral, which was not, I had said, strictly speaking, Liverpool itself. Still it had been a surprise. Neither of us could remember hearing any Scouse tones in Trisha's voice. Maybe a hint of something northern underneath her sing-song style, but that was all. She had disguised her origins well.

The funeral had taken place in some municipal crematoria. There were a large number of family members, finally accepting her in death. Along with a few others from the college, Catherine and I had clustered together at the back with Simon and Mark. It was the first time the four of us had all been together since the Five Feathers exhibition.

The service was short, and for the most part could have been for anyone. However there were a couple of things that did strike me as particular to Trisha – a mention by the vicar of her love of nature, God's infinite creation as he put it, and that at the end, she had found happiness before tragedy.

Afterwards, the four of us stepped out into the sunshine. The broken cloud of earlier having been swept away by a breeze that fluttered the petals of the wreaths placed down on the dull concrete flags at the back of the crematoria.

A thin middle aged woman approached us, her eyes dark-ringed with recent pain, squinting against the sun and the wind.

'Thank you for coming.' She said. 'I'm Trisha's mother. Please come back to the house.'

I was thinking she had made amends, to open a bridge between us. But then she moved onto some relative and did the same thing, except without the need to say who she was. And this time there was a smile – a forced smile perhaps, but a smile nonetheless.

I passed Catherine a tissue and looked back up the lawn again while she dabbed her eye.

Semi-detached, the house was as neat and ordered as the garden. Sunlight reflected off the windows, obscuring what was beyond. I wondered which one had been Bird-Girl's room, from where she had looked down at her bird table.

'Seems the wrong weather for a funeral, somehow' Catherine said.

'I was thinking that before.' I turned back to her.

Catherine sighed. 'Do you wonder why she did it?' She asked me.

I shook my head and shrugged. 'I've no idea.'

'I can understand depression… but I never saw anything like that in her.'

'None of us did. Try not to worry yourself over it.'

She looked up to the sky, shaded her eyes with one hand. 'I just wish I could see a bird.'

'The only thing… well, it just seemed that even when she was successful she could never let herself be happy. Be satisfied. She just worried and fussed and fluttered over everything all the time. Could never let anything go. Never find peace. Well, she's got peace now.' I let out a short bark of a laugh. I turned to Catherine. 'Dear God, that's far too sentimental – she'd hate me for that.'

Catherine looked back to me. She reached for my hand.

'No, it was nice.'

Simon and Mark walked down the lawn towards us. They were both in the same uniform as the rest – dark suits, dark ties and pale shirts.

'I don't want to be out of turn.' Simon said quietly, stepping up close to us. 'But while we are all together, we need to talk about this.'

'Talk about what?' I asked.

'What to do. About the collective. Now that Trisha's gone.'

'Carry on,' I said.'Anything else would be an insult.'

Catherine and Mark nodded their agreement.

'Still equal shares?' Simon said. 'The four of us? From now on?'

'I would have thought so.' Mark said.

'I think we'll have to ask the accountants. They'll know.' I said. 'We may have to do a new contract.'

Simon nodded at me. 'You take care of that?'

'Sure.'

'I think it will be a good idea to get back into the swing of things as fast as possible.' Simon continued. 'I suggest we have meeting later in the week to sort out anything hanging over from the exhibition. And get the plan to find a studio rolling.'

We all nodded.

'I think that's everything for now.'

Catherine turned to me.

'Can we make a move?'

'Sure.' I said.

'Heading back to London?' Mark asked Catherine as we started walking back up the lawn.

'Planning to stay in a hotel tonight. But,' She turned to me. 'Shall we go back now? It's going to be just depressing hanging around here any longer than we have to.'

'Yeah, good idea.' I took one last look back down the garden. 'I think Bird-Girl flew away from here a long time ago.'

The frozen water crystals clustered together, forming a snowflake. As it became heavier the air could no longer support it.

The snowflake slowly fell.

I was finishing a painting. I sat beneath the branches of one of the last large oaks that lined the driveway to Catherine's parent's house on a folding chair with a canvas on an easel set up in front of me. It was late afternoon and long shadows from the trees reached out towards the house, the autumn air warm, still and slow. At first I had felt somewhat exposed out in front of all those windows, but once I became absorbed in my work those feelings were forgotten.

I had sketched out the main details in a dark sepia ink with a dip pen, producing a pleasing, non-mechanical line. At the edges of the buildings, and with the trees beyond, I let the line peter out and loosely defined the light and shade with a brush. To that I had applied thin washes of acrylic paint. But I kept to a semi-monochrome, a reduced pallet based on the autumn colours of the surrounding trees – yellows and browns and reds and russets and ochres. Once dry I added final highlights with yellow and white chalk.

I was slowly looking over the painting again, trying to decide if it was finished or not, when I saw Catherine striding over the lawn towards me. She was dressed casually in jeans and an anorak. I briefly thought of adding her to the composition – it would have taken only a couple of quick dabs of paint – but changed my mind. However I decided it was better to leave the piece as it was, empty of people.

I packed away my paints and brushes into the plastic fishing tackle box I used to store them in but left the painting for her to see.

'Changing you style, then?' She asked me, after she had studied the painting for a few seconds. 'This is definitely something new.'

'Well, yes and no.' I said, standing and folded up the chair. 'It's just for me really. I was getting bored of doing the other stuff, the commercial stuff, all the time. Fancied a change.'

I lifted up the canvas and placed it down leaning against the tackle box, then folded up the easel.

'Want to do it now?' Catherine asked casually.

'Sure, if you want.'

'I'll take these.' She picked up the chair and easel while I took my painting and the tackle box.

'I thought you were going riding?' I said as we started walking back to the house.

'Decided to cut it short. It's pretty quiet now, so we'll be able to have our own little ceremony in peace. Before it gets dark.'

Once inside we dropped my painting things in the hall then headed back out the rear and over the lawn towards the arboretum.

I turned to look over at the new sculpture behind the pool house.

'Wow, it looks even better now, in this light.'

'Yeah,' Catherine smiled. 'I'm really pleased with it.'

The sculpture consisted of three oversized chess pieces – a brick-built fifteen foot high rook, a bronze ten foot high knight and a marble five foot pawn. All three were mounted on a concrete base that was the cut-off corner of a chess board. 'House, Horse and Humility', Catherine had called it.

Laugher and shouts came from a small group sitting around the pool. One particularly loud braying guffaw dominated.

'Oh god, not Uncle Rupert. I take it he's onto his third bottle of gin.'

Catherine smiled.

'He's not that bad.'

'Why wasn't he at the unveiling?'

'I didn't ask him – just wanted it to be intimate, that's all. Getting a bit tired of all those big art party things. So close family only.'

'You invited me.'

'You are part of the family now.'

'Really?'

'Well, unofficially.' She smiled.

We walked on into the arboretum. 'Now, another ceremony.'

Catherine led me through to the other side. A wind rose, rustling and picking up some of the yellowed fallen leaves that we kicked through.

'Oh yes, this is exactly right,' Catherine said.

We stopped at the other side and stood together looking out over the bare earth of the ploughed field beyond

Catherine reached into the pocket of her anorak and pulled out a plastic bag half-filled with feathers. A mixture of the left-overs from the publicity for the art show plus some others we had collected recently. She reached in and pulled out a handful. She dropped them into my cupped hands then reached back into the bag for more.

'Bird-Girl, rest in peace.' She said, throwing out a handful of the feathers into the air in front of her.

'Amen.' I said, doing the same.

Some of the feathers fluttered out onto the breeze, floating away, while others slip-sided down to the hedge in front of us or the field beyond.

Catherine reached back for my hand, gripped it tight. I looked over towards her.

'You know, when I was younger.' She said, looking out over the field as a few of the lighter feathers tumbled along and over the ruts of earth. 'When I was at my worst, I'd compulsively plan my own funeral. All sorts of alternative arrangements instead of the standard Christian thing.' She sighed. 'But I never thought I'd have to do it for one of my friends.' She finally turned to me. 'I'm never going back to that place, the dark place, that's for sure. Despite all this.'

'Let's go back.'

She nodded.

'Want to stop the night?' She said, as we walked back through the arboretum.

'May as well. Spend another day? Go back to London tomorrow evening?'

'Yes, I can go riding and you can do another painting.'

'Never fancy it yourself? Doing some more painting? I mean, I liked the stuff you showed me.'

'Oh no, photography only for me now. Not got bored with that yet.'

'It's not that I'm bored. Not really. It's just that I fancy doing something different now and again.'

'I liked it. You should put it in the next show.'

'Nah, I don't want to commercialise everything I do. And besides the buyers won't like it. Just confuse them. You have to pick something and stick to it. Variations on a theme, that's what sells. Not loads of different stuff. If you do move on it has to be a tiny steps. Keeping a clear identity.'

'Even if it's an ever changing identity? Like me?' Catherine laughed.

'Even that. You know I'd love to capture one of those identities sometime. Paint you.'

'No.' She turned and grabbed my shoulders bringing me to a halt. She suddenly looked very serious. 'No, paint anything else – paint my house – but don't paint me. Please. I don't think I'd like it.'

'Yeah, I'm not very good yet, am I?'

'No, it's not that. It's, that I don't ever want to see what you see in me. It's... can you just humour me over this...? Like the l-word?' She shook her head and gave me a little smile. 'I'm sorry I'm so bonkers about these things.'

'Hey, that's why I luuu – like you!'

She snorted and play punched me on the shoulder. Then, turning back to the house, she took my arm.

As we walked back across the lawn I saw the area around the pool was now deserted and cast in shadow as the sun set behind the house.

The room was dark but I did not bother searching for the light switch. I could see the decanter on the sideboard from the light from the hall.

'Catherine not with you?'

I spun around.

Someone was slumped down in a large armchair. As my eyes adjusted to the half-light I saw it was Uncle Rupert.

'She's gone to bed. Wanted an early night.'

He held up a glass

'Join me for a drink, then?'

There was another decanter on a side-table next to him. He put down his glass and topped it up.

I hesitated.

'Go on,' He said. 'I fancy a bit of a chin-wag. Before I hit the sack myself.'

'Er, sure. Okay then. Shall I put the light on?'

'If you want.'

There was a standard lamp near the door and I switched it on. I sloshed some whisky into my own tumbler from the decanter off the sideboard before sitting down in another armchair opposite Rupert.

Rupert pulled himself more upright.

'Sorry if I spooked you, old chap. I just like sitting in the dark, sometimes. Helps you to think, I find.'

All his normal bluster seemed to have gone. He suddenly looked much older to me.

He swallowed half the contents of his tumbler, then waved it over towards the curtained windows.

'A splendid thing she's built. Out there.'

'Yes, it's great. She's very pleased with it.' I said, sipping from my own glass.

'But a terrible thing. A terrible, terrible thing.'

'Sorry?'

'Your friend. Dying.'

'Yes.' I said.

He took another large swallow of whisky, then looked up past me, off into space, his eyes unfocussed.

'My wife. The first one, that is. She died. Cancer. One of those rare buggers that can grab you unexpected. And so damned quick – full of health to the grave in six months. I felt bloody awful for a long time. Went completely off the rails for a bit, I think. Many times I was close to taking a walk into the woods with my shotgun. And drinking far too much.' He laughed to himself, holding up the glass to me. 'I know that people say that I still do. But this was nothing to what I used to be like.'

He drained his glass.

'To bed, I think.' He said and slowly pulled himself to his feet. He stepped forward, swaying slightly. Pausing by my chair he patted me on the shoulder.

'Catherine. Look after her.'

A snowflake hit the ground and almost instantly disappeared, dissolving back into liquid and soaking away. But the temperature continued to fall.

As that autumn turned into winter we opened our collective studio in Hoxton. Working away on our own projects in our own studios, for long days and on into the night, we created work for out next show, to quickly build on the success of the first one and, I am sure, to help us cope with our residual grief from the loss of Bird-Girl.

In my mind I explored an imaginary landscape that would eventually produce what I called 'The K series'. K for Kastle – an alternate fantasy world where immensely intricate and complicated buildings raced across the landscape. I first drew plans of room after room in a semi-random manner, in top-down two dimensions, in patterns that were pleasing to me. Towers and turrets and connecting curtain walls I added as the mood took me. Then I brought them into an approximation of reality by drawing them out in perspective, turning my technical drawing skills into art. Finally I added loose semi-abstract landscapes around them.

For inspiration I worked my way through several libraries scouring books on architecture, incorporating features from all through the ages into the work – even, for a few days wandering around Catherine's father's company, to the bemusement of the other workers, seeing how it was done in the real world.

Catherine continued with her photographs. She started a series of ghostly reflections of herself in shop windows, quickly snatched from odd angles on busy streets. She roamed markets and vintage clothing shops for more props and costumes and travelled all over London scouting for new locations. Sometimes I went with her, but not often – I was usually busy with my own projects and watching someone else work, even when they are creating art can be pretty boring.

On the wall of our studio, behind the futon, we hung a blow-up of a photograph Catherine had taken one night of a gibbous moon hanging over the London skyline – so that we could have sex anytime, she had joked.

Early in the new year, we gathered our work together for another show. And this time we hired a proper gallery.

Simon had created an elaborate network of letters that he had sent out to random people picked out the phone book, asking them to send another onto someone else at random, sending copies back to him. Most had been unanswered but others had started chains of correspondence that had ended up looping right around the globe. He planned to mount them all around the walls of gallery, with string and ribbons and drawn lines following their various journeys through the various countries' postal systems. And to add to it throughout the exhibition, creating a multi-dimensional network that slowly gained complexity in four dimensions.

Mark created a new set of pieces. Dropping down to the other end of the scale from his previous work, he had produced a number of small spiky, roughly circular, abstract assemblies of scrap metal and electrical engines designed to slowly rotate on the spot or crawl around the gallery space on hidden caterpillar tracts or wheels.

Catherine had her 'Reflected' portraits and I my 'K Series' of paintings.

We had thought long and hard but in the end we only paid a small and modest tribute to Trisha, a page of the catalogue dedicating the show to an absent friend.

If anything it was more successful than the first exhibition. With my share of the profits I bought my dream bike – a lime green Kawasaki Ninja. I got the matching leathers and helmet to go with it, but felt a bit of a poser wearing them, so for most of the time I kept to my old helmet and scruffy leather jacket. I rode it alone. I tried to persuade Catherine to be my pillion but she was never keen. It was fair enough, she had never managed to entice me out horse riding with her.

'So how was Japan?' Simon asked.

'Fantastic.' I lined up the mallet then tapped my red ball. My aim was good but my ball rolled up just short of the hoop. 'Damn.'

As Simon took his turn I walked back to the garden table set up beside the croquet square to retrieve my Pimms and lemonade. While I sipped he knocked his black ball into my red. Then, after picking up his own ball and placing down next to mine, he whacked them both hard speeding my ball out of the square towards me. I stopped it with my foot, then placed it back on the square.

'*Hah!*' Simon cried. 'I'll have you know.'

I shrugged. I was not really taking the game very seriously. Although I was in the lead, several hoops ahead in fact – largely from the tactical experience I had gained from playing Catherine several times before – I was not playing anywhere near my best, due to my extreme fatigue.

I had flown in earlier that day from a one-man exhibition in Tokyo. Catherine had surprised me at the airport with a white Rolls Royce Silver Spirit she had hired for the weekend. Jet-lagged, I spent most of the journey to her parents' place asleep, stretched out on the leather seat in the back of the Roller. As soon as we had arrived at the house Catherine had raced off to get changed and prepare for a photo-shoot she said she wanted my help with..

Simon had arrived before us and Mark would be turning up that night for a 'welcome home party' followed by a more formal business meeting of the collective the next day.

It was a warm spring afternoon and I had suggested a quick game of croquet to Simon while I waited.

'Anyway, Japan was amazing.' I said. 'All those temples and shrines. And all the neon at night.

'Check out any art galleries?' Simon said as he aimed for his next hoop.

'Oh yes, loads. And what's really interesting, is that over there they don't have the same split between art and craft that we do.'

'In what way?' Simon's black ball rolled through the hoop.

'The art galleries, unless they are displaying Western art, or modern art are more like our museums. So instead of the National or the Tate they are more like the British Museum for example. They don't just display painting and sculpture but also examples of things like the finest swords, printed silk kimonos, scrolls of calligraphy – all are considered to be 'art', practically divine in some cases. And then there's things like the tea ceremony. Over there, everything – everything done well that is – is art.'

While I had talked Simon had quickly created a couple more free shots for himself.

'Everything done well is art, yeah I like that idea.' he said. 'See any geisha? Catherine told me she thought about surprising you at the airport dressed as one.'

'The Roller was enough of a disguise. But I did see a couple of geisha. Just in the street. When I managed a trip to

Kyoto.' I sipped from my drink. 'Missed her though, Catherine. First time we've really been apart.'

'Yeah, but you can't do everything together.'

Simon had missed a hoop and I had another shot at last. I put my glass down and walked back across the square to my other yellow ball.

'That's what she says.' I said pausing to plan my next move – to attack one of Simon's balls and try and knock him over to the other side of the lawn like he had done to me, try to get my other ball back in play, or to just play a long shot for the next hoop 'Wanted to take her. But she reckons we need to establish our own separate artistic identities. Outside the collective and as a couple.'

'She's right. And having a solo show abroad was a brilliant opportunity. The first one of us.'

'I'm sure you all won't be far behind.' I said.

I went for the long-shot, tapping my ball to send it running across the grass towards the hoop. It finished just short.

'Hope so.' Simon said hitting his blue ball to collide with the yellow one I had just played. He used his next shot to send my yellow hurtling over towards where he had sent my other ball out of play.

'Been away for a short trip myself. Back home.' Simon continued. As he talked we continued playing on opposite sides of the square to each other, taking turns to use our own balls to make some hoops without interfering with each other's play. I still stayed ahead, but he slowly gained on me. 'Saw someone I knew. Not seen them since school. He used to take the piss that I was the only male in the six form taking art. To be honest I think I only did it to be in a class full of girls, at first anyway. And the irony is he's ended up married to the girl in the class I most fancied. But he still can't appreciate what I've done. Just sees art as a hobby for his wife. I wonder if he ever realised his piss-taking made me take it all seriously.'

'Should have thanked him for it.'

'No, you—'

'Jason!' A shout interrupted us.

We both turned to see Catherine waving at us as she walked down the garden. She was dressed in the grey trouser suit of a chauffeur complete with peaked cap.

'Let's go. I don't want to lose this light. Be perfect for the location I scouted.'

'Finish the game later then?' Simon said. 'Think I've got you on the run.'

'Probably won't have time.' Catherine turned to me, putting her first two fingers up to her cap's brim in a salute. 'I imagine – as he has not seen his servant in such a long time – the master will want us to come back via the scenic route. The most scenic route.'

'More than likely.' I smiled as I slid my arm around her waist.

'I'll put this down as a victory to you then.' Simon said, as I started leading Catherine back to the house

'Didn't know you were keeping score.' She called back.

'Oh, you have to keep score.' Simon replied. 'Otherwise, what would be the point in playing?'

Another snowflake fell and before it could completely dissolve another landed beside it. More followed, with increasing frequency.

'Hello boys!' I called out to Catherine.

She was sitting slouched forward at the kitchen table wearing just her underwear – plain black bra and panties, suspenders, stockings. Her arms folded underneath her bra, created a noticeable cleavage.

There was an empty glass in front of her. Next to the fruit bowl was a half-filled bottle of vodka. Two ice trays from the freezer were sitting in pools of liquid. One was on empty; the other had a few shrunken cubes left floating in melt-water. The stereo was on low – Nirvana, 'Nevermind'.

Catherine did not look up as I dropped my bag down and closed the door behind me – just picked up the bottle and sloshed some vodka into her glass. She reached out to an ice tray with her other hand and clawed out two of the remaining cubes. She dropped the ice into the glass then took a large swallow.

There was a hand mirror at the near corner on the table. I noticed a small smear of white powder left on it, as I stepped closer.

'Christ Catherine, what's the matter?' I put my hand to her shoulder, then the back of her neck as her head tipped further forward.

'The news.' She said. 'Listening to it on the radio as I was getting ready to go out. I know I shouldn't be this upset, but–'

'What news? What's happened?'

She finally looked up at me, swivelling round in the chair. This close I could see her eyes were reddened and her make-up smudged.

'What? Don't you know? You must have heard?'

'I've been out all day, sketching.'

'What? Not seen a *Standard*? Must have been all over that.'

'No, got a taxi straight back. I've not seen or heard anything – just tell me.'

'Kurt's dead.' She waved her glass over at the stereo. 'Kurt Cobain. Shot himself.'

'Jesus.'

'I know I shouldn't be this upset.' Catherine said, turning to look up at me. 'But fuck, it was our song. And it reminded me… Trisha.'

'Oh, Cat.' I leaned forward to put my arms around her but she shook her head, gently pushing away.

'No, fuck it.' She said, wiping her nose with the back of her hand. 'Let's just dance. Like the first time.'

She stood and led me out into the middle of her section of the studio. Wrapping her arms around my back she held herself to me.

'But I think we should make it a slow one this time.'

We danced, out of time to the music, turning slow stately circles around each other – me still in my coat, her in her underwear.

'Jace?'

'Yes?'

'Don't let me fall.'

I tightened my arms around her.

'No, don't let me fall like Kurt.'

'I won't, I promise.'

A hot summer's day and I was planting a field. Planting it with art. Planting it with colours, artificial colours.

I knelt next to a cardboard box that held a stack of upright sheets of coloured pieces of paper, each one a foot square. I checked the list of numbers on the sheet attached to the clipboard wedged into the back of the box. The next five numbers were all the same. I selected five of the particular coloured pieces of paper – each a dull red – that corresponded to the number, long having memorised the code, then I crossed through the numbers with the pen tied to the clipboard.

Taking the first piece of paper I placed it down onto the short-trimmed grass, squaring it up with the last one I had placed and the string line in front of me. The string was stretched between the last two of each of the parallel rows of pegs that ran down the field. The pegs being the first things we had set out that morning with the help of a surveyor we had hired. He was now sitting in his car on the road near the entrance to the field, even though technically he was not longer working for us, just waiting until we finished. Also waiting were the gang of art students we had hired to help us with the placing down of the colours, lounging on the grass nearby.

There was some scattered cloud in the sky but rain was not forecast until tomorrow, and it looked like the forecast was going to be right. As a precaution there were rolls of plastic sheeting at strategic places around the edge of the field but it looked like they would not be needed.

I reached into the bag slung over one shoulder and pulled out four oversized pins. I stabbed one into each corner of the piece of paper, holding it down.

I went on to pin the next four squares down in rapid, smooth, well practised movements, then shuffled a few feet along, dragging the box behind me to where the next square would be placed.

I paused to look up over to the gate where Catherine was chatting with one of the students. I waited until she glanced in my direction, then waved her over.

Catherine had hired a digital camera and taken a shot of herself. I had copied it into my computer and over the next few days we had played around with the colours, smoothing them out to an acceptable number and changing the values of some neighbouring clusters of pixels to create the shimmering optical effect seen in the best of the Seurat's pointillism. Then a program I had written produced a list of numbers – each number representing the colour of each pixel – so we could recreate the image, row by row.

The last step was taking sheets of paper, coloured using vegetable dye, and guillotining them into squares – half a million pieces of paper, plus spares, to create one picture; one collage; one portrait.

I pinned down another square as Catherine made her way over to me.

'This is the final row.' I said standing up. 'I thought you might want to put down the last squares and finish it off yourself.'

'I was leaving that to you; as you did most of the work.'

'Thanks, but it was your idea in the first place.' I stepped away but pointed back to when I been, indicating for Catherine to take my place.

'Oh, all right then.' Catherine said as she kneeled down. 'Pity it's got so boring at the end.' She said, placing down and pinning the next square of paper. 'Nearly all the same colour, but I thought the red back drop would look good against the grass. A contrast.'

'It does. Could have finished with a highlight in the eye or something but there's no point painting yourself into a corner.'

'Phoned the pilot.' Catherine said. 'He'll be setting off about now. Should be arriving right on time. The bloke sounded quite excited – I think he's got totally board with photographing houses from the air.'

'Then we go up ourselves?'

'Of course. Have plenty of time to get to the airfield before it gets dark, take some of our own photos.'

'Decided on what you are going to call it yet?'

She laughed and shook her head.

'No. still can't decide between 'Landscape – Portrait' or 'Portrait – Landscape'.'

The rain came earlier than expected; it came that night.

Once we had taken all the photographs we could, when the sun had got too low, we made an appearance at the barn where the students were camping out.

We joined them for a couple of cans from the multiple slabs of beer we had provided and eat some of the food from their barbecue. Someone had just set up a ghetto blaster and several people has started dancing around it. I joined them, up for a party, but Catherine soon drew me aside.

She drove me back to the field telling me that she just wanted to spend a few more final hours with her artwork, before it was all cleared away tomorrow.

We felt the first fat drops of rain about an hour later.

We were sat down on the grass together on the far side of the field to where we had parked the car, smoking the latest in what had been a number of shared joints

Naturally we thought the rain was an absolutely hilarious development.

We ran – stumbling, shouting and laughing – for the rolls of plastic sheeting. A flash of lightning – followed almost immediately by a clap of thunder – announced the sudden shifting up of the rain from a slow but steady drizzle into a sudden cloudburst. Catherine took my hand as she veered off, pulling me towards the middle of the artwork, laughing; yelling at me that the sheeting was a waste of time now.

We charged, our feet slapping down on the suddenly damp pieces of paper, ripping and uprooting them. Catherine suddenly slipped. She fell down and took me with her. Together we slid and rolled down the slope; tumbling into each other's arms and rolling on, entwined together – the sheets of paper sticking to us as we ploughed down the slope, scarring the portrait.

And then – finally sliding to a stop, in the centre of Catherine's face – we were kissing each other and pulling at each other's clothes, while the rain still hammered down.

The next day was spent with us all scooping up paper sludge into refuse sacks, and pulling out pins from the ground. Once we were finished I had run over the whole field with a metal detector to catch the pins we had missed.

The rain had caused the dye to run from the paper – staining both Catherine's and my skin with multi-coloured blotches. Our explanation for that and the desecration of our image the next day had been we had both slipped running for the sheeting. Which was just about true if not exactly the whole truth.

The dye had also stained the grass, leaving a faint blurred ghost version of Catherine's portrait. Even though it was technically non-toxic we still compensated the farmer – though apparently it became somewhat of local curiosity until it finally faded.

Catherine eventually decided to call the work 'Landscape Portrait / Portrait Landscape'.

It would be the last piece we ever made together.

We took a holiday and toured Scotland. There was an offshoot of Catherine's family in Edinburgh she had wanted to visit. We climbed Carlton hill and Arthur's Seat. On one day we walked along the broad New Town avenues laid out in their strict Georgian geometries and another walk through the more chaotic streets, alleys of the Old Town to the Royal Mile and the castle. We browsed shops selling vintage whisky and tartan tourist tat; buying in the forming, nudging and pointing and giggling to each other in the latter. We visited the art galleries and the museums and finally finished with climbing The Scott Monument – looking like a Victorian moon-rocket ready for takeoff in the centre of the town. Then onto Stirling and Glasgow for more of the same. We drove out past Loch Lomand, heading north to explore further, staying in highland hotels, drinking in remote walkers' pubs and taking in a couple of distillery tours. We conquered Ben Nevis and walked through Glen Coe. Then we made our way along the Great Glen – spending an afternoon fruitlessly trying to spot the beast among the sullen waves of Loch Ness – to Inverness where more of Catherine's relations lived. Finally we made our way all the way up to the end of the country, to John O'Groats. Catherine photographed me by the Last House and then both of us threw a stone into the sea.

Then we drove all the way back south again.

We had talked briefly about staying up there, but we were never serious. The pull back to London, to the studio, to our work, was too strong for that.

Brit Pop came and we went to see the bands. We went to Manchester a couple of times to spend nights partying in *The Haçienda*. We both hated *Forrest Gump* but we were split over *Shawshank*. I thought it was too sentimental at first but came around later after watching it couple more times on video. We generally liked *Four Weddings* but the funeral scenes brought back some bitter memories that that kept coming back with that bloody song that never seemed to go away.

And like everyone else we watched the news in numb disbelief as the police carried out body after body from a house in Gloucester.

'Destruction is not creation!'

We had been climbing the stairs to our floor, coming home from the pub, when we heard voices coming from the open door of Simon's studio. Catherine and I looked at each other then peered in.

Simon had subdivided his floor leaving only a small work room at the entrance and a fully-fledged flat beyond – with separate spacious bedroom, bathroom, lounge and kitchen.

The workspace featured a row of grey metal filing cabinets and a large table, in a bland modern office boardroom style. There were several stacks of newspapers at one end. Mark and Simon were sitting at the opposite corner. The only decoration was a framed print of Helnwein's 'Boulevard Of Broken Dreams' – the reinterpretation of Hopper's 'Nighthawks' with Dean, Bogart, Monroe and Presley replacing the anonymous characters in Hopper's original diner.

'Look, I'm not saying it is,' Simon said. He glanced up as and waved us into the room. 'I'm just saying that so-called vandalism can change a piece of art into a different one, with a different message, a different meaning. So the act of destruction can be creative.'

'Are you drunk? Or on drugs?' Mark said shaking his head. 'It doesn't make any sense. And besides you wouldn't want your art being vandalised, would you?'

'If it made it into different artwork' Simon said, smiling. 'A better artwork… an act of collaboration. Maybe.'

'That's just nuts. It didn't make it better. It just ruined it.'

'But it brought it to the attention of many more people. That's art.'

'What are you two arguing about?' I asked.

"Away From The Flock'.' Mark said, turning to me and Catherine as we walked into the room.

'Well that makes perfect sense.' I said.

'The Hirst piece.' Mark said. 'The lamb in the vitrine. Someone's tipped ink into it.'

'See, he could call it 'Black Sheep' now. Be great.' Simon said.

'Besides being rubbish,' Mark said. 'That would set a terrible precedent. Get people running through galleries destroying the art, vandalising it.'

'No, you just don't see it do you?' Simon said.

Catherine took my hand. 'We'll leave you to it,' she said to the other two. 'I'm taking this artist here to bed.'

They ignored us, still arguing, as Catherine led me out the room.

'Vandalism isn't art.'

'What about graffiti?'

'That's different.'

'How?'

Catherine closed the door on them.

'It's the Vandals I feel sorry for,' I said.

'Sorry?'

'The Vandals. The German tribe the word came from. I think they were actually pretty civilized for the time. The Vandalism thing just came about because they sacked Rome.'

'It does give me an idea though.' Catherine said as we started climbing the stairs again. 'What they were saying. For a joint piece. Take an item of each other's work... Something non-essential, discarded, rejected... and alter it... change it somehow?'

'Vandalise it?'

'Not really, just modify it… somehow…' Her eyes narrowed. 'Not sure what though. Have to think about it a bit more. Something for another day'

'Hmmm, exchanging art…' I pondered, bringing a finger up to my lips, furrowing my eyebrows, nodding my head slowly trying to look like I was thinking deeply. 'Perhaps we could create something for each other, some token, some symbol, some jewellery perhaps… a ring? Maybe?'

She was grinning as she opened the door to our studio.

'You won't catch me out like that!'

'Ah, you see through my evil scheme then!' I said, waggling my eyebrows. 'Then I'll just have to have my wicked way with you instead, my dear!'

She put the back of her hand up to her forehead and fluttered her eyes like a silent movie actress.

'Oh no, who will save me now?'

'No-one, my dear,' I said in my best theatrical voice as I scooped her up in my arms. I carried her into the room, kicking the door shut behind me. 'No-one! Prepare to be vandalised!'

The temperature dropped further. The snowflakes started to settle without vanishing back to water, dappling the ground.

'Not many cunts in here, are there?' Catherine suddenly announced.

We were on one of our gallery tours around London. It was something we did every few weeks – visit a number of galleries and view a select number of paintings and sculptures in each, sometimes following a particular artist, or period, or theme or just taking in a random selection.

In the dull drab cold of a mid-week winter's afternoon, finishing at the Tate, we had decided on a cappuccino before heading home.

'What?' I said, looking up at her, momentarily confused. 'No, they seem quite nice. Most of the people.'

Catherine smiled at me over her raised cup.

'No, not cunt like that. I was just thinking, in the paintings, they never show the female ... well, cunt.'

I looked around, worried that we could be overheard, but the place was half empty at that time of day and no one was sitting near us.

Catherine raised an eyebrow, leaning towards me.

'What, embarrassed by a naughty word?'

'Not me, but others might.'

She put down her cup and sat upright.

'Ah, all right what do you want me to call it? Pussy? Beaver? Honey-pot? Twat? Hole? Crack? Snatch? Muff? Minge? Vulva? Pudenda? Va-gi-na?' She drew the last one out emphasising each syllable finishing with a wide grin and raised eyebrows on 'na?'

I just shook my head. 'This is something you've been thinking about this for some time, I take it?'

'Maybe they are too clinical?' She continued. 'How about something more poetic? What about Delta of Venus? Altar of Love? Heaven's Gate? Cleft? Yoni? Flower? That's it — a beautiful flower. A rose or a lily?'

'What about Berkley?'

'Berkley?'

'Thought you would know that one. Being a horsey woman. Rhyming slang. Berkley Hunt.'

'Ah, right.'

'Did you know that's were 'berk' comes from? It's a lot ruder than people realise.'

'Don't start nerding out on me there, partner.'

'And this is from the woman who knows ninety-nine synonyms for her nether regions.'

She laughed. 'Oh, I'm sure there's plenty more words than I could ever come up with.' She sipped her coffee. 'Like nothing. Forgot that one.'

'Nothing? Nothing, what?'

'Just nothing. As in much ado about. It was Elizabethan slang. So the play's title has a punning meaning of both 'it's a lot of fuss about nothing' as well as 'a great deal of fuss about getting pussy'. Learnt that at school, when we did the play.'

'I wish I'd gone to your school.'

'It was all-girl.'

'Even better.'

Catherine just rolled her eyes at that.

I sipped my coffee then put my cup down, thinking.

'Monkey!' I suddenly exclaimed.

'What?'

'Never heard that before? No one's ever asked you to 'show 'em your monkey'?'

'No, I've not had that pleasure, my dear.'

She finished her coffee then dipped her biscuit in the remaining froth and nibbled the end.

'Dear god, 'monkey'!' She shook her head. 'But joking aside you see what I'm saying? Hundreds of years of art and you won't see a glimpse of a woman's sex until very recently. There's not even any pubic hair for the most part.'

'I suppose it keeps it mysterious.'

'Untalked about, more like – hidden. Yeah, something to be hidden. If it had been shown more and seen as something just normal, just part of the body, as something of beauty, not just lust – maybe there would not be so much porn about.' She shrugged. 'I don't know – it's something to think about anyway.'

'Well for me you are an object of both beauty and lust.'

'You say the nicest things, shall we go?' She ate the rest of her biscuit.

I nodded, draining the last of my coffee.

'Remember that band, Fuzzbox?' I said as we stood up.

'No. Should I?'

'A great all-girl punk new-wave type of thing back in the eighties – a bit obscure but they had a couple of minor hits. Then they sort of sold out and went all pop. Actually they were still great even then. Their full name was – We've Got A Fuzzbox And We're Going To Use It.'

'That's subtle.'

'The thing is, in interviews, they said they named themselves after a guitar effects peddle... I mean it was years, literally years, before I realised it might have another meaning.'

She laughed, taking me by the arm.

'Fancy a duet?' She said, airily.

'What?'

'Perhaps you can give us a tune with the help of that guitar peddle, whilst I accompany you on the old pink flute?'

We were lying naked together, her back to my chest, propped up against one arm of our sofa, listening to Portishead's *Dummy* on repeat. The room was warm and stuffy, the heating turned way up. I took another drag then passed her the joint. Then I stroked my hand down from her shoulder along her arm, until our fingers locked together with my palm against the back of her hand, her elbow in the crook of mine. With the other hand she tapped the ash off the joint into the ashtray perched on her stomach then drew on it, pulling smoke into her lungs.

'You know,' I said. 'I remember someone once saying that elbow is the most beautiful word in the English language. To say, like – the sound of it in your mouth. But I don't agree.'

Catherine giggled, smoke coming out of her nose.

'Let me guess what your favourite is then,' she said, after breathing out the rest of the smoke. 'Pussy, vagina... no, fuzzbox!'

'Not quite. Melliferous.'

'Mel-li-fer-ous.' She repeated, slowly and deliberately. 'Yes, that is quite nice. What's it mean?'

'Something that produces honey. So, you were actually pretty close.'

She laughed and stubbed out the joint. Her hand left mine and she picked up the ashtray, placing it down on the floor beside the sofa. She turned and kissed me on the cheek. Then sliding down, she turned and rested her head against my chest.

Soon I heard her breathing become swallower and I knew she was asleep.

I cradled Catherine in my arms and carefully slid myself out from underneath her, gently letting her lie back down on the sofa. As I took my arms away she murmured something and moved slightly, turning more onto her front, but did not wake. I stood and turned off the CD then stepped over to the box at the end of the futon to pull out a blanket. On the way back to the sofa, I noticed she had again shifted slightly, her legs parting, one sliding off the side of sofa, foot resting on the floor. I made to lift her leg back with my free hand, but then paused with my fingers resting on her shin. I lifted my hand away and put down the blanket. I went over to my half of the room and returned with a pad and paper. I sat down on the floor at the end of the sofa and started sketching her.

I drew her, whilst she slept – whenever she fell asleep before me or if I happened to wake first. I kept the results hidden. At first I felt guilty, doing something she had asked me not to. But what was the harm? What was the harm in celebrating her?

Fred West hung himself alone in his cell as another year began. *Windows 95* started up and I was an early adopter, upgrading to a new PC. I started designing and building web sites for both the collective as a whole, and for each of us individually, but soon tired of it proving too much of a distraction from my art, so I passed the work on to some small local IT company.

We saw *Braveheart* and we hated it. We saw *Toy Story*, both of us stoned out of our heads, and we loved it. I saw *Pulp Fiction* time after time, once taking Catherine – she liked it but she never saw in it what I did, never had my obsession with the whole damned coolness of the thing. Catherine was thoroughly depressed by *Kids* but I was just annoyed, thinking it manufactured controversy. We both saw *Se7en* and *The Usual Suspects* and I smugly predicted their big twists to myself, well at least a full two minutes before you were supposed to.

Oasis won the 'Battle Of The Bands' with one of their worse songs but Blur seemed to be winning the war. I preferred Pulp to both of them.

Our media profile slowly rose – we did some interviews together, and not just the art press but a couple of the nationals' weekend supplements and there was also a mention in *Time Out*. The 'artist-couple' thing was hard to avoid but we preferred to do them separately, if possible.

Catherine's trust fund matured and more money came in from the art. We briefly discussed buying a house together but decided not to bother, both enjoying our studio-based life style plus there was always Catherine parent's house or a hotel when we fancied a break.

Sunday nights would see us sharing a bottle of wine, gripped by the OJ Simpson trial. The only other television we regularly watched was *The X-Files* and Catherine went briefly red-headed again off the back of it. We saw the creepy supposed Roswell alien-autopsy footage when it was shown late one night on television. I said it deserved to win the Turner Prize more than anything else, but when Hirst did eventually win I cheered him on with all the rest of us.

Early evening and I was sitting in front of the computer – inputting some figures into a spreadsheet for the accountants. Catherine, in a purple leotard, was finishing her exercise routine. Warming down, she bent over at the waist, stretching. As I was shuffling through some papers the PC's screen-saver kicked in – the now far too familiar music accompanying the series of static shots of the man dancing around the pint of Guinness.

'Getting sick of that.' I said to myself, flicking the mouse to cancel it. 'I'm really gonna have to take it off.'

'Heard the controversy?' Catherine called over to me. She was now standing with her hands behind her head, twisting her upper torso around and then back again.

'What controversy?'

'On the news. Some art student is claiming the advertisers stole that idea off him.'

'Really?'

I stood and walked over to the fridge, opened it then pulled out a bottle of Pills.

'They claim it's a coincidence.' Catherine said, wiping her face with a towel as she came over to join me. 'It is a similar idea but from the footage they showed it did seem quite a bit different, different music, just someone dancing around really, so they might be right. It worked anyway.' She smiled. 'The advert, I fancy one now.'

'I think there's some of the black stuff in the back of the fridge.' I said, taking a bottle opener from a draw and popping the cap off my Pills. 'I much preferred the old ones anyway – the adverts that is – with the *Blade Runner* bloke in them.'

Catherine draped the towel over the back of chair at the kitchen table then crouched down in front of the fridge. She pulled out a black can then took a glass off the draining board of the sink. She popped the can's ring-pull and poured its contents into the glass, then placed the glass down on the corner of the table in front of the fruit bowl. Then while the Guinness settled, Catherine started singing the theme of the advert – *'Dur-Dah! da, da-da, da-da Dur-Dah!'* – dancing next to the table, making some of the same exaggerated movements towards the glass as was in the advert. When the drink at last settled she pulled a final static pose, pointing at the glass.

'You're wasted as a photographer.' I applauded then pulled out a chair and sat down at the table. Catherine did the same. 'Should have done performance art. Or dance.'

'Not really, but I did have dance lessons when I was younger.' She said, drinking a mouthful of the Guinness then licking the foam off her top lip. 'Ballet, tap, modern. But I couldn't keep it up, not with the art and the riding. Also I was rubbish. I never got very far in the competitions I entered.'

'You'll always be a good mover to me, love.'

'Thank you.' She leaned back in her chair. 'You know sometimes I do miss the competition. Not the dancing but the stuff I actually wasn't too bad at – the show jumping and the other horsey things I did.'

'Could do it again, couldn't you?'

'No, I'd be hopeless now. You have to be at it all the time, plus you need to scrounge round for the right horse to do any good. Just miss the performing in public, that's all. I actually would do some performance pieces if I could think of any good ideas.' She drank again. 'But you know the one thing I always wanted to be though, as a kid?'

'Tell me.'

'A magician's assistant.'

'That's magic!' I said, with a Paul Daniels inflection.

'No, really.' She tapped my arm. 'They're the ones who do all the work, you know – the assistants. Have to be really clever and skilled and flexible – dancers and gymnasts combined. I always thought it would be nice to dress up in some spangled or feathered outfit and jump into a box and disappear then crawl out the back while the audience is distracted by the magician.'

'Couldn't you do some art piece based on that?' I suggested. 'I actually quite fancy myself as a magician. The top hat and the tails.'

I stood and lifted her towel from off the back of the chair.

'Now you see it.' I draped the towel in front of the Pills bottle standing on the table. With my other hand I awkwardly grabbed the bottle and hid it behind my back. Then with a flourish I swept the towel away. 'And now you don't! *Ta-da!*'

'I think it's up your sleeve.' Catherine said with a raised eyebrow.

'Oh, well.' I said.

'Anyway, time for a shower.' Catherine said, standing. She reached out and took the towel from me. She turned and he strode off down the length of the studio towards the bathroom. 'Not performance, not yet.' She called back to me. 'But I'm going to do something different for this coming exhibition. Something really different. Something radical.'

'Oh really? What?'

By the door of the bathroom she pulled her arms out of the leotard and rolled it down her body past her waist. Then she stepped out of it and dropped it to the floor. 'Strip it back. Stripping it right back'

'What do you mean?' I called over to her.

But there was no answer as Catherine, naked, closed the bathroom door on me.

Gradually the snowflakes covered the ground in a continuous thin frosting.

I came back from the party for the opening of a new comedy club alone. Catherine had slipped away earlier, saying she wanted to do this small piece that she had decided on, wanting to do it right then, alone.

Light had blazed down from our studio windows as I had walked across the yard but when I had climbed the stairs Catherine was nowhere to been seen. I called out to her.

'Oh, coming!' The voice, muffled slightly, came from the bathroom.

The door opened and she stepped out, naked except for a pink towel wrapped around her waist. She was drying her head with another. Her bald head, I suddenly noticed.

'My God, are you alright?'

'Of course,' She said, stepping back into the bathroom, leaving the door open. I saw her hang the towel she had been using to dry her head over the towel rail. 'I told you I was going to photograph myself nude, to strip everything back. I thought, why stop at just clothes?' She said as she came back into the main room. 'Don't you like it?'

As I looked again I noticed the lack of hair did seem to emphasise the other features of her face. Her eyes looked huge as she walked towards me, like a cartoon characters'.

'I suppose it's quite cute.'

'Oh, damn.' She gave me a smile. 'I was going for the hard skinhead look, like her in that terrible *Alien* film you made me watch.'

'I'm afraid it's hard to pass off 'hard' when you're topless. And with that towel.'

She did not say anything but unhooked the towel from around her waist and let it fall to the floor.

'The golden fleece! It's gone!' I cried out in mock horror, as I stared down at her now shaved crotch.

She looked down and slid her hand across her stomach to the arrowhead of reddened flesh.

'You know if feels really different, a bit weird.' She said. 'Not sure if I like it. Well, it will grow back.' She tipped her head to one side. 'Though it does feel strangely liberating.' She grinned at me, skipped back a couple of steps then leapt in the air. As she landed she spun around in a pirouette, hands about her head, one leg out. 'Like, I'm a spirit of something!' She cried. 'Of art, or beauty!'

'You might want to dim the lights or close the blinds, spirit of art or beauty.'

'Why? Many people will see me naked like this soon enough.' Catherine laughed. 'I'm thinking of doing the opening nude as well. A real bit of performance art that would be.'

'I'm not sure that's a good idea.'

She walked over to the light switches, flicking them off, turning the studio dark until the only illumination was from the lights beyond the windows.

'Oh, don't be such a fuddy-duddy. Now let's get you naked and you can see what it feels like.'

'There's no way you're shaving me!'

'No,' she said, walking back to me. 'What *I* now feel like… to *you*.'

'Ah.'

More snow fell, clotting into a sold mass, smothering and smoothing out everything it covered with white cold curves.

'Keep?' I asked.

'Get rid.' Simon replied.

I helped Simon pick up the huge, near life-sized, framed copy of the 'Marilyn Diptych'. We carried it through to the first room of his studio, the boardroom as I thought of it, and rested against the wall along with the rest of his belongings that were in the 'get rid' side of the room.

'That's the last of it.' Simon said. 'The stuff I needed help with, anyway. Thanks'

'No problem.'

I stepped back to look at the fifty head shots of Monroe in the screen print, one half of them in garish false colour, the other in various degrees of faded black and white.

'You know I never really appreciated Warhol before,' I said. 'But he's starting to grow on me now.'

'You can have it you want.' Simon replied.

'Oh no, don't want anything like this near me. Too distracting. And depressing – that I'll never do anything to match it. Love Monroe, though. She made some great movies. And she was so beautiful. Often forget that, her being an icon and everything. Got a real crush on a few years back, when I started appreciating those classic films more.'

'Not really.' Simon said. 'Beauty, that is. She was a brilliant actress – definitely underrated on that account. And I had that crush too. But she was not that beautiful. Not a natural beauty anyway.'

'What, all the make-up?'

'Yes, but not only that. She had plastic surgery, even before her first film. A chin implant to make her features look more even, more striking. She was an icon. But the reality? Not so great. Not a pleasant person by all accounts. Warhol did the best thing, making her this artwork. Making her all surface, all image.'

'Thanks, you're just destroyed all my illusions about her.'

'Sorry.' Simon smiled. 'But you've married your classic beauty anyway.

I laughed.

'We're a long way from husband and wife.'

'As good as and you'll have the place to yourselves now. Your own nest together.'

'What do you mean?'

'Mark said he's moving out too, told me this morning. Said he needs more space like I do. So he can sort the bugs in his 'meta-art' project, his art production line machine thing.'

'So it'll be just us two in our penthouse and the rest empty below.'

'You could get some more artists in. Or take a floor each.'

'No, we're settled as we are.' I waved around the room. 'And we can use this space for meetings and like for all of us. Not that there's that much we do now. As a collective together.'

'I think that was inevitable.' Simon said. 'Us drifting apart. At least with the art. But it's not like we are never going to see each other again.'

'No, but it still seems a bit like the end of an era.'

'Six today,' Mark said.

'Not bad,' Simon replied. He swayed back slightly, slumping against the wall. 'No, not bad. What's your high score again?'

'Twelve! Twelve in one day. That includes two in one carriage.'

'So how many days in total?'

'I think it's... yeah, fifteen now. Fifteen days without a break.'

'That beats mine by a long way. Twelve is the best I've done.'

'Yeah, but I have to get the tube to my studio every day, that's an advantage... but I've seen them other places now too.'

'I know... buses, cafés, pubs, parks, every-bloody-where. So I'm sure I'll get the record back soon.'

'What are you two talking about?' I said, interrupting.

'Corelli spotting.' Mark said, turning to me. 'Don't you do it?'

'What? No? What are you talking about?'

'*Captain Corelli's Mandolin.*' Simon said. 'Look, next time you are out check how many people you see reading it. We keep track of how many days in row we see them. A bit of friendly competition.'

'So what's it like?' I asked.

They both looked confused.

'What?' Mark said.

'The novel – *Captain Corelli's Mandolin*, what's it like?'

'Oh, god,' Mark said. 'You don't expect us to actually join them, do you!'

'The horror!' Simon cried out.

I laughed then drained my champagne flute.

We were all at Simon's party for his new show – *Are UFOs Ghosts From The Future?* The title was apparently taken from a book on modern myths and legends Simon had bought from some remaindered bookshop. He had placed adverts asking for stories of people's encounters with aliens. Then he had done exactly the same thing but with angels instead. The resulting correspondences formed the centrepiece of the exhibition that now surrounded us. It was hard to tell from which side the various letters and drawings he had been sent came from. The confusion had been deliberately increased by Simon sending items from the two different groups to each other, asking for comments, so that their beliefs seemed to mix and merge over time.

The exhibition was housed in a new space I had leased on behalf of the collective to show our art, two shops knocked together and converted into a number of display spaces – 'The Feather Gallery'. That night the place was packed out with all the usual faces. Music thudded through from the next room where Simon had installed what he said was an experiment in audio art. Several of the sharpest up-and-coming DJs had been invited via the hippest agencies in town. In addition there were a number of pedestrian wedding-disco types Simon had hired from the *Yellow Pages*. Each was taking it in turn to play their music and run their own light show. There had been some random and odd clashes but for the most part the two sides seemed to have found some common ground and had started working well with each other and there were quite a few people dancing. I was certain Simon was more than a bit disappointed by this outcome, but he was not showing it.

'So, Jason?' Mark asked. 'You still doing those castle things?'

'Pretty much. They keep selling.' I took another flute of champagne from a passing waiter. 'Though I've been thinking of using maps in a different way. That they can go way beyond just mapping the land, actually show peoples' lives – a narrative. Like there's this Victorian map that shows all the deaths caused by the water from a pump in London that was tainted with cholera. This was before they knew what was causing all the deaths, part of trying to find out why. One black dot for each death. Very moving, seeing it like that, the rows and clusters of them – especially where there's a block of them in one building, a whole family wiped out – the tragedy behind just a simple pattern. Plus also how they are used in war – for the planning, the execution and the aftermath, the redrawing of the map after the conflict. All those deaths hidden behind that one small change, all those black dots.'

'A whole life coming down to just one black dot.' Simon said. 'That's a powerful image.'

'And take Africa.' I took a swig of champagne. 'The way the continent was seized and all that effort put into exploration and claiming territory and all the people who were exploited and in the end it was just lines on a map. I mean don't worry about tribal boundaries that have existed for millennia. Fuck all that! They just redrew it and we are still living with the consequences – the civil wars and all that. There's loads to go on, but it's finding a way to do it in art. That's what's got me stumped.'

'Tell me about it.' Mark said. He lit a cigarette. 'All this time and I still can't get my bloody art production-line machine working how I want to.'

'You want me to take a look?' I asked 'I'm no expert, but I might spot something.'

'Thanks. But it's not so much that it doesn't work, it's that it's just not working how I want it. But I'll keep plugging away, get there in the end.' He turned to Simon. 'So what are you saying with all this? God is dead? That the way you going now?'

'Not so much dead as replaced,' Simon said. 'I was thinking of heading off and doing something on horoscopes, maybe print some fake ones. See what I can get people to believe.'

'What about those in the other room?' Mark said. 'The abstracts?'

'Yeah, I liked them.' I said. 'Didn't realise they were copies of photographs at first. Well, blurred and out of focus photographs. I suppose the 'rejected' stickers you had painted on were a bit of give away, though.'

'The thing is, they're too easy to do.' Simon said. 'I could keep doing them forever, if they take off.' He looked at me and smiled. 'I mean you do alright.'

'Hey, I do put some effort into it!'

'Only joking. But I want to create art with meaning behind it – something philosophical, something political. Saying something, anyway. Like the way you're heading. I think abstract is a dead end for me.' He took a sip of his champagne. 'Where's Catherine anyway?' He asked.

'Gone to powder her nose.'

'Oh, really?'

'Not like that!'

'You sure?'

'Yeah, I'm sure.'

'I thought you had to be together at all times now,' Mark said. 'Stand next to each other in case some journalist shows up – what was that article, 'The First Couple of Art'?'

'That was such rubbish! But I suppose it beats slagging off Catherine for doing that nude work.'

'Don't knock it.' Simon said. 'It's all good publicity. Embrace it. Being an artist is a much about the person doing it as what they actually do. For a long time now. Look at Warhol. Gilbert and George. I mean Mark's got that whole gay, working class, mechanic thing–'

'Thank you, duckie,' Mark interrupted with camp exaggeration.

'You've got the couple thing. I've just got boring me.' Simon said.

'So you are saying me and Catherine are Gilbert and George? I'd have said that was Fred and Ginger. They are here tonight, I take it?'

'Somewhere,' Mark said.

'Like we should dress the same, then?' I said. 'Well, Catherine actually does borrow my clothes now and then.'

'And you never borrow hers?' Mark asked with a wink.

'What are you lot talking about?'

I turned. Catherine was at my shoulder. She was dressed in black trousers and a plain, wine-coloured shirt. Her hair had grown out to just beyond stubble length. No longer a skinhead but a suedehead, she had told me. She had dyed it a very pale blonde, almost white. Her face was very pale as well, except round the eyes where she had used make-up to darken it right down – her panda-look she was calling it. More like Pris from *Blade Runner* I had told her.

'About me being a transvestite.' I said.

'Fair enough.' Catherine pulled a tissue out of her sleeve and wiped her nose.

'Still can't shake that cold?'

'No, you were right about being nude all the time. And I've just had a bloody nosebleed. At least this shirt is the right colour not to show it.'

'Oh, are you all right now?' I asked, concerned, a hand on her back. 'You want to go home?'

'No,' She stuffed the tissue back up her sleeve. 'I want a dance!'

She grabbed my hand and pulled me towards where the music was coming from.

I turned to look at Simon and Mark but they just smiled. Simon made waving away motions.

'Better do as the lady says.' Mark added.

As we approached the other room I put my arm around Catherine, feeling her ribs through her shirt.

'God, you are getting skinny.' I chided. 'You need to slow down on all that exercise, eat a bit more.'

'Got to burn up that energy somehow.' She said, voice loud. 'And I'm not skinny. I've been much worse than this. But don't worry, I won't lose any more. Don't need to, now we are the perfect couple!'

'Oh god, you're believing your own publicity!'

'Only the good stuff. Come on!' She said, leading me into the disco room just as someone cued up 'Firestarter'. I wondered which of the two sides it had been.

'And this is too perfect as well,' Catherine shouted as the first stabbing seconds of the song hit the room.

She laughed as she started to dance, as the skittering drum beat came in, aping the head-shakes from the video for each booming pulse of bass.

Then, as she grinned back at me under the disco lights, I realised what her new look, her make-up design, reminded me of – a skull.

Catherine went from the nude work to series of 'mask' pieces – photographing herself as a domino wearing burglar in striped top and swag bag over her shoulder, a guest at a Venetian masked ball, a balaclava-wearing terrorist, The Phantom of the Opera, Zorro and Catwoman.

After a brief *Tomb Raider* obsession she had flirted with doing something based on Lara Croft, but she backed out in the end, thinking it unimaginative.

From *Tomb Raider* Catherine moved on to *This Life*. I watched in sympathy but I could never get into it, even when I devised a drinking game around it: wobbly camera move – take a drink; character swears – take a drink; character moans about work, their love life or life in general – take a drink; character shags – finish your drink. The following mornings we would watch the *Telly Tubbies* nursing our hangovers.

I bought a pair of Levis off the back of the Babylon Zoo 'Spaceman' ad, feeling guilty afterwards for so easily falling for the pitch.

They finally caught the Unabomber and it really did turn out to be a mad genius living alone in a shack.

The country went mad when football came home with the European Cup. One hot night found me and Catherine screaming at the huge screen of a projection television – packed into a barn-like pub like it was a terrace – for our final penalty shoot-out. I actually felt slightly sad walking back to the studio, singing the 'Three Lions' song but substituting 'Football's Buggered Off' into the chorus.

An embittered ex-scout leader shot sixteen children and a teacher up in Scotland and then nothing seemed funny for a while.

By default I ended up running the Feather Gallery, with help from Catherine – using the experience she had gained from the part-time gallery work she had done while studying. It had been agreed – suggested by Simon actually – that we received a larger cut of the profits from it for all our work. We put on exhibitions by other artists whenever it was free of the collective's art. I found I actually enjoyed it almost as much as creating my own pieces, seeing satisfaction in others doing well.

I slowed down the rate of production of my own art, leaving behind the castle inspired pieces to start 'The Conflict Series' – maps based before, during and after a war between two imaginary countries.

Simon continued to gain interest with his new work, the abstracts sold very fast so he kept making them – farming out most of the grunt work to hired artists – but he still continued to work on increasingly complicated postal work. Mark, however, seemed to be producing almost nothing. But when asked about it, he claimed he was working on a number of new projects – projects he could not show us yet, but was certain would kick-start his career.

I was asked to redesign the interior of night-club, but did not enjoy the process. I had had plenty of ideas after another trip to Japan – this time taking Catherine with me – from both what I had seen and the cyberpunkish magazines and comics I had brought back with me. But I soon realised it was much easier to work in a fantasy land. The shaking heads of the builders, saying what I had drawn was either flat-out impossible, or the building would collapse if they went ahead with it, became a familiar sight. The continually redrafting of plans and swotting up from architectural textbooks seemed too much like a real job, though I did get a fancy coffee-table book of my designs out of it.

I went to see *Trainspotting* twice on my own, and twice again with Catherine. We both loved it, thought it was the first film in years that really seemed to speak to both of us even though we were neither junkies nor living in squalor, that the whole vibe of it just rang so true.

Hale Bopp went over and we went out to Catherine's parents' place so we could see it without the light pollution of the city, never imagining that on the other side of the world a whole cult could be killing themselves in the hope of beaming up to it.

Blair came to power; Labour in at last. They said we were living in Cool Britannia, the best time in years for the arts, a rising wave of creation that this new government would only encourage. Catherine and I turned down the invite to Number Ten but we did end up a minor footnote – inevitably the art-couple thing again – in the 'London Swings Again' issue of *Vanity Fair* with Liam Gallagher and Patsy Kensit on the cover.

We did not know it at the time, but that would mark the end of it, for Cool Britannia, for us, that the wave would soon come crashing down.

We were eating a curry at our favourite restaurant. We were on the final course, I dug a spoon into my *kulfi* whilst Catherine sipped her coffee.

'I just feel that's it all got away from me.' Catherine said as she put down her cup, and picked up a paper napkin. She had been tearing tiny pieces off it throughout the meal, sprinkling them into the ashtray.

Her hair was grown out again, and she had recently dyed it a sooty black. She had taken to wearing smart dark business suits along with expensive-looking bulky leather handbags and lots of make-up.

'I can't seem to concentrate,' she continued while I ate a spoonful of my almond-flavoured ice-cream. 'To knuckle down to it like I used to. Everything just rattles around my head. Nothing seems to stick. Nothing good, anyway.'

She looked down at the napkin in her hands and put it back down on the table, picking up her coffee again.

'Everyone has dry patches. What about video?' I asked

'I've only just started playing around with it.' She replied.

'Well, there you go. Just keep on playing around with it. Bound to lead to something.'

'Hopefully. Soon.'

I put down my spoon and reached across the table for her hand. 'I know what you need, what we both need. A holiday.'

'That,' she said, smiling fully for the first time that evening, 'is a splendid idea.'

The snowflakes fell thick and fast and steady.

A breeze picked up, swirling the flakes in the air. The breeze strengthened to a softly moaning wind that drifted the snow up into high banks.

I was lying face down on a beach in Ibiza, chin propped up on folded hands, staring into the sand, seeing universes in every grain.

We had rented a villa on one of the quieter parts of the island. The holiday so far had been trips to town for nights of heavy partying then lazing on our local beach or wandering around the nearby wooded hills during the afternoons after recovering.

Earlier that morning we had returned from yet another night of clubbing, collapsing together on the bed as the sun rose. I had woken a few hours later, drank down a bottle of lemonade then wandered out to the beach for a swim. After a few hours snoozing on the sand I had woken to a revelation.

'Hey, I was wondering where you'd got to!' I heard Catherine call out from behind me. I rolled over. Walking towards me, she shimmered in the sun. She wore a skimpy gold bikini and her skin was sun-bronzed and oiled. Her blonde hair was gelled up and scraped back. Big-gold framed sunglasses covering half her face. A faint smell of coconuts wafted off her.

'I've just thought of my next piece.' I said, shading my eyes.

'Let's get something to eat, and you can tell me all about it.'

'So I had the idea this morning. While lying on the beach staring up at the sky, staring up at the sun. Then rolling over and looking at the sand – the grains – in front of me. Then thinking back to seeing the night sky just a few hours before. Seeing the milky-way – which you forget about, living in town drowned out by the street lights. All those stars in it. Billions… And beyond that, billions of galaxies the same, with billions of stars in them in turn. Lying there just spacing out on the thought that our sun is just one of them. That big bright bastard that gives us everything is just one out of billions of billions. Like one grain of sand, not just in one beach, but every damn beach in the world!'

The woman sitting beside me nodded. Her name, she had told me, was Angelina.

'Yeah, I can see that,' she said.

'Anyway I remembered seeing this film when I was kid. Canadian, I think it was, but they showed it on telly several times. There's this kid on a boat with a dog and the viewpoint, well it zooms out and out and we are looking down on them like from a plane. Then from higher and higher and we see the country, then the whole earth. Then beyond that, to the solar system .Then our galaxy, then all the galaxies and on out to the edge of the universe. Then it stops and zooms back in, the music going backwards, real fast to the boy on the boat again. It pauses, then the music starts again and we zoom down to where we see this insect – a mosquito – on his arm. Then down into the mosquito. Then into its blood stream, into the red cells. Then down into their molecules. Then down into to the very atoms they are made up of. Then it stops again and zooms back up, music reversing, back to the boy on the boat with his dog again. Back to where we started. The end. Bloody amazing. Outer space and inner space all in one journey. So I do these maps and plans as art and–'

I glanced over to her but Angelina was looking away, looking down at the glass on the table, slowly turning it with the tips of her fingers on the rim.

'Oh god, I'm not boring you am I? I've got this terrible habit of going off and–'

'Oh, no. It's interesting.' Angelina smiled.

She was Hispanic but I could not decide if her unusually dark skin was natural or that she had just been working on her tan for some time. Her eyes were deep pools with very dark irises. Her straw-coloured hair has been plaited into corn-rolls. She wore a baggy white T-shirt with the outline of the island printed on it – my comments on the map had started the conversation – and a short white skirt. She was bare-foot with toes painted white, like her fingernails. Her legs were long and shapely and there seemed to be this strange heat coming straight off her.

She had told me she was Venezuelan, but grew up in California, which made sense of her exotic accent that I had not been able to place at first – half Valley Girl, half Latin inflections.

We were sitting together on the terrace of Space listening to the chill out-music, the night beyond us gradually blueing with the pre-dawn.

She looked puzzled for a second.

'That film? I think I might have seen it, but different, I remember.'

'Yeah, someone else remade it, a few years back. You probably saw that other version.'

'So you think about those kinds of things a lot?' She laughed.

'Yes, I'm afraid I do, I think my girlfriend thinks I'm a bit of an anorak at times.'

She reached over to me, her hand leaving her glass. Her fingers touched my bare arm, small intense patches of heat.

'An anorak? A coat isn't it?'

'Well yeah, but in Britain it's also a geek, a nerd… you know?'

'You are no nerd. I can see that. Where did your girlfriend go?' Her hand was still on my arm, resting casually.

'To get a drink. She's probably having another dance as well.'

'You don't dance?'

'Oh yes, just getting tired that's all.'

'I can help you with that.' She smiled reaching for her bag, her hand leaving my arm at last. 'I have some coke.'

'I'm not really into that.'

'Ah, but I saw your girlfriend, in the toilet. Actually I thought she might be, now?'

'No. Not if she's already done some.'

Angelina nodded, putting down her bag. She picked up her drink and turned to me. 'So tell me more about this art thing.'

'I'm using the film for inspiration. I've done maps before, but this time I want to use different scales. From the microscopic – well, right down to the atomic – upwards.' I looked up imagining the work I would soon be doing in front of me. 'Start with the diagram of a single atom. Then maybe a grid of them or the structure of a single silicon gate. Then the layout of a computer chip. The schematic of the computer itself. A plan of the room the computer is in. An architectural drawing of the house that contains the room. Then a map of the house's street, all its neighbours. Then the district. A city, region, country, continent. A world. Then a diagram of a solar system. A galaxy. A cluster of galaxies. Then… well I suppose that's it. All imaginary. A whole new universe. Can't wait to get back to get started. It's only that I promised Catherine a complete break from work that I've not started now – doing some sketches.' I looked back at Angelina. 'So, what do you do?' I asked her.

She had placed her drink down again and was staring right into my eyes. 'Oh, nothing as interesting as you – a bit of modelling. Taking acting lessons – a few bit-parts. Keep hoping for my lucky break. But nothing yet.' She rolled her eyes and that hand was back on my arm again. 'Apart from some offers I'm not going to take – not with me being a good Catholic girl.'

She leaned towards me, moving closer and I could suddenly feel the heat of her thigh pressing through my thin cotton slacks. I tried to move away from her but I was already pressed into the side of the seat.

'You know, pornography.'

Before I could form an answer to that the DJ came on with something about waking us up by 'taking it back to the old skool'. A song started, something I recognised… I glanced up. It took me a few more seconds to recognise what the track was, then I groaned.

'I never expected to hear that here.'

Angelina was giggling.

'The DJ was flirting with me earlier, asking my favourite record. I told him it was this.'

'The Macarena!'

She looked at me mock serious. 'It is a great song from my home country.'

'I thought it was Spanish?'

She waved that off. 'Pah! They stole it from us!'

Then she smiled at me. 'I also think it's funny because it's become a song for children's' parties when – if you listened to the lyrics – it is so filthy!'

'Is it?'

'Oh, yes. It is about a woman who wants an orgy.'

'What!'

'Listen to the lyrics! 'His two friends were so fine!''

Her hand returned to my arm and stroked along it and back.

'You know, I like you. And your girlfriend,' Her voice low, her head tilted to one side. 'I'm not that good a Catholic girl and you are both so fine.'

I pushed myself up out of my seat.

'No, I think–'

I turned and practically walked into Catherine.

'Ah, your beautiful woman returns.' Angelina said behind me.

Catherine looked from me to Angelina with a quizzical look.

'Glad you are back I was thinking of making a move.' I said quickly. 'I think I need to crash.'

'Right now?' Catherine asked. 'Really?'

'Yes, really.'

Later, while we undressed with the first rays of dawn stretching across the bedroom floor, I told Catherine what I thought Angelina was hoping for. She laughed for quite some time.

'No, I don't think I'm going to share you with any other women.' She said as she enfolded me in her arms.

'Actually, now I'm used to the idea… we could go back. I mean, I've always wondered what you got up to in those single-sex boarding schools you attended. Those long nights, crammed in together in those dorm rooms. All those girls and their torrid emotions. And– *Owww!*'

The next morning, the last full day of our holiday, we made our way into the local town for our usual late breakfast / early lunch. The place seemed strangely subdued, even for a Sunday. We wandered into a café we had eaten at before. The owner was leaning against the bar watching a small television placed up on the counter. I was surprised to see Tony Blair on the screen before it cut away to a local news presenter. At another table a woman was silently weeping.

'What's going on?'

The owner turned to me.

'She's dead.'

'Who?'

'Diana. Your princess. She's dead.'

We returned to a London choking with flowers.

At Kensington House I held Catherine's hand as we walked among the crowds. At the gate she let go, reached into a pocket to pull out a single, grey, tatty-looking pigeon's feather. She let it float down to the ground at the edge of the sea of bouquets.

Sensation, at the Royal Academy, with the cream of Saatchi's collection, featured singular contributions from each of us. I attended the opening with Catherine, but later went again alone, unofficially, as just another punter. It was shortly after 'Myra' – the Hindley portrait made of children's hand-prints – had been vandalised. The ink stain left on the floor, the gap in the hanging – they both had a power of their own, almost as much as the original had.

For a long time I stared at 'The Great Bear' – a reproduction of the London Underground map with the names of the stations on each line replaced by those of different groups of people – famous footballers, comedians, saints, scientists and many more. I had been briefly jealous when I had first heard about it, wishing I had had the idea, but in front of it I just felt quiet admiration.

The wind rose again, howling. Whipping the snow hard it created a snowstorm.

A blizzard.

White out.

'So you are staying with video then?'

'For the foreseeable,' Catherine said sipping on her vodka and tonic. She was sitting on the opposite side of the pub table to me. Tonight she had put a side-parting into her hair – dyed dark again – and wore a trouser suit. We were catching up with each other after both being away – her to shoot a music video in New York, me spending a few days with my family.

'There just seem so much more possibilities than photography. I got talking to a producer who turned up to the shoot about doing a short film.'

'Sounds great.' I said swallowing a mouthful of beer.

'The ideas slowly seem to be coming now – for something new and interesting, building on the self-portraits that–'

She was interrupted by a shout behind us. 'Nice one Tommo!'

Catherine winced.

The pub was not one we frequently drank in, but one we had fancied a change. And it had seemed quiet when we entered, which was what we wanted, to talk, with maybe a couple of games of pool later.

However, soon after we had sat down, a gang of male besuited after-work drinkers had arrived. Ties off, obviously several pubs into a crawl, they had taken over the pool table. But what was most annoying was they had programmed the jukebox for the whole of Oasis' *Be Here Now* – singing along to every track.

The current song finished in yet another meltdown of fuzzy guitars. The next one was a change of pace, though – Blur's 'Beetlebum'.

'Thank god for that,' I said. 'I wouldn't have minded so much if it had been one of the first two albums.'

'Who put this shit on?' One of the pool-players called out.

'Yes, I wonder who?' Catherine said innocently with a raised eyebrow.

'Oh, you're wicked.' I said my hand reaching under the table to squeeze her knee.

She just smiled.

I zipped my jacket right up as we left the pub against the cold of the night. As usual Catherine was not even wearing a coat, only her suit jacket. I linked arms with her and she leaned against me as we walked down a quiet side street towards the nearest Tube station.

'Yeah,' she said. 'I think I'll just take the camera out tomorrow. Go down one of the parks. Just set up the camera and film–'

'Oi!' A shout behind us.

I looked at Catherine as she stopped to looked back.

'Yeah, you!'

Three of the men who had been playing pool back in the pub were walking behind us.

'So high and fucking mighty, talking about your fucking art exhibitions and fucking videos and fucking what have you!'

The one in the middle jabbed a finger at us, his words a slurred Mancunian. His overcoat gaped open to show a beer-gut with his shirt half-out of his trousers. Next to him, one of his drinking companions – shorter, skinnier and rat-faced – sniggered.

'Just leave it, Mickey.' The man at other his side said – balding, obviously older – stepped in front of him.

'No Ed, it was definitely them.' He pushed the man to one side. 'Putting on fucking Blur when we were having an Oasis night. Been planning that for ages! I saw her do it. The fucking cow, thought it was a bloke at first though–'

'What, you own the fucking jukebox?' Catherine suddenly shouted, steeping forward towards them. 'The whole pub? Fuck off!'

I put my hand on her shoulder. 'Catherine, let's just go home.'

'Yeah, better listen to your man, 'Catherine'.' Mickey sneered. 'Though I say, 'man'. He probably likes you dressing like a bloke.'

I stepped past Catherine.

Mickey held up a fist, waving it at me

'Yeah, you want some do you? Art-queer!'

'Look, we don't want any–'

'Queer?' I heard Catherine laugh behind me. 'You're the one who's with all the other men.'

He took a swing at me. I saw the blow coming and instinctively stepped back outside it, my old martial arts' training kicking in. I grabbed his coat by the end of the sleeve of his flailing arm and yanked him forward, unbalancing him. I punched him hard with my free hand, catching him in the side of his jaw. He staggered, turning away from me. I kicked out, stamping my foot forward onto his backside. He stumbled, falling to the ground.

'Fuck.'

On his hands and knees he spat out blood.

'Do you want some more!' I shouted, stepping forward.

'No, no!' He spluttered, his hand to his mouth.

'Look, we're sorry mate,' His elder friend said, starting to help him up.

The rat-faced one was at his other side. 'Just too much to drink. No harm done, right?'

'Take him home.' I said, dropping my hands.

I watched them walk away while my breathing returned to normal, rubbing my knuckles.

'Oh god, I'm sorry.' Catherine said behind me. 'That was stupid, antagonising him like that.'

'No, it's alright.' I said turning back to her. 'It was alright in the end.'

'But you could have been really hurt! I'm sorry. It's just… at the worse of it. The bad times. When I was really thin. I used to get teased for looking like a boy.'

She looked down at her trouser suit.

'Oh, I never should have dressed like this.'

She put her hands to her hair, mussing up the parting, eyes closed against sudden tears.

I reached for her hands, pulled them away from her head. Then I held her.

'It's all right. It's over now. Dress how you want. He was just a pissed idiot. A bully.'

She brought up a hand to wipe her eyes and nose with her fingers.

'Yeah.' She gave me a small smile. 'You're my man, though… protecting my honour like that.'

I laughed. 'Not just an art-queer then?'

'No, my warrior!'

'Come on, let's go home.' I said, turning towards the Underground Station. 'I did kick his arse though? Didn't I?'

'Literally.'

'Wake up! Wake up, warrior!'

I stared around me, disorientated. 'Song 2' was pounding out – loud, booming, distorted.

Catherine was standing over me with wild eyes. Her hair was rough, spiked up. She was naked.

Lights flashed around us. A spinning glitter ball had been set up on Catherine's side of the room to send motes of light chasing each other around the walls and ceiling.

'Wake up! We've got to do it now!' Catherine urged me, pulling back the duvet. She seized my hand and tired to pull me up. 'It's going to be the perfect artwork. The greatest piece we ever did together! But we have to do it now.'

She let go of me and skipped away to the centre of her half of the room. All the furniture had been pushed back to one side. White sheets covered the floors. Lights and several cameras set up on tripods pointed back at her from around the edges of the space.

'Come on!' She shouted back at me over the music, waving me towards herself. 'Take me!'

I pulled myself to my feet. I looked around for the source of the music – so loud it blotted out all thought.

'Love me!' Catherine shouted. 'Make love to me now!'

'What?' I stepped towards her.

'Come on fuck me! Fuck me, I'm going to film it. 'A Prize For My Champion' it'll be called.' She spoke fast, the words crashing over each other in a gabble. 'Mix it in with film of you boxing, fencing, street fighting, whatever. It'll be brilliant. Now fuck me! Come on! Come on, I'm all yours!'

I grabbed her arms.

'Jesus, Cat... I can't think! Let's talk about it in the morning. Or at least let me turn that fucking music off!'

'No, I want to film us fucking. Right now! It will be our ultimate collaboration. Us, together, for the whole world to see! The perfect couple. The first couple of art!'

'No, Catherine!' I shouted back. 'I love you, but–!'

'I told you never to use that word!' Her eyes flashed. 'And it's not about love! It's about sex. Sex as art. Sex at its most brutal. The violence between man and woman. Fuck me! Fuck my cunt! Feel it!' Grabbing my hand, she tried to force down between her legs.

'No!'

I snatched my hand up and away from her.

'Do it!' Her fists, two tight knots of flesh, hammered against my chest. 'Do it, you cunt!'

I try to grab her wrists. 'Christ, you're acting crazy. I–'

I'm not fucking crazy!'

Shrieking, she suddenly clawed up at my face.

Without thinking I turned away, one arm swinging round, catching her across the face, open-handed.

She stopped. Suddenly very still, she looked back at me, breathing hard, as I turned back to her. There was a red mark on her cheek. Slowly, she brought up her fingertips to it.

'Oh god. I'm sorry I...' I held out my arms. 'Catherine, I–'

She stepped back and turned away from me.

'No, it's okay.' She said. 'I'm the one who's sorry. My fault. I was stupid.'

She stumbled off towards the bathroom.

'Catherine!' I called out, stepping forward.

'Just leave me. Go back to bed. Forget this ever happened.' She disappeared into the bathroom, shutting the door on me before I could stop her.

'Catherine!'

I tried the door but she had locked it.

'Catherine!' I rapped on the door, wincing from where earlier I had bruised my knuckles. 'Catherine!'

I shook my head and turned away. I switched off the CD, glad of the sudden silence. Walking to Catherine's side of the room I turned off the lights and the video cameras, the glitter ball motor. I went back to the bathroom.

'Catherine, please.'

Still nothing.

I had a sudden vision of her – wrist out, knife in hand.

'Catherine if you don't answer me, I'm coming in!' I hit against the door, harder. 'Catherine!'

I stepped back, then charged into the door shoulder first. I crashed through in one blow, the lock splintering out of the thin door frame.

She was kneeling on the floor, bent over the toilet, a rolled up banknote in her mouth. She was holding a small piece of silver foil, a lit brass Zippo lighter underneath it.

A faint vinegary smell and a curl of smoke.

I slapped the foil out of her hand.

Making an odd mewling sound, she dropped the lighter and twisted around, scrambling for the tinfoil on the floor. Bent over I grabbed her around the waist with both arms and pulled her back. The banknote fell from her mouth as I manhandled her out of the room.

'No, I need it! The calm! I need the calm!'

I spun her around, getting between her and what she was after. She squirmed beneath me like an eel as I pressed her down to the floor. She twisted round to face me.

'How long?' I held her to me hard.

'The calm!'

'How long!'

She looked at me, eyes wide. Tears. Trembled. Said nothing.

Then she looked away.

'Too long,' she whispered.

London was frozen. Smothered white from last night's snowfall. But its pristine beauty had already been marred, turned to slush by car tyres and footfalls.

I watched the car edge into the courtyard then I turned and stepped away from the window.

'Catherine, they're here.'

She was slumped against the far wall. Wrapped in our duvet. A faint bruise on her cheek. She stared out at nothing, lost to her Discman.

I touched her shoulder but there was no reaction.

I gently took off the headphones, recognising the track from the tinny sounds I could hear – 'Exit Music (For A Film)' from *OK Computer*. It finished then immediately started again on repeat.

I pulled at the duvet, but she gripped at it hard, knuckles white.

'I'm so cold.' She whispered.

'Keep it for now, but it's time to go.'

She nodded, the smallest movement.

I helped her to her feet.

'I'm never cold. Why am I cold?' She looked bewildered.

I turned her towards the door.

'Oh, it snowed.' She said, glancing over to the window.

'Yes.'

'Let me look.'

She stepped over to the window. The duvet fell to the floor. Underneath she wore jeans and two of my jumpers.

'I loved it when it snowed. When I was a kid.' She said, looking out, crossing her arms across her chest, hugging herself. 'Snowflakes. Snow crystals, really. Used to make them out of doilies at Christmas – fold then up then cut them to make the patterns. Paint then silver and hang them up. Perfect six-sided patterns. All unique. All perfect.' She looked back at me. 'That's what they tell you – show you in the books – don't they? But it's not true, did you know that?'

I shook my head. 'No.'

'My turn to tell you something, then. No, most of them are not perfect. Not at all. They grow misshaped and non-symmetrical, damaged, deformed. Far from perfect.' She smiled, but it did not reach her eyes.

'We have to go, Catherine'

'I know.'

I led her downstairs to where the car was waiting. Two men in sober suits were standing beside it.

I kissed her on the cheek.

'Get well.'

'I'll try.' She stepped towards the car then suddenly turned back to me, her face suddenly animated. 'Please don't tell my parents! I don't want them to know I've failed again.'

'Catherine, I already have.'

She stared at me, her face still and hard again. She said nothing. Then she turned her back to me. One of the men helped her inside the car.

'Don't worry, we'll look after her,' he said.

I watched them pull away, the car turning from the end of the ally into the road and disappearing. And I kept watching, my breath clouding in front of me, until finally the cold forced me back inside.

11 COFFEE STAINED MUG

An oblong of light reached up from the window to where the wall turned in towards the ceiling, then on out across the ceiling proper. I was lying back staring up at the delicate pattern of refracted light caused by rain streaming down the outside of the glass – an abstract, ever-changing canvas of grey on grey.

I had woken a few minutes earlier to the sound of the rain, alone in the bed. A sudden moment of panic until I realised where I was and the previous night's events came back to me. The bedroom door was open slightly and I could hear the woman – Louise, I remembered – moving around in the flat.

A knock. I twisted around, pushing myself up onto one elbow, the duvet sliding down my torso. Louise leaned around the door frame.

'You're awake then.' She was already dressed in jeans and a sweatshirt. 'Want a coffee? How do you take it?'

'Thanks. Black, no sugar please.'

I made a move to get up, but she held up her hand.

'No, it's alright – I'll bring it to you.'

And then she was gone. She returned a few seconds later with a steaming mug in her hand. She placed it down on the bedside cabinet next to an old paperback of *Jane Eyre*.

I sat upright and reached for the coffee. It tasted freshly ground.

'What time is it?'

'Just gone ten.'

'Damn, sorry. I'll get dressed and out of your way.'

'There's no rush. I've no appointments until later. You want a shower or a bath? Some breakfast?'

'A shower sounds great.'

I reached out to her, my hand against the curve of her hip, meeting her eyes. 'You want to join me?'

'No, I...' Her hand was on my mine, pulling it away. She stepped back.

'Ah, right.'

'No, sorry. Not now, but...' She leaned forward and gave me a quick peck on the forehead then quickly moved back to the door. 'I'll see you in a minute then.' She said before disappearing again.

Sitting together on her sofa, we spooned milk and cereal, listening to the rain outside.

After my shower, and dressing in yesterday's new shirt and trousers, I had rinsed out the coffee-stained mug in her tiny kitchenette. Louise had moved around me making us both breakfast. The inevitable minor collisions with each other were accompanied by small smiles and apologies.

Louise finished eating and waited for me, then took our bowls back to the kitchenette.

'I'll put some more coffee on.' She called out.

'Great.'

'So, what are you going to do now?'

'Start my life again, I suppose. Back to work… art of some kind, not sure what yet. But the ideas will come, eventually. I'll get rid of the studio though, definitely. Far too many bad memories there now… But as to what else? I don't know really.'

Louise came back into the room carrying two mugs of coffee. She was grinning.

'No. I meant, today? What are you going to do today?'

I smiled back as she handed me a coffee. She sat down beside me again.

'You said you had some stuff of Catherine's?' I asked. 'I'd better sort that out, take it off your hands.'

'It's in her locker. But I could handle that really, parcel whatever's there and send it on to you. Or her family. Whatever you want.'

'No, it's my responsibility.' I turned to her. 'Last night I was all for walking away from it. But this morning…? I'm not so sure. There's just so many unanswered questions still, The illustration. The tattoo. The prostitution… all of that behind my back. Why? I just can't accept I'll never know the answers. That I'll never know her, the real her. Not yet, anyway.' I sipped from my coffee. 'Oh and I'm sorry I jumped to the wrong conclusion about this place. Thinking it was a brothel or something.'

'That's all right. Problem with this profession. It could have been worse.'

'What do you mean?'

She slowly shook her head.

'The number of times, you've got a new customer – a guy, that is – lying there, you've told them all the details but ask them if there's any questions – out of politeness – and then they come back with, 'Do you do extras?', leering up at you like you're a piece of meat.'

'Oh, I see.'

'But the prostitution thing you say she was doing? I mean I thought she might not be telling me everything – why she wanted the work here and that – but I never thought she was hiding anything like that. Not at all.'

'Yeah. I know.' I sighed. 'I suppose I should go back to the studio. Go through all her stuff this time, see if she's got anything else hidden away. Any more clues to her other lives. Then there's her parents' place. I don't think they've touched her room – though we've hardly spoken since the funeral.'

'A pity I can't help you more,' Louise said. 'But she never mentioned anything about any of that. Never mentioned the art even. Just wish I'd known her more. Maybe I could have helped her.'

'Known her more. Yeah, so do I.'

I drank from my coffee and then looked down at the mug in my hands.

'About last night...' Louise broke the silence.

I looked over but she was looking away from me towards the window, holding her mug in both hands, elbows on her knees.

'The cards told me.' She continued. 'Very clear. But I thought you needed it too. Some extra physical therapy.' She smiled. "Extras', yes. And I think I probably needed it as much as you did. After hearing your story and... well I've been on my own for a while now. But...' She turned back to me. 'Anyway, let's just take it slow. I think it would be better for both of us. Yes?'

'You think I'm not over Catherine yet?

She just nodded.

'Yeah,' I said. 'I think you're right. Let's see how it goes.'

She finished her coffee then stood up.

'I know what you need.' She walked over to the book shelf and took down one of the packs of tarot cards.

Underneath was a folded dark blue cloth, and she picked that up too.

As she knelt down on the floor and spread out the cloth, I kept staring at the bookshelf, from where she had taken the cards.

There was something there. Something–

'A reading. Help you sort you head out.' Louise said.

I looked down towards her.

'What?'

'A tarot reading. To help you to decide what to do.'

She had taken the cards out of their box and spread them out face down on the cloth. She started swirling them around with circular sweeps of her hands.

'But I don't believe in any of that.'

She just gave a quick shake of her head then reached out a hand up towards me. 'You don't have to.' She beckoned with her fingers. I drank down the last of my coffee and put the mug down on the carpet. I slid off the sofa to sit down beside her.

'Don't think of it as telling the future.' Louise continued, taking hold of one of my hands and showing me how to stir the cards around like she had just done. 'Think of it as just something to, well, think about. A guide to what to do next. Like when you read your horoscope.'

I laughed. 'I don't read my horoscope!'

'What, never? Not once?'

'Well…'

'Exactly. Sometimes you don't see anything. Sometimes it's spot on–'

'But that's just chance.'

She shook her head. 'It might say. 'You are going on a journey.' And you hadn't been planning anything, but reading that you start to think, 'Actually, I've not been away for a while, perhaps I should book a holiday?' You see, it can affect you. Even if you say you don't believe in it. That's enough.' She put her hand on top of mine, halting my shuffling of the cards. 'Now the reading.'

'But–'

She looked right at me with a smile.

'Just try it, okay.'

I shrugged. 'Anything for a quiet life.'

'Pick a card.'

I reached for one and handed it face down to her. She turned it over and placed it down to one side of the cloth. The card showed an arrangement of thin double-headed arrows, plaited together to form an X-shape.

'Wands,' she said to herself. 'That's interesting. I don't think it's over then.'

'What? What's over?'

She turned to me. 'Come on, next card.'

I gave it to her and she turned it over – a skeleton with a scythe. 'Death'.

'That only means–'

'A change.' I said interrupting. 'I know that much. Not usually a death, just a change.'

She nodded. 'Another.'

This one was 'The Devil' – looking almost comical, a fat cartoon version with blue legs and wings.

'Great, you set this up?' I said, glancing towards her.

'Take it seriously!' She snapped back at me.

'Sorry.' I said, shocked to be so admonished. 'Look, if you want stop. I don't–'

'No, it's actually not that bad. The card.' She said, looking down at the cards, her tone returned to normal. 'It'd not evil or anything. Well… it represents self-bondage. You know, being stuck, not being able to make your mind up. That kind of thing. Another.'

The next card was a broken stone building – 'The Tower of Destruction'.

'That's change again.' Louise said. 'Looks worse than it is, but... no I should wait for them all before... next.'

I flinched when she turned over the card I gave her – 'The Hanged Man'.

'Again, it's not that bad.' Louise said, not realising the reason for my reaction. 'Just means a trail, a problem to solve that you will overcome. Something like that.'

'Right. It's okay, it's just...'

'What?'

'It doesn't matter. Let's finish this.'

I passed her the next few cards one at a time and she laid them out without further comment. Among them were several similar to the first one – wands, I remembered. Plus I noticed 'The Lovers' again, remembering it from last night. Finally a woman sitting on a throne – 'The High Priestess'.

'Is that you, then?'

She glanced at me, eyes hard. But then smiled.

'Maybe. She's a woman, one you know – a romantic connection.'

'Ah, I see. 'Maybe'.'

'She's fiery and passionate.'

'Definitely, then.'

Louise smirked. 'She's a key part anyway.'

I reached for the next card but Louise stopped me, a hand on my arm.

She turned to me. 'The next card is the last one. The result. I'll sum up what we have first.' She looked back at the cards. 'A lot of Major Arcana, the Minor dominated by Wands. It's all conflict. Struggle. With yourself, as much as anything else. An internal – a mental – as well as a physical, struggle.'

'That's what I've been doing, I suppose. Trying to sort out Catherine.'

'Yes, it's as much the past and the present as well as predicating the future.' She pointed to the cards. 'But the conflict. It's not over yet. 'The Devil' – shows you, or maybe someone else, but I'm sure it's you – trapped. Stuck. Think of it as something to fight against.'

'So it's a fight to break out of being stuck. Trapped, mentally?'

'Yes. But with all the wands… That makes me think it's going to turn physical.' She pointed to two of the cards. 'See these, the Seven and the Knight. That's a journey… a journey to battle.' She glanced back at me. 'That's all I can tell you.'

'The last one?' I asked.

She nodded.

I paused before picking another card, pondering my selection. Then I pulled one out at random and flipped it over.

The card showed a character dressed in jester's motley – 'The Fool'.

'The first and last card. End and beginning.' Louise said. 'Whatever happens, it'll be decisive.'

She turned over the cards I had drawn and started gathering them together with all the others.

'That's it?' I asked.

'That's it.' She said not looking at me, putting the cards back in the box. 'Do with it what you will.'

Louise folded up the cloth then stood and put it back on the shelf. I stood up too and stretched. She put the cards back on top of the cloth.

'I've not helped you, have I?' She said, still not looking at me.

'Well… I–'

'No, it's all right. I'll go get the master-key for the lockers. Get you Catherine's things.'

She moved towards the door.

'Louise.'

She stopped and turned back to me.

'Thanks. For that. And everything.'

She smiled. 'My pleasure. Honestly.'

'Do I have to cross your palm with silver now?'

She laughed and walked out the door without replying.

I smiled to myself and turned to look at the bookshelves, then frowned.

What was it?

It was just like when I was in the studio.

Not something moved this time, how could it be?

I scanned along the shelves.

Something...?

Then I saw it.

The book was end on, the title 'The Runes' running down its spine. But it was not the title itself that had drawn my attention but the way it was written. The typescript – some custom, hand-crafted font, all spindly black letters with lines intersecting at sharp angles – reminded me of...

I snatched the book off the shelf and flicked through it.

There! On one of the first pages, at the head of a list illustrating all the runes.

'Christ!'

'What?' Louise had just walked back into the room. She moved over to my side, looked down at the open book.

'That's it!' My finger stabbed down onto the page, at the symbol depicting the first rune. It was an upright line with two more extending away from it an acute angle – like half an arrow flight symbol or a stylised 'F'

'Catherine's tattoo!' I said. 'I mean it's a mirror image, but that's it.'

286

'The first one? *Fehu?*'

'Yes, what it's mean?'

'Money, I think. I'm not really into the runes. Not as much as the tarot, anyway.'

'Yes, it says here.' While she spoke I quickly flicked to the page that explained the rune's meaning. "Wealth, cattle'... well I suppose 'cattle' was money back then. But that doesn't make any sense. She was never that bothered about money. Didn't need to be...' I looked further down the page. 'Wait a minute, it says 'Reversed Meaning' here. That might explain it. *Fehu Reversed.* Loss. Slavery. Self-bondage. Devastation. Destruction.' Why would she want that tattooed on her?' I turned to Louise. 'Self-bondage – the Devil wasn't it?'

'It's not reversed. The symbol. Not from what you said.' Louise replied. 'Reversed means upside-down in this case. Some people do with it the tarot – well some, not me. You said it was flipped? The tattoo? A mirror image?'

'Yes.'

'That's not reversed then.'

I put the book back on the shelf.

'So, not an explanation after all. And I was sure I had just tied up a loose end.' I turned back to Louise. 'Never mind. You had better show me her locker then.'

She nodded. 'Follow me.'

Louise led me downstairs to the ground floor towards the reception where I had first entered the building. She opened the door of a small room with just a tiny frosted-glass window. There was a sink with a kettle and a microwave next to it. On top of the latter was a tray full of cups and mugs and jars of coffee and tea-bags. Opposite was a short row of upright lockers.

Louise went over to the latter, pulling out a key from her pocket. She slid it into the lock of one of the lockers but then she stopped and turned back to me as I waited in the doorway.

'Do you want to do this on your own?' She asked.

'No. I'd rather be with someone to be honest.' I said, stepping over to stand beside her. 'With you.'

'Thanks,' She said, patting my arm, then she unlocked the locker door and pulled it open.

Inside hung a short plain white uniform-like dress. Below was a pair of equally plain black mules. Above where the dress hung there was a shelf. I saw there was a small object almost hidden at the back. I reached in and pulled out a mobile phone, a standard looking Nokia. I tried to turn it on.

'Dead.'

'I've got a charger upstairs.' Louise said. 'It should work for that.'

'Yeah, I suppose it might hold some more secrets.'

I gave the locker one last check, pulling aside the dress but there was nothing else behind it. But there was something else on the shelf where the phone had been – a small scrap of folded paper. Some sort of leaflet, I saw when I unfolded it. A printed flyer for a night-club called 'Boiler Room' with an address somewhere in Clarkenwell. Below was *'THROB – every Tuesday. 8 till Late. Industrial. Noise. Punk. Goth. Metal. Alternative. And all things Dark. Dress: Leather, Latex, Lace. Comp One.'*

I passed it over to Louise.

'You ever heard of this?

'No. This her taste in music?'

'Nothing like this. Not the Catherine I knew, anyway.' I took the flyer back from Louise 'Tuesdays. That's tonight isn't it?'

'What? You're thinking of going?'

I shrugged. 'Most likely it's nothing. But if she ever went… there might be people there who knew her. Knew her in another identity. Might be able to find out more.'

Louise nodded down at my shirt.

'That's hardly leather, latex or lace.'

'You're right, better go shopping.'

I took the flyer back from Louise and folded it in half. I stepped back towards the door.

'Wait a minute.' Louise held out another key towards me. 'While I think of it. This is for upstairs, the fire-escape. I've not got a spare for the main door, but I'll get you one cut. I might be in bed when you get back tonight. If I'm asleep just wake me.'

'I was going to find a hotel. Somewhere close. Because—'

Louise took hold of my hand and put the key into it.

'I don't think you want to.' She was still holding my hand. 'I don't think either of us wants you to.'

'I thought you said to take it slow.'

'Not that bloody slow!' She laughed.

'All right then. I'll go and get my jacket.' I said pulling out my key ring to add the new key to it.

'It's on a hanger in the wardrobe.' Louise said.

'Got me domesticated already.'

'Hardly. Oh and the phone charger's in the lounge. Plugged in one of the sockets.'

She moved to the door and out into the corridor. I followed her.

'Come back down here and I'll let you out the front. Now, I had better get everything sorted before the girls turn up.'

Back in reception, after retrieving my jacket and leaving the phone on charge, I saw Louise was sitting behind her computer. She had a calendar program open. I could see a list of appointments for the coming afternoon.

'I'm free for a couple hours in the early evening, then another couple of appointments after that.' Louise said pointing at the screen. 'So you can pop back then if you want.'

She closed the calendar and clicked on an icon on the screen bringing up a small window showing CCTV footage of the alley and the street beyond it.

I turned up the collar of the jacket. 'Right, I'll see you later.'

'You've got no coat.' Louise said, standing. 'You'll get soaked. Hang on.' She went past me, back to the locker room.

I glanced back at her computer. I looked closer at the grey security camera view – cars passing along the road beyond the end of the alley plus a few pedestrians. I looked closer still, leaning forwards. I took the mouse and resized the window until it filled the screen. In the gaps between the cars, on the other side of the road, standing under the awing of a shop – a pale shape. It was blurred and grainy but I could just make out that it was a figure.

'Here you go!' I turned from the screen, Louise had returned with an umbrella. It was surprisingly masculine – long and black with a wooden handle.

'Lost property.' She said as she passed it to me, sitting down at the computer again.

Louise's hand went to the mouse, moving the cursor to close the window.

'No, wait!' The figure wore a pale long coat. Like before, returning from the Singh's shop to the studio. 'Fucking hell!'

'What?' Louise asked

I did not reply. I was already sprinting to the door. I twisted the lock back and yanked the door open then ran out into the alley, into the rain, the umbrella now forgotten. I ran to the street and would have sprinted straight out into the traffic but I could already see that she was gone.

If she had ever been there in the first place.

'I'm so sorry, about that.' I said to Louise after she let me back in. 'I thought I saw her. Catherine. Same thing happened to me couple of days ago.'

Louise had pulled up a freeze frame from the security footage. We both looked at it.

'It could be anyone. It's so blurred I'm not sure it's even a woman.' She turned to me. 'Seeing ghosts? And I thought I was supposed to the irrational one.'

'I must have looked a complete idiot.'

Her hand covered mine for a second.

'It's understandable.' She reached down for the umbrella where I had dropped it behind her desk and passed it back up to me. 'But it'll go away in time. Anyway, time you were away. The girls will be here any minute.'

'What, ashamed to show me off?'

She tutted. 'No, I want them doing some work, not fussing over you.'

I walked to the nearest tube station and travelled to Oxford Circus, thinking about the new identity I needed to create.

I started with buying a pair of black jeans from one of the chain stores along with some extra socks and underwear. I walked down Carnaby Street, and saw a pair of chunky scarlet motorcycle-style boots in a shop window, thinking them perfect. From the shop next door I bought a dark red shirt that had random streaks of black dye splashed across it.

I wondered on into Soho and found a retro shop. I left wearing a scruffed-up black leather jacket plus the clothes I had bought earlier, my suit in a bag. I hoped the obvious age of the coat would help disguise the fact that the rest of my clothes where brand new and that I was also totally new to whatever scene I was about to walk into.

The rain had reduced to a fine drizzle when I stepped out of the taxi. To my left was a car repair garage, shut up for the night. On the other side, behind a high wire fence, a short section of rough ground then a canal. I walked towards a glowing neon sign at the end of the road, the only obvious light. For a few moments I fumbled with the unfamiliar chunky metal zip of the jacket – my feet half-stumbling in my new boots as I had looked down. I managed to fasten the zip and pulled it right up to the neck. But then I stopped and pulled the zip halfway back down again. I deliberately pulled myself up tall and strode on forward, taking large confident steps this time.

I had returned back to Louise's after buying my clothes. She thought the outfit a bit much but her two employees liked it. Or at least they said they did as they fluttering around me as I posed making appreciative noises and ribald comments towards Louise. She had had to shoo them away eventually, rolling her eyes at me.

Then I remembered the phone. There was nothing in the address box but the voice mail had a number of messages that were variations on the ones I had heard back in the Nichola Lexington apartment. Plus there were a number of texts from Stephanie Smith, the woman at the publishing company I remembered – polite enquiries to get back in touch. I disconnected the phone from the charger and slipped it into my pocket.

Later Louise cooked me some spaghetti and we ate together. After, I went out into the gathering dusk while she waited for her evening appointments. I found a local pub and drank a couple of slow pints of lager, half-watching early evening television on the set above the bar, marking down the time until the club would be open.

The street had been deserted but there were a cluster of people around the club's entrance. Dressed in various dark coats, a mixture of male and female – their individuality was expressed through combinations of hairstyles and make-up, equally extreme for both sexes.

A couple gave me stares, but they seemed more in curiosity that threat, glancing away when I returned them. The bouncers were easy to spot with their cropped hair and bulked-out bomber jackets. I exchanged nods on the way in.

'You a member?' Asked the bored looking young woman with a severe dark bob and strappy blue dress from behind her counter inside the entrance.

'Friend gave me this.' I held up the flyer.

She nodded and with a flick of her fingers indicated for me to give it to her.

'Need to become a member if you want to come again.' She said as she ripped the flyer in half. 'Fill in a form on your way out.'

'Right,' I said, moving towards the muffled bass behind the swing doors on the other side of the entranceway. Beyond was the heat, noise and sweat-damped air of the club proper.

Though early, the place already seemed half-full. The space was roughly elliptical – three terraces leading down to a central dance floor with scattered tables and stools, most of them occupied. Music pulsed hard – something industrial that broke off every few seconds to a sampled German voice. The only part of which I caught was one word, 'Stukas'. Each pounding bass note was accompanied by a shift in the light show. Two screens behind the DJ console showed blurry archive war footage mixed in with what looked like a recording of the dance floor on another night.

I found the bar off in one corner and came away with a can of Red Stripe. Sipping from it, I made my way slowly around the club to the opposite side to where I came in, the carpet sticky under my boots, looking over the crowd. People appeared to be in clusters of similar dress-types, denoting sub-groups of the scene. I recognised metal, gothic and punk, but there were with several that I had no idea about. On the dance floor they either thrashed around, bouncing off each other or were just standing still on the edges, swaying. Their silhouettes – their hair high-plumed or falling in spiky cascades – cut through the shards of light.

'I've not seen you here before?' A voice beside me, loud over the music.

He was about my height, but a lot broader, a leather jacket open to show a bared, shaved chest with the slabs of muscle of someone who spends a lot of time lifting metal. His ginger hair was cropped very short, but you could still see it was prematurely thinning back at the temples – suggesting chemical enhancement to the weights. His moustache was thick and bushy, as if to compensate for his crop. Beside him was a slender woman with short blonde hair dressed in what looked like black PVC trousers and a similar, very tight, top. No make-up. She held a small leather bag in front of her with both hands, staring straight ahead.

'No,' I said. 'First time.'

'It's not bad.' He nodded towards the dance floor. 'Some interesting people, sometimes. Bit vanilla, but you can always meet people looking for something a bit different.'

'Oh, right.'

'So are you interested in something a bit different? Maybe join us? Move on to somewhere else?' He put his arm on my shoulder, casually. The woman at his side still seemed to be ignoring the both of us.

'I was a looking for a friend. I think she used to come here.'

'Ah yes, 'she'.' He shrugged and slowly took his hand away. 'Who? I might know her if she was a regular. What's her name?'

'She was... well, she went by a lot of names.'

'There are a few like that. What's she look like?'

'She changed her looks a lot too.'

He laughed. 'Not making it easy are you?'

'No. I–'

'Mr Gardner!' Another woman approached us. Tall, her generous curves were enhanced by some complicated looking buckled-corset arrangement. Below was a flared-out skirt made of several layers of grey lace-like material. Over the corset she wore a short cropped-sleeved jacket, of what looked like dark-blue velvet. A tattoo of a red and black banded snake ran along her forearm disappearing under the jacket's sleeve. Her long dark hair had been gathered into a high pony-tail. Her make-up was dramatic, giving her eyes a cat-like tilt.

She moved between the other two, a hand to each of their backs, but otherwise ignored them, speaking directly to me.

'This is the one place I did not expect to see you.'

She tapped the arm of the blonde with a single finger, who – while still starring ahead – passed her the handbag she was holding. The dark-haired woman took out a pack of

Rothman and a slim gold lighter. As she lit a cigarette, I finally recognised her, Stephanie Smith.

She inhaled deep on the cigarette, the tip glowing bright red, before exhaling the smoke out to one side.

'Come with me.' Stephanie smiled, grabbing my hand with one of hers. She stepped forward then turned back to the blonde, locking eyes for a second. 'Stay here.'

The blonde nodded once, the smallest gesture, but still said nothing.

'So, how goes the investigation?' Stephanie said, leading me through the crowd, her hand still holding mine, her handbag clutched in the other, along with the cigarette – poised between her fingers.

'It's progressing.' I said.

'I'm surprised it's led you to this place. Unless this is purely a social visit?' She laughed as if not expecting an answer.

Off to one side of the club there was a doorway I had not noticed before, which Stephanie led me through. Beyond was a short corridor, then a door. A bouncer stepped to one side as we approached. Stephanie offered him a smile in exchange for a nod that was so pronounced it was practically a bow as he opened the door.

Beyond was another room, much smaller than the main club space. At the far end was a bar and a small dance-floor but the majority of the space was filled with tables and chairs, with sofas off to the sides and beyond them nooks and booths. The place was crowded with most seats occupied. The lighting was low, the music a slower and quieter chill-out.

I let myself be led into one of the booths. A padded seat curved round a small table. In contrast to rest of the room the seat was completely empty. The table had a single tall drink sitting on a coaster.

Stephanie slid behind the table, and indicated with an outstretched arm to join her. She lifted up the glass from the table and sipped as I sat.

'So, is it a social visit?' She asked me again.

'No.' I took a swig from my own can of beer then placed it on the table in front of me. 'It's just I've got reason to believe Catherine may have visited here. Found a flyer along with her mobile in... an old cupboard.' I quickly lied, not wanting to explain about the health spa. 'I thought there might be people here who knew her... might know what other art she may have done.'

'I've never seen your woman, in here.' Stephanie said.

'You might not have recognised her. I've since found out she took on other identities. Disguises. Play-acting – that I think was part of her art.'

'Really? That sounds most intriguing.' She plucked at the sleeve of my jacket. 'You in disguise too?'

'No. Well, maybe.' I smiled back at her. 'So you say you've never seen her? Not even someone slightly like her? Anyone who could have been her?'

She inhaled from her cigarette. 'People do dress up to come here – sometimes excessively!' She said. 'But I'm sure I would have recognised her, especially after meeting her in the flesh as it were. I suppose if she came just a few times I might have missed her. I can ask around. I've still got your details.'

'I'm moving around a lot at the moment but you can leave message at the studio. Actually, come to think of it, I've just found her mobile phone though. You've got the number for that, right?' She nodded. 'But I suppose if you haven't seen her.' I continued. 'I don't suppose anyone else would have.' I pointed around the empty booth. 'You do seem you have a certain standing.'

Stephanie laughed. 'A 'certain standing'. Yes, I am something of a queen bee around here, I suppose. But I don't have to be like that. The boss.' She took another drag of her cigarette and breathed out a plume of grey above us. Then she slid across towards me, suddenly closing the gap between us in one smooth movement. She slid the arm with the snake tattoo along the top of the bench until her hand rested at my neck. 'Not unless you want me to.' Tiny wisps of residue smoke curled from the corner of her mouth as she spoke, her head very close to mine. 'Maybe I did know this woman. Maybe she was my lover. Would you like that?'

'What? No–'

Something caught my eye. I turned to look towards the entrance of the booth. As a figure passed I caught a glimpse of a sleeveless leather jerkin, one arm heavily tattooed – the other bare.

'Jesus, it's him! Scab!'

I pulled myself away from Stephanie and out from behind the table.

'Who?' She said behind me.

'He'll know! He's bound to have recognised her if she was here.'

'After him, then!' Stephanie laughed. I dashed out of the booth, seeing Scab was just leaving the room.

By the time I made it out to the corridor he was gone, but once in the main room I spotted him half-way across, heading for the exit. The place was really filling up, slowing me down as I made my way through the crowd. When I reached the club's lobby Scab was nowhere to be seen, nor was he anywhere in the street outside. The bouncer told me he thought he saw a guy with an armful of tattoos getting into a taxi. If so, he was long gone.

I walked out into the road. It had stopped raining and I breathed in the fresh air, glad for it after the smoke and sweat of the club.

A newly arrived minicab was disgorging two couples and I walked over, waving at the driver.

Ten minutes later, as I was heading back West, I felt the phone in my jacket pocket vibrating. I fished it out as the pulse of vibration finished with a beep. A text.

MR GARDNER, SOMETHING I REMEMBERED, FROM A LETTER FROM HER: '= = = = = = = = =' A CLUE? STEPH.

'STEPH' could only be Stephanie Smith.

'And let me guess… she wasn't there?' Louise asked me as she sat down next to me on the sofa. She was wrapped up in a baggy dressing gown.

'I went all the way back to the club but she was gone.'

'And you still can't get a reply?'

'Yeah, tried texting and calling several times, but nothing. I'll have to try her business tomorrow. Plus the tattooists. He won't be pleased to see me, but I need to find out if he knows more about Catherine from the club night.'

'You've not got a mobile phone?' Louise asked. 'Your own, before tonight?'

'No, I threw the last one away. Bad memories.'

Louise turned towards me, a serious look on her face.

'So this woman sends you some secret message. I suppose I should be jealous.'

'What! There's no need to be!'

Louise giggled.

'Only joking. She sounds crazy though.'

'I think she's just playing games. If she won't give me an answer straight away, she can stuff it. But... what with everything else I've found out about Catherine, it could be real.'

'What's it mean though? A row of equals signs?'

'Eight of them. You have any ideas? Like the rune? Something else like that?'

'No, nothing like that.' She furrowed her eyebrows in concentration. 'Eight equals...?'

There was something...

I looked up, something at the edge of my memory.

'Wait a minute...'

Eight equals. Equals eight. Equivalent eight. Equivalence VIII!

'Oh, fucking hell!' I cried out, leaping up from the sofa. 'No!'

'What?'

I turned to Louse, grabbed both her shoulders.

'It's the fucking bricks!'

'What bricks? What do you mean?' She said, confused.

I took a deep breath, relaxed my grip.

Then I sat down again and told her.

12 MISSED THE SUPPORT

'When's this band coming on, then?'

I nodded towards the stage of the cellar bar that was a couple of tables away as I placed the second pair of pints of Stella down. The stage was currently empty but the drum kit, keyboard and several microphone stands that were set up promised some sort of performance in the near future.

'Soon, I hope,' Mark said, already drinking from the first pint of the double round.

I started negotiating myself around the table to get to my seat on the other side. People had to stand or turn their legs away from me to let me pass, and I nodded thanks. As I finally sat down I jarred the table with my leg – partly due to the narrowness of the gap between the table and chair, but mainly because of the amount of alcohol I had already drunk. Mark automatically jerked his hands towards the glasses, but they stayed upright, just a splash of the lager spilling onto the table.

'Shit, sorry.' I pointed across to the nearest wall that was lined with people. 'Maybe we would have been better off standing.'

'Nah,' Mark said, 'This is a good seat here. And it's been too long a day to stand up.'

'Yeah, I know what you mean.' I said picking up my own drink. 'Think Simon's actually going to turn up?'

'He'll regret it if he doesn't. Reckon it'll be one of the last few chances to see them in a place like this before they hit the big time'

'Really?' I took a big swallow of my lager then looked around. Most of the chairs around the tables were now taken, and the rear of the bar was starting to fill up with standing people.

'So what sort of music is it?' I asked Mark.

'Hard to describe – better just to wait and see. Pity we missed the support though.

'Should have taken the tube, not a taxi.'

'Yeah, but I wasn't too sure were this place was and especially how to get here from the nearest station.'

'Well I've no idea where we are. Are we still in London?'

Mark laughed. 'I think so. Just.'

We were on a boys' night out. I had met Mark for a pub lunch – Simon had been expected to join us at some point but had never showed.

The session had extended into a long afternoon of drinking in several more places. The day was cloudless, so it had been pleasant to go from pub to pub beneath the winter sunshine. We had started drinking slow, but Mark soon began pushing for an increasing pace. I had kept up for the most part but had dropped out of a couple of rounds, where Mark bought himself and extra double.

Towards the end of the afternoon, catching myself reflected in a toilet mirror, I saw that I was visibly staggering.

However Mark did not seem to be showing any ill effects as he single-mindedly forged on.

At nightfall, as the air started to rapidly chill, we found ourselves in a City pub – settling down alongside a collection of recently off-duty stockbrokers and lawyers. I would have been happy to stay until closing but Mark had lurched to his feet, dragging me upright against my protests, and insisted on going to see this band he knew was playing.

He had phoned Simon again on the way.

'Sorry, it's taken.' I mouthed at the guy at the edge of the tables who was pointing down towards the seat next to me where I had dumped my jacket. I had just turned to reach inside the jacket to fish out an envelope from one of the pockets.

'I've not shown you these, yet.' I said as I turned back to Mark.

Inside the envelope were two photographs. I passed the first one over. It was Catherine, wearing a fake-fur fringed brown anorak with the hood up and blue jeans, gloves and boots. She was leaning back on a bench in the grounds of her treatment centre, with her hand behind her head, the other on her hip, with one foot resting on her knee. I had caught her laughing as she had struggled to hold the pose.

'You take this?' Mark asked.

'Yeah.'

'Wow, it's a different Catherine if she's allowing you to shoot her.'

The second photo was one she had taken herself, a trick using two mirrors to show a close-up of her smile endlessly repeated.

'She seems happy then. Home for Christmas?'

'Before then, I think.'

'Have to sort out a welcome home party.'

I shook my head. 'No, keep it low key. She wants to come back without making too much fuss. Just slip back into things. Well, not completely slip back.' I raised my glass. 'Be a bit less of this for a start.'

'She taken the twelve step and all that?'

'Not really. She wasn't actually addicted, they say. Just depression. Self-medicating with binges. I can't say too much, though... promised her not. Anyway she seems out of it now, planning to start working again. New ideas like these.'

'That's good.' He handed my back the photographs.

'I just wish I had done something sooner.' I said, 'Spotted the signals.'

'We all do. But don't kick yourself about it... no one saw the signs. She showed you when she needed the help.'

'Yeah, I think you're right. On the mend now anyway. Was worried for a while, though. Thought it was going to break us.'

'Nah, partners for life you are. That's one thing everyone can see. Going to do some more art? Jointly, I mean?'

'Maybe. Thinking about it.'

'You can put them away!' Simon's shout interrupted us. He pointed down at the photographs in my hand as he approached the table. 'Thought this was just lads together.'

'It is.' I said. 'And we were resigned to it being just being the two of us.'

Simon took his coat off. Underneath was a suit and tie. 'Yeah, sorry I'm late. Meeting with my business manager, my publicity people and a few others – thought it was never going to end.' He glanced down at the beer-filled table as he slung down his coat on top of mine. 'Better get to the bar, then.'

'Business manager. Publicity people.' Mark said when he was gone. 'Sounds like he's doing well.'

'Hey, we're all doing well!' I reached under Simon's coat to put the photographs back. Then I hung both coat and jacket on the back of the chair.

'Some more well than others, I think.' Mark said.

'Who you kidding? You got a new exhibition just around the corner.'

'If it's well received.' He shrugged. 'If the critics like it. If it sells.'

'Oh, cheer up, of course it will!'

'I suppose.' He took another swallow of lager.

'Not going to give me a sneak preview?' I asked.

He shook his head.

'You know, never before the day.'

'The amount of noise you've been making – sounds like you've got a proper factory down there!'

He turned to me. 'What? Thought you didn't mind me moving back in?'

'Course I don't. Pleased I'm not rattling around in there on my own any more. Just curious to see what you've been making.'

'You'll find out soon enough.'

Simon returned with a pint and squeezed himself into his chair.

'I take it I've not missed the band.' He said.

'Only the support.' I replied. 'And we missed them as well. But can't be long now for the main act.'

'What are you up to, Simon?' Mark asked.

'Just started working on the first in a series on myths and legends.' He replied. 'Starting with Greece. Cutting up all these books on Greek legends I read as a kid, and a load more I've found. Mix them up with other pictures, show how the real legends were a lot different to the censored versions I read as a kid. All the sex that was missed out for a start.'

Mark laughed. 'All the gay sex you mean.'

'I suppose so.'

'What was the meeting about, though?' Mark asked. 'That's what I meant.'

'Oh, I'm planning another big postal project in the near future. Going to have a hire a lot of people to sort it out. Be like a full time business, need support staff and everything. And proper premises. Thinking of somewhere out of town. Keep the costs down.'

'There's plenty of space back at the studio. Even though Mark's moved back.'

'I'll need much more than that.' Simon said.

'Pity,' I said. 'When Catherine's back it would almost be just like the old days. We really should do something together again.'

'A party would be good.' Simon said. 'When she comes home.'

'No,' I said. 'I was thinking of another joint exhibition. Something like that.'

'Unfortunately that's never going to happen now,' Simon said. 'Impossible to get all our schedules matched up.'

'More's the pity.'

'At least we're still talking to each other. That's something.'

'Yeah,' I lifted my glass up. 'And there's things like this.'

Simon leaned over the table looking towards Mark. 'Hey, you should have brought your boyfriend.'

'Nah.' Mark shook his head.

'I nearly brought Penny.' Simon said. 'But I thought you'd only moan.'

'That the blonde you brought to Jason's last thing?' Mark asked.

'Yeah, we're pretty steady now.'

Suddenly a ripple of applause through the bar and some whistling announced the band taking to the stage. Five women. The lead singer – dressed in a Hawaiian shirt and baggy green shorts, long blonde dreadlocks hanging down her back – took hold of the centre microphone stand. She held a tambourine in the other hand – black plastic and double curved, like the outline of a new moon. She looked out over the crowd with a hard stare, wielding the tambourine in front of herself like it was some offensive weapon. The bass player started a thudding riff. The rest of the band – all dressed in a mismatched confusion of styles that looked like an explosion in a charity shop – joined in one at a time.

The lead singer looked back to the band for a while, bouncing her head along to a beat that slowly increased in tempo. Then she turned back to the audience, and raised her tambourine high above her head, almost touching the bricks of the vaulted ceiling. Holding the pose, she remained motionless as the music built up to a complete frenzy.

Then she brought the tambourine down in one slashing motion, crashing it against the side of the mic stand.

The band stopped dead.

The lead singer leaned into the microphone – *Hi hooooo!*

She drew out the note, the rest of the band joined her to form an a cappella cord – *Hi hooooooooooooo!*

Again with the rest of the band coming in.

A pause, then with another slash of the tambourine, the song proper started.

Hi ho, hi ho.
We're home from the studio.
Where we made some art, that will break your heart,
Hi ho,
Hi ho, hi ho, hi ho!

Then, while the rest of the band went into a series of soft *Hi hos,* the singer spoke out to the audience, 'Good evening! Welcome to all our old friends – and it looks like some new ones too – and especially to any artists out there, you poor bastards. Later we'll be playing some stuff off our new CD, 'Songs About Love And Money', but first...'

She held up the tambourine again and the music died away.

'We are The Cocaine Dwarfs!' She screamed into the mic. *'And we are... Straight Out Of Hoxton!'*

As the music kicked in again – much harder and faster than what they had played before – a dynamic pop-punk fusion with lyrics rap-sung over the top, I turned to a grinning Mark

'This is great!' I shouted.

'I know, fantastic aren't they!'

I looked over at Simon, but he was sat with his arms folded, not looking happy at all.

We shuffled along in the taxi queue, exhaust fumes smoking around our ankles, our own breath visible.

My ears rang but I could still hear someone up towards the head of the queue singing the chorus from the band's encore song – 'Freddie Mercury's Dead'.

Can someone please explain to me,
why at the time I could not see,
Freddie's rather obvious,
homosexuality?

'That's true, you know.' I said to Mark and Simon. 'All those years and I never twigged. And some of the biggest homophobic fucks I knew were Queen fans.'

'Even I didn't see it at first.' Mark said.

'They were great though,' I said. 'Glad you dragged me here, Mark.'

'Oh, yes.' He said.

'You think so?' Simon said. 'Art school drop-outs taking the piss out of people who don't like art? Thought it was a bit obvious. And that sort of thing is dangerous.'

'Dangerous?' I asked.

'There're enough people who think art is rubbish without singing songs about it.'

'That's not what they were getting at.' Mark said, 'It was about people pretending to understand art when they don't.'

'But then they went the other way!' Simon said. 'What was that other one, 'All artists are wankers?''

'Perhaps we are.' I laughed.

'No,' Mark said. 'That one was like – The Bricks is just bricks to most people, but to a few like us it's different. But just because we can see it, it doesn't make us necessarily better than the rest. Only different.'

'But that's wrong.' Simon said. 'That's like saying being ignorant is a good thing. And what's all that taking the piss out of gangsta rap... is that really appropriate considering most of them were white?'

'Are you serious? Gansta rap's a lot more fake than what they're doing!'

Simon shook his head at that.

'I suppose we'll have to agree to disagree.'

'Well, I like them.' Mark said. 'The anti-Spice Girls... Art Spice, Art Spice, Art Spice, Art Spice and of course–'

'Art Spice.' Simon added but with the beginnings of a smile.

'Bricks...' I said, almost to myself. 'That's what started it with me. Back when I was a teenager.'

'What?' Simon said.

'On a television program, *Central Weekend*. Big thing in the Midlands. But local telly, so no one else has ever heard of it. It was a discussion program between some invited experts and an audience. Different thing each week, always provocative stuff – football hooligans, wife-swappers, things like that. Anyway, once they did art. Modern art. They'd got a bricklayer to arrange some bricks on the studio floor like 'Equivalent VIII', 'The Bricks'. Well, for a start they had used ordinary house bricks, not the pale fire bricks from the original and they weren't as precisely arranged – with gaps and some off-square, so it looked a right mess. The panel – critics and collectors like George Melly – talked for several minutes about how the original really was art. It was nothing too high-brow, all interesting stuff that made sense to me. Of course this wasn't good enough for the presenter so he turns to the brickie in the audience and asks if he thought what he had done was art. The brickie comes back in broad Brummie – 'But it's just bricks!' Which of course gets a big laugh – me too, to be honest. But at the same time I was thinking, 'You are so wrong!' Because I could see exactly what they had been talking about – that it was more than just bricks. That it was about geometry, the mechanisation of the world and the built environment. The extraordinary in something ordinary and how we overlook what we see all the time. How it fit into the history of art. The simplicity of it – Christ, even the beauty of it! I might already have been heading that way, but I think that was the moment where my love of art really began. As soon as I could I was straight down the library and reading everything they had. Yeah, that's where it started.'

'Wow,' said Mark. 'I never had that kind of revelation but–'

'Hey, you want this one?' Simon said pulling open the door of a taxicab. Unnoticed, while I was talking, we had reached the front of the queue.

I climbed into the taxi, Mark behind me.

'Not coming with us?' He asked back to Simon.

'No,' Simon replied. 'Going the other way. See if Penny is still up.' He leaned into the cab. 'Oh, do you know why they're called Cocaine Dwarfs?'

'Started liking them now, have we?' Mark asked him back.

'No, just curious.'

'You can work it out, Simon. It's easy.'

Simon shook his head. 'Always wanna keep us in suspense, don't you? Tell me next time.'

He slammed the door shut.

'Hey! Come up for a night-cap.'

We had just staggered out of the taxi into the yard in front of the studio, careful to avoid slipping on a pavement now raw with frost. I was about to follow the taxi back out to the street but Mark's shout as he was unlocking the studio door turned me around.

'I'm starving.' I said. 'Think we must have missed a meal out somewhere. I've got nothing upstairs… I'm going to the chippy.'

Mark laughed. 'The chippy? Going to seed without Catherine?'

'It's not like that.' I walked back over to him. 'We always shared the shopping and the cooking and all of that. It's just that cooking for one is a pain. But then sitting in a restaurant on your own is even worse. So I've been eating a lot of take-a-way.'

'Even I know the place doesn't shut for hours yet. And you can't be that hungry, we all got peanuts with the last round… Just one drink.'

'Oh, go on then,' I said.

Mark opened the door and we both stepped through into the stairwell out of the cold.

'Should have given me a shout,' Mark said. 'Could always go out together for a meal.'

It was my turn to laugh.

'I thought you've already got a boyfriend!'

But Mark did not laugh. He did not even smile.

'We've split up.' He sighed. 'Very messy. Didn't mention it before as I didn't want to go into all the gory details in front of Simon.'

'Ah, shit. Sorry to hear that.'

'And I thought this was the one. Never mind, just have to keep being the last free spirit for a while longer. Anyway, come up for a drink. Just the one.'

'All right,' I said. 'As long as you promise not to seduce me.'

'I'll try to resist.' Mark said as we started up the stairs.

At his door Mark held up his hand. 'You'll have to give me five minutes to cover a few things up.'

I rolled my eyes at him. 'Go on then.'

'Sorry.'

He closed the door and I sat down on the stairs.

It was more like ten minutes before I saw him again – leaning out the doorway, waving me in with a bottle of whisky.

'Come on, then.'

I pulled myself up and followed him into the room.

'I was about to go, you know.'

'I'm finished now.'

Inside, the large open area was more like a workshop than a studio. In front of me were rows of shelving units with tubs of nuts, bolts, washers and screws, lengths of pipe, motors and other electrical and electronic components. Behind were drills, lathes and other machinery with sheets of metal leaning against them. Fire extinguishers and gas cylinders were propped against one wall with the blank stare of a welders mask hanging above them. And over everything was the metallic smell – almost a taste – of manufacturing. Mark had only turned on a single bulb near the door and off in the shadows at the back of the room were large mysterious objects shrouded in sheets of canvas and dark plastic.

One set of shelves was filled with books, on art and design but also covering mechanics and electronics and a whole load of newer-looking ones on computer programing.

I pointed towards them.

'Taking up my old game?'

'Maybe.' He said. 'But that would be telling.'

I closed the door and saw behind it was a big stack of canvases.

'What's these?' I picked up one. It was covered in random lines and splashes of paint.

'Rubbish. They're going out soon. Gonna burn 'em.' He shrugged. 'It's what the art-machine produced before I gave up on the idea.'

'I'm sure you could sell these.' I said. 'Restaurant I was in the other night had some art on the walls. Got talking with the owner and he was looking to replace them, seemed keen to buy something by a 'name'. Plenty of money. I've got nothing spare at the moment, but I'm sure he'd take some of these.'

'I'm sure they would, but I'll only put my name to something that I thought was a success. Like that.' He pointed to the back of the room. He paused a moment then shook his head as if deciding against something. 'Ah, come on, let's get a drink.'

The only home comforts in the room were in a near corner by the windows, a couple of battered sofas facing each other, a low table in-between with some papers scattered across it. Mark slumped down, his back to the rest of the room.

I sat down facing him. Mark reached down and picked up a couple of tumblers off the floor. He poured whisky into one and handed it over to me. He was about to pour himself one but then suddenly seemed to notice the table between us.

'Whoops, forgot about these.'

He put the bottle and glass down and started gathering the papers together.

I leaned forward, caught glimpses of electrical circuit diagrams and drawings of metalwork with organic-looking flourishes along with some science fiction magazines.

Mark shuffled them all together as he stood and went over to a nearby shelf.

I noticed he left something behind, a comic.

'You've forgotten something.' I called out to Mark.

'That's just this week's *2000AD*. Nothing to do with the art.' He said as he returned to the sofa.

I pulled the comic towards me, spinning it round. The front cover was an illustration of a buxom, barely clad, future-babe – the word 'sex' written across her.

'*2000AD!* Judge Dredd and all that!' I said as I started flicking through the pages, looking over the artwork. 'I remember reading that as a kid.'

'Let me guess you had issue one, perfect, including the Space Spinner, but your mother threw it away.' Mark said.

'How did you know?' I smiled back at him as I put the comic down.

'Nearly everyone has that story.' He sipped from his whisky then looked back me his head tipped to one side. 'But, when you grew up you gave up childish things like comics.'

'Hey, I still read comics! Sometimes. Good ones. Well, you know, graphic novels. *Watchmen* for instance. That's genius.'

'Graphic novels, eh?' Mark said, knocking back his whisky. 'Light-weight.'

He picked up the bottle and poured some more into his glass. I had hardly touched mine and waved him back as he tried to add more to my own glass.

'You know? What Simon said earlier — about the band?' He held up an arm towards the rear of the studio, at his now shrouded artwork. 'I sometimes wonder about all this.'

'What do you mean?'

'The stuff we do. Does it really make any difference? And how do we know if it's any good, at all, in the long run. Like them old canvases you say some guy wants to buy just for my name. Like I'm a commodity, to invest in.'

'Some people buy just to make money,' I said. 'But I think most do because they like it. Because it appeals to them in some way. Intellectually or emotionally. That's good enough for me.'

'But what about our legacy? How do we know if we are any good in the long run?'

'The short answer is we don't.' I took a swallow of whisky. 'But people buy now. That means something.'

He sighed and pointed down at the comic. 'To most people, that's art. Not what we do.'

I shook my head. 'But most people will think that is rubbish too. Just a comic. Kid's stuff. Ask the average man in the street what is art and he'll probably say some crying clown painting from Woolies. Or if you are really lucky, 'The Hay Wain'. But fuck the man the street. 'It's just bricks!' Bollocks. What we do is art. It might be good art, it might be bad art — not up to us to decide that — but it *is* art.'

I picked up the comic.

'But one thing they are right about,' I continued. 'Is that this isn't art. It's illustration. Nothing wrong with that, plenty of room for creativity, for skill. But it's not art. It's not what we do. Not the art that can really make you think. That can turn your head inside out. That's open to interpretation and doesn't give you any easy answers. Or it gives you answers to a question you were not even thinking about. The physical philosophy of it. The puzzle. The conundrum. That's art.' I dropped the comic back on the table. 'Not that.'

'No, I can't accept that.' Mark said. 'The best comics, can move you, hit your emotions and make you think.'

'Yes, but it's like cinema, the pictures are just part of the whole. Used to tell the story, to create the narrative. I agree the best of it, the whole comic, graphic novel, whatever, can be art, like the best cinema. But almost all the time your thinking is being directed, so it's an entertainment. The pictures – there can be skill – but in the end it's just like one of those clown paintings. It's just an illustration of something.'

'Yeah, but it used to be all like that.' Mark said. 'I mean all the artists… Michelangelo, Rembrandt, Turner. All of them. All painted what was in front of them – portraits and landscapes. You are telling me that's not art.'

'But that was then. Not now. Not since the camera has done away with the need. Art was function. Paint people, illustrate stories – historical and religious, show places that people wanted to see, landscapes – things that needed to be shown, even some squire's favourite horse. But we don't need that now. So it moved on. To abstract. And on, into what we do now. Conceptual art. Modern art.'

'But some people don't see it…'

'I know not everyone sees it. Christ, sometimes I don't see it!' I laughed to myself. 'There's plenty of artists I don't like, can't see what they are doing. At all. Take Basquiat – to me it just looks like a load of scribble. I'm convinced he only got on because he was Warhol's friend. But others think differently. Can see something I can't. And they think… say Pollock is rubbish. In the end be happy to be creating something that someone likes. For whatever reasons.'

'I suppose so. I just hope they like the latest stuff I've done.'

'I'm sure they will. Everything you put up for sale always does well. In fact if you averaged it out per work, I bet you make far more than the rest of us.

'Yeah, you're right. Just lost a bit of confidence that's all. It's just… Fuck, don't tell Simon this, but it's what broke up my last relationship. Had a big argument over it. First time I had shown him anything – Jesus, first time I'd shown anybody anything before a show – and he said what I was doing was, I quote, 'A load of shit'. That it was 'sick and wrong'. Then when I got upset he started going on about how he thought I wanted him to be honest. Then I fell back on 'but you don't understand!' and it really went downhill after that. That what I was doing was 'just self-indulgent wank, when people were starving.''

'Oh God, that old chestnut.' I sighed. 'Yeah, we would be better off curing cancer, but we can't all do that. And you did tell him we give a great lump of cash to charity every year?'

'Too busy shouting. And too late now.' Mark said. 'I worry he was maybe right, not that it's complete rubbish, but…' He shrugged.

'Really? If you're worried, why don't you show me now what you've done.'

'Oh, you won't catch me out that easy!' He smiled. 'Fuck it… it's just pre-show nerves. Don't listen to me moaning.'

'Right, in that case,' I said, finishing my whisky before standing. 'I'll be off to the chippy while it's still open.'

Mark raised his glass to me. *Bon Appétit!*

At the door I turned back.

'Actually, why are they called The Cocaine Dwarfs? The band?'

'It's the Freddie Mercury thing.'

'Sorry?'

'Don't you remember the rumours? The parties Queen used to have?'

I shook my head.

'Supposed to be the ultimate in rock excess.' Mark continued. 'Tables laden with food. Enough booze to float a battleship. Strippers and prostitutes in fancy dress. And drugs of course, tons of them... They hired these short guys to wander round with plates strapped to the tops of their heads, piled up with charlie. So people could just lean over and sniff whenever they passed. The cocaine dwarfs. So, like a symbol of ultimate mindless hedonism?'

'Oh, I thought it was like if you do too much coke it stunts your creativity.'

'Maybe it's that as well. Art, remember? Open to interpretation.'

'Touché. Right, kebab time. You want anything bringing back?'

'No, I'm crashing.' He laughed to himself. 'A kebab, eh? You must be missing Catherine more than I thought?'

'What?'

'A donner kebab! Just look at it next time you buy one. That shape. All those folds of meat. It's just a big vagina substitute! Even I can see that. You're not the only one — thousands of guys go out Saturday night, and if they don't get lucky they go and bury their face in a kebab on the way home. And if they do get lucky then they just bury themselves in the lucky lady's kebab instead.'

I just shook my head. 'That bloke was right... You have got one sick and twisted mind.'

I shut the door on his laughter.

The inside of the phone box was a relief from the frozen streets. Though of the newer design – that were slowly replacing the tourist-loved old Scott *K2*s – and open to the elements at ankle height, it still alleviated most of the effects of a bitter wind that now gusted through the streets.

I had spotted it on the way back from the take-away and suddenly realising how late it was, thought it better to ring Catherine straight away rather than wait until I had got all the way back to the studio to give her a call.

I placed the brick on top of the shelf. Unfortunately it was not a 'Equivalent VIII'-style fire brick but a light-weight three holed red-brown construction brick. I put the kebab down next to it and reached into my pocket for the envelope with the photographs. I selected the one of Catherine on the bench and put it down on the shelf face up in front of the brick. Something better to look at than all the cards advertising unusual services from local women plastered around the inside of the phone box.

I picked up the kebab, tore back the paper and took a bite before dialling the number of Catherine's mobile phone.

As I chewed Mark's words came back to me and I shook my head as I listened to the dial tone.

'Hello?' Catherine's voice.

I quickly swallowed.

'Hello? Who is it?' Her voice continued

'It's me. Sorry, I was just eating. A kebab.'

'Right.' She sounded small and distant. Serious.

'Are you all right?'

'Yes, just tired.'

'Oh, sorry. But you said ring anytime. I didn't wake you did I? I know it's later than usual but I've been out with Mark and Simon—'

'It's all right… Actually, I'm glad you called because—'

'God, I really miss you Catherine. I'm so glad you'll be home soon. I've just got you a present? A brick.'

'What?'

'A brick. Saw this building work on the way to the chippy. Another conversion job of a warehouse. Jumped on a bin, then over the wall. Nicked a brick. You know the bricks, 'Equivalent VIII'… It's a bit complicated, but earlier tonight—'

'Jason.' She interrupted. Then a pause.

'Yeah?'

I heard her take a deep breath and expel it with a sigh.

'I've been thinking.' Another pause.

'What?'

'It's hard… but I need to go away. Right away. From everything. The obsessions I've got. The art. For a long time.'

'That's fine. Yeah, we need a holiday. We've got plenty of money. We can do anything you want.'

'No. You're part of it… I'm sorry. So sorry. I need to disappear. Forever. Don't try and find me.'

'What!'

The phone went dead.

'No, no, no, no, no. Don't do this.'

I redialled. No answer.

'No, no, no. *Please.*'

I dialled again. Still no answer. Voicemail deactivated.

'*No!*' I shouted.

I crashed the handset down on the phone.

'*No! No!*' I yelled as anger, panic and frustration seized me. I slammed the kebab against the glass side of the phone box.

Chilli sauce splattered me as meat and salad burst out. I flung the remains of the kebab down to the floor. I snatched up the brick and flung that against the side of the phone box. It just bounced back off the toughened glass. I lurched back to avoid the brick now falling towards my feet, flailing against the door and pushing it half open. The cold blast of air from outside brought an end to my destructive rage.

I looked down, at the mess of the kebab of my feet, at the brick, now split in two. Mind numb, I breathed harsh and ragged.

I reached out to Catherine's photo, peeling off a slice of tomato then brushing off the fragments of shredded lettuce that were scattered over it. Noticing, too late, that I had smeared a splatter of chilli across the photograph. Smeared a dark red streak right across Catherine's face.

13 STILL DARK EYES

He looked right back at me, his still dark eyes fixed on my own.

There was always a certain cool arrogance in that stare, in those eyes that never blinked, that never turned away from me. The arrogance that his position in society gave him and his money too, despite his relative youth.

Below, nestling in the flamboyant Vandyke moustache and beard combination, the lips were pulled into a tight smile... or was it a smirk? I could never decide, no matter how many times I stared at it.

I looked over the crowing silhouette of the hat, the curls of hair beneath it, the lace ruff and cuffs, the highlights and shadows of the folds of the cloth in the bulky plush coat, the detailing of the patterns of the fabric itself, at all the exquisite detail in the clothing depicted with such obviously loose brush strokes.

But it was that expression that I always ended up returning to, whenever I looked at 'The Laughing Cavalier'.

I waited standing before it, just one small painting among many others in the gallery and remembered back to seeing it with Catherine. Waited alone, but expecting to see Stephanie

Smith again any second, walking in through one the gallery's doorways.

In my pocket the phone vibrated then beeped as I pulled it out of my pocket – loud in the quiet of the space.

'One of my favourites.'

'Mine too.'

'And I swear,' I said turning to Cat. 'That expression changes as you look at it.'

Cat's hair was still dark and she was wearing the same long coat as on the night I had walked her home from the party. It had given me a deep thrill to see her wearing it all week in college, to see her in it now.

'I know. Though it never looks like he's actually laughing.'

'He's one of yours, isn't he?'

'What?'

'A cavalier. A posho. Think my ancestors would be more on the Roundhead side.'

'Oh, suddenly you are going all class consciousness on me. Up the proletariat and all that? Anyway he's Dutch. Nothing to do with the Civil War.'

'Don't worry, I'm not planning to declare war on you.'

'I should hope not.' She leaned in closer to the painting. 'I much prefer this to the 'Mona Lisa'. If you are talking enigmatic-smile portraits.'

'Oh, yes.'

'Have you seen it?' She turned back to me. 'The 'Mona Lisa'? In real life?'

'Yeah, on a trip to Paris a couple of years ago. Well, I suppose I sort of saw it. There was such a scrum of tourists in front I only bothered with a quick glance. Not so bad with the 'Venus de Milo' – though that's overrated as well. I mean there's loads of real good statuary around it that no one even looked at. Suppose it's because it's become an icon. Become more that just an artwork.'

'Hmm.' Her mouth was closed, he lips tight.

'So, is that a smile or a smirk?'

Her face broke into a full grin. 'Ah, that you will never know!'

I just smiled. 'Better be getting back, seeing my tutor this afternoon.'

I took hold of Cat's arm as we turned away from the painting. 'I've enjoyed today though. We'll have to do this more often. Come and look at art together.'

'Yeah, when we are not busy making it ourselves.'

The sky was overcast and a dull light had greyed out Oxford Street as I had crossed it, heading from Bond Street tube to Manchester Square and the Wallace Collection.

Though I had always liked 'The Laughing Cavalier', thinking it one of my favourite paintings, I was never really comfortable with the rest of the collection. The building itself was fine, a large brick-built Georgian house, and the more masculine side of the collection – the arms and armour – appealed to my inner schoolboy. But all the furniture and china, and most of the paintings were just too fussy and rococo, too chocolate-boxy and sweet for my tastes.

And as I had walked through the building again, to reach the gallery that displayed 'The Laughing Cavalier', the sweetness was soured as I realised it was the first time I was walking through there on my own.

'So then she disappeared?' Louise said when I had finished. Both of us were sitting close together on her sofa. She was lying against me, her arms around my shoulders. 'And that was when she…?'

'Killed herself? No. No, that was much later. She came back to me before that… It wasn't the end. But, it was the beginning of the end. That's obvious now. There's more,' I went on. 'But I don't think I'm ready for that yet.'

'That's enough for one night anyway,' she whispered. 'Come to bed.'

She let go of me and stood, turning from me but reaching back with one hand. I let her lead me to her room, into her bed and back into her arms.

The next morning we showered together and I dressed in the same clothes I had worn the night before. While Louise busied herself downstairs, I phoned Oyster Press, but there was only a recorded message. I also tried Stephanie's mobile number again in faint hope but there was no reply there either. I briefly cursed myself for not making note of the tattoo parlour's phone number. I slung on my new leather jacket and went down to where Louise was sitting in reception behind her computer.

'Much on today?' I asked.

'No. Very quiet.' She said. 'Nothing until tonight.'

'All right. I'll go visit the publishers, find out where she got the Bricks clue. Then the tattooist, see if he knows more about the club thing. It should only take a few hours. Then perhaps after we could meet up for lunch? Do something together this afternoon? I'd take you with me but I'm supposed to be the lone detective still. Though perhaps…?'

'Nah, I've got a pile of paperwork to catch up on. But yes, come back and we will do something. Any ideas?'

'I could do with some more clothes actually. But… a shopping trip isn't very interesting.'

'Don't forget, I am a woman.' Louise said to me deadpan.

I laughed. 'Fair enough, and if you are good girl I'll buy you something–'

I was interrupted by a vibration in my pocket and a beep. The phone.

I pulled it out.

'What is it?' Louise asked.

'Another text – *FROWNING ROUNDHEAD, NOT. 10AM*. What time is it now?'

She glanced back at the computer monitor

'Just gone nine.'

'Better be off then.'

'You know what it means.'

'Not a frowning Roundhead – a laughing Cavalier. 'The Laughing Cavalier'. It's a painting.'

'I've heard of it. This Stephanie again?'

I checked the number. 'Yeah. Looks like she wants to meet me at the painting for some reason.'

'Why is she messing you around like this? Is she mad?'

'Maybe. Perhaps it *is* from Catherine though. Something she left for me. Before… And Stephanie's only just found it. We did visit that painting together. I think it was the first time we looked at any art together, so it was significant, not as much as 'Equivalent VIII', 'The Bricks' was to me – but it still meant a lot to us. If it is from her… well, I have to honour her memory.'

Louise slowly nodded.

'All right.' She said. 'But just don't let that mad woman lure you away from me.'

I grinned. 'There's no chance of that!'

The horse was huge – life size, in fact. A truly splendid specimen, powerfully muscled, the anatomy perfect, his chestnut coat sleek, his flaxen mane and tail seeming to float in the air. The pose, reared up on his hind legs, looming over me, was so exact and finely balanced that he seemed to be perpetually moving against the plain background.

And though a thoroughbred, he did not have the look of a fiery spitting station. He seemed docile and friendly, looking almost embarrassed in fact, as if he had just been caught in this position, playfully prancing for his own amusement. 'Whistlejacket' was the name of this eponymous portrait.

Right at the appointed time the phone in my hand, buzzed and beeped. Just as I had expected. The next step in my tour around the art of London me and Catherine had shared – a final goodbye.

'That's the one, I think.' Catherine said. 'On a school trip down to London. I had always loved horses and I had started dabbling with paints, but him, that magnificent beast.' She pointed at the large painting of the horse on the other side of the gallery. 'Yes, that's what made me want to become an artist.'

She shook her head as we started walking up to the painting.

'But it's also, in the end, what led me towards photography. Because I knew that, deep down, I was never going to be able to paint something as good.'

'Oh, I don't know. Those paintings you showed me you did of your own horse and those others. I mean they were heading– '

'No. You're kind, but no.'

We stopped in front of the painting.

'I mean,' Catherine said. 'Look at the contrast between the brawn of the body and the featheriness of the tail and the mane. How that comes out of the colouring.'

'The brown and the blonde.'

'Well, chestnut and flaxen, to use the proper terms.' She ran her hand through her own blonde hair. 'I'm going to change this for the show. Another colour.'

'Chestnut with flaxen tips?'

'No, a different colour to that. You'll see anyway.'

The clue from the text had been – *CARRY A TUNE IN YOUR COAT. NEIGH? 12PM.* I first thought of a reversed meaning again, a negative. But then thought that 'neigh' was not as in 'no', but as in 'horse' and then it was immediately obvious, especially when thinking of art relevant to Catherine and I. 'Whistlejacket'. Two hours gave me plenty of time so I walked back to Bond Street then on to Piccadilly Circus and down to Trafalgar Square, to join the steady stream of tourists entering the National Gallery.

I stared through the frame into infinity, stared through each of them in turn. Nine blank portals. Nine huge frames within frames. Not portraits this time, unless you thought of them as portraits of the mind, of the soul, on its journey out to the ultimate. No, if anything these were landscapes. Landscapes of eternity. Of nothing and everything. Of all of art. Of all of us.

Hung against the grey walls – painted on red-stained canvases, in red or black or maroon – were frames. Or open squares and rectangles. Or gateways, or doorways, or windows. Or pillars and capitals. Entrances or exits.

The dim light shimmered off the paint as I moved around the room, creating new colours, new shades. This, and the feathered edges to the blocks of colour themselves – created from obviously vigorous brush strokes – gave the paintings an added dynamism, an unexpected life.

'The Seagram Murals'. One of the truly great works of modern art. So it was such a pity to see them in that new hang. In this new room, that seemed an afterthought, almost a long alcove off a corridor, with its two open entrances at the far end. Especially as the recently reshaped and re-purposed building they had been moved to was such a magnificent creation.

I sat down and waited, trying to ignore the stream of people passing through the other end of the room until the phone beeped with another clue.

A familiar clue this time.

To a familiar work. And one so close.

Catherine sighed. 'Did you know he killed himself on the day they arrived?'

She was dressed in a retro-styled navy-blue dress with dark blue tights and chunky shoes, a cornflower blue shawl across her shoulders. Her hair was back to blonde.

'No, I didn't.'

We were almost whispering to each other, despite there being no one else with us. The chapel-like atmosphere of the room, with its diminished light, seemed to demand it.

'I don't think it's connected, just one of those odd coincidences.'

'So he never saw them in situ?'

'No, despite supposedly loving the place and making all that fuss over how they should be displayed – one room, the dim light, not too high off the floor and all that – he never saw them here.'

'Seems a pity.'

'I think he was past caring about anything by that time. Just too old and too knackered with too much booze and too many fags making him ill. Just one last final colour field –

letting the blood from a cut in his arm pool out all around himself.'

She sniffed and I realised she was crying silent tears.

'Oh Jesus, Catherine.' I put an arm around her.

'Why did she do it? Why did she kill herself?'

'I don't know. I don't think we'll ever really know.'

She pulled away from me to reach into her purse beside her on the seat and grab a tissue. She wiped her eyes.

I heard someone push open the room's heavy door. I looked back to see a two young women entering speaking Spanish to each other.

'Come let's go.' Catherine stood.

We walked out into the high-columned central hall of the Tate.

'Sometimes I hate her for doing it.' Catherine said. 'That's terrible isn't it?'

'No, it's not. I often feel the same way.'

'Look, I've been thinking. I want to do my own memorial to her. Give her a better send-off than that awful funeral. Will you help me?'

'Of course I will.'

SPRING SUMMER FALL WINTER. 2PM. The use of 'Fall' instead of Autumn immediately caught my eye. An American work, then? Then very suddenly it was obvious. The seasons. The four seasons. The Four Seasons' Restaurant. The restaurant in the Seagram Building in New York that 'The Seagram Murals' had first been commissioned for. Not an official name – each painting was known individually as 'Red on Maroon' or 'Black on Red' and such like – but an obvious pointer all the same towards what the paintings had become collectively known as.

I knew they had been moved down the river, with the rest of the modern art, from the old Tate to the new building, Tate Modern. I had not been there before. I had been invited to the opening but I was too busy grieving for Catherine at the time and planning my supposedly final artwork – the cottage in the country.

There had been time to break my tube journey for a sandwich and a coffee and to ring Louise. I apologised that I would not be returning after all, that I was being led around to other works of art, but that this was all to the good, that it felt like a final closure on the whole thing. She told me not to worry, that she had a new unexpected client coming to keep her busy anyway, to just come back to her whenever I was finished.

Unfortunately the new spine-like footbridge – that reached out over the river from the shadow of Saint Paul's to root itself in front of Tate Modern – was still the 'wobbly bridge' and therefore shut. So I had had to approach the gallery from the rear after surfacing at Southwark tube station.

The station was itself a new construction and very impressive. With is metal-lined tunnels and airy modernist halls, I thought it looked like a bridgehead for an invasion by the Cybermen.

However it was nothing compared to Tate Modern itself.

I had seen pictures of that cathedral of a building but those had not prepared me for the reality. Like many a great artwork, you really had to stand in front of it to fully appreciate it.

As I approached I felt a growing excitement, sparking like the electricity this powerhouse had once generated. The walls towered over me, enormous expanses of brickwork, a cliff face of them, filling my field of view with thousands of bricks. And above, there was the tower, stabbing up into the gloomy skies, glazed at its apex like a lighthouse.

I descended down the long wide concrete ramp into the enormous space of the Turbine Hall. Dark girders reached up to the high ceiling like columns lining a nave-like space. The tall thin windows at either end only needed stained glass to make the transformation to an ecclesiastical building complete. I walked slowly, just letting the atmosphere of the place soak into me.

Halfway along an open mezzanine balcony jutted across the space. On top was a huge dark spider sculpture, rising up high on spindly legs. On the other side was the rest of the exhibition – three tall rusted metal towers of varying designs. There were long queues of people waiting to ascend. I thought about joining them, but then remembered why I was here. Checking the phone I saw that it was nearly the time when I should be standing in front of 'The Seagram Murals'.

I found a guide map and studied it as I rode the escalators up to the galleries.

I stood over it again. 'The Bricks'. One hundred and twenty of them, arranged in a ten by six by two slab – these bricks that were considered so special, in a building that was built from umpteen thousand other examples of their kind.

They were the prime exhibit in a room devoted to the concept of the grid. Straight, thin, narrow-gapped parallel lines have been ruled directly onto the walls above them, forming a work that consisted of different blocks of colour and direction – red, green, blue, black, yellow with lines drawn vertical, horizontal or slanting at forty-five degrees. Other grid-patterned pieces were repeated around the room, variations on the theme – a pattern that has been seen again and again throughout the last century – it did not need much imagination to transform them into networks of city streets, or rows of windows or a blank spreadsheet program waiting for its data.

I thought back to my own brief attempts at it, the chequered sheets of graph paper at our first collective art show.

The phone rang.

Not the beep to indicate a text but the full ring-tone but that familiar Nokia tune to show an actual caller.

Stephanie Smith?

I had almost expected it, right from the time I had received the first clue again, closing the loop.

'Hello?' I said.

But it was a man's voice that answered.

'Heard a weird thing the other day.' Catherine said, pointing down at 'The Bricks'. 'About this.'

Her close-cropped hair was just starting to grow out. She was wearing a denim jacket, jeans, and boots. Heavy make-up, as if to compensate for the tom-boy nature of her clothes and hair-cut.

'What's that?' I asked.

'Did you know some people think the artist's a murderer?'

'Jesus no, I didn't.' I said. 'What happened?'

'His wife, she was an artist too – but performance art, not minimalism like him. Anyway she fell from the window of their New York apartment. He said she killed herself, but there was a trial. I suppose they thought he must have pushed her or something. But he was acquitted. Thought you might have known though, I remember you saying it was such a big influence on you.'

'No, I've never heard that. But it's not the sort of the thing they usually put in art books, murder-suicide scandals like that.'

'Just thought it was a strange contrast, the order and regulation of his work, the chaos of that event.

She reached up to scratch behind her ear.

'Still itches?' I asked her.

'A bit.' She turned towards me, caught my eyes and then pointedly looked down towards the crotch of her jeans. 'And other places, too. But that's not so easy to scratch, in public.'

'Better go home then. See what we can do about that.'

'Yeah, we better.' She grinned.

The text had been eight equals signs again, the same clue as I had last night, plus 4pm. So the next artwork was 'Equivalence VIII' – 'The Bricks'. Which conveniently was also in Tate Modern, moved out from the original Tate along with the 'Seagram Murals'. So I had a spare two hours to explore the place.

I wandered the galleries, mingling with the other people, the tourists and students and other art lovers. The layout was refreshingly different, the work arranged into theme-based rooms, instead of the more typical chronological arrangement, a clever way to get around the gaps in the collection.

And then I found myself staring at one of my own pieces – in a small room devoted to art based around maps. There was a map of the UK that had been cut up and re-arranged to create an alternate Britain, with metropolises in the highlands of Scotland and acres of green space in the South East. Another piece had a map of the USA where everything, bar a couple of states, had been stripped away to leave them floating like islands, and another where the only towns indicated where the ones named Springfield.

My example was a plan for an imaginary war. On top of a fake map – a garish tourist planner – were numerous, carefully labelled rectangular symbols representing each side's regiments of infantry, artillery and tanks. Down the sides were illustrations of the highlights of the region – the majestic castles, pretty thatched villages, quiet woodland glades and river valleys that would all soon be smashed down and ground out to mud under the coming conflagration.

I never paid that much attention to where my work went once it was sold so I had not been aware that a piece had made it into the Tate's collection.

I gazed at my work from across the room, but I also looked at the people that viewed it. So different from a show, when everyone came up to you to tell you how great it is after giving it studied attention – but not too much attention, of course. Here it was glanced at, stared at, pointed at by school children. Some read the description by the side of the work, were I was supposedly 're-envisioning the imaginary landscape by the use of maps' and showing 'the depersonalisation of the destruction of war'. But more often than not it was just ignored because something more interesting had caught the viewer's eye. And finally it was laughed at by a pair of Japanese girls.

I shook my head and smiled to myself. Then I made my way towards the room labelled on the map as *The Grid* and to 'Equivalent VIII', 'The Bricks'.

'Hello?'

'Ah, Jason. Enjoying your little journey? Your little tour?' The voice was male, deep, breathy. 'Not sure what I'm going to call it yet–'

'Hello, is this Stephanie Smith's phone?'

'Stephanie. No. It's not.'

'Look, who is this? Is this some sort of joke? Because if it—'

'It's a long way from a joke.'

There was something familiar…

No…

'I thought of you, of all people, would recognise what I've done.' The voice continued. 'But obviously not.'

No, it can't be.

'Nothing more to say…? I must say I'm disappointed. Can't even guess who I am?'

I almost hesitated to say it out loud.

'Simon?' I hissed.

A short bark of a laugh.

'At last.'

'But… but…'

I just could not say it.

'I'm dead? Obviously not.'

A wave pulsed through the grid patterns on the wall in front of me. I looked down at bricks and they seem to blur out into one large block of concrete.

A tombstone…

I quickly turned and rushed out of the small room. I had to get some air. I almost ran through the galleries, ignoring the people around me, as that voice from the past whispered to me.

'No, not dead, not by a long way. Very much alive in fact.'

'But how? I saw you in the video. You jumped…'

'The eye can be deceived. You should know that. A so-called artist.'

I had reached the balcony that looked out over the turbine hall. One hand grabbing the railing I stared down at the floor far below. Stared down at the enormous black spider below me.

'But if you… then Catherine?' I almost cried out the last word.

'Oh, yes. She didn't jump either. I'd put her on now but she's a bit tied up at the moment.'

That hateful laugh again.

Then the voice altered, became hollow and echoey as if he'd taken the receiver from his mouth, and was calling out to someone else – 'It's Jason on the line. Want to speak to him…?' Then he's back close again. Breathing in my ear. 'No. No, she's shaking her head.'

'Look, you sick fuck, I don't know how you are doing this, how you got Catherine's number, or Stephanie's phone– '

'Ah, some balls at last.' The voice interrupted me, suddenly harder edged. 'You really still think it was her texting you? Giving you these clues? What the fuck does a pornographer know about art? But, I really don't care if you think it's me or not. It doesn't matter. Not for the end game. The final work in the series. Just adding the final touches to it now. Oh, you are going to love it.'

He paused. I heard a deep breath almost a sigh. Then, before he cut the connection, his final words dripped in my ear like acid. 'But, I'm sorry about your whore. That was a mistake and I apologise.'

Red and silver. The steps up to the flat. Silver metal. Tubs of red flowers. Silver and red. The key in my hand.

I had tried phoning Louise on the taxi over. Nothing, just the recorded message. I had promised the driver double his fee to get me back to Chelsea as fast as possible, but he still seemed far too slow as we were snarled up in the rush hour traffic.

No, she must have gone out, that's all. The twisted fuck is lying to me.

But as soon as I entered the flat I knew. When I saw in the main room her tarot cards spilled out across the floor.

I found her downstairs, in the reception area, lying face up. Her uniform ripped open at the front, bruises on her arms, her neck and her face. One of the shelves above her swept bare of toiletries, the bottles scattered over her and across the floor. A patch of blood behind her head, that flowed into the thick pale liquids that had spilled from where some of the bottles had smashed or split. She stared blankly at the ceiling with dark still eyes.

A card thrown down on the floor next to her.

A tarot card.

'Death'.

14 ERROR

Should have called them from the phone box.

I strode back into the yard, rubbing my hands together, my breath bright in the cold.

Running out of there like a frightened rabbit. It's not like they are going to let her leave in the middle of the night. What were you going to do...? Jump on your bike, pissed, and ride through the night to her? On iced-up roads?

I saw there were lights on in Mark's studio. Faint light's that flickered like Christmas illuminations – white, blue, green, in regular pulses, forming some sort of ordered sequence.

Phone them up, then bed. Then get round there in the morning. When I'm sober enough to drive without killing myself.

I unlocked the door and climbed the stairs. On the third floor the door to Mark's studio was ajar. Light flickered on the wall opposite, shining through the gap between door and frame.

I pushed the door back and stepped into the room
'Mark?'

The illumination was coming from the back of the room. From behind the shelves.

Lights beamed out, projecting square blocks of colour with text streaming down then onto the walls, floor and ceiling — white on black, black on white, green on black, white on blue. Computer code, I realised.

I stepped around the shelves.

Saw his artwork, now uncovered.

A ring of computers screens, some melted and twisted like Dali watches, connected by arcs of plastic and metal, radiating out from the centre so it looked like the hardware was exploding outwards. A frozen explosion, like an ultra-fast shutter speed photograph of a splash of water.

In the centre was a sphere of lenses, a compound eye, from where the light show was being projected.

One by one, the computer screens and the projected blocks of light, displayed the same single word. Streaming down in a continuous cascade it filled the screens — blinking, flashing, green on black — *ERROR*.

I saw Mark, lying on the floor in front of his artwork, the words crawling across his body, just before they broke up into random code again.

I rushed over. He was face down in a pool of acrid vomit. Vomit that was speckled with half-dissolved gel capsules.

He was cold, as cold as the night.

15 SHADOWS IN SHADOW

The inside of the top deck of the bus was brightly lit. Outside, there was light too – the slabs of illuminated shop windows, the lines and dots of street and vehicle lights. But the rest, in the darkening twilight, was all murk, shadows in shadows.

Down below, an abstract shape resolved into a queue of people shuffling forward to board the bus – only their movement giving them definition.

I had a whole seat to myself but I was sitting right up against the window. My head, resting against the glass, vibrated with the bus's engine, but there was also a slower pounding in my head.

As the bus pulled off I focused on the scratches in the glass, not what was beyond. Trying not think back to where I had just come from, what I had just seen but trying to answer the question – how?

How are they still alive?

I saw them die. Saw them jump.

I had hoped the journey would help me to solve it. I had often used bus journeys in the past, when I wanted to come up with new ideas for art, sparking inspiration by looking over my fellow passengers, or from the streets of London outside. But I could hardly see the streets now and most of the passengers were buried behind newspapers, books and magazines. And the same thought just kept spiralling round my mind. *How?*

The bus halted again. Bags were picked up and newspapers cast aside or folded up under arms as passengers stepped into the aisle and on towards the stairs. Someone walked past from behind me. I glanced up and saw dark curls of chestnut hair. And before I realised it, I was back there again.

I had no idea how long I stood over Louise. Seconds? Minutes? Could have been an hour for all I know. Just to see her here there, silent and unmoving, for a while, time had no meaning. I thought back to before, but this was far worse than with Mark and I kept imagining the terror of her final moments – her fighting back but finally being overpowered.

For one long moment I truly felt like joining her.

Then I remembered the phone call.

Catherine is alive? Probably lies, but…

I had to know either way.

I reached into my pocked for my keys, removed the one Louise had given me and dropped it onto her desk. I opened the reception door and stepped outside into the evening. I let the door shut behind me.

I was about to walk away, but there was something…

What had she said? That she had customers tonight? Her girls, I could not let them find her like that…

I pulled out the mobile phone and dialled three nines.

As soon as I was asked what service I required I cut in with, 'There's a body…' and rushed out the address then closed the call on any further questions.

Then I really had to move. I had cut off any choice in the matter.

Again I had left everything behind – my other clothes, my folder with Catherine's art. I felt a twinge of regret at the latter – but I just had to be moving.

I walked down the alley to the street, then on towards the main road. At the end, on the Kings Road, I saw a bus pull up. I ran to join the end of the queue.

The bus stopped again, jerking me out of my memories back into the same questions.

How? I saw them jump. I saw them die. How are they still alive? I saw it all in that video.

And now?

Were they really alive?

The only evidence was a voice on a phone.

Could it be some trick, someone impersonating Simon, recreating his voice somehow?

No, those artworks I had been sent around were too personal to me and Catherine. She must have told him.

Then I realised. Remembered. Remembered seeing her. Before, on the way back to studio. And outside the health spa. Not a ghost. Not my imagination.

It had been her, alive! I had to find her! Get to her!

I pulled myself upright. Breathing hard I gripped the top of the seat in front of me.

But where? Those texts… that phone call. They could have come from anywhere in the county. In the world, even.

I plunged my hand into the jacket pocket and grabbed for the phone.

But what was the point of that? He had never answered before. And even if he did, then what? What could I do except curse him, swear at him then plead with him to tell me where he was?

No. I shook my head and taking my hand out of my pocket forced my breathing under control.

I had to be calm and logical and out-think him. He had manipulated and tricked me for too long.

How long?

The texts were to the phone in the locker of the health spar... Which must have been planted for me to find. And the health spar I had discovered via the calendar in the flat, the flat from the tattooists, the tattooists from the photo at the publishers, the publishers from the drawings in studio...

How far back? The cottage? The video?

The video.

Yes, that had to be the biggest trick of all.

I had been waiting in the pub for half an hour before he arrived, glancing up every time the door opened. But I instantly knew this had to be the man I was waiting for. Everything about him said copper, the short cropped hair, the bomber jacked zipped up over a plain white shirt., the hard gaze that scanned the whole pub. The only exception was the scrunched-up Tescos carrier bag he held in one hand.

I gave him a nod as he was looking in my direction and he strode over to my booth. Sitting down opposite he casually dropped the bag down at his feet.

'Drink?' I asked.

'No, I won't bother. Got the money?'

'Yeah, of course.' I reached for the coat on the seat beside me and pulled out an envelope.

'Under the table.'

It had been much easier than I had expected.

At first the liaison officer had not seemed sympathetic to my hints. But the second time we met he casually mentioned the name of a desk sergeant, suggested I might have a word with him. The desk sergeant had seemed non-committal too. But there had been a phone call a couple of days later from someone else, someone who said they could help me and a meeting was arranged.

I held out the envelope under the table. But the man opposite did not make a move.

'Last chance,' he said. 'You sure? I know people think they wanna see things. Clothes. The body. But sometimes it makes it worse. Sometimes it's better not knowing it all. Letting it rest.'

'No, I want it.'

He just nodded then reached out for the money. He slipped it inside his coat and stood, all in one easy movement. He walked back to the door leaving the carrier bag on the floor behind him.

A burst of white noise – the screen seethed and boiled with static.

Then an abrupt switch from chaos to order as the static was replaced with colour bars and a single pure sine-wave tone.

A cut to random dark shapes and muffled sounds. The view swung and jerked sharply as the camera was moved – glimpses of a cloudy night sky then swung down towards grass.

The view was grainy, contrast poor. Not a professional-standard camera, or tape, I had been told.

A face suddenly filled the screen, distorted.

Catherine.

She moved further back. The view was now fixed, the camera obviously having been mounted on top of a tripod. Grass reached out to an abrupt edge that cut across the screen about twenty metres away. Night sky above, a few stars between the clouds.

Catherine wore a long dark coat. She held something in her hand, a sheet of rectangular white card about the size of a large envelope. Wind ruffled her hair, dyed black.

'That's it. It's running.' Her voice was hard to hear over the wind noise on the camera's cheap microphone. And there was also a constant rolling hiss on the soundtrack – the sea, breaking against the bottom of the cliffs.

A light was turned on behind the camera. For a few seconds Catherine blinked against the glare, holding a hand up to her eyes. A long shadow now reached out behind her towards the cliff edge, where the white cone of light started to grey out and the sky beyond turned to a pitch black.

The camera was adjusted, panned slightly so I could see the rear of a car. His car.

Simon came into shot beside her. He wore a similar long dark coat. They kissed. It was brief, but it still sickened me. Shocked me.

Catherine stepped forward. She held up the card to the camera then flipped it over. On the other side, hand-written in thick black felt-tip pen – '*LEAP OF FAITH*'.

Catherine stepped back, threw the card aside, and started talking again but I could hardly hear. Did not want to hear. Most of it made no sense anyway. That this was not a destructive act but a creative one, the ultimate artistic action. That they were about to take the final step – the leap of faith – the leap into the imagination that would live in our minds forever. That by launching themselves off these pristine white cliffs, this blank canvas at the edge of the world, they would become symbols of pure art.

Halfway through I saw the tears glistening on her face. She did not seem to notice, though I was certain at one point she choked back a sob when she apologised. Apologised to me. Apologised for the hurt she knew it was going to cause me.

But then she went on to say that in the end it would save me, set me free, release me from her. Save me from her life, from all her lives, from everything. She said much the same again, addressing it to her family.

Finally she stopped. Turned to Simon. He just shook his head, said there was nothing more to add. They kissed again. Longer this time. More passionate.

'Let's do it.' He said when they parted. And she nodded, stiffly.

Holding hands they walked towards the cliff. At the edge of the cone of light they turned to two grey smears against the blackness of the sky.

And then they were gone. Just gone. Dropping down behind the edge of the cliff, the coats billowed out briefly.

Then, nothing… just the same shot, steady, unrelenting. The only movement was the wind running invisible fingers through the grass.

I fast-forwarded. The view became ragged – ripped across by two thin bars of static – but nothing else changed all the way to the end of the tape.

I rewound and it watched again. And again. And again.

The bodies were never found. The tide had been high. The sea rough. Speculation that they had weighted down their clothes. The family had been told that they might end up washed up on a beach somewhere but there never were. Empty coffin funerals.

'The eye can be deceived,' Simon had once said. He was right there.

The video had been faked, then – could have been created days before and just left at the site.

Did they step out of frame for a second as they walked back and another shot edited in? Dummies falling? Easy to hide in the roughness of recording… if you were not looking for it.

I could not check. Not now. I had ripped out the tape and burnt it, turned the casing to a lump of melted black slag, then thrown it out with the rubbish. It had been my last impetuous act before leaving the studio for the cottage.

How could she? How could they!

I punched the back of the empty seat in front of me, hard.

I looked up and around at the now sparse collection of passengers but no one seemed to have noticed. Or were ignoring me at least.

I shook my head. This was hardly thinking logically and clearly, rethinking bad memories.

And the question was not how they faked the video, or even why that had done it.

No, not how? Or why? But where?

Where are they?

He had talked of an end game, I remembered. Preparing something. Where would he do that?

Our studio? No, I could have gone back to that anytime. No, it had to be somewhere else.

He had sent no texts. Left no clues. Not this time. Unless, the card? The tarot card. The Death Card. But what sort of clue was that? She was dead.

The card. Just the card itself?

A trick. A card trick. 'Find The Lady'. His magic-tricks video.

That afternoon. That journey. The Shed. His big new studio. For his greatest projects. That's what he had said.

It had to be.

The bus had stopped again. I pulled myself upright. Out of my seat. Ran down the bus's steps. Out into the street.

The Shed. That's where I had to go.

I stopped. Looked around as the bus pulled away. Another row of shops, houses. Somewhere out in Metroland surely, but I had no idea where. Nothing I recognised, I realised. I could not remember what bus I had been on, what its destination might have been.

I was lost. Lost for the first time that I could remember.

But that did not matter. What mattered was I knew exactly where I was going.

Get a bus back to the city...? No, too slow. Find the nearest tube station then straight to Kings Cross. Plenty of trains this time of the evening. Taxi at the other end?

I watched the traffic that ran past me then shook my head. *No.*

No, there was only one way to travel to The Shed.

I felt into my pocket for my key ring.

Yes, I could feel the keys were still there, next to those for the studio – the keys to the lock-up garage and, more importantly, what was inside.

I opened the door of the garage and turned on the light.

It was alone, exactly as I had left it in the middle of the garage, draped in a couple of blankets. I uncovered it and spent just a few seconds looking at the perfection of its lines and curves in lime green and grey. I ran my hand along from the high rear seat, rising like a tail above the back wheel, down to where the cowling curved around the circumference of the front tire like an open mouth.

My motorbike. My Kawasaki Ninja. My green shark. My steed.

I swung one leg over and straddled it

It had been so tempting to get rid of the bike, after everything. But in the end I had left it alone, like the studio, when I had retreated to the cottage.

I put the key in the ignition and fired up the engine. It was rough and throaty after standing. Probably needed a tune-up, an oil change at least, but it would do for now.

I got off the bike, leaving the engine ticking over. At the back of lock-up was a high wooden shelf where there were two bike helmets alongside two pairs of boots. From hooks underneath there hung a leather jacket alongside another full set of leathers. One helmet was lime green, the leathers were the same colour – with the addition of swatches of sage, yellow and white jagged across the chest and down the side of the thighs. The matching boots were green and white. The other jacket was plain black leather, same as the other boots – the other helmet was a dull red.

I reached for the red helmet. Then stopped. I turned back to look at the bike. Looking at it as if seeing it for the first time.

My steed.

I took down the green helmet, pulled out the gloves folded inside. White with green flashes to match everything else. A damp musty smell, but no actual mould. The same with the leathers. I changed quickly.

I joined the rest of the traffic heading north up the duel carriageway.

I rode steadily, keeping a constant seventy, taking time to get used to the bike again.

I remembered another journey north, with Catherine sitting behind me, holding me tight. A journey, when I had thought up 'Blindsight', and we had visited the Shed on the way home.

Blindsight, when I had been so blind.

Those final months, came back to me in fragments – Blindsight, the Turner, and those final days.

That final day.
High in the sky I saw the moon. Full.
I'm coming. I'm coming for you.

16 BLINDSIGHT

'I'm going to call it 'Blindsight'.'

I shaded my eyes as we stepped out from the shadow of the statue into bright sunlight and gusting wind.

'What? Hang on a second.' Catherine stopped.

I turned to her. The wind blew her dark hair across her face. She ignored it, pulling the strap of her rucksack off her shoulder and reaching inside her jacket for her cigarettes and lighter. She fished a cigarette out of her the packet with her mouth as she turned away from the wind. She wedged her helmet between her knees sweep her hair back before cupping her hands round the cigarette to light it.

Although the leather trousers and boots she was wearing were plain black, her helmet was a bright candy pink, matching her jacket. The pink was a garish contrast to the rust colour of the great iron man that towered over both of us.

I was wearing my leathers too – my bright-greens, the matching helmet in my hand. As this was a special occasion Catherine had persuaded me to wear those instead of my old scruffy gear.

Catherine turned back to me, puffing grey smoke.

'What did you say?'

'My next piece.' I said 'I'm going to call it 'Blindsight'.'

Morning. The thirtieth of November, nineteen ninety-nine. The day was so special but it had started just like any other with me waking, dozing in bed for a few minutes, then getting up, a piss, clean teeth, shave, a shower, breakfast – the usual cereal, toast and coffee.

The one difference was that I was alone.

Catherine had left a note – that she had to nip out to film something for a new art project, that she would be back later, that she would be back for tonight.

I had found Catherine curled up on a sofa, asleep. She was hidden away at the back of the plush reception area of the hotel, the concierge having pointed me towards her. She wore a thick white cable-knit sweater and indigo coloured jeans, white socks. Dark brown ankle boots were standing in front of the sofa next to a leather bag.

When my hand stroked her shoulder she made a slight snuffling noise. Waking, she turned and stretched, her feet slipping to the floor.

'Oh shit, sorry.' She said, rubbing her eyes as she sat upright. 'I didn't mean to fall asleep. I've been travelling all night.'

'How...?' I started, sitting down beside her. 'God, Catherine–'

'I came back as soon as I heard.' She said quickly, a hand running through her blonde hair. 'I rang the studio, but only got the answerphone. Your business people said you had moved out here. I'm so sorry, I should have never fled like that...' Her voice trailed off as she looked down and away from me.

I slipped an arm around her shoulders and silently she turned back to embrace me.

'It's all right now.' I said. 'Now you are back.'

'Back for good.' She breathed into my shoulder.

'I tried to find you...'

'I didn't want to be found... But then I heard, on the news, on the radio... and I realised everything I was worrying about was just bullshit.' She sighed and turned her head back to face me. 'Do you know any more? Was it like Bird-Girl?'

'Suicide?' I shook my head. 'They don't know yet. Not officially. But there was no note... the policeman in charge told me the general feeling is misadventure. Too much drink on top of the pills. The door was open so he may have tried to get help or something.'

'And you found him?'

'Yeah. Right after I phoned you.'

'Fuck.' Her voice low.

She turned and reached down for her bag and pulled out a packet of cigarettes – twenty Silk Cut – and a brass Zippo lighter. Next to the sofa was a small table with a lamp and ashtray. Catherine dragged the ashtray closer to her as she lit a cigarette. After taking a long drag and exhaling it she turned back to me.

'I'll quit soon.' She said, glancing towards the cigarette in her hand.

'Jesus, don't worry about that. I'm just glad to see you... I worried. Your parents...?'

'I've rung them. It was hard but... I think it's going to be all right. I was so selfish. Going off like that. But I thought that place was messing up my head up even worse. The treatment centre.' She looked again at the cigarette between her fingers. 'They gave me a proper addiction for a start. Everyone smoked like chimneys in there. But I think talking to some of the others did help, gain me some perspective at least. Then the time on my own... in a hotel on the south coast – well hotels, I kept moving on from town to town – walking alone along the beaches. That got my head together.'

'I never should have sent you off. I panicked when...'

'I know. That's the past now anyway.' She flicked the ash off her cigarette then swept her hand round to include the whole of the reception area before returning the cigarette to her mouth. 'This is very smart.'

'I had to. The police were all over the studio at first. And then... Well, bad memories, you know? I couldn't go back.'

'But we must.' She interrupted me. 'Go back. Can't let bad memories haunt us. Destroy us. If there's one I thing I've learned it's that.'

She placed the cigarette on the edge of the ashtray then reached for my hand, taking it in both of hers.

'Do you forgive me though? Can you forgive me?'

'Of course I do.'

She nodded, just once. Then smiled.

'Good. I've got loads of new ideas. For art. Video work mainly. Must go and buy a camera. But first...'

She reached for the cigarette and took a final drag before stubbing it out.

She turned back to me, her hand on my thigh.

'Your room, I need a shower and...?' She said, hesitantly. 'If you want? If you can–'

I leaned forward and kissed her.

'That'll take a bit of getting used to.' I said after we parted.

'What?' She frowned.

'The taste of ciggs.'

'Oh sorry. I–'

I kissed her again. Then gave her a smile.

'See, I'm getting use to it already.'

'It's impressive. Up close.' Catherine said, crouching.

Holding her cigarette tight in her lips she placed her helmet on the ground in front of her and slung off her backpack. She pulled out her video camera and holding it one-handed, the cigarette between the fingers of the other hand, she pointed it straight up at me. Then slowly she panned the camera across to the statue, then up along the deep ribs of the legs and torso, on past the broad reach of the wings, to pause again at the head.

'Impressive, it certainly is.' I agreed. 'Though I think I preferred seeing it last night from the road with the sunset.'

'Yes. That was beautiful.'

'He would have loved this.' I said. 'Mark.'

'Yeah,' Catherine said, still filming. She had panned the camera up until it was almost vertical, shooting the thin scudding clouds above the statue. 'Although a bit too representational? The human form. An angel a bit obvious?'

'I was thinking more of the scale of it. This great lump of metal. The sheer splendour of all that hard engineering.'

Catherine turned off the camera and put it into her bag, then looked up at me.'So what's this 'Blindsight', then?'

I held out my hand to help her stand up again. 'Let's take a walk to the bottom of the hill and I'll tell you all about it.'

Mid-morning. The phone rang.

I put down my coffee and turned down *News 24*. The report was all about the coming trade conference in Seattle and the protesters gathering, plus a feel-good report that T-bone steaks would be un-banned by Christmas. I tried to think of the last time I had actually eaten one as I picked up the phone. It was Catherine.

'Where are you?' I asked.

'Sorry, just realised, I had to get out for something. Had to film it now. What with us going away.'

'What is it?'

'You'll see, if it works out. Don't worry, I'll be back for tonight. What are you up to?'

'Not much, just lounging around, watching television. Tried to do some work but can't concentrate... not with tonight. Stupid really. It's not like I'm going to win.'

'No, I suppose...' He voice trailed off.

'What?'

'Sorry.'

'Look, are you all right, Catherine?'

There was a pause. Silence down the line.

'Last night.' I continued. 'If you think—'

'No, it's not that. It's just....

'What?'

'No, it's nothing.'

'Are you sure? Because you sound—'

'Yes. Of course. See you tonight. Got to go, bye.'

And then the line went dead.

Blindsight — seeing without seeing. I had come across the concept in an article on consciousness in the *New Scientist*.

I had heard the word before, I was sure, and I thought I knew what it meant. That it was the way the blind can 'see' without vision — walking around a familiar room avoiding all the furniture from memory or using other senses to tell where things were like Ray Charles knew when he passed an open doorway in the street because the sounds of the metal taps on his shoes against the pavement would subtly change.

Or so I thought. Turned out I was wrong.

Blindsight was a technical term for something else entirely.

The processing of sight is not a single discrete function in the brain, it comes from a number of systems working together – while one set projects the images into our consciousness, another processes that information for other parts of the brain to use.

With blindsight a person suffers a particular rare form of brain injury that leaves them blind in one eye. However the eye itself is undamaged, the blindness being due to damage to a specific part of the brain than handles one aspect of visual processing. In tests, their good eye is covered and they are shown a number of dots on a screen. Though they are unable to actually see them, if asked to guess how many dots there are, they still invariably give the right number.

So those with blindsight may not be able to actually 'see' something – have pictures of it in their mind – but they can react to it.

Later I found myself wondering if the opposite of blindsight could be true, 'sightblind' as it were. That instead of reacting to something you did not see you could see something but not react to it. That there might be something really obvious, something that was right in front of you, but which you just ignored.

Catherine and I moved back into the studio.

In a meeting with ourselves and Simon we all agreed that the collective was now effectively over and allotted out the remaining assets between us, the studio coming to me and Catherine. We hired some people to clear out Mark's section, then sealed it up. For a long time I had to suppress a faint shiver every time I passed the door.

However, although the studio officially remained our main base of operations we actually found ourselves spending little time there. We moved from the hotel there had still been reporters and photographers lurking so went to Catherine's family home for a bit of privacy, taking over a cluster of rooms in a distant wing for our sole use – the 'no sleeping together' rule quietly forgotten. And even when the news agenda moved on we ended up spending most weekends out there – those stays occasionally extending into whole weeks at a time, a month or so in the summer.

Also, Catherine's new direction in art – her video work – took her out and about to gather footage, much more than her photography had ever done. And when she was not filming, she would spend days away in hired video-editing suites, putting it all together. I would receive excited mobile calls telling me how well the editing was going.

Her first pieces consisted of long single takes of the inside of abandoned buildings with a fixed camera. Catherine would occasionally enter the shot, walking or running or crawling, dressed in a mix of ragged old clothes, never acknowledging the camera. She mixed in short splices, almost freeze-frames, of walls splattered with stage blood. The soundtrack was just amplified muffled breathing. 'Existential Horror Films' she called them. I was initially worried about their subject, but later I realised it was just something she had to get out of her system.

She eventually exhibited her films and received a muted, but positive, reception. However by that time she had already moved on to a much bigger project shooting candid footage from hidden cameras all over London: inside offices, shops, pubs, sports halls and cinemas, theatres and libraries, out on the street and down the underground. Catherine was always in shot, usually just a small figure in the background. She electronically scrubbed out all the details from the visible faces in the scenes, turning each one into a soft blur.

Simon told us he was working on something big, though his next exhibition was rather smaller scale. He had advertised for wedding photographs from people who had since divorced. He carefully split each one in two between bride and groom and their respective families. He re-matched each bride with a groom from another wedding, mixing up class and race, young and old, high church and registry office.

I was kept busy disposing of Mark's estate – being named as his executor – selling off the pieces he had finished. Most of the profits went to various AIDs charities, as his will had specified. In the end I did not have the heart to burn the paintings his machine had made, as he had planned. I wanted as much of his work as possible to live on.

However the one piece I could not deal with was 'Error'. I just could not see it again, and Mark's solicitors found another dealer to handle it.

Art-wise, I only produced a few simple drawings and paintings of the streets around the studio, waiting for the next big idea.

Then one day Catherine and I decided to go see the new 'Angel Of The North'.

'Want to go back now?' Catherine asked.

We were walking towards my motorbike parked on the road outside the entrance to the Angel site.

'Hell of a long way to London.' I said. 'I was thinking that maybe we could stay another night and set off first thing tomorrow. Break up the journey – stop off at Simon's studio and have a quick look at what he's up to.'

'Good idea.' Catherine said, then glanced back towards the statue. 'I'm glad we came.'

'Oh, yes'

'Going back during the day will be good. I want to try and get some footage of the statue from the road as we leave.'

'Thought you did that yesterday?'

'You noticed?'

'I could hardly not, your squirming around about behind me. You might have warned me, I thought you'd have us over at one point.'

'Yeah, well, sometimes you have to take a risk for your art.' She looked down sheepishly

'I don't mind you taking risks for your own art, it's me taking risks for yours, that I do mind about.'

She laughed at that, then reached into her jacket for another cigarette.

Late afternoon. I had torn the dry cleaning bag off my suit and unwrapped my new shirt and ironed it. I wondered again if I should a wear a tie, but as Catherine had said, I was supposed to an artist now, with an image to keep up and ties were for just funerals and weddings.

I tried phoning her again but there was no answer.

Once an interviewer asked me, 'After all that death, what kept you sane?' I automatically answered, 'My art. My art keeps me sane.' Seeing her confused expression I had to explain it came from a film, *Scanners*. And then her confusion turned to shock because, for most people, that film is just one scene, the only one they remember if they have seen it, the only one they have heard about if they have not – the exploding head. But there is another scene that resonates with me much more now, a scene that I actually overlooked on the first viewing when I was crammed into a friend's front room with half a dozen others shouting-out 'Rewind!' at the gory bits. However, years later, during my time at art college, I watched it again, on my own, when it came up on late-night television. I was in a more reflective mood and it was another scene that stood out for me then. The film's hero, a telepath, was talking to another telepath, an artist, at his studio, asking him how he stopped the voices, what kept him sane? They were sitting inside the sculpture of a giant head that the artist telepath had built. The artist pointed up at the sculpture then to his own head and simply said, 'My art, my art keeps me sane'.

After Mark's death I was at first lost in grief, feeling myself on the edge of sanity, especially with Catherine gone, but what eventually calmed me was the thought that I had to continue. That I had to go on with the process of creating art. That my art would keep me sane.

And eventually I realised that the art that I wanted to create next was for Mark. A memento-mori. Create an artwork that would both celebrate and remember him. Something that was of my work and his. But also something that would assuage my feelings of guilt. Guilt that I could have saved him. That I should have seen. That I was blind.

I started studying death art, visiting churches and cemeteries as well as galleries, trying to seek inspiration from the most ancient of tombs all the way up to Andy Warhol's car-crashes and electric chairs.

I thought of the traditional memento-mori images: a pile of skulls; clocks – broken, their cogs, springs and other workings scattered; hourglasses, smashed, their sand cast out across out the gallery floor. I considered just showing an absence – perhaps by changing the art-space itself, having the gallery empty, or unlit, the door ajar to show just blackness beyond. Or some sort of performance art? A ceremony like Catherine and I had done for Bird-Girl – scattering the feathers – but something more public. But I soon realised I did not want to dilute the effect of that act on both of us by repeating it.

Nothing seemed right.

Then, when I first saw it from the road, that iron avatar, that Angel Of The North, poised with wings outstretched as if about to zoom up to heaven, several ideas suddenly started to coalesce in my mind, to flow together like scrap metal melting in a furnace.

I thought of other angels I had seen, the stone angels at Highgate and the other cemeteries. And then on to other grave markers – the rectangular solidity of tombstones. Monuments that marked a life, represented a life.

I thought of Mark's art and his sculpture.

I thought of my own art – not the recent stuff, the maps, or architecture – but back to my earlier work, my grids and geometry.

Grave-markers. Sculpture. Geometry.

Together they merged and out-poured one pure idea.

Three-dimensional geometry.

Objects of three-dimensional geometry to both celebrate and commemorate a life. All life.

The Platonic solids. The set of five basic regular solids. Each one made of a different element of life. But not the modern chemical elements of the body – the hydrogen, oxygen, carbon and the rest. I thought of something simpler, more ancient, more primal, to match the Platonic solids – the Greek elements – air, earth, water, fire, adding a couple more to reflect the changes in the world since those ancient times.

Once I returned to the studio, once I started sketching and planning, I soon realised there was no way I could learn all the skills that I needed, to create all that I wanted myself.

So I spoke to a number of sculptors and visited the places – the metal fabricators, the joinery shops – they recommended to discuss my plans.

I designed then had fabricated a collection of sculptural objects. They were all three meters high so they would dominate whatever space they were placed in.

The first was 'Ve'. An icosahedron – a twenty-sided solid, each face an equilateral triangle; gem-like, almost spherical. It represented information, knowledge, memory. Each side was plastered with printed pages – each side a different source – ripped from old horror novels, from a *Complete Works of Shakespeare*, from dictionaries, the phone book, sheet music for a Beethoven sonata, diagrams from a Haynes car manual, pages from newspapers and more.

'Double You' was a dodecahedron. Twelve sides, all pentagrams. This was metal. And again each side was different: cut from pure sheets of steel, aluminium or lead – left dull or buffered to a high shine; from sections of blackened brass or green-tarnished copper; from pieces cut from the doors of old cars, the sides of washing machines and other scrap, some rusted or still flecked with paint.

'Ex', was an octahedron. Eight triangular-shaped sides, like two pyramids stuck base to base. This one was wood – elm, oak, ash, chestnut, pine, birch, walnut and maple – all polished to show off their grain and fitted together seamlessly.

'Why' was a cube, a simple glass tank filled with its one element, water.

'Zed', the last platonic solid, was a tetrahedron, a pyramid shape with three triangle sides extending up from a triangular base. This one was earth, to be assembled on site. Shuttered behind bands of toughened perspex it would be slowly built up in different layers of cobbles, gravel, sand, slit and mud, collected or imported from all parts of the country.

And there was one more. A sphere. Technically not a Platonic solid at all but it would be the full stop to the whole work. And also – like the angels I had seen – I wanted something to symbolise the idea of renewal with a shape referring back to the almost sphere-like icosahedron at the start.

I called it 'Alpha/Omega' – the first and the last. Made from frosted glass it was lit from the inside by an array of lights that were linked together and computer-controlled so that seemed to flicker and pulse and throb, producing the subtle effect I wanted, to give the impression of an unearthly mix of fire and air, plasma like the sun, or the spark of life itself.

That was 'Blindsight'.

And that was what won me the Turner.

Catherine was lying back against the beanbags and cushions that were piled up in one corner of the small room, watching television. She had a dark blue towel wrapped around herself, her damp hair pulled back and tied with a black ribbon. Bright summer sunshine seeping through and around the edges of the drawn curtains illuminated her in a haze of light.

The room was just off our bedroom in Catherine's parents' house, one of the small suite of rooms we used whenever we were there.

The sound of the television had woken me. After strolling naked into the on-suite bathroom for a piss and to clean my teeth, I had pulled on a pair of combats before opening the door of the television room.

I sat down beside Catherine as she shifted across to give me more room. On the television screen cartoon cars were chasing each other.

'What's this?' I asked. *Wacky Races?*

'Close. *Penelope Pitstop*. Her own show. Though she was always my favourite on the original, too.' Catherine brought her hand up, pressing the back to her forehead, tipping her head back. *'Hee-elp! Hee-elp!'* She cried, putting on a broad Southern Belle accent.

'Hmm, don't know who my favourite was… The gangsters, the Anthill Mob was it? Though they were a bit creepy. Actually it was probably Dick Dastardly or Muttley.'

'Definitely Penelope Pitstop for me,' Catherine said. 'Though I think she was the only girl. I remember always wanting a pink car like hers. Never got one though.'

'You could get one now.'

'Nah, I'm past all that. Like when I was a princess. Talking of which…' She pushed herself to her feet and stepped over me heading back towards the bedroom. 'Won't be a tick.'

A minute or so later she returned, holding a couple of old school exercise books in her hand.

'Mother found these the other day.' Catherine said. She dropped one of them into my lap as she stepped back over me and returned to her previous position on the floor. 'Meant to show you them before.'

I picked up the book and slowly paged through it. It was filled with drawings of knights, dragons, and castles and similar, mostly in pencil crayon – obviously done by a child but still showing some precocious skill.

'Nearly my very earliest work.' Catherine said.

'Not bad.' I said, turning to her. 'You can see your later talent here.'

She smiled. 'Thanks. They were fun, my own fantasy world.'

She flicked through the book she had kept hold of until she found a particular page and showed it to me. A fairytale princess in the viewing stands at a joust accepted the colours of a knight on horseback, reaching out for the green scarf tied to the end of his lance.

'This was supposed to be me,' She said, pointing at the princess.

'Obviously,' I nodded. The princess had long blond flowing hair and I recognised some of Catherine's features in her face.

Her finger went down to the knight. 'And this was you.'

'What?'

'Yeah, I always dreamed of someone coming to rescue me. Especially during the bad times, the anorexia and all that.'

'But I'm no knight. I'm a commoner, a peasant.'

'Oh, I wouldn't say that.' She leaned over to kiss me on the cheek. 'Anyway my knights were all from poor backgrounds, not poshos like me. Warriors who had been rewarded by the king for success in battle – not ones who had been born into it.'

'I'm no warrior either.'

'But you told me you did martial arts?' She cocked her head to one side, raised an eyebrow. 'Didn't you?'

'That was ages ago.' I pointed at the drawing, at the knight. 'And I don't have a horse? I can't even ride.'

'You've got a steed.'

'What steed?'

'Your iron steed… Your motorbike.'

'Ah, right. Yeah, I suppose so.'

'You'll have to take me out on it sometime.' She closed her book and put it down on the floor besides her.

I reached over and put the book she had given me on top.

'Thought you didn't want to.' I said.

'Think I've changed my mind about that. It can't be any worse than a galloping horse. And you don't leap over fences do you?'

'Not usually. Have to get you a helmet then. Jacket and boots as well.'

'No problem.' She pushed herself to her feet and stepped over to the television. The cartoon was just finishing, the titles streaming up the screen. Catherine leaned down to switch it off. 'I can get a pink jacket and helmet like Penelope.'

I smiled. 'If you want. But don't expect me to go riding with you in return. I still don't fancy getting on a horse.'

She turned around, looking down at me.

'Oh, don't worry, there's some rides I want to keep to myself.'

'Yeah?'

She untied the ribbon, dropped it to the floor and shook out her hair. She unwrapped the towel and let it fall to her feet.

'*Some* rides…'

'Is this it?' Catherine asked, her voice slightly muffled as she took her helmet off.

I pulled the bike back and up onto its stand and then pulled my own helmet off. Ours was the only vehicle in a small car park labelled 'Visitors Only' in front of a huge grey box-like building. The building was in the middle of a light industrial estate on the edge of Peterborough.

'I'm sure it is.' I said, pointing over towards the entrance that was in the middle of a stretch of single-story office buildings squatting up against the nearest corner of the main structure. Blinds were pulled down in all the windows of the office section. 'SHED' was spelled out in bold block capitals on a sign next to the door. 'That's what he said he'd called it.'

'Bit bigger than the garden shed I was expecting.' Catherine said as we walked to the entrance. 'It's enormous.'

'See if there's anyone home.' I said, stepping forward.

I found the door unlocked, it swung open as I pushed against it.

Inside was a small empty foyer. On the right was an open window through to an office behind which was sitting a middle-aged overweight man in a security guard's uniform. He had a motoring magazine spread open on the desk in front of him. He stood up.

'We're friends of Simon.' Catherine said. 'He's expecting us.'

He traced his finger down a printed list on his desk.

'Catherine and Jason?' He said looking up, and we both nodded.

He picked up a mobile phone. While he made a call I glanced around. Facing us were a set of two heavy red fire doors in the far wall. To either side of them a pair of corridors led off out of the foyer. The only thing on any of the walls was an electronic time clock. There were no chairs or anywhere else to sit, no plants or anything else to try and humanise the space.

The fire doors suddenly swung open and Simon strode out towards us. He was wearing blue overalls and work boots.

'Glad you could make it!' He grinned and shook both of our hands. 'Found us all right?'

'Went past it at first.' I said. 'Thought this couldn't be the place. Far too big.'

He shrugged.

'Yeah, maybe it is a bit excessive. But I couldn't resist it.' He led us back over to the fire doors, pushing them open for us. 'Anyway, I'll show you what I'm up to.'

Beyond the doors was an enormous open space, lit from high above by lines of strip lighting. The space was mostly empty but close to us were several long metal tables. Around the nearest couple were a dozen or so people of both sexes, mostly young, all dressed in the same overalls Simon was wearing. Each were busy taking objects from small plastic hoppers in the middle of the tables and adding them to boxes that they passed from one to the other. As we approached I could see some of the objects were novelty items like you might find in a cracker – spinners, mini jigsaws, dice. Other hoppers were filled with mysterious looking pieces of plastic that had no obvious purpose. At the far end of the table the boxes were being sealed with packing tape, labelled and then stacked onto a pallet. A forklift truck was carrying a full pallet swathed in plastic wrap to the other end of the factory space, where several more stacked pallets were arranged in a neat row in front of loading bay doors.

'It's very industrial.' Catherine said.

'Mark would have liked it.' I added. I turned to Simon. 'I'm planning to do something for Mark by the way. My next art work. Some sort of tribute.'

'Good idea.' Simon said.

'I was inspired by the statue.'

'Impressive is it?' Simon asked.

'Oh, yes!' Said Catherine. 'We both liked it.'

'I'll have to go and have a look myself.' Simon said. 'When all the tourists have seen it.'

'So?' Catherine asked Simon. 'What exactly are you doing?'

Simon started walking down the length of the table, past the backs of the workers and we followed.

'A new art project. Postal art – similar to what I've done in the past. But with this one I started with random objects that I sent out with a letter asking people to add their own and to send it on to a friend of theirs. A certain number of passes and it comes back here. Most disappear of course, but quite a few do make it back and these I add to and I send out again.' He pointed to half-way down the length of the building where I could see a sizeable stack of boxes. They were all battered and worn to some extent – they had obviously been through the post. 'Not had a chance to check the latest but I'm sure some of them have been right round the world several times.'

'Pass the parcel?' Catherine said.

'Yeah. Pass the parcel.' Simon replied. 'That's the idea.'

'What are you sending?' I asked him.

'Started with mainly novelties. Recently I've starting adding in plastic parts, lightweight stuff – spares from white good manufacturers, electronics companies. I realised it doesn't really matter.'

'Did you really need all this space?' I asked.

'Oh yes, it was nearly full at first. But there's quite a fall off since the early days. It's just the hard-core participants I'm catering for now. I'll wind it up soon, then create a show out of it with what I've been sent.'

'Then all these people will be out of a job.' I said.

'They are only temporary staff.' Simon said. 'Some art students… look good on their CVs'

'And then?' I asked.

'I've got a few more ideas for this place.'

'What, more art like this?'

'No, I'm going to divide it up. Portion out the space for other projects. Sublet for studio space. And I've been thinking of turning at least part of it into a television studio or two, with full lighting rigs, sound proofing. Add a couple of editing suites in the offices. Hire them out – for visual arts stuff, corporate videos. There're loads of independent production companies springing up. Plenty of work.'

'What stuck out here? Who's going to use it?'

'We're only an hour from London on the train. Not much more by road. And we'll be a lot cheaper than any other facilities. Reckon it'll be a gold mine.'

'Well, it's your money.'

'Don't worry, I'll do you a cheap rate.' He said with a smile.

'I'm not very likely to be using it. Catherine, though — she's moved over into video. Did you know?'

'Yeah. It was Catherine who suggested it.'

I turned to her. 'Did you?'

'Thought I mentioned it?' She said. 'I mean, it wouldn't hard for me to come up here. Thought you could come up with me, see your folks for once, while I'm working.'

'I'll show you. Already got something basic set up. To get the feel of it.' Simon said, as he started walking back to the fire-doors, beckoning us to follow him. He led us back to the foyer and down one of the corridors, opening the first door we came to. Inside a young man was sitting in front of a mixing desk, facing a row of four television monitors, all blank except one. On that screen someone was manipulating playing cards. We could only see his hands. As we watched he fanned the cards out and pulled out three — the two red aces and the queen of spades — discarding the rest of the deck. He turned the selected cards face down and then swapped two over. He turned over a card — it should have been the queen, but now it was an ace. He turned over the next card, another ace. Then he turned over the final card and that was also an ace too, the ace of spades, the queen having vanished. The footage then finished with colour-bars and then static.

The video technician glanced up at Simon.

'Nearly all the tapes logged.' He said.

'Great,' Simon said.

'What's this, Paul Daniels?' I asked.

'Could be,' Simon said. 'Been gathering all this footage of magicians doing tricks anonymously. I just like the idea of doing something about magic. You know, simple tricks of the eye. Misdirection and all that.'

'I can see that.' Catherine said. 'I liked magic when I was kid too.'

'Might not work out though.' Simon said, picking up a tape off the console. 'Not got any ideas how to make into art. Not yet anyway.'

'If you want any help, any tips, let me know. I'm learning a lot at the moment,' Catherine said. 'About video that is, not magic. Though I actually thought about doing something about magic a while back.'

'Really?' Simon said, putting the video down and turning to her.

'Yeah, it's difficult though, hard to find a new way of dealing with it.' She said. 'Others have gone there before.'

'Who?' I asked.

'Yves Klein for one.'

'What him and his patented blue colour?' I said. 'Great canvasses of it. What's that to do with magic?'

'It's not just that he was famous for. He did this photograph – 'Leap of Faith' it was called. It shows him jumping out of a window, suspended in mid-air. Even now it's not exactly obvious how he did it.'

'Right,' Simon said. 'I'll have to look into that.' He turned towards the video technician. 'I'd better start looking through the stuff you've logged, that might give me some ideas.' He turned back to us. 'Unless…?'

'No, we had better be getting moving, anyway.' I said. 'Wanted to miss the rush-hour traffic.'

'I'll see you out.' Simon said, walking over to the door. Then he turned back to us. 'Catherine? You don't mind me doing this, do you? Video, I mean? Didn't want you think I'm treading on your toes.'

'I don't have exclusive use of the medium.' Catherine said with a smile.

Simon grinned back.

'That's always assuming I can get something out it. Just have to keep going and see what happens I suppose. Make my own leap of faith.'

Early evening. At the Tate. I had just peeled away from the main crowd and headed back towards the entrance.

I pulled out my phone. Checking it every few minutes had become a nervous tick. No messages. No missed calls. Again.

I tried her number for the umpteenth time, leaving yet another whispered message to please call back, to let me know where she was, to tell me when she was going to arrive, that I was worried about her, that I was truly sorry about the other night.

There had been a message earlier that I had missed making a final trip to the toilet before leaving. She had told me she was working on a special piece of art, her masterpiece she thought, that I would be amazed by it. But also that she would make the ceremony, that she was on her way back right then, that she would meet me at the Tate.

But there was something about her voice that worried me – sounding too flat and measured for what she was telling me.

I had called back immediately. But there had been no answer, then or since, and no other calls.

I reluctantly slipped the phone back in my pocket, resisting checking it yet again.

Looking up I saw two people approaching me, the two clowns Fred and Ginger, but out of costume. They were wearing close-fitting matching suits of a metallic-looking dark blue, almost black cloth, ivory shirts and deep red ties. No make-up.

'On your own?' Ginger asked. 'I heard Simon's away abroad, can't get back or something. Jealous of you?'

'Don't be daft.' I said.

'And the darling Catherine?' Fred added.

'Soon, I hope. Got delayed with some art project.'

'Oh, don't worry,' Fred said. 'She'll be here. Not going to miss her man's big moment!'

'I'm only making the numbers up.' I said, shaking my head. 'Not clowns tonight, then?'

'No,' Said Fred. 'We are the clowns no more. Finished with that.'

'Definitely. Time to move on.' Ginger continued. 'We still go to all the parties… though they seem to have moved on too. Not as interesting as they used to be.'

'Nothing stays the same, does it?' Fred said, not aiming his remark at anyone in particular.

'No, I suppose not.' I said.

Ginger looked back towards the main part of the building. 'Looks like they are making a start.' She said.

I glanced around, the crowd did seem to be making a general move forward towards the tables laid out for the pre-award meal.

'Well good luck, old man.' Fred said, his hand grasping my shoulder.

'Yes,' Ginger said. 'Good luck.'

I smiled. 'Tracy's going to win, everyone knows that.'

'Maybe,' Said Fred, giving me an exaggerated wink. 'But you got closer than we ever did, just being nominated. One of the Five Feathers finally triumphing.'

'No, not of one us,' I said. 'All of us, well that's the way I'd like to think of it.'

'See,' said Ginger, as we started walking towards the crowd. 'He *does* think he's going to win. He's practising his speech already!'

I shook my head, trying not to laugh, as I felt again for my phone, but this time to turn it off. We had all been given dire warnings about ring-tones during the live television broadcast of the announcement.

Catherine turned to me to after studying the work in silence for several minutes. 'I'm impressed'

'Really?' I said. 'Think they work at a reduced size?'

'Might even be better, they are more of a set here.'

We were at the Tate, at the Turner Prize exhibition, standing together, in the single gallery that showed my contribution, 'Blindsight Too'. It was a smaller version of the original with each of the Platonic solids a metre high, spaced out a metre apart in a line running down the centre of the gallery. But except for size, all identical to the original, the print clippings, the wood, the metal, and all the rest. I had decided – rather than just show one or two of the original sized solids in the limited space I had been allocated – to show the whole piece at a reduced size.

It was early on a weekday and there were only a few other viewers in the galleries for the short-listed artists and for the moment we had my piece to ourselves. I was in my normal combats and leather jacket, Catherine in black slacks and a grey bulky padded jacket. She wore a black floppy hat, the brim pulled down to just above her eyebrows. Her hair, natural coloured now, spilled out to her shoulders.

We walked together to the head of the line where the sphere flickered.

'Tracy's bed's going to win though.' I said, pulling a mock frown.

Catherine put her arm around me and pulled herself close, resting her head on my shoulder, still looking at my work.

'Yes. I'm afraid so, love. That's the winner. But congratulations anyway.' She said.

'Thanks. Think he would like it?'

'Who?'

'Mark.'

'Oh, I'm sure he would.'

'But maybe I abstracted the ideas out too much? I worry that people just won't see it. What I've tried to do.'

'I'm sure they will. And even if they don't, well… everyone sees art differently, brings something different to it. If it was too obvious then it wouldn't be art in the first place.'

'True.'

'Doing any more? Copies of this I mean.' Catherine said waving down towards the row of sculptures.

'I was going to do a miniature version, like each one an inch or so, but decided against it.'

'You could do other types of solids, I suppose. Other combinations of substances.'

'No. I'm going to draw a line under it. It's my tribute to Mark and I want to leave it at that. And I think I can move on now. Finally forgive myself.'

'For what?'

'For thinking I could have seen something, saved him somehow. Him and Bird-Girl.'

'Yeah.' She took my hand and led me down the other side of the gallery, towards the exit, of both my display and the exhibition as a whole. 'It's strange. I've been wondering if there's something odd about us artists. Some of us anyway, that the urge to create is tied up with an urge to destroy ourselves. There's Van Goth, Gorky, Nicolas de Staël. Many others not so famous. And if not committing suicide directly, then there's the ones who lead such careless lives they may as well have. Take Manzoni for instance.'

'The canned shit guy?'

'Yeah, died in his twenties. Cirrhosis. Drank himself to death, basically. Then there's Jack The Dripper – Pollock, heading that way as well, before he crashed his car whilst pissed out of his brain. And I suppose there was me, on the same road. Living on the edge can be fun – the mad booze and drug fuelled bursts of creativity and all that – but it's not worth the lows that come after. I'm glad to leave it behind. Be happy to live a more balanced life.'

'Steady as she goes, you mean.'

'Yeah, I think so.'

We walked from the gallery leaving the main part of the exhibition space.

In the room beyond was a wall covered with slips of paper for comments, each one held up by a pencil stub slotted into holes drilled in a board behind. Catherine took a slip down, I saw her scrawl, *Jason is the best fucking artist in the UNIVERSE!!!* I smiled, turning away to the pair of televisions mounted in the wall oppose. They were soundlessly showing a loop of brief documentaries about each of the short-listed artists. In front, a few people benches with headphones on were sitting on solid watching the screens. I suddenly appeared in the film, in my studio, mouthing silent words.

'Coffee and cake?' I heard Catherine whisper in my ear.

'Of course.' And we left before my segment finished, before there was a chance that anyone watching could turn around and recognise us.

I started arranging the exhibition of 'Blindsight' by dividing up of the rooms of the old Feather Gallery so I could display each solid in a space of its own. At the same time I also started work on the new idea I had had, The 'Real World' project – the mapping of an imaginary land onto the topology of our studio.

Meanwhile Catherine broke off from video for a few weeks, going back to photography for just one piece of work. Another self-portrait. A tight macro close-up of her face, cropped to show just her eyes. In colour, but so over-exposed and with her grey irises, that it looked black and white. She had it printed up at a huge scale – the final work measured six meters by one.

The final year of the century and the 'Blindsight' exhibition was a huge success. Soon the rumours started that I would be Turner nominated but I just dismissed them, especially to myself, as ridiculous. But that did not make them go away.

There were other rumours circulating – worries about the possibly of the millennium bug, then more justified worries about public transport, after a number of train crashes. The latter hardly affected us; when we were not using my bike or Catherine's car we just jumped into taxis.

Music seemed to just fuzz out for me with all those Brit Pop bands that had seemed all-conquering just a few years back seeming to be spent forces. One exception was Pulp's *This Is Hardcore* which I played frequently, especially the title track. Another track I became obsessed with was the remix of Run DMC's 'It's Like That' which never seemed to be off the radio.

Both of us together went to see *Fight Club* and *The Sixth Sense* and *The Blair Witch Project*.

The day before the Turner prize, I woke to find Catherine leaving for a photo-shoot. I was not in the mood for work, or to just hang around the studio. Over the last few days, deep down a tension had slowly started nagging at me – that there was a slim chance I might actually win. Plus autumn was turning to winter and soon the time would come when riding the bike would be more of a chore than a pleasure. So I went out for a long ride that looped out of the city into the country using technically challenging back roads wherever possible. I returned in the dark.

From the yard below I could see just a dim glow of light in our studio's window so I knew Catherine was back before me.

I did not hear the music until I opened the door – Madonna's 'Frozen'.

Catherine was sitting on the leather sofa, lit from the side by the kitchen light. She was smoking, the ashtray full besides her. She wore a sweater and jeans as when I had seen her in the hotel. With one hand she held something close to her, clasped across her stomach. She stubbed out the cigarette and reached for the stereo's remote on the sofa. Suddenly the room was silent. She turned to me, her face expressionless.

'What is it? What's the matter?' I asked, stepping into the room, closing the door behind me.

'How could you?' Her voice was tight. She held up what she had been cradling against herself. My sketchbook. The one I had filled with drawings of her. 'I mean now could you? I asked you never to draw me and you fill up a whole book with the fucking things.' He voice seemed to crack on the final words.

'I just wanted a record of you.' I moved towards her. 'Something that I did with my art. I love you, I want to keep–'

'Don't fucking say that!' She cut me off, her voice shrill. Then she sighed, deep and ragged, and something like her old voice returned, but tinged with sadness. 'I just thought I could rely on you.'

'You can! Of course you can!' I sat down beside her. 'If I'd have known,' I continued, urgently. 'That it would upset you this much... I'm sorry, I'll throw them away.'

Catherine put the sketchbook down and turned to me.

'No, don't. Keep them now.' She looked away her lips pursed.

'How did you find it?' I asked.

'The other night, I woke and saw you. But the next day I thought it was just a dream. Then, earlier today, I saw it – the sketchbook – poking out from under your notes.'

'Oh, it's the damn Turner thing, I can't think straight. I should have hidden it away properly. I–'

She suddenly turned back to me, wrapped her arms me, hugging me tight. 'I'm sorry. It was stupid. Telling you not to draw me. Then getting upset about it. I'm just not a nice girl.'

'No, Catherine.'

She sat back from me. 'I don't want to know how others see me, that's all. But it's silly thing for me to get so upset about.'

'Ca–'

She stopped me with a finger on my lips.

'I'll tell you what. Fuck me and I'll forgive you.'

And she leaned forward again to kiss me. After a while I made to pull up her sweater.

She broke away from me again, her hands snatching at mine.

'What? What is it?'

'It's just that... today, after I found the book, I went out filming again. At this semi-derelict building site... Anyway there was this girder jutting out of a wall, I didn't see it at first and I caught my bloody arm on it.' She pulled the sweater up over her head. Underneath she wore a dark sleeveless singlet. I could see a bandage high on her arm. 'Can't be helped, but it's a bit tender, thought I had better warn you. Bet it leaves a scar.'

'Oh Jesus, I'm sorry. I really am.'

She shook her head, 'Not your fault. Me being stupid.' She pointed down to her forearm where I could see the faint line of the scar running down to her hand.

'Don't worry it will match up with this one.'

'I used to wish I could do that.' Catherine said, lifting her helmet over her head.

The low sun now cast long shadows across the car-park outside Simon's Shed.

'What?' I asked.

'Disappear. Like a magic trick.'

'Don't mean that do you?' I said with raised eyebrows.

'In the past maybe... no, not now.' She pulled her helmet down over her face. 'Let's go home.'

'Forgive me now?' I said once our breathing returned to normal.

'Definitely.' She whispered, her slick body against me.

'Catherine...'

'Yes.'

'Let's go on holiday. Fly off straight after the Turner. Well the next day.'

'Scotland?

'No. I fancy something warm for a change. The Caribbean, a bit of winter sun. Just lazing on a beach.'

'Ah. yes...'

'And also on the beach. But only if you want... I've been thinking for a while... but...'

'What?'

'On the beach… a wedding?'

She answered me with a kiss. 'That's a beautiful idea. Now, fuck me again.'

Night. I got the final message when I returned to the studio, when I could finally pull myself away from all the well-wishers, the congratulations, the party invitations and the interview requests. The first time I could turn my phone on – planning to call her, planning to leave a message of my own telling her of my triumph – I had heard Catherine's penultimate message, a sobbing, almost incoherent, 'I'm sorry. So sorry. There's an explanation at the studio'.

The final message was hand-written on the last page of my sketch-book.

The 'Dear John'.

The one that started, 'By the time you read this I will be dead.' And then went on to tell me she would be soon be leaping, arm in arm with Simon, from the top of a cliff.

Then the phone rang. The police this time.

The next day. Waking in a daze mid-morning, after finally getting to sleep in the early hours. Feeling sick. Needing air. Staggering out into the day.

And seeing her. Everywhere. On the front of every newspaper. Those grey eyes staring back at me from her final photograph.

And then it came to me, in a flash of sudden inspiration, seeing a cottage in the country, back where I came from, filled with paintings and drawings, another memento-mori, my final piece.

17 BLACK AND WHITE

I watched him work. Watched him paint her at the centre of his maze.

Catherine was standing on top of a pedestal, a solid metal block about a metre square. She was naked except for the body paint that covered almost all of her, dividing her into black and white. Her arms were widespread and raised up above her head. Loops of rope held her wrists at the edge of the white-painted circle of board she was standing against.

Her hair was cropped and slicked back with black paint. Her face was painted white except for a curve of black that ran down from the middle of her forehead past the outer edge of one eye to her chin. The dividing line crossed to the opposite side of her body before swooping back — leaving her neck and breasts black — then vertically downwards at her navel to the slit of her shaved sex. One leg and one arm were black, the opposite white.

She was motionless except for the slight rise and fall of her chest as she breathed. Her eyes were closed.

Simon — dressed in the same blue overalls he had worn the last time I had visited the Shed — was bent over, brush in hand, filling in the one bare patch of Catherine's skin at the side of her torso.

The space was walled by the same sheets of white and black canvases that had formed the rest of the maze. In addition to the one I had just walked down, two other canvas lined corridors led off to either side of me.

Pointed at Catherine were still and video cameras mounted on tripods. On either side were an array of studio lights and reflectors on high stands. I stepped out in front of them.

Catherine suddenly opened her eyes. She looked right at me and gasped.

Simon turned towards me. 'Oh fuck, you're early.'

The car park had been empty, just as it had been when I first visited the place. But this time the door was locked. I kicked it twice, hard – jumping at it with my full bodyweight. I felt the door give with the first impact – wood splintering around the lock. The second time the door flew open.

The foyer was a dark void lit only by the high full moon and distant streetlights. The room behind the window was completely empty. There was not even the desk or the chair where the security guard had been sat.

The wall opposite was different. Two maps had been posted up there – even in the dim light I recognised the rough triangular outline of the British Isles, and next to it London, the city a ragged oval divided by the Thames. Both maps were marked. I pulled off my helmet, placed it on the floor and steeped across the room to look closer.

On the British map there was a black cross drawn in thick felt-tip at the edge of Lincolnshire, just in from the coast – right where the cottage had been, where I had planned to create my final artwork. I looked across to the London map and saw there had been multiple crosses added there. I ran my finger from one to other, the studio in Hoxton, out to the Oyster press office, down to the tattooists in Croydon, up to the flat in Camden, the Carlton Health Spar in Chelsea, the art galleries – The Wallace Collection, The National, Tate Britain, Tate Modern. All the points on my journey. I checked back to the UK map but there was no cross on Peterborough, no cross for this latest stopping point.

I turned from the map and walked to the rear of the room. There were no signs of life down either of the corridors but at the bottom of the fire doors there was an edge of faint light. I pushed against them and stepped through into the factory space beyond.

In front of me hung a white sheet of canvas, three meters high. It was joined with metal rings to eyelets hammered into the floor and to more canvases on either side to form a long parallel barrier about two meters from the main wall.

Over towards the centre of the space a bright glow shone upwards. Against it I could see the canvases were attached to wires hanging down from the roof – hundreds of wires filled the whole space, forming an intricate metallic web.

I walked along the corridor formed between the outer wall and the canvases, heading in the rough direction of the light. Black painted sheets started to intersperse the white ones, to turn the canvases into a line of Morse-like dots and dashes of light and dark. Ahead I saw a gap in the sheets – another corridor formed by two walls of the black and white canvases, turning in towards the centre of the space.

I turned and walked down it, towards where another corridor split off, heading towards the heart of the maze.

Simon moved quickly away from Catherine. There was a table over to one side, close to one of the canvas walls – one of the large metal tables I recognised from the last time I visited – and Simon headed towards it. At the far end was a collection of paint tins and a number of brushes – from fine art size up to the large flat ones more suitable for house decorating, some standing upright in jars and glasses. Some of the glasses, judging from the smell were filled with turps and paint thinner. There were rolls of paper towel and bundles of rags. Simon searched among this detritus for a few seconds before holding up a large efficient looking hunting knife.

As I made another step forward he waved it up at me. 'Don't get any ideas!'

I stopped.

'Bloody early, but perhaps it is better that you see my work – my 'Catherine Wheel' – in the flesh, as it were.' Simon jabbed with the knife towards the cameras. 'Rather than seeing the film and the rest once we were gone.'

He called over to Catherine. 'Kate, want to take a break for a minute?'

Catherine slipped her hands from each of the loops of rope. Now I was closer I could see that they were not that tight and she had merely been using them to take the weight off her arms while she posed. The circle turned as Catherine removed her second hand and continued to slowly spin as she stepped down off the plinth and towards the table. The disk was fixed at its centre to a frame behind. Where Catherine had been there was a pale silhouette in the primed unpainted board.

At the table Catherine reached for a packet of cigarettes. I noticed as she had turned away from me that the tattoo, the F-shaped flipped rune, had been redrawn in contrasting paint on her shoulder. Her back, buttocks and the backs of her legs were unpainted, the skin bare.

She lit a cigarette with her brass lighter as Simon turned to her.

"Catherine Wheel'," He said. 'Hmm, still not sure about that. What else did we think? 'Moon Goddess'? 'Hecate'? 'He-cate'?' The second time he pronounced it as two separate words. 'Something on those lines?'

'Or perhaps just call it 'Gibbous Moon'?' Catherine turned back to me breathing out a cloud of smoke.

'Perhaps, 'Untitled'? Just leave it unfinished?' Simon said. 'Like your quest. To get back your Catherine. Of course she was never your Catherine to begin with.'

'Is that right?' I said, trying to keep the emotion from my voice.

'Oh, yes,' Catherine replied, in a light tone. She leaned back against the edge of the table.

'And you two?' My voice still calm, I pointed from her to Simon.

'Oh, since the first exhibition,' Simon said, moving to stand beside her. 'Dragged me into one of the Portaloos as soon as the guests left. But wouldn't let me fuck her. Not then anyway... But I don't have to tell you she has other skills besides art. And then nothing for a while, what with all the fuss over that lunatic Bird-Girl. Then just off and on. But the last few years? Let's just say it's been entertaining.'

Catherine took another drag on her cigarette then flicked the ash off the end onto the floor. She leaned over towards Simon and they kissed. His tongue slid into her mouth, a fat red slug.

'You see Jason,' She said to me when they had parted, when she had taken another drag on her cigarette. 'I'm not the person you think I am. Not Cat, certainly not Catherine. I'm Kate. Kiss-Kate. He-Kate. I thought it might be interesting to attach myself to someone conventional for a while. To have someone to go back to. But I could never stick to the straight and narrow. And you can never give me what I want. What I need. Deep down. What Simon gives me. What he does to me.'

'You sick cunts – both of you.' My voice came close to cracking, no longer able to keep the anger and the loathing in check. 'You fucking killed Louise!'

Catherine flinched at that but Simon just shook his head.

'I'm sorry but, no.' He said, shaking his head, sounding genuinely apologetic. 'I really was going to leave her for you, just put my mark on her. But she fought back, too hard. And I struck out. It was an accident.'

'Bird-girl? Mark?'

Simon smirked at me.

'What? You think I'm some sort of serial killer? Bird-Girl? That mad bitch took herself out without any help from me. And Mark? He was just a stupid self-pitying queer who had too much booze on top of his happy pills. When I saw him there, after seeing that stupid band, in front of that pathetic sculpture, gagging on his own puke, and him taking the piss all night... I just thought, 'Yeah well, who's the real artist now, you fucking puff?''

'What?' I said, astonished. 'You were there?'

'Oh, yes.'

'All those years, I thought I should've saved him!' I shouted, my anger flaring. 'When you could have!'

I stepped towards him.

He flicked the knife up, holding his arm outstretched towards me.

'Now, now. Temper, temper. He just should have shown a little respect. After all he owed his whole career to me. You all did. You would have all been nothing if I'd not set up the collective in the first place. I'm better than all of you. You Jason, especially. You might have the Turner prize, but I've manipulated you, tricked you, into performing my greatest artwork. Well, second greatest work, after Kate here.' He pointed with the knife towards where he had redrawn the tattoo. 'See, even signed her with my mark, the money rune reversed for ownership, slavery, submission.'

'You got that wrong,' I said, my voice calm again. 'It should be inverted not flipped.'

'Really?' There was a brief flash of annoyance across his face, then a smile – but a smile that did not reach his eyes. 'No matter. Anyway, one thing I want to know before we depart – Why are you so early? What brought you here before I could send the final clue?'

'The card you left. The Death card. I remembered the card trick you showed me. The video. Here. A card trick. Find the lady.'

He shook his head. 'Ah, well, that wasn't the plan. Just felt the card was the right artistic touch. Wasn't intended to be a clue. That was to come later, once we were ready.'

'Plus the suicide video.' I continued. 'That pointed to here as well, once I thought about it, realised it must be fake. I presume this was were you doctored it, in your editing suit. More of your manipulation. Another trick.'

'Of course!' He said. 'My idea, but mostly Catherine's work. Getting rid of the rope harnesses we wore. It's not perfect, but it didn't have to be. Just to give us enough time to plan and set all this up and then find a place to go to afterwards. Someplace you'll never find us, by the way, so don't even try. Of course you had to leave that house before we had completely finished. With all those old movies you liked to watch, we knew you would easily fall into playing the detective, start looking for clues. Just didn't expect it so quickly. Yes, very shocked when we saw you coming back to the studio. Luckily we had just planted the first clue but you nearly spotted Kate outside.'

'I did see her. I thought it was my imagination. Or a ghost.'

'Had the place wired for sound and vision by the way. Monitors in Mark's old place. For a long time. I suppose a lesser man might be jealous. Catherine put on quite a performance with you, those nights she wasn't with me.' He pointed to a case full of videos on the floor under the table. 'Been filming you from afar too. A couple hid in the Camden flat. All there; all part of the piece.'

'Jesus,' I breathed.

'So you might have got ahead of me at first but I soon had you moving around to plan, criss-crossing my map of London, showing you all the sides of my Kate, the pornographer, the masseuse… the whore.'

I glanced at Catherine, but her face under the paint has unreadable. 'And the tattooist?' I said. 'And that woman at the publishers, Stephanie? Both of them? In on this?'

'Oh no,' Simon said. 'Old friends though. From the club. Where Catherine took me to show me her wild side. They were very easy to manipulate though, Stephanie especially. I knew she would latch on to you if you went to the club asking questions. So it was easy to make you think those texts were from her. Just had to sneak into the massage parlour at night with Kate's old key and leave the phone in the locker, that flyer – get you to the club in the first place. Piece of cake. And then have you visit all the art galleries via the texts while I set things up back at the massage pallor, sign the woman. Set up and film this final piece then give you the final clue. Unfortunately that didn't work out. I suppose you can't plan for everything… I certainly didn't expect you to spend the night there. Two nights, in fact. Didn't mourn my Kate for long, did you?' He smirked with the final remark.

'I thought you were dead.' I said to Catherine, my voice flat. She just looked back at me and for the first time I thought I saw something of the old Catherine in her eyes before she took a final drag on her cigarette and stubbed it out on the side of an empty jar.

Simon ignored me, turning to towards Catherine. 'And she tells me that when she once virtually threw another woman at you but you turned it down flat?'

'When?' I asked Catherine. But then I remembered. 'That time in Ibiza? The Venezuelan girl?'

Catherine gave just the slightest nod.

'But why?' I asked her. 'Why didn't you just tell me. And why all of this?' I pointed open-handed at the canvas walls around me. Then back towards Catherine, my hand sweeping up to indicate all the body paint, finishing at the tattoo. 'Why all this? When obviously, for years.... Why now? Don't tell me it was just because you found out I drew you? Because I proposed? Art? It has to be more than that!'

'Jason—' Catherine started, then paused while she lit another cigarette before adding more softly. 'It's difficult.'

'Kate—' Simon started in a warning tone.

'No,' Catherine said. She moved back over to plinth and sat down on the edge of it. 'I'll have to tell him. I owe him that much.' She looked up at me. 'It was the last time I let someone paint me.'

18 WHIPPER-IN

'I hear that you paint, yourself.'

'I try,' I said, leaning back into the couch, trying to look around the edge of the canvas at this far too handsome artist with his wave of blonde hair and tight-jeaned legs.

'No, no, no! Sit upright!' He scolded me, then continued in softer tones. 'It's just that I like the way the light from the window catches the side of your face.'

'Sorry,' I said, pulling myself upright again. 'Yes, I hope to go to art college when I finish my A-levels.'

'Good luck with that.' He said absently as he stepped back. He looked from me to my work and back again for a moment, then continued painting.

'In fact,' I said. 'I'm glad you are here. Hope to watch you work later, painting the rest of the family. Learn from a pro. And I was hoping to show you some of my work. Get some advice?'

'I'll be glad to.'

He painted on in silence

'This is not the first time I've sat.' I said, after a few minutes. 'At school, my boarding school… A few of us girls who do art sit for each other. In our own time. For figure studies.'

'That can only help,' he muttered without looking up, now absorbed in his work.

I looked sidelong at him, trying not to turn my head. 'Nude occasionally.' I said, attempting to dip my voice low and add bit of husk to it. 'You know, I could pose nude, for you.'

A small laugh. 'I don't think your parents would approve.'

'We could keep it to ourselves. And you don't even have to paint me. I can just *be* naked. And... we... take it from there. After all, if you are going to help me. I should–'

He laughed fully this time.

'Oh, I don't mind giving some help with your art. For nothing.' He looked up from his canvas right at me. 'And while I can appreciate you aesthetically, artistically, I don't really appreciate you in any other way.'

'Ah. Oh. Right.' I said. 'You're gay.'

'No, I'm not. Sorry if that's a disappointment. Now, lift your head back up again!'

'Kate!'

'Uncle Rupert!' I cried out, turning my grey towards where he was approaching on his large bay stallion, its breath fogging in the morning chill.

'Oh, just Rupert, please.' He said. 'Anyway, glad to see you here.'

He pulled his horse up alongside mine. The whole hunt was gathered around us in front of Shorely House, mostly mounted, on grey, black, brown, dun, and chestnut with a plethora of red and blue jackets, riding hats, top hats and bowlers. The hounds – a sea of black, white and brown patches – were milling around the horses, tails raised high, snuffing and yelping, excited for the off. To one side were a whole extra contingent of hunt supporters in barbers and padded coats, headscarves and hats, next to their Land Rovers and Land Cruisers.

'So, what brings you out today, then?' Rupert said.

'School is going well,' I said, 'Thought I deserved a bit of a mid-term break. Pop back for a decent ride-out.'

'Ah, bunking off. Very good!'

'It's not like that!'

'You'll be able to see the paintings, then. Of the family.'

'Finished are they?'

'So I heard; he's bringing them up tomorrow.'

'Great.'

Then I noticed his ready smile seemed a little too fixed and looking closer I could see an extra darkness around his eyes.

'How's everything else for you.' I said, concerned. 'How are you coping?'

'Ah, well, one copes. You know?' He shrugged.

There was silence for a moment until Rupert spotted one of the hunt supporters walking past with a tray filled will small glasses.

'Ah, drinkies!' Rupert called out to him. 'Over here, my good man!'

I took a cherry brandy as Rupert reached for a sherry.

'*Ahh,*' Rupert said, smacking his lips after he drained half his glass. 'That will take the chill off!'

'Yeah, I did have to choose the first proper frost of the year!' I said. 'Hopefully it will warm up later on.'

'Yes, soon as this fog rises.'

'I must say you do look rather dashing, Rupe. New jacket?' I asked.

'Oh, yes. I'm a whipper-in now. In fact I better go see to the hounds.' He knocked back his sherry and placed it back on the tray of the supporter making another round. Then he kicked his horse into a trot, turning it away from me.

'Nice talking to you though,' I said. 'Good hunting!'

'And you! *Tally ho!*' He waved back at me. I reached down and selected another cheery brandy.

I sipped my drink until there was the sound of horns and I followed the rest of hunt away from the house.

It happened just when I was really starting to enjoy myself. The sun had come up and burned off the mist and my horse, after a bit of early hesitancy, was now starting to stretch out and jump freely.

There was a high hedge at the far end of the lightly rutted field. I was at the back of the pack, off to one side, as I cantered towards it. The ground at the approach – in the shadow of the hedge, where no other horse had loosened it – was still frosted hard. That may have been it. Or maybe the hedge was too high at that point. Or it was just my own incompetence. Whatever, the result was that my horse stumbled then refused, stopping dead. I went straight over its head, into the top of the hedge itself. I fell down through it to the other side, brambles scratching at my face and catching at my clothes. Something hard and sharp and unyielding – a branch or a fence post – snagged my left sleeve, pulling my arm back, and, before my weight and momentum tore me free again, I felt something sharp rip into the back of my hand. I slithered down into a pool of muddy water on the other side just about face first.

I pulled myself to my feet waving at the nearest rider who had stopped to show that I was all right, for them to carry on without me.

I was half soaked – the front of my jacket plastered in mud. The left sleeve had been shoved up to my elbow. As I went to pull it down I saw blood dripping from my fingers. There was a gash on the back of my hand and wrist. I swore to myself as I found a handkerchief in my pocket and tied it over the wound, before putting my jacket back on.

By the time I found the gate and gone back to collect my horse, the hunt was long gone. I had started shivering so I remounted and headed home.

I was taking a shortcut along a bridle path, approaching a small cluster of trees, where the path met a road when I realised I could no longer resist the urge to empty my bladder. I dismounted and tied my horse up at the edge of the copse. I made my way through the trees over to where they were thickest, carefully stepping through the tangle of ivy choking the ground. There was a bare patch of dumped rubble, a television with a smashed-in screen off to one side. A damp smell of old decay. I pulled down my jodhpurs and knickers, squatted and pissed.

'Hello! Kate! Are you all right!'

'Fuck!' I jerked up at the voice, losing my balance. I staggered backwards a few steps, jodhpurs still round my ankles, before I fell back down right on my arse, something sharply stinging. I twisted round as I pulled up my trousers and knickers. I saw I had fallen back right into a clump of nettles. Frost-blackened, I had not noticed them before. I stood up rubbing my backside.

'Bloody bugger!'

'That you Kate?'

Standing among a strand of silver birch at the edge of the copse was Uncle Rupert.

'Are you all right? We were just coming across the end of that field.' He pointed behind him as I approached. 'But I was sure I saw you tying up your horse. Told the others I'd check if there was anything wrong.'

'I was just heading back. I fell, got soaked. Stopped off for a pee. Then I bloody fell again when you called out and now I've nettled my bloody fanny!'

Rupert chuckled. 'Oh dear, not a good day then?'

'It's not funny!' But I found myself laughing too. 'Think we can catch up?'

'Maybe? You alright, though? You look frozen.'

'I am frozen!' I said, rubbing my hands together.

'Here.' He pulled out a hip flask, unfastened it and passed it over.

I took a swig of its contents — some thick fruity spirit with a touch of almonds. A spirit that was new to me, both in flavour and strength. I coughed. Rupert smiled and held out his hand, but I took another drink from the flask before handing it back.

'That's certainly not cherry brandy.' I said.

'It's sloe gin. Old family recipe. A proper drink. After all, you're not a little girl anymore.'

'No, and I think it's doing the trick.' Warmth from the alcohol was starting to seep through me.

'You've hurt yourself?' Rupert said.

I looked down to where he was pointing, blood dripped from the handkerchief tied around my wrist.

'Oh fuck, I ripped my hand open when I fell.'

'Let me take a look.'

I pushed my sleeve back up. The cut had reopened, probably when I had just stumbled.

'I thought you were only supposed to be blooded on your first hunt.' Rupert said as he slipped my bloody handkerchief off. He dabbed at the wound with his own then tied it in place of mine.

'Very funny,' I said. I dropped my hanky to the ground.

'You know you look a lot better with some meat on your bones.' Rupert said. I was suddenly aware of how my mud-plastered jacket was clinging to me, showing off the outline of my breasts. 'All that nonsense in the past now?' He continued, smiling at me.

'Oh, yes.' I smiled. I reached down and pulled my jodhpurs up higher. Then winced, rubbing at my bottom again. 'Fuck, that smarts. I need to find a dock leaf.' I tried to joke.

'Like a covered mare.' Rupert said with another smile.

'What do you mean?' I asked.

'After the stallion has covered the mare – to sire a foal – they use nettles on her... well, it swells up, increases the chance of pregnancy. Sorry, that's a bit... '

'It's all right. I'm no blushing virgin, Rupert. Not for a while now.'

'We had better be going, if we–' He looked away from me and made to step back.

'Do you really want to?' I asked.

He looked back at me. I reached up behind his head and drew him forward to kiss him. He did not resist.

'No,' I whispered just as our lips met. 'I thought not.'

'Kate,' he said, when we parted. 'We shouldn't–?'

'Shouldn't we?' I breathed, my hand stroking up his thigh. 'As you say, I'm no little girl anymore and you're not my real uncle.'

I unbuttoned my jodhpurs, started to pull them down to my thighs, twisting my hips to get them off.

He hesitated for a second then grabbed my hips and spun me around. I reached out for the thin trunk of the sliver birch now in front of me. He yanked down the jodhpurs. Then my knickers. Cold air cooled my irritated flesh.

I felt him enter me in one smooth movement then suddenly stopped.

'Are you on the pill?' His mouth close to my ear.

'It doesn't matter!' I gasped.

'Shit!' He pulled out.

'No! No, don't!' I tried to reach back for him.

Then I heard him hawk and spit. Felt wet, slimed fingers slide in-between my buttocks. One finger, probing.

'This?'

'Oh, god.' I breathed.

He held me by the hips with both hands as he pressed against me, struggling to slowly open me. I cried out as I pushed back against him, against his searing penetration.

He slid back then powered himself into me, again and again. His hands gripped me hard, fingers digging in as he levered himself against me. I bent lower arching my back. I held the tree in front of me so hard the edges of the pink flesh beneath my nails went white. I let go with one hand, licked my fingers then reached back between my legs to finger and tug and pinch at my flesh there. I closed my eyes against burning tears.

I hissed as he panted, pain and pleasure fighting against each other, each holding the other back in a hot tension. Then the pleasure started to edge out in front, rapidly increasing, until with a flash of red in front of my eyes, I came, screaming.

I lost my grip on the trunk and started to fall forward. Rupert grabbed me by the shoulders, hauled me upright. Then, pressing me up against the tree, he swore and gasped and grunted out his own climax.

Eyes now wide open I saw another flash of red. The fox was in the copse.

Rupert turned from me, fumbling with his clothes. I frantically groped downward for my own.

And suddenly we were in the middle of the barking, yelping, crying pack of hounds that ran and jumped up all around us in pursuit of their quarry.

That afternoon we had one, very embarrassing, half-conversation agreeing there was no fault on either side and to never mention it ever again.

The next day I saw the completed painting of myself, my portrait. Everyone else said it showed me as a fine young woman. But to me it was as if the artist had seen right through to my very core. They all saw the nice girl, remarking on the confident tilt of the head, the demure glance and the full-lipped smile. But I saw in that haughty lifting of the chin, those sly half-closed eyes, that pouting sneer the nasty girl within.

Later, during the bad times – during the worst of the bad times – in the middle of one night, I slashed the painting with a kitchen knife, ripping it beyond repair.

19 GREY

I looked straight into Catherine's grey eyes as she looked back at me. When she had finished her story she had returned to the table for another cigarette, the lighter now smeared with paint from her hands.

'I'm not the woman you think I am. No matter what I appear on the outside.' She leaned back against the table, and with the cigarette in her hand, she first indicated the white-painted half of her body before moving over to point at the black side. 'Underneath I'm dark. I try to suppress it… and for a long time I can – be the good girl that my parents would have wanted – but it always comes out in the end. Then I just end up hurting people. It's for the best if I just disappear.'

'Disappear. With him?' I glanced over to Simon. He was moving to stand next to her.

'He completes me.' She said.

'No,' I said quietly, stepping forward. 'We were happy, most of the time. We can be happy again. All this nice girl, nasty girl, is just bullshit. I'm not going to let you do it. I'm not letting you go. You're coming with me. Now'

'What?' Catherine gasped. 'You can't mean that? What about everything I told you?' She made to step towards me but Simon was now right next to her, the knife pricking into her side. Closer now I could see tears welling in her eyes. Her voice broke. 'It's not just him. It's everything. I lied to you, so much. I have slept with strangers. I've whored myself! I'll give you a horrible life. I've given you a horrible life!'

Her hand slashed across her eyes, wiping tears, smearing the paint on her face.

I shook my head, taking another step forward. I held my hand out to her.

'When I was a kid, I nearly died. Nearly fell of a roller-coaster, of all things. So, everything since, no matter how bad you might think it's been, has been a bonus.' I glanced over at Simon. 'Don't try and stop us.'

'Don't be idiotic,' Simon started. 'I'll kill–'

'Jason,' Catherine's voice was suddenly calm and steady. I looked back towards her. Our eyes locked again. The cigarette fell to the floor. 'I love Simon.'

'You see!' Simon cried. 'She–!'

I snatched the jar up off the table. The one I had been slowly moving towards. The one with the brushes soaking in paint thinner. I grabbed the brushes out of it and flung the rest of the contents straight into Simon's face. He shrieked, bringing his hands up to his eyes.

I grabbed Catherine and pulled her forward.

'Run!' I shouted.

She took off immediately, dashing down the nearest of the canvas lined corridors.

I stepped back as Simon, eyes tightly shut, lunged at me down the table. Tins, jars and glasses, toppled or smashed, thinner and turps spilling out across the table and floor.

I took another step back as Simon blindly scythed at the air with the knife. He blundered against one of the light stands and brought it crashing down across the table – sparks flew, then flames licked up.

I turned and sped after Catherine. She was nowhere to be seen. I ran up to and turned the first corner, peering into the shadows. Nothing.

I raced on. Stopped at a junction. Each corridor led only to darkness.

'Jason?'

I saw her crouching down, her eyes wide. She sprang up and flung herself into my arms.

'Oh god, Jason! He said he would kill you unless I did what he said. It was all–!'

'It's all right! I know. You used the 'I' word.'

There was a scream from back where we had come from – 'You fucking bastards!'

The lights went out plunging us into near total darkness, just a faint flicking glow from the fire back behind us remaining.

'We have to go back.' I said.

'No!'

'It's the only way I know how to get out. Unless you?'

'No.' I felt her pull her body off mine. 'I don't.'

'Stay behind me.' I whispered, reaching for her hand.

Together we slowly crept back to the centre of the maze.

I paused at the edge of the corridor. Flames were now spread over half of the table. The canvas behind had caught, the fire spreading to its neighbours. The box of videos underneath crackled and spat, smoke rising.

'Where is he?' Catherine harshly whispered.

I looked around again but Simon was nowhere to be seen.

'Fuck it, we've got to get out of here, the whole place will be up soon.' I strode out into the open area moving over to the table. I snatched up a handful of brushes then I grabbed all the rag I could see that was not already alight. I tied the rag around the end of the brushes. I dipped my improvised torch in the nearest flame then held it up above my head.

I led Catherine down the corridor.

'Just round the next corner, I'm sure.' I said, back to Catherine.

Two wrong turns – with two dead ends and having to double back twice – meant the light from the burning centre of the maze now glowed brightly behind a thickening haze of smoke.

'It's alright as –' She started.

Simon barrelled out of the darkness behind us and crashed straight into me, knocking me to the floor. His lips where pulled back in a snarl. His eyes, the skin round them, were a livid red.

'You're not taking her!' He shouted, turning to Catherine as she cowered away from him. The knife sliced against her arm as she brought her hands up in front of herself. She tried to kick out at him but he slashed her again across the stomach.

I grabbed for the torch, yelling, pushing myself upwards. Simon turned, stabbing out at me. The blade caught against my leather jacket. I brought the torch round, connected with the side of his head. I held it there just for a few moments until his hair, soaked with the paint thinner, burst into flames.

He shrieked, battering his hands against his head. I brought the torch down to his chest, set the front of his overalls alight, the flames licking up towards his face. He ran from me, back towards the centre of the maze, arms flailing against himself.

I went to Catherine. The cut on her arm was superficial but her hands where already wet with blood where she held them to her stomach. Back behind us something exploded, sending a sheet of flame roaring up towards the roof of the factory.

'Come on!' I helped Catherine to her feet.

Half carrying, half dragging her, coughing from the smoke, I soon made it out of the maze to the factory wall.

I crashed out through the fire doors into the foyer then out of the building and across the car park

Behind us I heard more explosions. Looking back smoke was starting to pour out of the door. A fire alarm rang.

I laid Catherine on the ground. She still clutched at her wound. The red of her blood was smeared into the black and white of the paint, but the bleeding did appear to be slowing.

I took of my jacket, spread it over her, the quilted lining against the wound, brought her hands round to press down on it.

'I'm going back for him,'

'You can't!' She cried.

I ran into the foyer but the smoke was too thick to go any further. I staggered back out, coughing and spluttering. I could hear more alarm bells.

I returned to Catherine. I found the mobile in my jacket pocket, dialled three nines, asked for fire, ambulance, police, the fucking lot of them. I dropped it to the ground and took hold of Catherine's hand.

'Oh, fuck,' She gasped.

'It's alright,' I said. 'It's over.'

'He said he would kill you. He made me lie.'

'All of it? All of it, lies?'

She looked away from me.

'No, not all of it.'

'The affair?'

She nodded, stiffly.

'You as a prostitute, it was real? Not some artwork?'

'Yes.'

'And it was it all his idea?'

She did not reply to that.

I still held her hand, now feeling the heat of the burning building on my back. I heard sirens in the distance.

She looked back at me.

'What now?'

'Hospital… then long conversations with various people in authority, I imagine. A lot of long explanations.' I sighed. 'Jesus, what a fucking mess.'

'No, for us two. What now, for us? We can be happy! You said!'

This time it was me who looked away.

'I don't know, Catherine. I just don't know.'

20 BLANK CANVAS

They found Simon in the centre of the burnt-out shell of his warehouse, lying across a blackened disk of wood. When they removed the charred body it left a pale silhouette behind.

The police kept us for more than a long time. There was talk of charges. But Catherine's family enlisted some high-class legal muscle and they eventually let us go. We both went straight to Catherine's family house. We talked a little during the following days, walking together in the grounds, without really saying anything.

We slept in separate rooms.

I woke from a nightmare of fire and suffocation that still seemed to cling to me like cobweb as I lurched out of bed. I staggered from my room and down the corridor to where I knew Catherine was sleeping.

But she was awake, staring back at me with open eyes as I flung open the door. I ripped back her bedclothes. She was naked underneath.

I grabbed hold of her, twisting her over onto her front.

'Is this what you want?' I spat the words as I climbed onto the bed and over the top of her, kicking her legs apart.

My hand went around her throat wrenching back her head. 'Is it this that turns you on? Gets you wet? Is it?'

My other hand went down between her legs.

She was totally slack, I suddenly realised. She was not resisting me at all.

I froze. I breathed hard to control the waves of nausea that now rose within me. I rolled away from her.

'I can't give you that.'

Her voice was small beside me. 'I don't want it. I don't need it... if you don't.' I felt her hand reach across my chest. 'You're the knight who rescued his princess. Everything we did, you came through it. Everything I did, you overcome. *Christ, you've fucking killed for me.*' She groaned. 'I'm yours now. Completely. Forever.'

'I can't–' I moved further away from her, twisted round to sit on the edge of the bed. 'I have to go. I–' I slumped forward, my head falling into my hands. 'Oh fuck, who am I kidding? I'll never leave. It's you that always left me. I love you... despite the pain. Despite everything.' I laughed, a short sharp humourless bark. 'Perhaps I'm the fucking masochist. It *was* you, wasn't it? Not him. *You* manipulated me, like you manipulated him–'

'Jason, please!' Her voice cut through mine. I said nothing and she continued more softly. 'I just kept things from you, at first. I... I just wanted pain, punishment. For what I had done. For what I was. The bad girl. And the pain I caused you – to try and drive you away from me. It made me want it – need it – even more. I tried to get away, to stop it. To stop all your pain… but I couldn't. Because… Because I love you too.'

I looked back over my shoulder at her. 'Cat, Catherine…'

'I love you.' She said again, with complete conviction.

I turned, reached over to her and cupped the side of her face with my hand. She reached up to cover my hand with her own.

'I don't want a slave, but…' I paused. 'Just be who you are. Who you were. Before all this. The white without the black; the good girl without the bad.'

'I'm not sure I know what that is.' She gasped. 'I'm… *I'm scared.*'

I slipped my hand from under hers and lay back down on the bed beside her, facing her. I pulled her to me.

'Tell me it all, tell me everything.' I said. 'And we'll start again. A blank canvas.'

'Yes,' She said, a sigh.

I held her to me all through the night while she whispered a long bittersweet confession. Then, in the soft light of dawn, I moved against her, loving away our tears.

Cat, Catherine, Kate, Nichola Lexington, Nicks, Fanny Dore, Lauren Ibsen, Jane Doe, Kitty-Cat, Horse-Girl, Princess Peculiar and all the rest, took another name.

A final name. My name.

It was a quiet service in the church where we had once fucked under a gibbous moon.

We healed, slowly, together – rediscovering ourselves anew.

We healed almost completely but there were scars – both physical and mental – that would take a long time to fade, if they ever did.

We discussed lasering off the rune tattoo but in the end Catherine covered it with a new tattoo — a stylised feather that I designed.

We never went back to London, at least not to the studio, not to the life we had known.

Back up in Scotland for an extended holiday, in Edinburgh we passed a small vacant shop premises, not far from the Royal Mile. I stopped, tuned to her. She nodded.

We turned it into a coffee shop and café, called it *The Uranium Raven*. We filled our days serving from behind the counter. And that was that, for a while.

Then one day, through the door came a young woman — a shock of brown hair, long home-made dress, bold canvasses held under her lanky arms. She was all stuttering enthusiasm as she explained she was from the local art college and asked if she could put up paintings in the café, offer them for sale and give us a share of the profits.

I hesitated and looked over to Catherine where she was sitting at the table with a coffee and a cigarette. She just raised her eyebrows batting the question back to me. I smiled and said of course.

The next day I bought a sketchpad, and between serving I started drawing the view through the café's window, the grey stonework of the Old Town.

The day after Catherine did the same, but drew portraits of our waitresses, a couple of the patrons.

There was a room above the café, empty most of the year, only really used as a performance space during the Festival.

We turned it into a gallery — taking on more staff at the café as we found ourselves spending less and less time working there.

I paint the city and Catherine paints the people in it. — both of us taking a basically realistic approach but adding a surreal or gothic or expressionist touch as the mood takes us. Occasionally we paint each other too.

We are mainly too avant-garde for the tourist trade and too traditional for the main art market back down in London, but we find favour with some.

We just hope they are not buying them entirely because of the notoriety of our pasts.

EPILOGUE

One morning I wake to find all the ashtrays in our apartment gone.

Catherine is in the kitchen, leaning against the side of the window looking out over the city towards the humped green and greys of Arthur's Seat. She is wearing just a really old black ripped T-shirt I thought she had thrown out years ago. Her hair is natural-coloured, shoulder-length, simple but stylishly cut, haloed by the bright morning sun behind her.

It is a view I have painted several times, often with her standing there – smoking, usually. But not today.

I slip my arms around her and she twists her head back to kiss me.

'Quit?'

She nods.

'That was sudden.'

She does not reply but reaches for my hand and slides it under the T-shirt. I briefly feel her scar but then she slides my hand lower, down past her navel and holds it there. Holds it there until I understand.

'Work of art.'

ACKNOWLEDGMENTS

Many thanks for all your help and support, occasionally unwittingly, in pushing this project along – Doug Bell, David Brunt, Michael Carroll, Mike Donachie, Floyd Kermode, Mike Molcher, Gordon Rennie, Paul Scott, Simon Spurrier, Andrew Wilson, Arthur and Heather Wyatt and my parents.

ABOUT THE AUTHOR

John Black lives in the UK. *Work of Art* is his first published novel.

Please visit www.johnblackwriter.com for more details on current and upcoming projects.